TROUBLE &
TRIUMPH

TROUBLE &
a novel of power & beauty
TRIUMPH

Tip "T.I." Harris with David Ritz

WILLIAM MORROW
An Imprint of HarperCollins*Publishers*

HarperCollins books may be purchased for educational, business, or sales promotional use. For information please write: Special Markets Department, HarperCollins Publishers, 10 East 53rd Street, New York, NY 10022.

A hardcover edition of this book was published in 2012 by William Morrow, an imprint of HarperCollins Publishers.

FIRST WILLIAM MORROW PAPERBACK EDITION PUBLISHED 2013.

Library of Congress Cataloging-in-Publication Data has been applied for.

ISBN 978-0-06-206769-2

13 14 15 16 17 OV/RRD 10 9 8 7 6 5 4 3 2 1

There's only three things for sure—
Taxes, death, and trouble

—MARVIN GAYE, "Trouble Man"

THE SETUP

The Ritz Hotel, Paris, France

Kato Yamamoto looked out the window of his suite at the Place Vendôme into a misty moonless night. The Ritz was his favorite hotel and Paris his favorite city. He wished he had brought his girlfriend, Beauty, with him, but she was too busy. As the creator of a new boutique and extensive line of clothing within the empire of Fine/Bloom stores—the retail chain Kato ran—Beauty had responsibilities that had kept her in New York. Kato also knew she was worried about Power, the man she called her brother. But Power wasn't Beauty's blood brother—he and Beauty had merely been raised together—and Kato had concerns about that relationship.

Beneath Beauty's sisterly concerns for Power, Kato detected something that felt like passion. When it came to Beauty, it was hard for Kato not to be jealous and possessive. He was obsessed with this woman and had every intention of marrying her. It would happen. Soon he would bring her to Paris and marry her. Now wasn't the time to press his case. So far he had done everything right. He had not rushed her. He had cultivated this relationship with a cool mixture of patience and perseverance. Beauty was not only working for him but living with him. It was inevitable that they would marry. Kato had it all under control.

He ordered room service and dined in his suite. With a critical meeting with a French financier set for eight A.M., he was eager to get to bed.

At two A.M., he was sleeping soundly when the ringing of the phone next to his bed startled him. It was Beauty.

"What's wrong?" he asked.

"Call your people in Tokyo." She wasn't asking; she was telling— she was giving *him* an order.

"What people?" Kato asked. He especially wanted to know how much she knew.

"The people who helped you buy Bloom's. The people they talked about in the newspaper. Call them right now." Kato understood that Beauty was talking about the Yakuza, the Japanese mob, whose money had made the purchase possible.

"And say what?" he asked.

"Have them find Power. They have to find Power. They can. They can find anybody anywhere. Or if they can't, they have connections with people here who can. I know that. You know that. Make it happen."

"Beauty, I know you're desperate to help him, but I'm afraid—"

"Do you want to marry me?"

"What?" Kato couldn't believe his ears.

"I said, do you want to marry me?"

"Of course. You know I do."

"Then do this and I'll marry you."

"Beauty, it's the middle of the night here in Paris and I feel like I'm still in the middle of a dream—"

"This is no dream, Kato. I've never been more serious in my life. I will be your wife. I will agree to whatever kind of wedding you want. In Tokyo. In New York. In Paris. Wherever. Just find Power."

"Couldn't the service find him?"

"They did find him. And a minute before I got to him, he was thrown in a car. I saw it happen."

"Beauty," Kato said with alarm, "they could have gotten you."

"They didn't see me. I don't think they know me. I don't think they care about me. Power is Slim's boy."

"Then maybe Slim will protect him."

"Goddamn it, Kato, you don't get it. Slim's men were the ones who got him."

"Then maybe he's no longer alive," said Kato.

"I refuse to believe that. You have to find him. You have to put your people on it—now!"

"*My* people?"

"Yes, stop stalling and start calling. You want to marry me, don't you?"

"Are you serious about this, Beauty?"

"Dead serious. This is your only chance. You're Power's only chance. Call me back when you've made contact with Tokyo. Tell me when the wheels are in motion. I need to know everything. Call Tokyo this very minute. It's all up to you. If you want a life with me, you'll do what I'm asking. If not, you'll never see me again."

Cascade Heights, Atlanta, Georgia

Power was back where he started, in the apartment above the garage that had been built for him by Slim, the man he had once seen as mentor, savior, and surrogate father. The difference, though, was that he was now locked in, with two goons outside his door, the same goons who had kidnapped him, thrown him in a van, and flown him back to Atlanta in a private jet.

From the minute he was pulled from the street, Power figured this was it. He was dead. Beauty had been right. Slim had gone mad. Slim was killing anyone and everyone who had once worked for him. As the van traveled through the tunnel on its way to a small airport in New Jersey, Power expected to be shot and dumped in the river. In the backseat, guarded at gunpoint, he anticipated his own death. He wondered just how they'd kill him. Knife? Gun? Strangulation? His greater fear, though, was for Beauty. Was her life also in danger? Did Slim's paranoia extend to Beauty? Seeing her there, running to him on Charles Street, brought back every dream he had ever dreamt. She looked more beautiful than ever. As he went to his death, this was the image he would hold to his heart.

But he didn't meet death. He met a luxurious Learjet and overheard the pilots say that they were heading to Atlanta. Power was convinced that, in the city of his birth, death awaited him. The goons had been silent from the minute they had captured him. They answered no questions. But after they landed and put him in a Cadillac Escalade, the route soon became clear. They were heading to Slim's compound in Cascade Heights. Driving into the property, Power noticed that the cage that held the black leopard was empty. He was escorted to his former living quarters and told to wait.

"Wait for what?" he asked.

No answer was given.

His apartment hadn't changed. The décor was just as he had left it. His high school trophies still sat on the shelves. The schedule for his last season of basketball games still hung on the closet door. He looked around, drained from this daylong assault of confusion and fear. He got into his old bed, closed his eyes, and drifted off into an uneasy sleep. He didn't know how much time had passed when he heard the door open. He looked up and saw Slim.

"Get up, son," Slim said. "There's a new suit, shirt, and tie for you in the closet. We're going to Dre's funeral. That man loved you. We got to pay him our respects. Take a shower, get dressed, and meet me in the house in a half hour."

A half hour later, one of the goons accompanied Power to the main house. Everything was in place—the sculpture of the life-sized mermaid swimming over a waterfall; the paintings of Hank Aaron, Evander Holyfield, and Dominique Wilkins; the ice-white walls and white marble floors. Slim was sitting at the dining room table, wearing the same matching diamond wristbands he always wore. His wavy hair was black as ever, not a spot of gray. He'd started dyeing it. His pin-striped suit was double-breasted and his cologne had a dusky fragrance. He had put on another ten pounds and looked noticeably heavy. His eyes weren't right.

"Let's get going, son," he said. "I told my man Cutler Jefferson to spare no expense. Dre gonna be laid out in a manner that's respectable and right."

Cutler Jefferson was the man who'd organized Power's mother's funeral.

With two goons in the front, Power and Slim sat in the back of the Maybach 57, the same car Dre used to drive. As they rode over to the chapel, Power finally spoke.

"Why'd you bring me back?" he asked Slim.

"Didn't you want to tell Dre good-bye?"

"You could have just told me to come. You didn't have to have your flunkies throw me in the back of a van and bring me here at gunpoint."

"For your own protection. Can't let nothing happen to you. All for your protection."

"And where's Wanda?" asked Slim. Wanda, an employee of Slim's, had been a friend to Power's mother—and a good friend to both Power and Beauty.

"Wish I knew. Got me a crew out there looking for her now. They be conspiring, boy. Conspiring big-time. You don't know nothing about those conspirators, do you?"

"No, I don't."

"The ones who say I don't know how to fuck a woman. You heard about that?"

"No, I haven't."

"They out there. They telling everyone in Atlanta that Slim Simmons can't fuck no woman. They calling me a sissy. They hired women to go around saying that shit. You ain't heard nothing about it?"

"No."

"Well, you will. You stay around here and you will. Whole town's talkin' 'bout it. Talkin' 'bout how I bust my nut before I even start fucking. Imagine hearing shit like that. Imagine what it does to a man. Lies, son. Motherfuckers tellin' lies on me."

"Dre wasn't telling lies on you," said Power. "Dre was loyal."

"He loved you, Power. Dre always talkin' 'bout how smart you was. Dre always defending you."

"Defending me against who?"

"No one could say nothing about you when Dre was around. No, sir."

"Who killed him? What happened?"

"Shit went bad. Real bad. I told you I got motherfuckers conspiring against me."

"You think Dre was working against you?"

"You never know who's working against you, son, but we here to wish this good brotha good-bye. This is a brotha who thought you hung the moon. Hate to see him go like this. But Cutler Jefferson, he knows how to throw a funeral. He's the best. I said, 'Cutler, buy all the flowers they got in the state of Georgia. Buy a casket made out of the finest wood. Hire that lady over at the First Baptist Church who sings like Aretha. Get her to sing "Amazing Grace." Get the whole fuckin' choir. Spare no expense, brotha, 'cause Dre, he going out in style.'"

The singer and choir did show up. There were flowers everywhere. Slim and Power took seats on the front pew next to Gloria, Dre's white wife, whose eyes were filled with fear. She came over to Power and, through her tears and sobs, whispered, "You need to get away."

"What'd she say to you?" Slim asked.

"She thanked me for coming."

"Gloria's set. She's set for life. She'll never have to worry about nothing. Dre's leaving a wealthy widow. He sure is. Go up there and take a look at him, son. That man loved you."

Power walked to the casket. Dre was set out in a black silk suit and white tie with a diamond stickpin. You could see that work had been done to cover the gaping wound on his neck, but the work was excellent. The scar was well hidden. He looked at peace. Remembering how many times Slim had taunted and embarrassed Dre, Power felt a flood of rage overcome him. He suppressed the rage but could not control his tears. Putting his hand to Dre's cheek, he was weeping openly as he returned to his seat.

"Good to cry," said Slim. "Man's got to cry sometimes. Ain't no shame in crying."

Slim kept looking at his watch as Reverend Nolan Everett, Slim's jackleg preacher, the same man who spoke at the funeral of Power's mom, spoke of Dre's loyalty. His words about Dre were vapid and clichéd. When he was through, he asked if anyone else wanted to speak on behalf of the deceased.

"You go on up there, son," said Slim, urging Power. "He was your man. Testify for your man."

Power rose and walked in front of the pulpit. He looked out at Slim and Gloria and fought for his composure. "Dre was a good man," he said. "He was all-state in high school and proud of being recruited by the Atlanta Falcons. He would have been a star fullback if it weren't for an injury. To me, he was a star. Always a good word. Always encouraging. Never lost his temper. He took a lot. He held it in. He had a beautiful heart. I loved him. I'll miss him. God bless Dre."

While Power was speaking, Slim had slipped out of the chapel. His two goons were now sitting in the pew, the same goons who would drive Power back to the house and his apartment over the garage.

They continued to guard him. For reasons he himself didn't understand, Power stayed dressed in his suit. He sat at the desk where he had once worked on his high school homework and waited.

An hour later, Slim arrived carrying a leather-bound chess set, the kings, queens, rooks, knights, bishops, and pawns carved from Italian marble.

"This fuckin' thing cost me four thousand dollars," said Slim. "Was worth it, though. Ain't nobody beat me on this board yet. I figured it's time you gave it a try. Before you left, you were getting halfway good. You thought you were hot shit, didn't you?"

"Don't feel like playing chess."

"If I was playing against me, I wouldn't wanna be playing neither. No fun getting your ass kicked, is it?"

"Whatever."

"Ain't whatever. It's what's happening. You and me in a battle to the death. You ready?"

"You've won that battle."

"Baby boy, I'm the cat who's keeping you alive. You don't seem to realize that. 'Bout time I got some gratitude up in here. Now let's play us some chess."

Slim set up the board and set out the pieces.

"Your move," he told Power.

Power tried to concentrate but couldn't. Early on, he made several bad moves. Slim nailed him easily.

"You're a joke," said Slim. "You used to know this game—at least a little. Now you're fuckin' pathetic."

"You won," said Power. "Enjoy your victory."

"I intend to, son. I intend to enjoy it like I've never enjoyed nothing before. But you got to understand that I see this here life like a chess game. You know that about me. I taught you this fuckin' game and here you thought you could beat me. You thought you could get five or six moves ahead of me. You thought you could set Sugar Ruiz against me. He was plotting before you got there, and once you got there, you joined the plot, didn't you? You got right into the thick of things with that asshole. You told him shit about me that no one knew. Just like your mama was about to tell shit on me that no one knew.

"They say don't get bit by the same dog twice, but I got bit more than twice. I made you, you fuckin' little piece of shit, and you were looking to unmake me. You and your mama's friend Wanda. You think I didn't know she was part of the plot? You don't think I've always been five moves ahead of you? Well, think again, mother-fucker, just like Dre had to think again when I saw how many times he was calling you on the phone. You don't gotta deny it, 'cause proof is proof. Numbers don't lie. Motherfuckers lie. Dre lied like a moth-erfucker. Wanda, that cunt, is a liar. Your mama was a liar."

"You killed her!" Power screamed as he grabbed Slim by the throat and started to choke him. The goons outside heard the commotion and ran into the room, wrestling Power to the ground.

"Get him out of here!" ordered Slim as he caught his breath. "Take him where you took Dre. Let him bleed out slow. Real fuckin' slow."

"You're so goddamn crazy you're gonna wind up killing these assholes who you want to kill me," said Power. "You're gonna think that before they got me, I turned them against you. And you know what? You'll be right. There's no one left who's not against you. Think about that when you go to sleep tonight, Slim Simmons. The world is out to get you. The entire world."

Slim considered killing Power right then and there, but he had a better thought, one that gave him an added measure of pleasure. "You know what?" Slim told his goons. "Don't do shit to him tonight. Give him the night to think about what's going happen in the morning. Wait till the morning. Even better, wait till the afternoon, till he's good and hungry and had a whole day with no food, no water, no nothing. I'm flying out tonight. Got me some out-of-town business. Enjoy your evening, Power. Enjoy your day tomorrow. It will be your last."

That night Power faced two kinds of fear. The fear of dying—he had felt this before when his mentor Sugar Ruiz (who himself had been mentored by Slim) ordered him to kill Gigante. Gigante had accidentally murdered a young woman Power thought he loved. The ordeal leading up to the assassination of Gigante put Power in touch with his own mortality. There was no guarantee that he wouldn't be killed himself. But because Power was the predator rather than the pursued, he'd felt in control.

Now he had no control. Loss of control was his second fear. No control over his fate and fear. In looking death in the face and imagining the void, he tried to comprehend the disappearance of self. He couldn't. Instead he sought to bring forth the faith of his mother, who believed in a loving and eternal Jesus. She'd prayed to that Jesus ever since he was a small boy; Power had been told that Jesus was the Great Protector.

But where was the Great Protector when Slim murdered his mom? Where was the Great Protector when Slim manipulated Power into believing that Slim was protecting him? Where was the Great Protector in this hour of Power's greatest need?

Slim's dark sadism was something Power had observed for years. Slim had loved to publicly humiliate Dre, his most trusted lieutenant, forcing him to speak in public so that the world could laugh at his severe stutter. Time and again, Power had seen Slim demand that any perceived enemy be dealt with as cruelly as possible.

Power was now such an enemy. He tried not to imagine the torture that waited for him, a horror beyond his comprehension. He hoped he could pass out early on so that he might be free of all feelings. He didn't want to think about it, yet thought of nothing else. He tried to bring his mother back to mind. He tried to remember what it was like being in her arms, like a little boy, calling out to Mama.

Suddenly Power remembered a long-lost lesson he had learned in Sunday school. Jesus was seated in a garden, awaiting his torture to come the next day. He prayed to God the Father to free him from the horrible fate of crucifixion. But his prayer was not answered. Jesus suffered a death of unspeakable pain. It was his death, though, that saved the world. And then he defied death. He came back to life and walked the earth like a natural man.

But Power wasn't Jesus. Power knew there was no noble purpose in his torture. There was nothing but pain. Jesus cried that God the Father had abandoned him. Power's silent cry said the same thing.

As Power paced back and forth in his room like a caged animal, his thoughts went from his mother to Jesus to Beauty. Beauty was the first to warn him that Slim was a killer. She had told him, even before they had moved into Slim's house, that the man was no good. She wouldn't even talk to him, wouldn't even look at him. Shortly after moving in, Beauty escaped, urging Power to do the same. But he thought that she was being stubborn and self-deluding. Power was drawn into Slim's lifestyle—the glamour, money, and women. Power was lulled into his own destruction.

More than anything, he wanted to avoid that destruction. He wanted to find a way out. He had to find a way out. But with two goons at his door and another stationed under his window—all three armed to the teeth—there was no way out.

This is what Slim wanted—to give Power time, second by second, minute by minute, hour by hour, to feel the fear wash over his head, mind, body, and soul. Sleep wouldn't come, couldn't come—just the sweats and the images of what it was going to be like to experience the cuts in his flesh and the blood draining from his veins.

He went from the bed to the window, from the window to his desk. He turned on the TV, turned it off, started to play a CD, stopped, closed his eyes, opened his eyes, breathed heavily, began hyperventilating, managed to bring his breath under control when his heartbeat felt like a jackhammer inside his chest—louder and faster and faster and louder until an explosion rocked the room. At first Power thought it was a figment of his imagination until his desk tumbled over and his bed collapsed and the sound of gunfire came from every direction and the goons were hollering out, cursing wildly, and then a silence fell. Power went to the window, where he saw a goon on the ground below, blood gushing from his head. Seconds later, the door to Power's room burst open. Two Japanese men stood there in full battle gear—helmets, bulletproof vests, AK-47 assault rifles.

"You Power?" asked one.

"Yes."

"Where Slim?"

"Gone."

"To where?"

"Don't know."

"You, come with us."

Member of the Wedding

Beauty had learned of Power's rescue seconds after it was complete. Alone in the lavish penthouse that she shared with Kato Yamamoto in New York City, she had been called by a man in charge of the detail.

"Paul Clay is safe," he said. "He is with us and, as promised, he will be brought to you in New York."

"Was he hurt?"

"No."

"What about Slim Simmons?" she asked.

"Wasn't there. Nowhere to be found."

There was a pause in the conversation. The thought that Slim was still at large frightened Beauty—but at least Power was alive and well.

"Thank you" was all Beauty could say. She hung up the phone and burst out in tears.

For the past twelve hours Beauty had been beside herself. What if the rescue attempt failed? What if Kato's people got there too late? In her mind's eye, she saw a dozen different ways that Slim would murder him—or have him murdered. She hadn't been able to sleep or eat or even speak on the phone to anyone. She knew that Kato had heard the desperation and determination in her voice, but would Kato be able to do what needed to be done? The questions plagued her, even tortured her, as the hours slowly ticked by until the phone call came, delivering the news that had Beauty sobbing uncontrollably.

With a deep breath, she got hold of herself. She thanked God and all the forces that had brought Power to safety. She walked to her window and looked down thirty stories below. The nightlights of the city blazed in every direction. The streets of Chelsea were crowded with people. Soon Power would be among them.

An hour later, he called.

"What the hell happened, Beauty?" he asked. "Who are these people you sent? They saved my life."

"I'm so glad, Power. I'm so, so glad."

She quickly explained the circumstances—that her husband-to-be had remarkable resources.

"Your husband-to-be?" asked Power.

"Yes," said Beauty. She explained about how Kato owned a large chain of luxury stores financed in Japan. "I'll explain everything when you get here."

"Can't wait to see you, Beauty."

"Can't wait either."

She imagined what would happen when they finally got together. She had imagined that reunion for many years. It was all finally coming true. Power was on his way to her.

"I'm on my way back," said Kato, who was calling from the plane taking him to New York.

"I thought you were going from Paris to Tokyo," said Beauty.

"Change of plans. Missed you too much. Besides, I want to be there to celebrate with your brother. I understand he's landing around the same time as me. We'll be together and celebrate—his safety and our engagement. Isn't that great?"

Beauty paused longer than she knew she should have. "Yes," she finally made herself say. "That's great."

She got a few hours' sleep that night, but the sleep was not restful. Her dreams—deep erotic dramas in which she and Power played leading roles—left her with a sexual hunger that both excited and disturbed her. She prayed that Power would arrive before Kato.

He didn't.

Beauty hugged her husband-to-be with as much enthusiasm as she could muster. The hug was not entirely sincere—but her gratitude was.

"You did what I asked," she told Kato. The fragrance of his cologne, although fresh, was too strong for Beauty. She wanted to tell him that it was too early in the morning to wear that much cologne, but she restrained herself. Instead she asked Aasta, their Norwegian housekeeper and cook, to fix breakfast.

A half hour later, while Beauty and Kato were in the dining room eating omelets, the doorbell rang. Unable to contain herself, Beauty jumped up and ran to the door. When she opened it, Power was standing there, a smile on his face.

They held their embrace for a long, long time. Neither would let go. Beauty knew that Kato was watching, but her relief at seeing Power alive overwhelmed her every thought. Finally they stepped apart, and she introduced Power to Kato.

"This is my brother," she told Kato.

The two men shook hands. "I'm glad you're well," said Kato.

"Hey, man," said Power, "I can't thank you enough."

"I'd do anything for this woman," said Kato, putting his arm around Beauty and kissing her on the cheek. "You're family, Power, and we're just glad you're safe."

Beauty looked at the men as they stood side by side. Power was several inches taller. His shoulders were broader than Kato's, and while

Kato was an attractive man whose elegant clothes highlighted his thin silhouette, he lacked defined muscles. During the long embrace, Beauty was reminded of—and immediately excited by—Power's body. Unlike Kato, who smelled of cologne, Power didn't disguise the natural scent of his body. That scent had Beauty's head spinning.

"Come," said Beauty to Power, "have breakfast with us. You've been through hell. You must be starving."

Aasta quickly prepared a cheese-and-tomato omelet that Power wolfed down. The dialogue between Power and Kato was cordial.

Beauty hadn't been with Power since they were sixteen. Now they were twenty-two. She marveled at how articulate he had become. He displayed the social ease of a man who had gone through a world of experiences. He had acquired a conversational charm that, as a teenager, he lacked.

For his part, Power saw that Beauty's physical allure had deepened. Her looks had matured and blossomed in a way that quickened his desire. But in her hardened eyes, he perceived that she had been through ordeals he could only imagine. They were still gorgeous, but the innocence was gone. Secrets lurked in her eyes—secrets that Power felt compelled to unearth.

The sexual tension at the table was evident. A stranger could have walked into that dining room and felt the chemistry between Power and Beauty. But Kato didn't want to see it, didn't want to admit it, didn't want to face an emotional fact so potent that it would undermine his faith that Beauty was his and his alone. Denial was his protection. She loved Power only as a brother; brotherly love was different than romantic love. Beauty was a devoted sister and nothing more.

After breakfast there was talk about the next steps. Power had told Kato and Beauty that he had enrolled in college and taken courses in psychology. He didn't tell them that he had been working for a woman named Holly Windsor who ran a national escort service. He didn't say that Holly's financial supporter had been Slim Simmons. He didn't explain how he had moved into a high-paid position of executive management for Holly, evaluating not only the female escorts but their male customers as well. Psychological insights into people had become Power's specialty.

That insight enabled him to see Kato as a man hopelessly in love with Beauty. He saw Kato as a somewhat spoiled son of rich people who had ambitions beyond his parents' success. He knew that Kato's folks owned Fine's in Atlanta and that Kato had parlayed that into the purchase of Bloom's. The fact that Kato needed Japanese mob money to make that purchase was of great interest to Power. In Power's eyes, Kato had much in common with the characters he had met through Slim. He had worked with such characters and knew them inside out. They were schemers who required more than their own cunning to get by. They required brute force supplied by others. Kato looked good on the surface—he played the part of the brilliant young corporate genius—but underneath the façade was a criminal. Power was sick of criminals.

Yet Power's own criminal past was nothing he wanted to reveal to Beauty. It would hurt his chances of reaching his goal—to get her away from Kato and bring her into his life where she belonged.

"Will you be staying in New York?" Kato asked.

"No," he said. "I'm going back to Atlanta."

"That's crazy," said Beauty, her voice filled with fear. "You need to stay as far away from Atlanta as you can."

"I've stayed away long enough," said Power. "I've got business to conclude there."

"That business is over," said Beauty.

"It's not," said Power. "It won't be till I find him."

"He'll find you first," said Beauty.

"If he does, he does. But I can't stop looking."

Kato said nothing. He liked the idea of Power going back to Atlanta to seek out Slim. The notion that Power was endangering his life did not bother Kato in the least. He wanted him as far away from Beauty as possible.

"Stay here, Power," said Beauty. "Stay away from Slim."

"When you first told me that six years ago, you were right," said Power. "I didn't believe you. I didn't see what you saw. But you saw the truth. He killed my mother. Now he's killed Wanda and Dre and God knows who else. I should have stayed away from him, but I didn't. Now I have a responsibility that won't let me stay away. I couldn't live with myself if I didn't meet that responsibility."

"Kato's associates can do it," said Beauty.

"They're hardly associates," said Kato. "I have no real connection with them."

"They did their job," said Power, "and I'll be grateful to you forever, Kato. But now it's up to me."

"That's macho talk," said Beauty. "You're going to risk your life to prove what?"

"I'm not looking to prove anything," Power said. "I'm looking to end this story before it gets worse."

"You need to get out of the story," said Beauty.

"I can't."

"Say something, Kato," Beauty said, urging him. "Tell him that your people will find Slim."

"I can't do that," said Kato. "I don't control them. I don't even know them. I'm not really involved in any of this. I can't just—"

"Kato's right," said Power. "The man's done enough. I don't want to hurt him in any way."

"But you're the one who'll wind up hurt," said Beauty. "I'm scared you'll wind up dead."

"I couldn't be any more scared than I've been these past two days," Power said. "I went beyond the point of fear to some other realm."

Beauty just shook her head. Kato remained silent. Power kept talking. "I've got to get back to Atlanta. The sooner the better."

"And what will you do when you get there?" Beauty asked Power.

"Find him."

"Tell him not to do that, Kato," said Beauty. "Tell him your people can do that for him."

"I have to wash my hands of this whole thing now," Kato said.

"I understand," said Power.

"And I understand," Kato told Power, "that you have to do what you have to do."

"You're encouraging him?" Beauty angrily asked Kato.

"We each live our own life," said Kato. "What can I say?"

"You'll stay here for at least a few days," Beauty said to Power. "We have a guest suite on the other side of the apartment."

"Just tonight," said Power. "Just to give me time to make arrangements to return to Atlanta."

"You can stay as long as you want," said Beauty.

Kato began to protest but, again, thought it best to stay silent.

"You don't mind?" Power asked Kato.

"Not at all," Kato lied.

Exhausted from his near-fatal ordeal, Power slept all afternoon and into the early evening. When he awoke, Aasta cooked him dinner.

"Mr. Yamamoto and Beauty have gone out for the evening," she told Power. "They said they won't be back till late, but they asked me to tell you to make yourself comfortable."

Beauty had wanted to cancel their plans, but Kato insisted that they attend the dinner party at the Tribeca loft of a powerful fashion magazine editor. Beauty realized that it was a smart thing to do for her business—this editor had been generous in publicizing Beauty's line—but she didn't want to leave Power. The next day, however, Kato was returning to Paris. That would give her at least a few hours to try to convince Power to stay in New York.

"I'm not going to Paris tomorrow," Kato told Beauty. They were riding back to Chelsea in their chauffeur-driven Mercedes. A heavy rain was washing over the city. The streets were slick, and from the tinted windows of the car, the neon lights of the city were a blur of red, yellow, blue, and green.

Kato was waiting to hear Beauty's reaction. He realized that she might be disappointed. He sensed that she wanted to be alone with Power. But knowing she was being tested, Beauty covered up her true feelings.

"Good," she said. "You've been traveling too much."

"I want to stay here so we can start planning our wedding," he said.

"Fine," said Beauty.

"You don't sound too excited."

"Kato, I've been through a lot these past days."

"But there is the promise of our marriage, isn't there? Nothing has changed on that score."

Beauty didn't respond.

"I asked you," Kato repeated, "if anything has changed on that score."

"You don't need to ask. I gave you my word."

He squeezed her hand and kissed her cheek. She knew she should reciprocate but didn't.

Back in their penthouse, Power was watching an old Eddie Murphy comedy on TV.

"I remember we saw that when we were kids," said Beauty.

"Sit down and watch it with me."

"Mind if I join you?" asked Kato.

"Of course not," said Power. "It's your place. I'm just passing through."

Power and Beauty were seated on the couch, a respectable distance between them, while Kato sat in an armchair. Power and Beauty laughed at Eddie's antics while Kato missed much of the humor. He forced himself to laugh. He felt out of it, an intruder in his own home. He was also tired but not about to go to bed and leave them alone.

When the movie was over, Beauty got up and, without touching Power, merely told him good night.

"We'll see you in the morning," said Kato. "If you need any help in making arrangements to return to Atlanta, just let me know."

"Thanks, man," said Power. "I will."

Beauty and Kato went to their bedroom, where she changed quickly into a nightgown, slipped into bed, and turned off her night-light. Her mind was overwhelmed with thoughts of Power sleeping in the guest suite. Kato soon joined her, wanting to make love.

"I'm too tired," Beauty said.

"It's been a while," said Kato.

"I'm really exhausted," Beauty said, protesting. "Please understand."

Power went to bed an hour later. His mind was on Beauty, wondering what she wore to bed. He tried to sleep, but sleep wouldn't come. At about four A.M., he wandered into the kitchen, wearing only white boxer shorts.

He opened the refrigerator and took out a half gallon of milk. He poured a glass and heated it in the microwave, hoping that warm milk might help him sleep. He was seated at the kitchen table when Beauty, wearing a black silk robe, walked into the kitchen.

"I see you couldn't sleep either," said Power.

"You shouldn't be walking around here half naked," said Beauty. "Please put on a robe."

"I didn't exactly have time to pack. I didn't bring a robe."

"I'll bring one of Kato's."

Beauty left and returned with a terry-cloth robe with the fancy insignia of the Ritz hotel in Paris. She handed it to Power, who put it on.

"That better?" he asked.

"Much," she answered. "Warm milk?"

"Yup, just like our mother gave us."

"I should have some myself," said Beauty.

"Have a seat," said Power. "I'll make it for you."

He heated a glass of milk and handed it to her.

"Let's make a toast," he said.

"To what?" she asked.

"Us."

"An unwise toast."

"Let's make it just the same," said Power.

They clinked glasses and each took a sip of warm milk. It felt good, comforting, but it did not break the sexual heat between them as they sat across from each other at the kitchen table.

When Power moved his toe to brush against Beauty's calf, she felt a jolt surge through her. She moved her leg away.

"Don't," she said. "Please."

"Do you know how long I've been waiting to be with you?" he asked.

She didn't answer.

"You've been waiting just as long," he added.

"We don't need to have this discussion," she said.

"If we didn't need to be together, Beauty, you wouldn't have done what you did. You would have let Slim slit my throat."

"Don't even say that."

"Well," said Power, "isn't that true?"

"I couldn't let anything happen to you."

"Isn't that what they call love?"

"Of course I love you. I've never said I don't. You're my brother."

"No, I'm not. We grew up in the same house but with different fathers, different mothers."

"Your mother was my mother."

"Only by adoption," said Power. "Only through her love of your mother."

"It's a family love I'm talking about," she said.

"Call it what you want, Beauty, but for six years I've dreamed of no one but you. Tell me you've never dreamed about me and I promise I won't say another word."

It was Beauty who didn't say another word. She couldn't deny it.

"Girl," said Power, "I know what you've been dreaming. We both have."

"It happened once," she said, referring to the moment they had made love the night after Charlotte Clay, Power's mother and Beauty's adopted mother, had been killed. "It can't happen again."

"Why? That's the question that's been killing me all these years. All this time has gone by. We're no longer two teenagers. You've gone your way, I've gone mine. I can see you've been through hell and back. I know I have. I want to hear what happened to you. I want to tell you what happened to me. If we were just two people meeting somewhere in the world, you know damn well we'd hit it off, we'd start talking, we'd start dating, we'd fall in love, and we'd promise to be together for the rest of our lives. You know I'm right."

"But it didn't happen that way, Power. We just didn't meet like a normal girl and boy would meet. There was nothing normal about my mom dying so young and your mom taking me in. There was nothing normal about how Slim murdered her and lied to you; nothing normal about how I came here to escape all that; nothing normal about Anita Ward, the woman who mentored me; nothing normal about what she did to help me and confuse me and bring me to where I am now."

"I want to hear about her," said Power. "She's Wanda Washington's friend, isn't she? I want to meet her."

"She's dead."

"I'm sorry."

Beauty took another sip from her milk and sighed. "So much has happened, Power, I don't know where to start."

"Start wherever you want. Take all the time you need. We have the rest of our lives to hear each other. I could listen to you forever."

Beauty sighed again. "It's too late," she said.

"It's still early," he argued. "Early in our lives. We've just made twenty-two, and with everything we've learned we're a world ahead of everyone else our age. If we join forces, there's nothing we can't achieve."

"Join forces to do what?"

"Make a life together."

"I have a life," said Beauty. "I'm here with Kato."

"You don't love him. I can see it when you look at him."

"We're engaged."

"Break it. Come back to Atlanta with me."

"If it weren't for Kato, you wouldn't be here. He did what he did because I gave him my word. I promised him."

"What . . . that you'd marry him?"

"Yes."

"You gave yourself to him in order to save me?"

Beauty nodded her head.

"You know something, Beauty, if I had known what was happening, I would have let Slim kill me."

"You don't mean that, Power."

"I've lived my life two ways—with you and without you. Without you it isn't worth a damn."

He got up from the table and took her hand. More electricity, more shock jolting through her system. He took her in his arms, brought her to him, held her against his body. She felt his excitement, he felt hers.

"No, don't, please . . . ," she said, protesting. "Not here, not now."

"Then when?" he asked, stepping away.

"Never."

"I'm never giving up."

"It can't happen like this," said Beauty. "It's unfair to Kato. He's done everything to make me happy. He's given me the career I've always dreamed of."

"Your talent gave you that."

"This is his home. I won't violate it."

"I'll move into a hotel tomorrow. I'll wait for you there. Take a day or two to get ready to tell him."

"Tell him what?"

"That you can't marry him. That you're going back to Atlanta with me."

"And give up everything?" Beauty asked.

"Give up nothing. *Get* everything—everything we both want."

Beauty said nothing.

"You'll think about it?" Power asked.

"How can I think about anything else?"

He smiled. He'd made his point. He approached her again, took her in his arms again, kissed her again, this time his mouth open. She opened hers. Her resistance melted. Their robes opened. He couldn't stop. Neither could she. She put her hands around his neck. Inside her robe, he slipped his hands around the smooth skin of her naked buttocks and brought her to him. He backed her up against the stainless steel refrigerator. She was afraid that Kato might hear them and walk in, but the sensation of Power slowly entering her—a sensation she had imagined and reimagined for six long years—threw her into a state of ecstasy that ruled out reason. She was frenzied. He was gentle but persistent, her resistance melting, her heart beating, now seeking, now demanding, now receiving his deep thrusts with muffled cries of crazed pleasure.

The pleasure went on and on and on.

As he sat on a chair, she lowered herself on him.

The floor, the countertop, her back against the wall.

The leather couch in the den where, for the third or fourth or fifth time—Beauty lost count—she released with an intensity that drove her higher and higher, tears streaming from her eyes . . . until . . .

She got up; she pushed him away; she found her robe; she grabbed a towel to clean up the residue of their passion; she hurried back to the bedroom, grateful that Kato was still sound asleep; she slipped into bed. She tried to stop shaking, but the pleasure was still on her; the madness of the passion wouldn't let her sleep.

In the morning, Power was gone. He left a nice note, thanking Kato and saying he'd be in the city for a few more days at the Regency Hotel. He would try to call before he left, but if he didn't, it was only because he was in a hurry to get home

"Strange," said Kato to Beauty, "that he never mentions you in this note. Do you have plans to see him before he leaves?"

"No," she said abruptly. "No plans at all."

"He didn't want to tell you good-bye in person?" asked Kato.

"I've got to get to the office for a meeting with a buyer," said Beauty, ignoring his question while pushing Power—and last night's insane passion—out of her mind.

Power was in his room at the Regency. He had showered and ordered up breakfast. In his mind, he was still reliving what had happened the night before. He was still feeling Beauty. Usually sexual fantasies don't match reality. But in this case, reality had been even greater than the fantasy. Beyond the explosive nature of the physical encounter, there was also love—he was sure it was love—that contributed mightily to their union. It was love, not just pleasure, that they found in one another's bodies. It was love that would bring Beauty back to him today. Love would make her leave Kato. Love would convince her to be with Power. Love would do what only love can do—change their lives for the better.

He would wait in that hotel room until she arrived.

· · · ·

When Beauty arrived at work, her mind was on Power. Her body was still tingling, images from last night still reeling in her mind. She did, in fact, have a meeting with an important buyer from California. She needed to focus on selling this buyer the Young Beauty line of teen dresses for next season. But concentration didn't come easily. She thought about Power in his hotel room. She wanted to go there. She wanted to be with him. She wanted him again. Sex in the kitchen was incredible, but it was also restricted. She couldn't cry out; she couldn't do everything she wanted to do to him; he couldn't do everything he wanted to do to her. A hotel room had no restrictions. It was there for the very purpose of having uninhibited sex. She wanted uninhibited sex.

The buyer entered her office. She was a mousy woman with a pretty smile and fashionable shoes. She spoke with a French accent. She expressed genuine interest in Beauty's line. Beauty thanked her and began to show her the new designs. The buyer asked a number of questions. Beauty answered them succinctly, eager to get the meeting over with. She knew she could have been far more charming with this buyer, but her charm was exhausted. She wanted this woman to leave so she could go back and daydream of Power.

When the woman left, Beauty asked her assistant to bring a cappuccino. Coffee would help. She was tired, nervous. Just for the hell of it, she got on the Internet and went to the website of the Regency Hotel. The rooms looked lovely. She wondered whether Power was on a high floor. She looked at the telephone number of the hotel, studied it, memorized it, and then tried to forget it. She had to forget it. She had to forget Power. But she knew that was a silly thought, that was impossible; he was there and would continue to be there, deep in her soul, forever. Or would he? Wasn't that just a silly romantic convention that needed to be challenged? He needed to be forgotten. He would be forgotten. She would forget him because remembering him did nothing but confuse her mind and upset her life. She had plans that were working; she had a fiancé who not only had given her everything she desired, but wanted to give her even more.

Sex was fine. Sex was wonderful. Sex was ecstasy, but sex wasn't real life. Sex was something that happened between her and Power on a super-intense level. It was good between them—she had to admit it was sensational—but those sensations die and life goes on. Life is about practicality. She had struggled for years to get where she wanted to be. And why, in the name of reason, should a single sexual encounter throw her life into chaos?

It shouldn't. It couldn't.

But what about one last sexual marathon? What difference would that make? Couldn't she allow herself a few more hours of pleasure before telling him good-bye forever?

No, that was foolish and selfish. The truth, she thought, was the very opposite: The more you get, the more you want. The more you yield, the more you want to yield again. Temptation doesn't disappear when you act on it; it grows stronger.

The strength of her relationship with Power was rooted in sex and sex alone.

But was that true? When she reached out to save him, was she saving him so she could enjoy sex with him? No. At that moment she didn't even think of sex. She thought of him—his decency, his sweetness, his consideration and compassion. She cared deeply for him. But caring isn't necessarily love. Or is it? Was she capable of leaving Kato and everything he had provided? Could she really run off with Power?

Of course not. Which is why she couldn't run off to spend a few hours with him at the hotel. She owed him more than that. She owed him her respect. And so if she did decide to visit him at the hotel, it would only be to tell him just that.

I respect you, Power. I admire you. I wish you well. I've come here to say it in person because the phone is too impersonal. Good luck. Good-bye.

Beauty looked at her watch. Noon. She'd run over to the Regency and be done with this dilemma once and for all.

"Have lunch plans?" asked Kato, standing at her door.

She was flustered. She guessed that he knew she was thinking of running over to the Regency. He had come to save her just as he had saved Power.

"No plans," she said.

"Great, I've made reservations at the Four Seasons."

The Four Seasons restaurant, one of the classiest in the city, sat at Park Avenue and Fifty-second Street. The Regency Hotel, at Park and Sixty-first, sat only nine short blocks to the north.

Beauty was aware of the proximity. She wondered whether Kato was as well. She didn't want to ask him. She didn't have to ask him. He had a list of questions he was asking her, all about their wedding.

"Paris is right, don't you think?" he asked.

"Paris is fine."

"And the Ritz hotel?"

"The Ritz is beautiful."

"We'll get the grand ballroom. I hope you won't think it's vulgar if we make some discreet overtures to select members of the press."

"There's no reason why we shouldn't get coverage."

"You don't think that would commercialize the event?" Kato asked.

"We're in commerce, Kato. We want to expand our commerce. We want to broadcast our brand. I say invite all the press you want."

"I was hoping you'd see it that way."

"I do."

"I love hearing you say those two words."

Beauty tried to smile, but a smile wouldn't come. Instead she took a sip of wine and had a chilled oyster. She looked around the room and, at separate tables, spotted Barbara Walters, Bill Clinton, and Julia Roberts.

"What about early December?" asked Kato. "That'll give us two months to plan. Is that enough time?"

"Good," said Beauty. "Let's get it over with."

The comment struck Kato in the heart. Beauty immediately saw her mistake.

"I didn't mean it that way," she said. "I just meant let's get all the tedious arrangements out of the way."

"If you don't want a big splashy wedding, we don't have to have one."

"I want whatever you want, Kato. I really do. I'm sorry I made that remark. It didn't come out right."

"I understand," said Kato.

Beauty wondered whether he really did. She wondered what Power was doing at his room at the Regency. All during lunch her thoughts drifted back to last night and all she had felt. During dessert, she wondered whether she could make up an excuse—*I have a dentist's appointment, I'm getting my nails done, I'm going to the spa*—that would allow her to visit the Regency.

"Why don't we go by the Regency on our way back to the store so we can invite Power to our wedding and tell him good-bye in person?"

Kato had read her mind. Or at least part of her mind. The problem was, Beauty didn't know her own mind.

"You go," she said. "I have a crazy afternoon. A million things to do."

"I'd rather not go without you."

"Then don't go."

"But he is an awfully nice guy, and he is your brother, and I really hope he can come to our wedding."

"Then go," said Beauty.

"I will."

. . . .

When the phone rang, Power jumped. He was certain it was Beauty calling him from the lobby.

"Power?"

"Yes."

"It's Kato. I was hoping you were there. Come down and we'll have a quick cup of coffee."

Taken by complete surprise, Power hesitated. He didn't know what to say. Had Beauty told Kato about last night? He couldn't imagine she would have. Had Kato heard or seen them making love? That wasn't likely, given Kato's friendly tone of voice. On the other hand, maybe Kato was one of those guys who hug you before they plug you. Power couldn't be sure.

"Okay," he heard himself saying, "I'll be right down." Curiosity proved stronger than caution.

Kato was waiting in the lobby, a smile on his face.

"Beauty wanted to come to tell you herself," said Kato, "but she has a load of work. She asked me to apologize for her."

"What's up?" asked Power.

"Let's go to the bar."

Kato ordered an espresso and Power a Coke.

"We're getting married in Paris in December and we want you to be a member of the wedding."

Power's heart was on the floor. He tried to keep his eyes fixed on Kato, but it was hard. His eyes wanted to close, tear up, roll into the back of his head.

"Congratulations," Power said weakly. That was all he could manage.

"I'd love for you to be in the wedding," said Kato. "I'm sure Beauty feels the same. Would you honor me by being a groomsman?"

Power was trying to keep his emotions together. On the surface, Kato was a nice guy—polite, considerate, smart. He was a nerd, but

Power had come to respect nerds. He saw Kato as someone who got the job done. It seemed like Kato had no idea that Power and Beauty were lovers.

But maybe that was just a cover. Maybe he really did know, and by showing up in person to announce his engagement to Beauty he was letting Power know that he, Kato, had won the war for the lady's heart. If this was the case, then Kato was a son of a bitch and, right then and there, in this fancy bar in this fancy hotel, Power wanted to level him. On the other hand, Power wasn't sure. More than anger or even suspicion, he felt grief. He felt sadness for learning that what seemed so right to him last night—that he and Beauty were fated to live their lives together—seemed so wrong to Beauty.

"Hey, man," he finally found the strength to tell Kato, "it's good of you to ask, but I don't know where I'll be in December. I gotta put my life back together."

"Just be careful," said Kato. "None of us want anything to happen to you. You're family. If there's anything we can do, we're here for you."

"I think you've done enough," said Power, allowing the hint of warning to hang in the air.

Back in his room, alone and downhearted, Power searched for hope. Just because Kato came to say good-bye didn't mean that Beauty might not come later. Kato had no notion of the incredibly intense attraction between Power and Beauty. Or even if he did have a hint, he couldn't know that it was strong enough to change Beauty's life. Beauty was getting ready to shock Kato like he had never been shocked before. She was getting ready to leave him. After this cordial meeting at the bar of the Regency Hotel, Kato would go back to his store and find that Beauty was gone. Or later that night he'd go home and find a note from Beauty saying she had left him for Power.

It was going to happen.

It had to happen.

But it didn't happen that afternoon, and it didn't happen that night. When Power tried calling Beauty's cell, he got the voice mail. His message was short, "I'm waiting," but there was no return call.

That evening he ate in his hotel room alone. He was tired of waiting. He was exhausted from hoping. He thought of actually going over to Kato's penthouse and confronting Beauty, but he knew that was a mistake. There was nothing more to say or do. He simply had to wait until she came to her senses and saw that she needed to be with him.

When morning came, Power had barely slept. He had to go out. He also owed a call to Holly Windsor, the woman who had employed him before he was kidnapped. He ran her escort business in New York, the most important branch of her business. It was a multimillion-dollar enterprise and he needed to explain his absence.

Holly already knew. She had just flown in from Miami and gotten to her New York office when Power called.

"Darling," she said—Holly called everyone "darling"—"thank God you're all right. I've been getting reports from all over. Where are you now?"

"New York."

"You must come over, darling. We must talk in person."

Because it was Slim who had set up the job with Holly, and because Slim had originally underwritten Holly's enterprise, Power was hesitant.

Sensing his reluctance, Holly said, "You're safe here. I severed financial ties with Slim a long while back. My loyalty is to you, dear Power, not Slim. Come quickly. I have a lot to tell you and I know you have things to tell me."

Holly Windsor

Holly Windsor was a proud lesbian and wildly successful business-woman who had perfected the art of selling escorts. She dealt strictly with high-class women and well-heeled clients. Her service had no Internet presence; there were no advertisements in any form. Clients could not view pictures of her escorts online or make inquiries other than by meeting Holly or the men and women who ran her offices in Chicago, San Francisco, Houston, Miami, Dallas, and New York, her headquarters and most lucrative location. It was there that she had trained Power to oversee the operation. His job was to scrutinize both the women and their clients. The goal was to avoid all drama. A scandal-less, smooth-running business is what Holly had worked diligently to perfect. And, at least so far, she had done just that.

She was a tall thin woman who made the most of her plain looks. Her short-cropped hair had purple highlights. She wore silver neck-laces designed by avant-garde artists, dressed in elegant black pant-suits, and favored purple Adidas sneakers. Her deep-red, nearly black lipstick and fingernail polish made a statement: She was both serious and fashionable. She was unique.

Her office had no traditional furniture—no desk, just two matching black suede couches and a silver love seat. Purple drapes extended from the ceiling to the floor. Holly was on the phone when Power walked in.

"Oh, darling," she said to her caller, "I must run. The love of my life has just walked in. He looks tired but radiant all the same. This is the man all men hope to become. Yes, darling, it's my Power. My Power has returned."

She got up and gave Power a long hard hug.

"I can feel tension running all over your body," she said. "I'm having Evelyn, my massage therapist—the best in the city—work on you tonight for two hours. Evelyn will set you free. Now sit down and tell all."

"I hope I haven't caused too much chaos here," said Power.

"You know me well enough, darling, to realize that I calm chaos like mother's milk calms babies. When you didn't show up I knew something was terribly wrong. I went into emergency mode and made sure we were on schedule. Thanks to your exceedingly conscientious preparation, we were. The mark of a distinguished executive is preparation. You, darling, are a distinguished executive. More important, you are a *living* distinguished executive. If I believed in God, I would thank God for that. If I believed in fate, I would thank the gods of fate. But since I believe only in our personal strategies for survival, I am thankful that your strategies proved brilliantly effective."

"How did you learn what happened?" asked Power.

"Miami is all abuzz about the event. Slim is in Miami."

"Did you see him?"

"No, but I spoke to the man who is caring for him."

"Who?" asked Power.

"Your dear friend Irv Wasserman."

"You have to tell me everything you know, Holly. I need details."

"Not before I hear the details of your ordeal. The reports I've gotten are sketchy. Pray tell, darling, what the hell happened?"

Power took a deep breath and told the whole story, beginning with what happened six years ago when his mother was killed. The words came spilling out. He told it all. What happened between him and Beauty the night his mom died. The way Beauty escaped Atlanta and he stayed. How Slim trained him, sent him to Chicago to work for Irv Wasserman, then to Miami to work for Sugar Ruiz—the part of the story Holly already knew. How he was abducted in front of his professor's apartment building, and how Beauty, through Kato, had arranged his rescue. He thought about stopping there, but he didn't. He described what had happened two nights ago in the penthouse with Beauty. He told Holly how Kato had broken the news about his upcoming marriage. He didn't hide the fact that he was devastated.

Holly listened intently and when he was through said, "I'm going to say something that I don't believe I've ever said before. I'm speechless. Holly Windsor is speechless. This story is far beyond anything I could have imagined. And yet, darling, you stand before me as a man who does not show signs of breaking. Sad, yes. But broken, no. You are made of sturdier stuff than any other male I have known, Power. You must know that and revel in that fact."

"I feel broken."

"And I said that I feel speechless, but I'm speaking, aren't I, darling?"

Power had to laugh.

"Yes, I'm speaking," said Holly, "and I'll continue to speak no matter what negative feelings get in my way. We carry on; that's what we do. And we carry on with the certain knowledge that we can change. Today we're broken, tomorrow we're fixed. We change."

"Do you really think people change, Holly? Beauty has been this way since the first day she came to live with us—headstrong, the most goddamn headstrong person I ever met."

"Except for me."

"You're different," said Power.

"Because I love women and she loves men?"

"I don't know if she loves at all."

"And yet you love her."

"I always have."

"What does the psychology professor you admire so much say about people's capacity to change? She's an expert, isn't she?"

"I never asked her."

"Well, darling, if you did, I can tell you what she'd say."

"What?"

"She'd say, 'I don't know.' Look, most people don't change. But others do. You, for example, you're a changed man from when I first met you."

"How?"

"More discerning, more sophisticated, better judgment about our employees and their customers. You can spot a nutcase from a mile away. You've changed your perception of the world."

"I'm not sure."

"I am, darling. I know that your world will continue to evolve. You'll grow beyond this obsession with Beauty. She may or may not change. Her focus is obviously on her career and doing everything she can to further it. God knows I relate. You, on the other hand, are a romantic motivated by a vision of domestic bliss. I applaud that vision. It's a beautiful thing to watch on the movie screen. But you have—and are—moving past that vision into hard-boiled reality. That's where I continue to be of help to you, my dear. I am the hard-boiled realist, not the psychology professor dealing in abstracts, not the relationship counselor dealing in theory. I am here to tell you that not only can you change, but you can and will change for the better."

"One thing will never change," said Power.

"What's that, darling?"

"How bad I want to kill that motherfucker."

"Understandable but unsuitable as a top priority. You must remove that from your mind."

"I can't."

"This is the change I was discussing. This is the change, dear Power, that you must realize if you are to succeed. The physical removal of Slim Simmons from this planet will do nothing to further your goal. In fact, pursuing him will blind you to that goal. Physically he is already gone from Atlanta, which is where a world of opportunity awaits you. He will not be back."

"How do you know?"

"I spoke with Irv Wasserman. Irv is caring for Slim. He is in a mental hospital."

"Give me the address."

"Darling, darling, darling. You are missing the point. Even if I had the address, I wouldn't give it to you. Slim is a broken man, not you. He suffered a complete nervous breakdown. When he heard about the attack on his compound, he ran from the city like a frightened child—a crazed child. He ran to the only father he's ever known and trusted."

"Irv?"

"Precisely. There is a bond between the men. Irv is convinced with proper care, Slim can change. He thinks he can be brought back into his right mind. Whether that's true or not, the fact remains that his Atlanta empire is in shambles. That's an empire you know intimately. You know it better than anyone. That's the empire he trained you to take over one day. Miraculously that day has arrived. Go home and assume the role that awaits you. Put on your crown and become king of Atlanta."

Power didn't know what to say or think. He thought of Beauty. He wanted her. He'd do anything to have her, but that wasn't happening. He thought of Slim. He wanted him dead and had every intention of killing him with his own hands. Nothing short of that would satisfy the rage that boiled within. Slim had killed his mother. Slim had killed Dre and Wanda. Slim had tried to kill him. Power lived to see Slim die, and yet Holly made sense. What would that do for his future? What would be accomplished by devoting his life to an act of revenge?

"Darling," said Holly, "I understand vendetta. Blood feuds aren't simply dissipated by a few pleasant thoughts. I realize that the kind of monstrous betrayal you have suffered must be answered. It's a question of timing, however. I am proposing to you, sweetheart, that now is not the propitious time. Now is exactly when he and those who protect him, including Irv Wasserman, will be waiting for you. Consequently, you will do better to fill the void that Slim has created in Atlanta. Tend to that business. Take it over. If Slim ever returns to reality—and that, my dear, is an open question—lull him into believing that, rather than strike back, you have decided to strike out on an entrepreneurial path unlike anything the city of Atlanta has seen. His operation will simply be your base. Secure it, darling, and then build upon it. I don't simply see you in an office suite, I see you in the penthouse office of a skyscraper, the tallest in the city. Atop that skyscraper for the entire world to see, in riotous red neon, is one word and one word only. The word is 'Power,' blazing night and day, never growing dim, lighting up the sky, an endless affirmation of your brilliant success. Do you feel me, Power? Can you see it, darling?"

Power first chuckled, then sighed. Holly was without doubt the greatest salesperson he had ever encountered. At this moment he didn't mind. He needed to be sold a vision that said his life wasn't over; he needed to feel that he could go on without Beauty, that his sense of possibilities was not exhausted, and that an adventurous future really did await him. As Holly broke down her ideas, his spirit began to rise. But his spirit also sank when he thought of the large strain of criminality that marked Slim's enterprise. There were legitimate operations—car washes and restaurants, beauty salons and barbershops—but there was also a heavy involvement in drugs. It was one thing, as Holly had said, to be the new king of Atlanta. But to be the new drug king?

When he mentioned these reservations to Holly, she said, "Darling, you can divest and reinvest as you see fit. That's the beauty of assuming control. You can do a complete reevaluation of which businesses you find worthwhile and which you wish to discard. Meanwhile, it's all waiting for you. I'd advise you to hurry, though. If you don't fill the void left by Slim quickly, someone else will."

"I'm not sure."

"Well, I am. In fact, sweet Power, I am so sure that I'm asking you to kick things off in Atlanta by opening an office of the Holly Windsor Agency there. I've been targeting that market for months now, and you're the perfect person to lay the foundation for a profitable southeast presence for me. You know the territory. At this point you're a seasoned pro and I frankly wouldn't trust anyone else with the job. In interviewing escorts you may well find just the kind of woman who will help you forget Beauty."

"That's never gonna happen."

"It won't if you cling to the past. It will if you seek the thrill of the future."

"I thought I knew my future," said Power.

"We always think that," said Holly, putting a cigarette in her fancy white holder and lighting it with a bejeweled gold Zippo, "and we're always wrong."

Tiffany & Co.

P aisley was one of the best restaurants in New York City. It occupied its own three-story brownstone on a quiet tree-lined street in Greenwich Village. The first floor was reserved for celebrity clientele who, no matter how famous they were, had to make reservations months in advance. The building itself, constructed well over a hundred years ago, was a historical landmark. The interior walls were covered in sheets of billowing cognac-shaded, hand-painted silk with swirls of forest-green paisley. The tables and chairs were precious antiques from the Edwardian period in England.

Kato and Beauty were seated in a front booth that overlooked the street. Outside, the evening had turned chilly. A brisk breeze was blowing the orange and brown leaves from the trees. Inside, the restaurant was packed. Sade occupied a table not far from Kato and Beauty, where she was engrossed in conversation with her attorney. Martha Stewart sat across from a handsome man who looked young enough to be her grandson. Perhaps he was. Anderson Cooper ate alone.

Kato and Beauty were fresh from their workout at the exclusive Perfection Fitness Center on Fifth Avenue. It was the first time that

Beauty had been able to exercise since Power had rocked her world two weeks ago. She was glad for having made herself do it. It was good to build up a sweat on the Stairmaster, good to lift a few weights, good to stretch, and especially good to have a ninety-minute deep-tissue massage.

Her body felt better, but her mind was still on Power and their explosive night together. She was glad that she had not caved in and gone to his hotel. She was also regretful. She was still on an emotional roller coaster. One minute she congratulated herself for avoiding another encounter; the next minute she imagined the ecstasy another encounter might have involved. She was high on the fresh memory, she was low on her weakening willpower. Why had she let him do what he did? Why had she let herself do what *she* did? Because she liked it; because she loved it; because she loved him . . . but no, it wasn't love, it was lust, burning crazy lust that led her to redo what they had done six years earlier. She wanted to redo it again, even though fourteen nights had passed since the night of nights.

In these fourteen nights, still fueled by the flames ignited by Power, she had made love to Kato no less than six times. Kato was surprised and delighted at Beauty's overtures. He didn't want to believe that Power had unleashed this great passion; he wanted to believe that it was their impending marriage—and Beauty's commitment to their relationship—that excited her into this deeper phase of intimacy.

Beauty couldn't lie to herself. Not once during those six times had she made love to Kato; it was Power who was consuming her—his mouth, his arms, his motions. Satisfaction came through memory and imagination, not through the man whom she had promised to marry.

That marriage was on Kato's mind as she sat across from her fiancé at Paisley.

"My parents pushed for Tokyo," he said. "But I said we were both committed to Paris. They were hurt, but they'll get over it."

"I don't want to hurt them," said Beauty. "If Tokyo is what they want . . ."

"It's not what I want, though," said Kato. "Paris is the city of light, the city of romance. I've always dreamed of getting married in Paris."

"So Paris it will be."

"Do you want to go over the press list?" Kato asked excitedly.

"I'm sure it's fine."

"And tomorrow we'll be selecting a wedding planner."

"You'll be selecting the planner, Kato. I'm super-busy tomorrow."

"The planner is critical, Beauty. I want you to be happy with the person who'll be coordinating everything."

"I will be happy," said Beauty unhappily.

"You don't seem happy."

"I'm famished—that's what I am. Let's order."

After dinner, Kato kept discussing the wedding—the music, the flowers, his groomsmen.

"I'm hoping Power will change his mind," said Kato, "and participate. I know that will make you happy."

He waited for Beauty to respond but she didn't. She couldn't even manage a smile.

"Have you heard from him?" asked Kato. "I presume he's back in Atlanta."

"I guess so."

"So you haven't heard from him?"

"No."

"And you haven't called him?"

"No."

"I don't understand why not."

"And I don't understand why you're pressing this, Kato."

"When I think of the trouble you went through to save this man, it makes no sense that you suddenly are so uninterested."

"Let's talk about the wedding. Do you really think you can get

Mariah Carey to perform at the party? I'm not sure she does that sort of thing."

"For the right money, anyone will do anything. That's something you understand quite well."

Beauty didn't reply. Kato's blunt statement was cutting and, in her mind, deservedly so. Why bother to argue? Why bother to sit here through this tedious dinner?

"Can we go home?" she asked.

"Sure. I'll call the driver."

Nothing was said on the ten-minute drive between the Village and Chelsea. In the backseat of the Mercedes S65, Beauty sat as far from Kato as possible. Her body language said that she didn't want to be there. She spent the trip texting Solomon Getz, her close friend and vice president of merchandising for the Fine/Bloom chain. Kato had given him the job to make Beauty happy.

A light rain had started to fall when they arrived at their building. The doorman was there with a waiting umbrella. They rode up the elevator in silence. Kato took the key from his pocket and opened the door. Kato asked Beauty if she wanted a nightcap. She declined. She said that after her workout and dinner, she was tired. She walked to their bedroom. When she turned on the light, she noticed a small aqua-blue Tiffany & Co. box that had been carefully placed on her pillow. She sat the bed, undid the bow, and opened it. A tiny card read, "Our engagement with destiny. Love forever, Kato." Under the card was a velvet ring case. She opened the case to discover the largest square-cut diamond she had ever seen. It had to be twenty carats. The white-gold setting was beautiful. At first she thought the diamond was too big, far too showy, even vulgar. But when she slipped the ring on her finger and saw that not only did it fit perfectly, but it sparkled with a brilliance—a shimmering radiance—that absolutely thrilled her through and through, she gave out a small cry of joy. By then Kato was standing in the doorway.

"Do you like it?" he asked.

"It's overwhelming."

"Overwhelming good or overwhelming bad?"

"Overwhelmingly beautiful!"

She went to him, kissed him deeply, and led him to the bed. Again, they made love, the fabulous ring still on her finger.

When her climax came, Kato asked, "Are you with me? Are you thinking of me?"

"Yes," she lied. "Yes, I am."

The Art of the Orgasm

Soon after arriving in Atlanta, Power learned that Holly Windsor was right. Slim's empire was in shambles. In fleeing the city, Slim had also fled from his responsibilities to some dozen separate businesses. The pattern was clear: As Slim began sinking into deeper paranoia, his operations sank into fiscal chaos. The brick-and-mortar establishments—the restaurants, barbershops, car washes, and beauty salons—were still standing, but because payroll hadn't been made for weeks, their doors were closed. Slim had abandoned his employees.

Ed Kingston, a man with whom Slim had had a nasty falling-out, succinctly explained the situation to Power. Some years earlier, Slim had helped Kingston, a young banker, get elected city councilman. He threw Ed a fund-raising party at his home and contributed generously to his campaign. Once in office, though, Kingston found Slim's demands for tax breaks based on false tax returns too fraudulent to handle. In order to survive politically, Kingston had to separate himself from Slim. At the same time, the bank where Kingston was a vice president—Southern Security—continued to handle Slim's money. The bank's president, Ajay Lock, took over Slim's considerable account.

Power knew Ed Kingston well. A thirty-eight-year-old light-skinned, blue-eyed brother who stood at six foot eight, Kingston had been a basketball legend at the high school Power attended some twenty years after Ed had graduated. He and Ed had always enjoyed a cordial relationship, and when Power called about meeting him, Kingston readily agreed.

The executive headquarters of Southern Security were on Peachtree Street in downtown Atlanta. Kingston occupied a high-floor corner office with a sweeping view of the city. When Power walked through the door he got up and greeted the younger man warmly.

Ed was dressed in a black pin-striped suit, pale yellow shirt, and dark blue tie. He looked like he owned the bank. Power wore a black blazer, khaki trousers, and a plain white silk T-shirt bearing the small insignia of Louis Vuitton. Each man was impressed with the other's carefully chosen outfit.

"Good to see you, brother," said Ed. "I'm glad you called. Been wondering where you were."

"Thanks for seeing me, Ed."

"What would ever keep me from seeing you? We've always been cool."

"I know you had your problems with Slim."

"Not *had,* good brother. *Have.* If I'm not mistaken—and maybe you're here to tell me that I am—your man is still around."

"He's moved to Miami," said Power.

"Permanently, I hope."

"I don't think he's coming back, Ed. At least that's what I hear. The best information is that he's lost his mind."

"I never thought the man was ever in his right mind."

"That didn't keep you from taking his campaign contributions."

"I gave those back, Power. You know that as well as anyone. As a politician responsible to the public, I couldn't have his heavy strings attached to me. At first I didn't see those strings. Soon as I did, though,

I cut 'em loose. But that was years ago when I harbored political ambitions. Now I'm all about business."

"That's why I'm here, Ed. I want to know about Slim's businesses."

"No one knows more about them than you, Power. You should tell me."

"He did his banking here."

"Not with me, with Ajay Lock."

"I don't know Ajay Lock."

"You will soon. I see him as the next mayor. He's getting ready to run. Rhodes scholar, Yale graduate, PhD in finance from Stanford."

"A brother?"

"Yes, sir. Straight from the old Fourth Ward before the 'hood was gentrified. Give him four, five years and he'll run for governor. Then who knows?"

"How old is he?"

"Early fifties. Had been head of the biggest bank in Birmingham."

"Surprised I didn't meet him."

"He and Slim didn't like to publicize their relationship."

"Lock had a close relationship with Slim?"

"Well, Ajay's smart. He's discreet. He knew to keep Slim at arm's length. He realized the value of Slim's account and used it to consolidate his position at the bank. He was clever enough to keep a healthy distance from Slim, so if there came a time to remove himself from the equation, he could easily do so."

"And he has?" asked Power.

"I'd be shocked if he hasn't."

"And what about the businesses? What will become of them?"

"They'll fall into receivership. The bank will take custodial responsibility."

"This bank?"

"Unless you know of other banks where Slim kept his holdings."

"So I've come to the right place," said Power.

"Maybe you have, maybe you haven't. Depends upon your goal."

"You said I know more than anyone about those businesses, and you were right. I can run them and keep the operations from going under. I can protect the bank's interests in those operations. I just need help."

"I'm sure you do."

"Can you help me, Ed?"

"I can't if I'm still believing that Slim sent you here. After all, everyone in Atlanta knows that you're his boy."

"Just as anyone knows he went crazy and tried to eliminate me like he eliminated anyone close to him."

"And if that was all a big show to divert attention . . ."

"Attention from what? In the aftermath of what Slim has done to his so-called friends in Atlanta, he could never show his face here again. I'm not part of any show, Ed. Look, the truth is that I'd like to spit on Slim's fuckin' grave. I'd like to put him in his fuckin' grave if I didn't think that would divert my attention from cleaning up the mess that he left here. There are dozens of people who are urging me to do just that. Dozens of businesses waiting to get up off the ground. Dozens of workers who need to get back on track and earn a living wage. I need some short-term financing and a plan to parcel these properties together. I need to put it all on a sound financial footing. You know what I've been through, Ed. I have the training, I'm your man."

"The training had two sides to it," said Kingston. "One side was straight and the other was crooked."

"Forget Slim's illegit shit," said Power. "I want nothing to do with that crap. Let those businesses rot on the garbage heap. I'm not touching them."

"You're going to have to come up with some initial capital of your own," said Ed. "We're not going to finance this enterprise with a partner who's broke."

"I agree. And I'm far from broke. Whatever plan we devise to bundle up these businesses under a single umbrella will be partially underwritten with my own money. If I'm asking you to run a risk, I've got to run the same risk myself."

"How much, brother," asked Ed, "are we talking here?"

"I can risk a hundred thousand of my own money."

"And how much would you need from Southern Security?"

"That's what I need you to tell me. I need your expertise to figure out what it's going to take to put these businesses on an even keel and give me a chance to turn them profitable again."

"You're talking about big money—ten million, maybe more."

"Partnering up with me will double the bank's money and make you a hero."

"I like the way you talk, Power. Slim really did give you the gift of gab."

"Slim didn't give me shit, Ed. I'm here because I want to work with you. All I'm asking you is, do you want to work with me?"

Ed did. He especially did when he saw the $100,000 check that Power handed him. The money had come from Holly Windsor— seed money, she called it, which would allow Power to take over Slim's empire. There was one condition to the loan, however: Power had to lay the groundwork for a Holly Windsor Agency in Atlanta, a booming market for high-paid escorts.

As Power left Kingston's office, his mind felt clear for the first time in weeks. Holly had helped his thinking enormously. She had set him on the straight-and-narrow path back to where he had once belonged—Atlanta, Georgia, city of his birth and education, a city he knew better than any other, a city where his mother had taught him a set of values that, once she was gone, were overturned by the man who murdered her. Now Power saw himself returning to those values. He was not going to sell drugs. He had seen the enormous profits Slim had realized through the underground market; Power himself had moved large quantities of cocaine in Miami, hand-delivering the goods to Sugar Ruiz's premier customers. But the profits weren't worth it. The risks were too great, the criminality too intense. As a drug-taker himself, Power had had his fill. He never saw the stuff as manna from heaven. He could—and would—easily live without it.

He had a slightly different view of the escort business. Of all the mentors he had encountered—Slim, Irv Wasserman, Sugar Ruiz—he considered Holly Windsor the most sensible. She was crazy but also practical and wise. Her operation deftly avoided all illegalities. Her staff of top-notch lawyers made certain that her women signed contracts that never obligated them to do anything against their wishes. And while Power had no interest in continuing Slim's drug dealing, no matter how profitable it was, he felt different about opening an escort service for Holly in Atlanta. She had, after all, bankrolled him, increasing his chances of getting hold of Slim's operations. Beyond that, he liked interviewing prospective escorts. He never hit on any of them. Holly had taught him not to mix business and pleasure. Do that and the business is ruined. His attraction for the women—and many times he was attracted as hell—was trumped by his professionalism. As a professional, he enjoyed the process of evaluation of who would and would not make a successful escort. The criteria were fascinating.

He never forgot Holly's lessons. "Women are actresses," she'd told him when she began indoctrinating him into the business, "and the bed is their stage. The audience in the bed is comprised of a man who is viewing the drama in a heightened state of excitement. His critical powers are low. His dick is hard. He wants to be pleased—that comes first. But as you well know, darling, he wants to please. He wants to satisfy Mama. All you little boys want to satisfy Mama. You want Mama to get off on you. So Mama perfects the art of the orgasm."

"You mean, she's able to come every time she gets fucked?"

"Not at all, darling. Granted, such women do exist. They are healthy stable creatures. But the women you and I meet as prospective escorts often have a history of instability. Their relationship to their bodies—and to their ability to climax—is usually hidden behind a dark curtain. Our job is to look behind their curtain."

"Why?" asked Power.

"Well, darling, because her attitude will ultimately make her a winner or loser as an escort. In other words, has the lady perfected the art of the orgasm?"

"The art can actually be perfected, Holly?"

"A smart woman can come awfully goddamn close. For example, if she sees that her gentleman friend lacks staying power, she'll anticipate that and lower the level of excitement so that he might hang on for a minute or two longer. If that fails, she'll scream out her pleasure at the moment of his, showing him that his single penetrating stroke was all she needed. Conversely, an astute escort will sense when a man is having a hard time coming. Man wants release as much as woman, isn't that true, darling? Such a difficult client will be made proud by the number of orgasms he is generating in his partner, even as his own climax is long in coming. Some men require a whack on the ass, others a bite on the lip. The number of necessary stimulants is infinite, but you get my point."

"During an interview in an office," asked Power, "how in hell do I know if a woman is good at the art of the orgasm?"

"You ask."

"Just like that?"

"Well, darling, subtlety is always recommended. And I see you as a subtle conversationalist. You can read people."

"But, Holly," said Power, "that's really a deep read."

"Deep but delightful," said Holly. "What could be more fun than questioning a woman about the emotional disposition of her vagina? I call it the pussy probe."

Power had to laugh.

"Humor helps," said Holly. "When it comes to sex, humor is the only salvation. Take it too seriously and it becomes some grueling test. With humor, it's a hoot and a holler."

That conversation had taken place well over a year ago. Since then Power had interviewed dozens of prospective escorts, discovering that Holly was right. He was good at it. He did find a way to engage women in discussions that touched on sexual congress. It didn't take long to detect their sensitivity—or lack of sensitivity—toward the art form Holly valued so highly.

"A good escort requires objectivity about what she does," Holly had said. "She can't take it personally. She must separate herself from the act. She has to know that, as an actress, she is dealing with a script. If she can't analyze the script, she can't enact the role."

These were the thoughts in Power's mind when he started interviewing potential escorts for the Atlanta branch of the Holly Windsor Agency. After the debacle with Beauty, Power thought this work would help him forget her. It didn't work that way, though. The most important qualities in a good escort were looks, sophistication, and smarts—all Beauty's best characteristics. When Holly had told Power that Beauty was acting as a high-priced hooker, he argued against the notion. He didn't want to see her that way.

"I understand, darling," Holly had said, "that it's a bitter pill for you to swallow, but examine the facts. The facts indicate, at least to this old business broad, that your Beauty is the ultimate escort. The truth is that she has been bought not only for an evening, but for a veritable lifetime. She has found a man who can make all her dreams come true. Beyond the security of unimaginable wealth, he is sponsoring her career as a designer and fashion executive. What more could a girl want?"

Power had wanted to say, *Me,* but restrained himself. He recognized Holly as someone who understood the world of women far more accurately than he. But he also knew that Beauty was different. Power had made love to his fair share of women. Yes, on many occasions he may well have been fooled by the art of the orgasm. But no, there was no artifice attached to Beauty's sexual releases. It was pure passion. It wasn't calculated or contrived. It was the real thing. Power would bet his very life on that truth. When they loved and came together—when they came repeatedly—the explosions were real.

Power tried forgetting those explosions. He tried focusing on the task at hand—interviewing escorts. He sat in an office suite in a building close to the Ritz-Carlton hotel in Buckhead, the exclusive section of Atlanta where he was renting an apartment. The interviewees had been selected by Holly through her network of contacts—friends of current escorts employed in other cities, names given to her by various business associates, women she had met in the course of her work and travel. Some, in fact, recognizing the lucrative potential of an affluent metropolis like Atlanta, had flown in from faraway cities.

The interviews were spaced far apart during the day so the women would not encounter one another. Each meeting took over an hour, some went on as long as two. The process continued for a week. Power, a serious student of psychology, was fascinated. Who wouldn't be? These were women, anywhere in age from their early twenties to midthirties, who possessed charm and poise. One was in medical school, another studying law, a third in a program for a PhD in cultural anthropology. They were all beautiful. They were all eager to earn. Several made the mistake of coming on to Power—an understandable mistake, given his status as the boss. He let them know, though, that such a move would get them nowhere.

Power's line of inquiry had been developed by Holly. They were questioned about their mothers. Holly was certain that the key to a woman's relationship to sex—good or bad—could be traced back to her mother. They were questioned about their loss of virginity. According to Holly, a happy encounter boded well for success as an escort. A negative encounter increased the chance of failure. And of course there was a series of questions about their attitude toward men.

The balance between beauty and brains was a delicate thing, thought Power. The overtly beautiful woman got by on what seemed to be a slight intellect. He hired three such women, realizing male customers would be wowed by their looks, and although the conversation might lag, there would be no complaints. A certain category of men welcomed an evening of little talk. On the other hand, Holly had taught Power that some males valued sexy talk more than a sexy body. No Holly Windsor escort could be homely, but a plain-looking woman, well dressed and attractively made up, could make big money utilizing the gift of seductive gab. Power hired two chatty women. He was convinced that—linguistically at least—they had what it took.

On the Friday of the last week of hiring, Power saw he had one final appointment. The woman's name was Skyla. As she walked through the door, she made an immediate impression. She was of medium height and wore a draped loose-fitting pantsuit in red that contrasted brilliantly with her dark brown skin. Her hair was cut close to her scalp, left natural, and tinted with a shade of red far subtler than the hue of her pantsuit. Her figure was superb, but her outfit did not trumpet that fact. Her extra-long silver earrings formed exclamation points. When Power noticed them, he smiled.

"I have to say—your earrings. They make a point," he commented.

"That's their intention."

"And exactly what point are you trying to make?" asked Power.

"That I'm here."

"You sure are," he said, widening his smile.

Skyla had not yet shown her smile. It was as though her eyes did the smiling for her. Her lips, seductively large, glistened with a reddish copper gloss.

"I see you met Holly in San Francisco a few months ago," he said.

"That's right."

"And the two of you have kept in touch."

"We have. I think she's hysterical."

"Have you been living in Atlanta long?"

"Five years."

"And before that?"

"Birmingham. We moved to Atlanta because of my father's job. After I graduated from high school two years ago, I decided to go to Georgia Tech."

"Majoring in?"

"Finance."

"You like school?"

"I was my high school valedictorian."

"But did you like it?"

"Actually no. I never fit in."

"And college?"

"Still don't fit in."

"But you want your degree?"

"I'll get my degree, and a graduate degree as well."

"I presume you no longer live at home."

"I have an apartment off campus."

"Tell me about your mother."

"Is that a necessary question?" asked Skyla.

"Wouldn't ask it if it wasn't."

"She's wonderful."

"And your dad?"

"Not a factor."

"In what sense?" Power asked.

"In no sense."

"I don't understand."

"Next question," said Skyla.

"Sorry," said Power, "a sensitive issue, I see."

"Let's talk about the work I want to do. I've done it before."

"With another agency?"

"No, on my own."

"And?"

"I liked it. It excited me. It intrigued me. I'd have to say it was fun. Putting it out front like that—saying there was a price. Made everything easier. The lines were clear, the boundaries neatly drawn."

"Then why come to an agency?"

"Holly made a good point when I met her. For a woman on her own, the danger in client selection is too great to risk. That's where you come in—and why I'd like to ask *you* a few questions."

Amused that Skyla was turning the tables on him, Power nonetheless was agreeable.

"Shoot," he said.

"What's your criterion for a suitable client?"

"Safety for the escort."

"And not money?"

"Safety first," said Power. "Suitability is also key."

"And how do you judge the suitability between the client and your employee?"

"Cultural compatibility."

Skyla finally broke into a smile. "Oh, please," she said. "You sound like it's a college course."

"Well, you've been to college. And so have I. And I'd guess many of your clients will be college graduates as well."

"So I've passed the test," said Skyla.

"I always have to consult with Holly."

"Holly's my girl. We understand each other."

"Then we should have no problems, Skyla."

"Good."

"One final question, though. I see your last name is Lock. And you mentioned that you moved here from Birmingham. Just wondering if you're related to Ajay Lock at Southern Security Bank."

"Oh, you mean good old dad?" Skyla asked coyly.

Dr. Trina Mappleroot

"Several years ago I moved my office to this beach house on Montego Bay," said Dr. Trina Mappleroot as she faced Irv and Slim across her expansive desk. "I find water has a calming effect on both my patients and myself."

The doctor was a big woman in her fifties. Her ample upper body was covered with a freshly laundered white smock with "Dr. Mappleroot" embroidered in flowing script in black thread above a pocket holding a Montblanc pen-and-pencil set. She wore white trousers and white lace-up shoes with thick pinkish-red soles. Her oversize horn-rimmed glasses highlighted her alert brown eyes. The doctor had a pretty face, wide and youthful. Her skin was medium brown. She spoke with a slight Jamaican accent. She spoke authoritatively, but her manner was soft. Her voice was comforting.

"I see, Mr. Simmons," she said, turning to Slim, "that you've just come out of the hospital. How are you feeling, sir?"

Slim heard the doctor's words, but his head was not clear. After six weeks in a hospital mental ward, his emotional equilibrium was still radically off. Although he had gotten past the point of being totally incapacitated by fear, he still was not well. The precarious stabilization, brought on by heavy psychotropic meds, went only so far. He no longer thought that all medical professionals had been hired by his enemies to kill him. At his lowest point, there was only one man in the entire world that he felt he could trust—Irv Wasserman.

Back in the day, Irv had given Slim money when no one else would. He had often come to his aid. Slim also knew that Irv's gratitude toward him was deep: It was Slim who sent Power to Chicago, and it was Power who saved Irv's life. Irv had no reason to harm Slim. Rather than compete, their businesses had always augmented one another. Over more than three decades, they'd made money together. They had never haggled, there was no history of double-dealing, and trust between the two men was absolute—so absolute that, in his acutely fearful state, Slim ran to the man whose words he had never forgotten: "You're black, I'm Jewish, but we're brothers, blood brothers. I'm here for you no matter what."

Irv had struggled with his own fears. When a cousin accused him of being paranoid, Irv's response was "Maybe, but even paranoids have enemies." Irv was right. More than paranoia, his scrutinizing nature led him to understand that those closest to him were looking to rob him blind. By pretending to slip into dementia, he caught his enemies red-handed and quickly eliminated them. In Slim's case, those enemies were largely figments of his fabrications; in Irv's case, they were real. But in both cases, the men felt cornered and alone.

Irv saw that Slim was sick. Understanding the root of his sickness, though, allowed him to be especially sympathetic. When Slim called Irv, crying that his house had been shot up and his bodyguards murdered in cold blood, Irv identified with his crisis. That's when Irv directed Slim to leave everything behind, come to the airport, and fly to Miami. Irv wasn't aware that Slim had kidnapped Power, who, facing his own death, had been rescued in the assault. Irv knew of some of the recent murders ordered by Slim against his so-called enemies, but he didn't realize the extent of the purge. All he knew was that, for all practical purposes, his friend Slim had lost his mind.

As they sat in Dr. Mappleroot's office, Irv reflected on how Slim's presence in Miami had given him new purpose. His isolated retirement made him feel useless and bored. He had divested himself of all his businesses, he had tens of millions of dollars stashed in banks all over the world, and yet mistrust had driven him to an extreme solitary existence. He moved from one luxurious penthouse to another and, before Slim had called, was on the verge of leaving Miami altogether for a seaside home in Jamaica. Slim's arrival temporarily changed his plans. Slim became his pet project. In helping Slim, he thought that he could help himself. If paranoia, no matter how justified, had nearly driven Irv mad, loneliness was doing the same thing.

He was allowed to visit Slim for a half hour each day. The other patients who populated the ward were all ages and races. There was a young black Latino woman who wouldn't stop talking; a middle-aged Asian man who wouldn't stop crying; a white lady, with the composed appearance of a TV news anchor, whose eyes displayed raw terror. For his part, Slim was withdrawn. He had lost considerable weight. Without his flashy clothes and bling—his trademark matching diamond wristbands and eighteen-karat-gold-and-diamond Rolex—he looked ordinary. In his hospital-issued drawstring pants and collarless shirt, you might have mistaken him for a custodian.

During the initial visits, Slim told Irv that they had to talk in the hallways. His room wasn't safe. There were microphones and cameras recording everything. The nurses were giving him the wrong meds; the doctors were conspiring against him. He wanted Irv to sneak him out. If not, he'd be dead in another week.

Irv listened to him with sympathy. He didn't argue, knowing that logic would make no difference. Maybe medicine would. Maybe individual and group therapy would help. Maybe time would heal and bring him back to reality.

Irv Wasserman was not devoid of sentiment. He dearly loved his daughter, Judy, in spite of the fact that she had conspired with his closest adviser against him. Irv had eliminated the adviser but did not stop his daughter from running to Dubai, where she was living with a wealthy Arab. How could a Jewish girl try to cheat her own flesh and blood and then flee to a country where they hate Jews? Irv couldn't fathom such a thing. At the same time, according to the way Irv thought, he couldn't possibly hurt his own daughter.

When it came to his enemies, though, Irv was as ruthless as Slim. The fact that an adversary had a family—and was a devoted father or son—made no difference. If someone was out to get Irv, Irv got him first. This strategy for survival had worked for over six decades but left him friendless. At this point in his life, he felt the need for at least one friend, another human being to care for.

Little by little, Slim began showing signs of progress. This gave Irv a sense of satisfaction. He knew that his daily visits helped. Slim saw that there was someone genuinely concerned about him. And when Slim finally got to the point where he was told he could be released within a week, Irv made plans to fly to Jamaica.

Irv's Jamaican home was a rambling ranch-style villa that sat on two acres. There was a massive master bedroom suite and a lavish guesthouse in back. There was a lap pool, sauna, Jacuzzi, and spectacular view of the Caribbean. Large electronic gates protected it on all sides. Irv had a staff of five—a maid, a cook, a driver, and two brawny veterans of the Jamaican special forces. All of this gave Slim a feeling of safety.

During his first days in Jamaica, Slim sat on the veranda and looked at the water. The scene calmed him. Other than Irv, the only person he spoke to was Rashan Guyot, one of the bodyguards and the son of Melea, Irv's cook. Perhaps because Slim bore a resemblance to his own father, Rashan treated Slim with special kindness. He could feel how Slim was hurting. At one point, he took the liberty of telling Irv how his own mother had been immobilized by a deep depression and, through a teacher at his school, had found help in the person of Dr. Trina Mapperoot.

"She's a wonderful woman," Rashan told Irv, "with special powers."

Irv thought it strange that someone like Rashan would go out of his way to make such a suggestion and decided it'd be foolish not to follow up. He went alone to meet Dr. Mapperoot and was immediately encouraged. He thought Slim would be comforted by the fact that she was black. He also liked that she didn't mince words.

"I don't know if I can help your friend or not," she said. "As far as I'm concerned, Mr. Wasserman, fear is a mystery. How it imprisons us and how we break free of that prison are not easy questions to answer. Have I treated people who were able to change to where they're living less fearful lives? Yes. Have I treated people who, over time, became ever more fearful? Again, yes."

"Well, I don't know much about psychiatry," said Irv.

"Neither do I," said Mapperoot. "I'm not a psychiatrist."

"Then what kind of doctor are you?"

"My degree is from the Jamaican Institute of Folkloric Healing."

"What does that mean?"

"We heal through stories."

"What kind of stories?" asked Irv.

"The kind of stories brought to us by our patients. A patient comes to us with the story that has driven him to sickness. The story has diseased his mind. We show him there is another story, another way of viewing his life. Do I make sense?"

"Not really," Irv confessed.

"Let me give you an example. You have come to see me today with a story. What is it?"

"I have a friend who needs help."

"Exactly. But look what happens if the story is told differently.

Look what happens if the story is told like this: You, Mr. Wasserman, a caring man with a burning desire to do something good for someone else, have come to seek my advice. When you hear the story that way, how does it make you feel?"

"Better."

"So do you see my point?"

Irv didn't answer right away. But in thinking about the exchange, he decided it was a good idea to bring Slim to see this woman.

Slim's first reaction was positive. Just as Slim had reminded Rashan of his father, Dr. Mapploroot reminded Slim of his mother. She had his mother's girth and gentle manner.

"Why didn't you tell me that the doctor was a sista?" he asked Irv with a smile on his face.

"I wanted to surprise you," said Irv, who hadn't seen Slim this animated since he left the hospital.

When Dr. Mapploroot asked Slim how he was feeling, he was still unsure why he was there.

"Are you a heart doctor?" he asked.

"You might say that."

"So you're going to listen to my heart?"

"I'm listening right now."

"I don't see no stethoscope."

"I'm trying to listen with *my* heart," she said.

"Okay, baby, you got my attention."

That was the first time Irv had heard Slim use the word "baby" since he was put in the hospital. Slim was starting to sound like his old self.

"How do you like Jamaica, Mr. Simmons?"

"It's okay to call me Charles. That's my real name. Everyone calls me Slim, but my mother called me Charles."

"What was she like?"

"Nice lady. Good lady. God-fearing lady. Probably one of the best ladies to ever walk the earth. Never would do nothing to hurt me. Never did."

"What was her name?"

"Lucille Mae Jackson."

"Is she still living?"

"Oh, Lord no. Mama died when I was eleven."

"That's a young age to lose your mother, Charles."

"Remember it like it was yesterday."

"Please tell me about it."

"Came home from school and she wasn't there. Now, that was unusual, 'cause one thing about Mama, you could count on her to be there when you got home. She had seven different kids by four different men—I was the oldest and the one she loved best—and no matter where those men might be, Mama was home looking after us. Yes, ma'am, count on that. I could sure enough count on my mama."

"Tell me what happened the day she wasn't there."

"My three little brothas and three baby sistas, they was running around like crazy, crying and carrying on. I had to tell them to shut up and make 'em believe that Mama would be right back. I fed 'em their dinner. Acted like I knew what was happening even though I didn't. Then this here man comes to the door and says he's from the city. Says he's gotta take us away. I say, 'Look here, mister, we ain't going nowhere without Mama. We don't know who you are. You could be one of those men who fuck with little children. You ain't touching us.' He says Mama ain't coming back 'cause Mama has done passed on. I say, 'What does *pass on* mean? *Pass on* to another house? *Pass on* to another city? I don't understand.' He say, 'Pass on to heaven. She dead.' 'She what?' 'She dead,' he say. 'Oh, yeah? Well, you gonna be dead.' And I run to the kitchen and grab the biggest butcher knife and go after the motherfucker. Well, when he see me coming at him with that knife he takes off. No matter that I'm only eleven. He sees I mean it. Hour passes and here comes a whole load of policemen.

This time it ain't no game. When I see them, I still got the knife in my hand, but they take it from me. They take me and my brothas and sistas down to some orphanage house where we supposed to wait for God knows what. I ain't crying, but all my brothas and sistas, they hysterical, they want their mama. The different daddies—shit, nobody knows where they are. The folk at the orphanage say they out looking for them. Meanwhile, I keep asking what happened to Mama, is she really dead? How she die? No one's saying nothing, and I'm trying to keep the kids halfway calmed down when a social-worker lady, a white lady, she comes in and sits down with us.

"She says it ain't gonna be easy to hear this. I say I'd rather hear something than nothing 'cause up till now no one has told us shit. That's when she describes what happened. Mama was at the corner store buying us our food. She was hurrying back to the house when a bus jumped the curb and ran into her, ramming her head against a tree. Lady say that the bus driver was drunk. First thing I say is 'Where is he? I'm gonna kill him.' Lady say he's in custody. I still wanna kill him. Ain't thinking about nothing but killing him. The screaming and crying coming from the kids is so bad the lady knows she got to do something. She finds us a big room where we all gonna sleep together. 'What's gonna happen to us tomorrow?' I ask her. 'Who's gonna take care of us?' 'You'll be taken care of.' 'How?' 'We gonna find your fathers.' 'Our daddies ain't gonna take care of us.' 'We'll see about that,' say the lady.

"I was right. Our daddies didn't give a shit. A couple of them came by the orphanage to see us but then disappeared. My daddy showed up to take us all to the funeral. That's the first time I ever laid eyes on the man. He was an asshole. Hardly talked to me. I remember saying only one thing to him, 'Can you keep us kids together?' 'Can't do that, boy,' he said, ''cause I don't even stay around here. I stay in Macon.' 'Well then, take us to Macon.' 'That ain't gonna happen, son.' I said, 'Don't call me "son." I hate your fuckin' ass.' He turned and slapped me, right there at Mama's funeral. I made my mind up not to cry—and I didn't."

Slim stopped the story. His emotions got the best of him. His eyes teared up, and for a second, Irv thought he was going to break down and cry.

"There's nothing wrong in crying, Charles," said Dr. Mappleroot. "Sometimes crying is healing."

Slim blinked his eyes, took a deep breath, and regained his composure. But when he started to speak, he lost it again, this time breaking down in sobs. Irv was amazed to see this man—among the coldest and most calculating he had ever met—reduced to weeping like a child. Irv was touched to the point where he got up and put his arm around Slim's shoulders. After a while the sobbing subsided.

"Thank you, Charles," said Dr. Mappleroot.

"What . . . what are you thanking me for?" asked Slim, still breathing heavily.

"I thank you for sharing your story. It's a privilege to hear it, a privilege to watch you let go of so much pain."

"Shit," said Slim, "when Mama died, the pain was just beginning. See, none of these fool men, including my own daddy, had no interest in keeping us kids together. So the court split us up. That was the part that hurt the most. Some judge who didn't even know us, didn't know shit about our family, suddenly this old white motherfucker is running our lives. He got my brothers living with some distant relatives over in Alabama, got my sisters in a foster home, and got me moving in with an aunt—least she said she was an aunt—who only wanted me 'cause the state gave her money. Her name was Marlene and she was half blind. That was a good thing 'cause it meant she couldn't see that her husband, Floyd, was pimping bitches and selling smoke out the back bedroom. Floyd hated me 'cause he knew I was smart. He worried that I'd tell Marlene what was up. He'd come up to my room in the attic with the rats and the roaches and no goddamn heat and he'd beat the shit outta me just for the fun of it. He'd say, 'I see you peepin' 'round, I see you looking over my shoulder, I know you think you slick, but believe me, boy, if I ever hear a fuckin' word outta you I'll cut off your nuts with a razor blade and shove 'em up your ass.' Scuse my language, doctor, but that's how the man talked."

"You're entitled to tell your story any way you want to, Charles," said Dr. Mappleroot. "I appreciate your concern, but my ears have heard worse."

"Well, there wasn't nobody no worse than Floyd Bixby. That was his name. He killed Aunt Marlene for the little insurance policy on her life. Don't think it was worth more than twenty thousand dollars. Imagine smokin' your wife for twenty thousand dollars. She had said something to him about how she was tired of him forgetting to pick up her prescriptions at the drugstore—a little nothing comment like that—and he beat the shit outta her. Next day she had a stroke that the doctors said killed her, but it wasn't no stroke that killed her, it was Floyd Bixby. He made me go to the funeral 'cause he said it wouldn't look good if I didn't go. He said I could keep staying there, not 'cause he wanted me but 'cause he wanted that monthly check from the state. It got to be summertime and it was so hot up in that attic, without no fan or nothing, that I thought I'd die. I asked him if I could move into Aunt Marlene's bedroom—Floyd and Marlene kept separate rooms— but he already had his biggest-earning ho living up in there. When I told him I was going to sleep on a bench in some park rather than up in that sweltering attic, he said I wasn't going nowhere. Just to make his point, he took an iron cord and beat my back until he cut through the skin and I was soaked in blood with welts from my neck down to the bottom of my butt, welts so big that when I went to school I wouldn't take off my shirt for gym class 'cause if the authorities found out what happened and went to get Floyd Bixby, he wouldn't think twice about killing me."

Slim stopped talking.

"Could I have a glass of water?" he asked.

Dr. Mappleroot went to a minifridge and retrieved a bottle of water, handed it to him, and went back to sit behind her desk.

Slim took his time in drinking down the water. It was as though his story couldn't restart until all the water had been consumed.

"Where was I?" he asked.

"Telling me that you were afraid that Floyd would kill you."

"I wasn't afraid of nobody, least of all that weak-ass motherfucker."

"That's not how you were telling the story before," said Dr. Mappleroot. "Before you gave me the feeling that you were afraid of him."

"Well, I'm telling it different now."

"I like that, Charles. I like for you to see how there are lots of ways to tell a story—and when you tell it differently, you feel differently, don't you?"

"I feel like if I was really afraid of that evil motherfucker, I couldn't have done what I did."

"Which was what?"

"Figured a way to do to him what he wanted done to me."

"Tell me *that* story, please."

"That story is about patience. See, by then I was thirteen or fourteen and knew enough to plan. Later on I became a champion chess player 'cause of my talent for planning ahead. Did you know that, Irv? Did you know I played chess?"

"Yes," said Irv.

"Do you play?"

"I never have. It looks too hard."

"It *is* hard, man," said Slim. "Very fuckin' hard. I taught Power and he thought he could beat me, but that sucker never did. I look for college professors to play me 'cause no one else is smart enough to give me a good game. See, chess is about patience, and God blessed me with lots of patience. I knew patience was the only way I was ever gonna figure out how to get Floyd. Patience also showed me that it'd be better not to get him personally. It'd be better to get someone else to get him. That's where Barbie came in. Boy, Barbie was something else."

"Who was Barbie?" asked the doctor.

"Barbie was named after the doll 'cause the bitch looked like the doll. No joke. Blond, tall, and white as snow. She was a junkie whose real name was Virginia. Never will forget her. Bixby's biggest earner. He pimpin' her out to niggers, to white cats, even a few lesbians. Man, everyone wanted some of that fine Barbie ass and Barbie didn't give a shit who she be fucking long as they be paying. Am I offending you with this story, Dr. Mapperoot?"

"You're intriguing me, Charles. I told you before. You tell it however you like. No one is judging you here."

"I appreciate that because going back in my mind, like I haven't in years, is having me remember some shit that I done forgot. Shit I didn't wanna think about. I'm not sure I even wanted to think about Barbie."

"Why not, Charles?"

Slim stopped again. "Think I could have another water?"

"No problem," said the doctor.

He drank down the second bottle and closed his eyes. "Feel like I've been saying too much."

"To me, Charles, it feels like you've been waiting a long time to put these things in story form."

"Ain't no story," said Slim. "It's the truth."

"I don't doubt that," said the doctor. "All I mean is that when you tell it, it becomes a story. I have a feeling, for example, that there are things in this story you want to leave out."

"You right. I do."

"What parts do you want to leave out?"

"The parts about Barbie."

"Well, Charles, it's your story and you're free to leave out whatever you want."

"Then I wouldn't be telling you the whole truth."

Dr. Mappleroot said nothing. For several seconds, the room turned silent.

"You wanna hear the truth?" asked Slim.

"It's not what I want to hear, Charles, it's what you want to tell."

"Barbie was my first."

"Your first woman?"

"Yes, she was. I was thirteen, then, maybe fourteen, can't be sure, but she liked me. She liked young boys. She liked young boys who were big down there and I was big. You understand?"

"I do."

"Yeah, Barbie took a big liking to me. I didn't know nothing about no good sex. I'd done had sex with myself, like most boys that age, but I was a little scared of doing it with a lady, especially a big tall grown white lady like Barbie. But one day when Floyd was gone, she started fooling with me. She said she liked being with young guys who had a little boy's face and big man's dick. That's how she put it, Doctor. I ain't lyin'."

"I believe you."

"The next thing that happened is the part that I'd like to leave out."

"Feel free to leave it out."

"But if I do, you won't understand something that no one has ever understood. Not even Irv. That's why if I tell it, I'd have to ask Irv to leave the room. Would that hurt your feelings, Irv?"

"No, of course not," said Irv. "I'll step outside. You two talk."

When Irv was gone, Slim said, "I tried to do it, but the second I put it in, I came, I came so quick I couldn't do what she wanted me to do."

"That's understandable, Charles. You were young."

"Barbie didn't understand. She got mad. She said she didn't get no pleasure. When I went soft, she tried to raise me up again, but much as I tried, I couldn't get hard. And that's when things really got bad. Turned out Barbie was as evil as Floyd. She went around telling the other girls that I came even before I could get my dick in her pussy. Other girls thought it was a big joke, and every time I passed by they'd start in laughing. That made me hate Barbie and made me think of a plan. See, I was good at planning. This plan would turn Barbie on Floyd and get rid of 'em both. Because I never missed a trick, I saw that when Barbie turned her tricks she put her money inside the hollow left heel of her thick-stacked high-heeled shoes. I'd seen her do this twice, so I knew she did it all the time. I waited and waited for months, until one Sunday morning after she'd been tricking all Saturday night she went out to get something to eat with the girls. I snuck in her room and saw her shoe filled with money. I took the money and ran out the house. I knew that when Floyd woke up—he didn't get up till noon—he'd want that money first thing. I wasn't there when it happened, but I heard they had one helluva fight when the money wasn't there. He beat her real bad. She swore the money was stolen, but since I was gone there was no one to accuse. I knew one time wasn't enough so I waited another month, maybe two, until another good opportunity came up for me to steal that Saturday-night cash from inside Barbie's heel. This time he really did kill her like I knew he would, but I was close by and called the other girls to come running. I also called the cops to tell them what was happening. The girls got there in time to witness him beating Barbie to death, and the cops got there before Floyd knew what the fuck was happening. First-degree murder. And the beautiful thing was when he got to the pen some guy he'd cheated back in the day was waiting for him. Slit his throat. Motherfucker bled to death in the yard. Bled to death like the pig he was. End of story."

"Is it?" asked Dr. Mapploroot.

"Well, end of Floyd's story."

"Sounds like the beginning of yours."

"You might put it that way."

"Maybe that's something we can talk about next time, Charles. You're good at telling these stories."

"Am I really?" he asked like a little boy getting approval from his teacher.

"Very good. You have me on the edge of my seat. Can we ask Mr. Wasserman to come back in?"

"Sure thing."

When Irv reentered the room, Dr. Mappleroot said, "Thank you for referring Charles to me."

"What happens now?" asked Irv.

"I hope he keeps telling me stories," said the doctor. "I hope to see him this time next week."

The Ritz, Paris

Mariah Carey wasn't available to sing at Beauty's wedding, but Rihanna was—as long as her astronomical fee was met and she could stay in the Coco Chanel Suite of the lavish hotel where the wedding was taking place. Originally, the wedding planner had reserved the Coco Chanel Suite for Kato and Beauty, but the betrothed were only too glad to switch to the Elton John Suite—anything to accommodate Rihanna.

Beauty liked Rihanna's music and admired how she had widened her brand to include perfumes, lingerie, and sportswear. Rihanna was a savvy business lady who, as far as business opportunities were concerned, knew the sky was the limit. Beauty knew the same. For the most part, she had put those nagging thoughts about Power behind her. He had gone back to Atlanta to do whatever he needed to do. She took comfort in knowing that Power finally understood what she had realized the first day she met Slim: that he was a murderous thug not to be trusted for a second. Power was now on his own. Power could take care of himself. She didn't know whether Slim was gone forever or planning his revenge. That was no longer her concern. Having fulfilled her responsibility with Power, she could wash her hands of that part of her past. Power and Slim were ancient history.

"Modern history is being made in Paris this weekend," reported the gossip magazine *Up-to-Date*. "The Kato Yamamoto–Beauty Long wedding is being called the most expensive in the annals of the Ritz hotel. The floral bill alone is reportedly $150,000. The four hundred guests, flying in from five continents, include Karl Lagerfeld, Cindy Crawford, Naomi Campbell, Drake, Kelly Rowland, and Japanese minister of finance Nomo Hisaki."

A week before the wedding, after having received special consideration from the French government, Kato and Beauty flew over in a private jet along with a hairdresser, makeup artist, wedding planner, and publicist. Kato's parents, Mr. and Mrs. Daicho Yamamoto, who had once employed both Beauty's mom, Isabel Long, and Power's mom, Charlotte Clay, were flying in from Atlanta, where they still ran Fine's department store, now part of the Fine/Bloom chain created by their son with unconventional Japanese financing.

On the plane over, Beauty's mind was on one thing: her gown. Her obsession with Power had been replaced by an obsession with her wedding gown. The style was radical, geared to get the maximum publicity. The gown itself, Beauty's own creation, was a tight sheath of white silk with strips of black satin whirling from top to bottom. There was a long train that carried the same white-and-black swirling pattern. When Kato saw it as a sketch, he had his doubts.

"Why the black?" he asked.

"Why not?" Beauty replied.

"I'm not sure it's appropriate."

"I don't consider it inappropriate."

"But what kind of statement are you trying to make?"

"It's not a statement, Kato, it's a gown."

"Oh, come on, Beauty, I don't have to tell you that clothes make a statement."

"And I don't have to tell you, Kato, that's a cliché."

"I just don't like the black."

"What's wrong with it?"

"There's something sinister about it."

"Sinister?"

"Yes," he said, "something dark. Wedding gowns are white for a reason."

"What reason?"

"They symbolize purity."

Beauty laughed. "Well, that leaves me out."

"You are pure, darling. You're purely wonderful."

"Thank you," she said, "but part of my wonder has to do with impurity. Maybe that *is* the statement I want to make. In any event, it'll be all over the fashion news—and that's the aim of this wedding, isn't it?"

"The aim of the wedding is to declare our love to the world."

Kato waited for Beauty to validate his statement. Instead she stayed silent.

By the time their plane landed in Paris, everyone was nervous. There was far more than the normal high tension that precedes a wedding; this affair had everyone on edge. Kato was concerned about Beauty's attitude. She was treating the occasion more as a press event than holy matrimony. She and her publicist were in constant consultation. Beauty had a tight schedule of interviews, before and after the wedding.

"You're like a movie star publicizing your new film," said Kato.

"I want to be professional," said Beauty. "I want this to work."

"The wedding or the marriage?"

Her hesitation before answering worried Kato. "Both," she finally said after several long seconds.

During the day they barely saw each other. She was always in meetings. He had meetings of his own, but he felt that something was amiss. Something was very wrong. Then, the day before the wedding, the activity having built to a fever pitch, Kato woke up that morning, reached over to touch Beauty, and discovered she wasn't there.

He always got up before her. Kato was usually out of bed by seven, and Beauty never before eight. Not once in their relationship had she risen before him. He quickly got out of bed and searched the suite. She wasn't there. He got dressed and went downstairs. Maybe she was having breakfast in the hotel dining room. She wasn't. He repeatedly called her cell. No answer. He rang the rooms of everyone in their entourage. No one had seen her. He asked those working the front desk if they had seen her leave. They hadn't. The concierge hadn't seen her and neither had the doormen. By eight A.M., Kato was in full panic mode. He even called the room of his parents, who had arrived from Atlanta, to see if, for some unknown reason, she had decided to visit them. She hadn't. Now his parents were alarmed.

"She probably just took a walk around the block and no one noticed her leave," said the publicist.

"She doesn't take walks around the block like that," said Kato. "That's not her style."

"It's early in the morning, Kato. Just relax. She'll show up any minute. I bet she's at a nearby café having a croissant."

"Why go there when she could order all the croissants she wants in the hotel?" he asked.

"We women have our whims," said the publicist. "Everything's fine."

Kato knew that everything was not fine. He thought about the whole ugly affair with Power, Power's nemesis Slim, and the intervention of the Yakuza. Maybe Slim had regrouped his forces and was after revenge. Maybe Slim had her. Or, worse yet, maybe there was something more between Power and Beauty than sibling affection. Maybe there was love, even passion. Maybe she had flown out of Paris to be with Power. Maybe that's what all her detachment had been about. She tried to go through with the wedding as a publicity event but at the last minute realized it was a sham. Beauty was leaving him, Beauty never really loved him anyway, she was just in it for the money, and now even money wasn't enough.

She was gone. But why? And where? Kato was going crazy.

At ten A.M., three hours after he had awoken to find his bed empty, Kato called the police, the American embassy, and every powerful person he knew. His wife had been kidnapped. His wife was missing. They had to do something. Put out a dragnet. All-points bulletin. *Now! This very moment! Do something before it's too late!* He was screaming as he had never before screamed in his life. He knew Beauty's life was in danger.

Blackland Road

*L*eave him!" Skyla screamed at her mother, Louella Lock, one of the most preeminent socialites in Atlanta. "Leave him and get the hell out!"

"Leave him for what reason?" asked Louella, who had grown up in a prominent Creole family from New Orleans.

"For what he's doing to you!"

"You're hysterical, darling, and saying things that make no sense."

"How can you live in denial this long, Mother? How long can you keep pulling the wool over your eyes? He has other women. You know he does."

"I know nothing of the kind."

"Then you're the only one who doesn't know."

"Skyla, you seem to be the only one who does know."

"Why are you afraid of facing the facts? It makes me crazy how he abuses you."

"Please . . ."

"You're his trophy. The former Miss Louisiana he puts on his arm when he goes to his banquets and award dinners. He's used you ever since he married you."

"This isn't a conversation I want to have, Skyla. Besides, you're screaming so loud the servants will hear."

"Let them hear! They know the truth! They've seen what he's done when you're out of town."

"Enough! That's enough, Skyla. If you've come over to ruin my day, you've succeeded beautifully."

"Mother—"

"I said that's enough, child. I don't want to hear another word out of you."

"What's it going to take to convince you?" Skyla screamed. "What's it's going to take to get you to leave that man?"

Louella Lock didn't bother to answer. She walked out the sun-drenched glass-enclosed breakfast room of the $8 million Buckhead mansion that her husband had bought last year on Blackland Road. She ran up the grand staircase to the palatial master bedroom suite on the second floor. As president of the board of Atlanta's famous High Museum of Art, she had a meeting with the new curator, a man recruited from London, and she needed to shower, dress, pick out her accessories, and make certain that her driver got her there on time.

Meanwhile, Skyla went to her old bedroom, which she hadn't occupied for two years. The day after her high school graduation she had moved out, vowing never to live there again. The room was much the same. The collection of porcelain dolls that her mother had given her remained on the dresser. The fancy canopy bed, imported from France, was untouched. The only change was her posters of Lil' Kim that she had hung over her father's objections. He had taken them down. She looked at the room in amazement. It was still hard for her to believe that she had lived in this household for so long. As an only child, she felt enormous pressure from her parents to excel in all areas. There was never any question that she would become a deb-utante. Her mother, who cherished her pedigree, had even written a short book called *Cotillions of Color,* a history of black debutante balls in the South. Skyla's flat-out refusal to participate was not the first dramatic confrontation with her parents.

In Birmingham she had watched her father's aggressive social and financial climb. She hated the stuffy private school she was forced to attend. By age thirteen, she had lost her virginity. When her father chastised her for coming home late and grounded her for a month, she flung the fact in his face: "I was with a boy tonight and let him do what he wanted to do, and I wanted it too, and I liked it, and I'm going to do it again." That wasn't the first or the last time her father slapped her across the face.

She liked sex and didn't care who knew it. She liked scandalizing her parents' society circle. She seduced several of the sons of their friends. The wilder she became, the more she infuriated her father, the stricter he became. At the same time, she made the best grades in her school. She knew academic success would confound her parents even more. She was proud of being smart. Her brilliance only boosted her confidence.

Skyla had long suspected that her father had outside women. He often came home past midnight with lame excuses. She didn't believe that all his out-of-town trips were, as he claimed, for business. The thought that her mother was being duped infuriated Skyla. What gave him the right to cheat on a woman who had stood by his side? It was her mother who had elevated him into a social set far higher than the working-class status into which he'd been born. If Ajay had any class, it came from Louella. He owed her. He needed her. And the last thing in the world this woman deserved was deceit and betrayal.

Ever since she was a young girl, Skyla had suspected something else: that Louella was not her biological mother. Skyla's skin was even darker than her dad's. Her physical features, though beautiful, were nothing like her mother's beauty. Their facial characteristics were completely different. There was no doubt that Skyla bore a resemblance to her father—she had his nose, mouth, and liquid eyes—but the older she grew, the more she believed that her mother wasn't her mother. Every time Skyla brought it up, though, Louella laughed the accusation away.

"Then why aren't there any pictures of you when you were pregnant with me?" Skyla began asking when she became a teenager.

"What woman wants to see herself bloated like that?"

"There has to be one picture somewhere," said Skyla.

"Well, if there is, I haven't seen it."

"No one has. That's because you've probably never been pregnant. You and dad have been lying all this time, haven't you?"

"I don't understand how these foolish ideas got into your head, Skyla. I really don't."

Now that she had moved out of the mansion and into an apartment near Georgia Tech, Skyla had her goals in order: get her degree in finance; expose her father for the fraud he was; get her mother to leave him; learn the identity of her real mother; and make so much money she could live even larger than her father.

"Did you meet Skyla Lock?" asked Holly Windsor, calling from New York.

"I did," said Power.

"What did you think?"

"She's fine, she's super-smart, she's savvy about men."

"That was my impression when I met her," said Holly. "It took her only fifteen minutes of chitchat to figure out what business I was in. The idea of being an escort excited her. It was like she'd been preparing for this a long time."

"But there's only one thing," said Power.

"What's that, darling?"

"Do you know who her father is?"

"No."

"President of the bank where I'm looking for financing."

Holly laughed. "Wow. That's wonderful."

"It is?" asked Power.

"Of course it is."

"Why do you say that?"

"Don't you see, darling? It's clear as day. Skyla's a mad rebel like me. She wants to scandalize the world. In doing so, though, she's given you the ace you need. In any game of poker with her father, you're holding the winning cards."

"But she could also undermine our business. Isn't that kind of dangerous, Holly?"

"Of course, but danger is what makes life exciting."

"So hire her?" he asked.

"God yes, darling. Do it now!"

Dream

Beauty opened her eyes and did not recognize her surroundings. She was alone in a narrow bed. A gray cat was asleep on her chest. The purring sound of the animal reassured her that she was all right. She looked around and saw that the bed was in a tiny apartment. Seated on a threadbare couch across from the bed was an elderly woman, frail as a bird. When she got up to approach Beauty, she was severely stooped over and walked haltingly. Immediately Beauty thought of Anita Ward, the woman who had cared for her in New York. Their deformities were similar.

The woman began speaking to Beauty in French but soon saw she wasn't being understood.

"I know no Japanese," said the woman, "but a little English. We can try English. English is your language?"

"Yes."

"*Bien*. English is good. I have good English friend. Maybe I call him, no? Maybe he helps."

"Where am I?"

"You come to my home."

"When?"

"You are here, I mean, I bring you. You cry, 'No, no, no!' But I take you, your hand, I see you, so I take your hand. I lead you."

"I was staying in a hotel."

"Hotel?"

"The Ritz hotel. Do you know the Ritz hotel?"

"You dream. Is 'dream' the right word?"

"I'm not dreaming of the Ritz hotel, I was actually staying there. I *am* staying there—with my fiancé."

"You speak fast. Fast, fast, fast. Please . . . slow is better."

"Do you have a telephone?"

"No telephone."

"I need to leave. I need to leave right away."

Beauty got up and realized she was wearing only a nightgown.

"Stay," said the lady. "You can . . . calmness . . . you find calmness."

For reasons she couldn't explain, Beauty felt a wave of tiredness pass over her. She got back in bed, closed her eyes, and rejecting the confusing reality she faced, fell back into an uneasy sleep.

In her dream she was running on a beach. It was a familiar dream, one of those dreams where she knew she was dreaming—and yet the fear brought on by the dream didn't go away. She was running away from a group of people hard on her heels. She didn't know who they were. She was running toward a house, but the faster she ran, the farther away the house got. The frustration was maddening. The people chasing her turned into animals, tigers and jackals, screaming hyenas. She felt their breath on her neck. She woke up in a sweat. The gray cat was still asleep on her chest, purring gently.

Beauty's eyes opened. The old woman was gone, but seated in her place on the couch was a middle-aged man weighing some three hundred pounds. A black beret was not large enough to cover his enormous bald head. He needed a shave and emitted a foul body odor. He looked at Beauty with curiosity. She looked at him with fear.

Trench Town

B ob Marley came up in Trench Town, the funkiest ghetto in Kingston, Jamaica. So did Peter Tosh and Bunny Wailer. Slim Simmons had heard these names, he'd heard their music, but it wasn't an interest in reggae that brought him to the back alleys of a part of town that tourists avoided like the plague. Walking through Trench Town, especially in the dead of night, you took your life in your hands.

Slim was on full alert, but he wasn't afraid. After all, he was the product of several ghettos. Their poverty might not have been as devastating as what he saw in Trench Town, but they were filled with the same kind of danger. Besides, walking next to Slim was Rashan, a big muscular man who had grown up in these back alleys. Rashan, who had told Irv Wasserman about the healing properties of Dr. Trina Mapploroot, was taking Slim to see the other person who had helped his mother when depression had attacked her so viciously. His name was Father Noel Peters, and he had a church.

"Ain't going to one of them crazy Rasta churches where they be smoking weed all night," Slim had told Rashan. "I ain't down with none of that."

"No, Mr. Simmons," said Rashan. "The church is not like that. Father Noel's mother was an American who married a Jamaican teacher. He speaks in the American way. He prays in the American way. You will like this man. He will help you."

Slim's condition was steadily improving. He had been to see Dr. Mapleroot again, and in telling her stories about himself, he was beginning to make some sense of his life. He felt a little bit more like himself. The fact that he was willing to leave Irv's compound without Irv, who had been his constant companion, indicated a growing confidence.

A yellow moon cast an eerie light on the makeshift shacks that lined the dirt roads. Stray dogs and cats roamed here and there. Little boys kicked a tattered soccer ball. The sound of a crying baby filled the air. Rashan walked quickly toward his destination.

"Slow down, youngblood," Slim told him. "I ain't moving as fast as I once did."

"Sorry, Mr. Simmons," said Rashan, who did slow down, "we're almost there."

A few minutes later they approached an old building made of wood and tin. Inside was a large single room with rows of rickety folding chairs. At the end of the room was a large high-backed armchair made of torn red velvet. Seated in the chair was Father Noel Peters, engrossed in the open Bible he had in hand. He didn't look up when Rashan and Slim came in. Other than Father Noel, the place was empty.

Rashan led Slim down the center aisle. The two men sat in folding chairs closest to Father Noel. Not a word was said. Slim looked around the room and saw that the walls were covered with crude Crayola-colored pictures drawn by children, all images of Christ—feeding the poor, riding a mule, protecting a woman by a well, suffering on the cross.

When Father Noel finally looked up, Slim saw that he was probably in his seventies. He had a long thin face, high cheekbones, and a four-day growth of gray beard. His skin was light brown and his dark eyes so intense that Slim had to look away. Father Noel, though, kept staring at Slim. Several minutes passed before the pastor, still seated, spoke in the booming voice of an actor. There was no trace of an accent.

"You have come here for forgiveness," said Father Noel, looking directly at Slim, "but I can't grant that."

Astounded, Slim said nothing. His heart beat wildly. He didn't know if he was feeling fear or wonder.

"You have stolen men's money," said the preacher, "and you have stolen men's lives. Because of that, the devil has stolen your mind."

Slim had heard enough. He got up to leave.

"It makes no difference to me whether you stay or continue to hide your sins," said Father Noel. "I can offer you love. My love is not dependent on your contrition. But I cannot offer you the freedom of forgiveness. Only God can do that."

As Slim reached the door, people started streaming in—women, men, teenagers, children. The entering worshippers made it difficult for Slim to exit, and for reasons he couldn't explain, Slim turned around and went back to sit in the chair next to Rashan, who, putting his arm around him, whispered, "You are safe here."

Slim stayed seated as Rashan, along with everyone, stood and started to sing. A few of the older women brought tambourines. There was no choir, instruments, or musical director. The singing happened spontaneously. It reminded Slim of his mother's Holy Ghost church, where people moaned rather than sang. Here in Trench Town it wasn't a sad moan, but a moan of comfort and release, a moan of relief. They were relieved to be in a holy place where joy replaced fear.

Slim began feeling that joy until he found himself, along with everyone else, on his feet. He heard a moan coming out of him that he hadn't heard since he was a child. It was okay to release it because everyone else was releasing. It was okay to moan loudly because everyone else was even louder; no one was holding back—the adults, the kids, the teens. They liked this moaning, they liked this letting go, they liked not having to put words to their feelings and sending these feelings into the air with the sounds of shaking tambourines and feet beating on the loose planks of the floor, stomping down a beat that went with the moans and had some folks falling out, some folks weeping, others smiling and laughing, others dancing and jumping, while Slim was feeling a looseness, a freedom, a goodness inside his body that had him shouting, had him stomping, had him up and out in the aisle praising the Lord like a man possessed while Father Noel, seeing the work God was doing, stepped out and laid hands on Slim's head.

"Are you ready?" he asked Slim.

"Yes, sir," Slim answered.

"Really ready?" asked the preacher again.

"Ready, ready, ready!" shouted Slim.

And then, as though he'd been struck by lightning, Charles "Slim" Simmons fell to the ground. Rashan went to help him up but Father Noel stopped him.

"Let him be," said the pastor. "Let him deal with it."

Everyone around Slim kept singing their wordless song, kept on with their mantralike moaning, kept raising hands and beating feet, paying no attention to the fallen man from Atlanta who was caught up in a kind of convulsion. He shook, he cried out, he teared up, he went to a place he had never been to before, far away from any world he had known, his heart overwhelming his mind, his soul overwhelming his hurt, until he stood back up and with both hands reached to the ceiling and said, "Thank you, thank you, thank you!"

Slim sat back down along with the rest of the congregation. His eyes were still wet with tears as he focused his attention on Father Noel. The pastor spoke of cleansing. Slim felt cleansed. The pastor spoke of forgiveness. Slim felt forgiven. The pastor spoke of compassion. And Slim felt compassionate. When the service was over, Slim felt new.

Before leaving, he walked over and embraced Father Noel. He looked at the old man and before he could say anything, the preacher stopped him. "I understand," said Father Noel. "You are changed."

Slim and Rashan followed the crowd out the door into the night. The trade winds were fresh. Slim felt invigorated. He felt alive. As they walked through Trench Town to where Rashan had parked the van, the sound of reggae caught the attention of both men. It was coming from an outdoor nightclub where a band was playing that brand of island music that captures the hypnotic rhythm of a planet at peace. Slim was at peace. He wandered over, Rashan by his side. The two men sat at a table close to the musicians. Rashan ordered Slim an exotic Jamaican drink.

A woman got up to sing. To Slim, her smile seemed divine. Her smile warmed his heart. She was in her early thirties, short, compact, dark skinned, and proud of her full figure. She had large brown eyes and a pretty, chubby face. She wore a wig of shoulder-length straight black hair with bangs over her forehead. Her voice was sultry. Her song said that a "night without love is a sky without stars." She called to her man to bring "love to her night, love with all his might." She looked at Slim as she sang, and afterward she came to his table.

Rashan brought over a chair so she could join them. The conversation was brief. Her name was Besta. She worked as the assistant manager of the luxury Serenity Seasons Resort in Ocho Rios, where from time to time she also sang in the lounge. Music was her passion. She longed to make music her profession. Slim praised her singing and told her that this was the most amazing night of his life. He described what had happened in his encounter with Father Noel. She herself went to Father Noel's church on Sunday. She hoped that she and Slim might go together. She said she lived not far from Trench Town in a small apartment.

"You live alone, baby?" asked Slim.

"Yes," Besta answered. "I like solitude, but I also like company."

Slim offered to give her a ride home.

"I rode over in my new Vespa motor scooter," she said. "It's lime green."

"Besta in a Vespa," said Slim with a laugh. "We can put your Vespa in the back of our van."

"Or follow me home. I like being watched from behind."

"I'm watching, sugar," said Slim.

"I have another song to sing," said Besta.

"I want to hear it."

"I want to feel all right," she sang onstage. "I want a man tonight."

Rashan and Slim followed her as she rode her Vespa around the mountain roads that led to her apartment. Her lime-green helmet matched the green of her Vespa. When she arrived and motioned to them to come up to her apartment, Rashan said, "I'll wait here, Mr. Simmons."

Slim went up. That night he stayed up and in longer than at any time in his life. The problem that had haunted him for so long—coming too soon—was gone.

He knew that he was a changed man—changed forever.

The American Hospital of Paris

The fat man in the beret and the frail birdlike woman spoke to the doctor in French.

"I found her walking the streets in her nightgown," said the woman.

"Was she talking?" asked the doctor.

"No," the woman answered. "Just walking. Her eyes were open. When I addressed her, she didn't answer. But when I took her by the hand, she let me lead her. She did not resist. I took her to my apartment because I knew she would be safe there. But all the while, she didn't speak. When we got to my place, she fell asleep immediately."

"How long did she sleep?"

"All night and much of the next day," the woman said. "When she awoke she spoke a few words that I recognized as English, so I ran to my friend Jean, who speaks her language."

"What did she say to you, Jean?" asked the doctor.

"At first she was fearful," said the man. "She was disoriented. She thought I was going to hurt her. I explained that I was there to help, but my words didn't register. She fell back to sleep, as though she were in a trance or a coma. I felt her pulse and her vital signs were strong. Her body showed no signs of trauma. So we decided to let her rest a little longer. A few hours later she woke up and began screaming. I'm certain she'd had a terrible nightmare. I asked what was the matter, but before she could answer—maybe the sight of me caused her more fright—she fell back into her sleeping trance. That's when we decided to call an ambulance and bring her here."

"And in the ambulance did she say anything at all?" asked the doctor.

"Nothing," said the old woman. "When I gave her my hand, she held it tightly. But her eyes remained closed."

"I've examined her," said the doctor, "and can find nothing at all that is wrong. You are right, Jean. Her vital signs are strong and there is no indication that she suffered any kind of blow. The only explanation is that her breakdown is emotional. I've called in a psychiatrist who speaks English and another who speaks Japanese since she may be more comfortable in one language rather than the other. At this point we just don't know. I've also asked my assistant to call the police to see if any missing-person report fits her description. Since she has no identification on her and will not—or cannot—speak, perhaps we'll be lucky and learn that someone is looking for her."

"I've been looking for her for two goddamn days!" Kato screamed into the phone. By then he was a nervous wreck. "What the hell took you so long to call?"

"I am sorry, sir," said the official from the American hospital, "but we've only had her a few hours."

"What's wrong with her?"

"We don't know."

"What do you mean, you don't know? How can you *not* know? What is she doing in the hospital?"

"She was brought here."

"Why?"

"She was lost."

"Lost?" asked Kato.

"Yes, lost."

"I don't understand."

"We don't either. We can't find anything wrong."

Impatiently Kato said, "I'm on my way over now."

In the car, he had a thousand conflicting thoughts. He had been more than half crazy ever since Beauty turned up missing. He was sick with worry and frantic from the ordeal of canceling the wedding. The publicist put out word that it was due to a sudden illness that overcame Beauty. No details were disclosed because no details were known. The media didn't buy the explanation. They assaulted Kato to the point where he couldn't leave his room. His parents tried to comfort him, but there was no comfort to be found. This woman, the most important person in his life, had disappeared. This event, the most significant he had ever planned—and the most publicized—had turned into a devastating humiliation. The questions never stopped running through his head: Why did Beauty leave their room? Where was she going? What or who was she looking for?

When he arrived at the hospital, he ran down the hallways until he found her room. The fat man and the frail woman were seated in chairs across from the bed where Beauty was sleeping. Her breathing was normal and she seemed at peace.

"Who are you?" Kato asked the strange-looking couple.

"My friend found her," said Jean. "She brought me over to speak to her in English."

"Found her where?"

"On the streets."

"Doing what?"

"Wandering."

By now the resident physician had arrived. He explained to Kato that they could find nothing and suspected that she had been sleep-walking. Did she have a history of sleepwalking?

"No," said Kato. "I've never seen her do it and she never mentioned it. But even if she was sleepwalking, do sleepwalkers open locked hotel doors?"

"It's been known to happen," said the doctor.

"But how did she leave the hotel without the front desk taking note of a woman walking out in her nightgown?"

"Hotels have back stairs and back exits."

"But wouldn't that mean she wanted *not* to be noticed?" Kato asked. "Wouldn't she have to be awake to decide that?"

"There's no easy explanation."

"How long has she been asleep?"

"A very long time. Other than a few waking moments, nearly two days."

"Doesn't that mean something *is* wrong?" said Kato.

"I suspect heavy depression. Has she been acting depressed?"

"No."

"Has she been under unusual stress?" asked the doctor.

"Yes. We've come to Paris to marry. The wedding is—or was—going to be an international affair. Hundreds of guests have flown in from all over the world. There's . . ." He stopped himself from going on. What was the point?

"I understand the stress."

"The hell you do," snapped Kato. "Just wake her."

"We've tried. She opens her eyes and just goes back to sleep."

"Well, open her eyes now. When she sees me she won't go back to sleep."

Gently the doctor shook Beauty until slowly her eyes began to open. Kato leaned over her so his would be the first face she saw. Her eyes did open, she saw Kato, but then she closed her eyes again, falling back into a sound sleep.

"Beauty," said Kato. "It's me, darling. I've come to get you."

He kept repeating her name, but her eyes remained closed.

"This is insane," said Kato. "Give her something that will bring her back. There has to be some kind of medicine."

"There are many medicines," said the doctor, "but before we do anything we are awaiting the results of blood tests."

Kato struggled to keep his composure. He felt like falling on the floor and crying, more confused and frustrated than at any point of his life. After a few minutes, the doctor left and Kato, not knowing what to do, sat down next to the frail woman who had found Beauty.

"You two don't have to stay here," he said to Jean.

"We want to," Jean said. "We want to make sure she is all right."

"She's fine," said Kato. "She's just tired."

That's the thought he clung to—the thought he tried to convince himself was the truth. But no one is *that* tired. No one suddenly decides to walk out right before her wedding and wander alone through the streets of a strange and dangerous city. No one falls asleep for three days.

There was nothing to do but wait. At one point the woman left and brought back some salami, bread, cheese, and coffee. Kato thanked her. At another point Jean left for a breath of fresh air. He suggested that Kato do the same. Kato refused, wanting to be in the room when Beauty awoke. Nurses came in and out with clean bedpans. But even when they changed her nightgown Beauty didn't awake.

When he returned, Jean said to Kato, "There is a story that the English call 'Sleeping Beauty.' Maybe she is caught in that story."

"When the prince kisses her, Beauty awakes," said Kato.

"Then by all means kiss her."

Kato went out and softly kissed her on her cheek, then her lips. She did not respond. All that night she slept.

Kato was himself asleep in a chair next to the bed when he heard her call his name. He was startled.

"Beauty! You're awake!"

"Where am I?"

"In a hospital."

"Why?"

"You don't remember?"

She looked over at Jean and the old woman. "I know these people," she said. "They were in a dream I just had. They found me in some meadow. I dreamt I was lost in a field of flowers. But it was a dream."

Kato called for the doctor. "You need to be examined, darling," he said. "You've been through hell."

"I have? I feel wonderful. I feel better than I've felt in my life. Like I've had the most peaceful sleep of my life."

"You've been sleeping for days."

"Days? Oh my God, our wedding. Our wedding in Paris. Are we in Paris?"

"We are, but our wedding day passed."

"How can that be?"

"We didn't know where you were. We had to cancel."

The doctor arrived and asked, "How do you feel?"

"Wonderful." Beauty was all smiles. "I feel absolutely marvelous."

Kato was disturbed that the news of the canceled wedding hadn't bothered Beauty.

"Have you ever walked in your sleep?" the physician asked.

"Never. Is that what I did?"

"We think so."

"That's funny," said Beauty.

"It wasn't to me," Kato snapped. "And it wasn't funny to my parents or the guests or the hundreds of people working on the wedding."

Beauty sat up in bed and aimed her comment at Jean and the old woman, both pleased to see her fresh and alert.

"I missed my own wedding," said Beauty, releasing a small but distinctly happy laugh. "How amazing!"

Ajay Lock for Mayor
The Man Means Business!

The campaign, like most, was all about money. Lock positioned himself as a seasoned executive who, through his extensive banking experience, would bring prosperity to the average citizen. His opponent, Monica Page, had served on the city council for years. Before that she'd been an educator. She was among the most respected black women in Atlanta and a formidable opponent. The contest was heated. Page was liked among her constituents, but her funds were limited. Lock had money to burn.

Ajay saw no reason to resign his position as president of Southern Security Bank until—and if—he was elected. Meanwhile, he carefully avoided any conflicts of interest. His wife, Louella, campaigned by his side. When he asked his daughter to make several appearances with him, she refused. He left a message on her answering machine that said, "A show of family unity is important."

Her return message was a single word: "Bullshit."

Meanwhile, Power's relationship with Southern Security had turned sour. His request for financing had been refused, not by Ed Kingston, Lock's subordinate, but by Lock himself. He wanted no further connection with Slim Simmons or anyone who had ever been close to him. Other banks in the city felt the same. Power was rejected wherever he went. No one would even consider putting up the kind of money required to take over Slim's empire. Months after his return to Atlanta, Power had nothing to show for it except his job as the manager of Holly Windsor's local escort agency.

Skyla had never been in love. She viewed love as a luxury she could not afford. Some women see men as dogs; others see them as pigs; Skyla saw them as a means to an end. For several years now, she'd been fascinated by loveless sexual intercourse. She liked to see how long a man could last and whether he had the sensitivity to give as well as get pleasure. The vast majority of men failed that test. They came, they left. She laughed at them, sometimes to their faces, sometimes behind their backs. She enjoyed her reckless abandon but, after meeting Holly, realized there was a way to keep enjoying it while profiting at the same time. To be a professional beguiler of men appealed to her. The fact that they would pay big money for the mere pleasure of her presence in and out of bed thrilled her to no end. She also imagined the outrage this would cause her parents if and when they ever found out. That thought only added to the thrill.

Holly was Skyla's kind of woman—clever, forthright, practical, and successful without the help of men. In fact, her success was at the expense of men. She didn't mind working for a woman like that. What Skyla hadn't counted on, though, was meeting a man like Power.

During the initial encounter she responded to his physicality in a way she had not experienced before. It wasn't simply that he was tall, lean, and handsome. There was something deeply romantic about Power that got to her. Maybe because he wasn't trying. Or maybe he got to her because he was the last man she expected to meet in such a position. The truth is that she was surprised that Holly had trusted a man, and not a woman, to manage her Atlanta agency.

In being interviewed by Power, she sensed his practicality and cold intelligence about a woman's sexuality. That coldness excited her. How could a man that attractive be so objective? What was his history? Who was his woman? Those were questions she wanted to ask but knew not to. They were hardly appropriate. But when he asked whether Ajay Lock was a relation, she suddenly saw that his interest in her might go beyond the business of his escort service. She guessed that her father would give her an advantage in dealing with Power.

Her first assignment as an escort was hugely successful. Her date was a professor from Stanford University visiting Atlanta. Marcus Copeland was an African American economist who had written a famous textbook that he was amazed to learn Skyla had read—and understood—in her first year of college. He told Skyla over a private dinner in his hotel suite that his wife was frigid and his marriage loveless. Beyond that, she was a professor herself, a botanist, who had never bothered to read his book. Sexually he was shy and inexperienced. Skyla was pleased to take the lead. He considered their physical encounter spectacular; she considered it ordinary. He asked her whether he could see her again before he left the city, and she lied, saying she was all booked. She realized this would motivate him to offer her more. He did, in fact, offer her twice the rate, and with great satisfaction, she agreed. The second encounter was sexually more stimulating for him and financially more stimulating for her. She thought Power would be pleased with the extra money she brought him and was surprised when he wasn't.

They met in the agency office the morning after.

"Why did he pay double?" Power asked.

"Because I told him that was the only way he could get me."

"You lied."

"Of course I lied. What's wrong with that?"

"We're running an honest business here—that's what's wrong."

"Oh, please. Don't get high and mighty on me."

"It's Holly's guiding principle—be straight with the client. Tell him the absolute truth. That way no one gets hurt."

"If I told this tweed the absolute truth it would go something like this: 'You're a pathetic little man who can't fuck worth a shit. The only way you can get decent pussy is to buy it.'"

"You think you're shocking me?" asked Power.

"No, I think I'm telling you the absolute truth. The truth is that this business is about money and I just brought you a shitload. I thought the way this works is when baby brings her pimp big money, her pimp pats her on the head. When she doesn't bring big money, pimp beats her ass."

"Is this supposed to be some kind of role-playing?" Power asked.

"No, I'm just sticking to the absolute truth—just like you asked."

"I don't consider myself a pimp."

"Then you're the one who's running from the truth."

"And I don't consider you a hooker. You're an escort. You're an educated and sophisticated young lady."

"More bullshit to make me feel like I'm something better than I am."

"If you get off on seeing yourself as hooker, fine."

"And if you get off on pretending you're not a pimp, I don't think that's fine at all. I think that's self-deception. If you knew I was with two or three guys this week and didn't come back to you with two or three thousand dollars, you'd beat my ass, just like any pimp."

"You're wrong. I don't beat women."

"Because you haven't been provoked by one."

"You want to provoke me?"

Skyla smiled before saying, "Maybe."

Power shook his head. "You know what I think, Skyla Lock?"

"What?"

"I think you're a privileged bourgie chick getting her kicks out of playing the part of a whore."

"That might be true, but that still makes you my pimp. And if you're my pimp, I'm here to serve at your pleasure. I'll do anything to make you happy."

Power had to laugh. "What makes me happiest is seeing this business run smoothly. What doesn't make me happy is to hear back from your Stanford professor, like I did just before you got here, that he's staying in Atlanta for another week so he can see you again."

"That should make you deliriously happy."

"It makes me think we're gonna encounter trouble."

"Why do you say that?"

"I've seen it before. He's falling for you. You're the daughter he never had or the wife he never gets to fuck. You're his everything. Next he's gonna propose that you return to Cali with him so he can set you up in an apartment. It's no longer straight business. It's turned into love."

"I guess I'm just too good at my job, Mr. Pimp—I mean, Mr. Power. What are you going to tell him?"

"I'm going to say no. I'm going to say that you're all booked up."

"Am I?"

"No, but we can't afford any messy entanglements."

"May I express my gratitude for your wisdom?"

Before Power could answer, Skyla went over to where Power was seated in his reclining high-backed office chair, fell to her knees, and, in record time, had his dick in her mouth. The fact that he was already hard proved to her that the combative conversation had turned him on. After the initial shock, he didn't resist. Few men could resist the pressure of her lips and movements of her tongue. When it was over, he leaned back in amazement.

"What do you have to say now, daddy?" she asked.

"Only that you give the best blow job in town."

. . . .

"Are you still here?" asked Ajay Lock. He was on the phone in his office at the Southern Security Bank. He looked out his window, where a driving rain had darkened the afternoon sky.

"I found I had a bit more business here and have delayed my trip for another week," said Professor Marcus Copeland.

"Must be a woman you met," said Ajay.

"No such luck," Copeland lied.

"In any event, I'm glad you're staying a while longer. I'd love to have you out to the house. Louella wants see you, and we'll go over some of those papers on the economic outlook you prepared for me."

"Aside from this other matter I must pursue, I'm at your disposal."

"Are you certain that the other matter doesn't have a vagina?"

"Not everyone chases willing women like you, Ajay."

"Please, Marcus, we've known each other too long to hide our vices. I remember that conference in Boston a few years back when you fell in love with that little call girl."

"I'm past all that."

Ajay laughed. "You can't bullshit a bullshitter."

Cable News

Irv Wasserman had never been addicted to television before he decided to retire from the world. In the past, when he was actively involved in his wide web of illegal enterprises, he didn't have time for anything but business. His mind was on one thing—making certain his organizations turned big profits. He understood that he needed knowledge of what was happening in the world, but only as it impacted *his* world. Politics were important, and it quickly became clear that politicians were for sale. So he bought all the politicians he needed. He didn't need television to teach him about politics; he had advisers who did that. He didn't need television to entertain him; he was a man who didn't require entertainment. His only use of television was to put it on in his bedroom when he went to bed. The sound of Jay Leno or David Letterman quickly put him to sleep.

But retirement changed all that. Irv didn't simply stop working. With the exception of a few Swiss bankers, he cut himself off from everyone he had ever known. Because he had been so blatantly betrayed, he decided relationships weren't worth it. His only comfort was in knowing that his enemies had been eliminated, leaving him with total access to the tens of millions they had tried to steal. Winding up with an enormous treasure chest was comforting—yet not as comforting as he had imagined it would be.

Like lonely people everywhere, Irv turned to TV. The sound of another person in the room—whether he was spending time in a two-thousand-dollar-a-day suite on the French Riviera or the Fiji Islands—made him a little less lonely. Or maybe it made him lonelier because he was forced to realize how alone he really was. He could have bought sex, but in his old age he decided that he was through with sex. The drive had disappeared, and he was glad for it. Sex had brought him a certain amount of pleasure, but women had only brought problems. He was glad to be free of those problems.

That left television. At first he tried game shows, but they were silly and stupid. Soap operas were out of the question because they were geared toward women. He had never been a sports fan. Once in a while an old gangster movie might interest him, but dramatic stories weren't his thing. Big-time talent shows only reminded him of the corrupt music business that he had left. He wanted to forget about the hassles of his past.

That left news. News was delivered in sound bites, perfect for Irv's short attention span. He found it fascinating that the main goal of the news seemed to be creating fear. In the way people like horror movies, people like news that frightens them. If a hurricane is coming, the news will make it sound like the worst hurricane of the century. If the economy is bad, the news will make it sound like soon there'll be no milk for the babies. Scary news sells, and Irv loved watching how the news organizations built up fear to boost their ratings.

Cable news was the worst. From Irv's perspective, though, they were the best because they were the most entertaining. He preferred the right-wing stations, which were better at scaring the viewers than the left-wing ones. He'd sit back and laugh at the newscaster's outrage at taxes or government regulations. He knew it was an act and admired the actors' skills. Sometimes he tried to watch the proceedings in Congress on C-SPAN, but he needed more theatrics than that. He saw that cable news understood the art of packaging political theatrics. After a while, though, even those theatrics began to wear thin.

That's why he had welcomed Slim into his life. Slim was a real character with real problems. Slim needed Irv at a time when no one else did. They might make an odd pair, but Slim could make him laugh. Slim's ghetto smarts had always been impressive to Irv ever since the two had met some thirty years earlier. Seeing Slim slowly come back to sanity had given Irv a sense of accomplishment that he sorely needed. What else had he done lately except watch cable news?

Irv understood how Dr. Mapperoot had helped Slim open up. Even if Irv wasn't able to express his own feelings in front of a stranger, he could see how doing so had worked to Slim's advantage. It was like cleaning cobwebs from the closet. But when Rashan mentioned something about taking Slim to a preacher, Irv wasn't sure.

Irv was proud of being Jewish. He'd never denied the existence of God. At the same time, he couldn't claim to know much about God. All he knew was that God was something good. But he also knew that when it comes to God, people could get fanatical and compelled to convert everyone they knew. That's the last thing in the world he wanted to hear from Slim. Irv Wasserman was not about to embrace Jesus Christ as his Lord and Savior.

It was noon and cable news was blasting from the television in the living room of the main house of the well-guarded compound. Irv looked up and saw Slim and Rashan walking through the door.

"You just getting up?" Irv asked Slim.

"No, man. I'm just getting in."

The guesthouse, where Slim was staying, had its own entrance, so Irv wasn't aware of Slim's comings and goings.

"Getting in from where?" asked Irv.

"The night of nights. Ask brother Rashan here. He'll tell you."

Rashan was by Slim's side. "Oh, I don't know, sir," he said. "All I know is that Mr. Simmons seems very happy."

"Come in and sit down, Slim," said Irv. "Let me turn off this fuckin' news. This TV is driving me crazy."

Slim fell into a chair across from the couch where Irv was sitting.

"Want a cigar?" asked Irv.

"Hell yes," said Slim.

The two men lit up Havana-made Cohiba cigars, among the world's best.

"I thought you went to church, Slim."

"I did."

"And?"

"God answered my prayer, Irv. Just like that."

"What was your prayer?"

"That I love a lady good."

"I don't get it."

"I'm about to tell you something I never told no one except Dr. Mappleroot."

"Don't tell me that you're a fag."

"I ain't no sissy. Never was and never will be. That wasn't the problem."

"Then what are you talking about?"

"All my life I'd bust a nut before I'd ever get to fucking. One look at the pussy and I'd pop."

"That's no problem for a preacher, Slim, that's something for a urologist. I got a good one back in Palm Beach, Dr. Meyer Nussbaum. I'll take you there next time we go to Florida."

"Don't need him. Got cured by Dr. Jesus. Yes, Lord, Dr. Jesus done the trick."

"Well, that was quick."

"But that's not the best part. The best part is after this preacher set me free, I met a woman."

"At church?"

"After church. I saw her singing."

"And?"

"Irv, I boned that bitch like I ain't boned no bitch before. I fucked her until she had to scream for me to stop."

"Well, that's good, Slim."

"Not good, Irv, it's a goddamn amazing miracle."

"So you'll be going back to church."

"I don't know about that," said Slim, "but I sure as shit will be going back to Besta."

"Besta?" asked Irv, blowing out a thick stream of smoke.

"Besta's the bitch. And she's beautiful. Sweet as honey. Soft as silk. Can't get enough of me."

"So you have a girlfriend, Slim. That's nice."

"I want you to meet her, Irv."

"I don't need to meet her."

"You do. I told her we'd help her."

"How we gonna do that?"

"She wants to record. She needs to record, Slim. Besta's *bad,* I guaran-goddamn-tee you. We gotta help her."

"*We?*"

"Look, Irv, I seen you sitting 'round here bored as a muthafucka. You ain't doing shit except staring at the television screen. Ain't nothing happenin' on that screen you care about. Am I right or am I right?"

"I travel. Travel is interesting."

"Travel is just as boring as that television. You on this island, you on that island, they all the same. You in this fancy hotel or that fancy hotel, you still bored. You still up in there with the TV on. I say let's go back and do a little business and help this lady become the star she was born to be."

"The music business is murder, Slim, I don't have to tell you that."

"With our brainpower, we can murder the business and get her where she needs to be."

"I'm gonna have lunch and then take a nap," said Irv.

"Will you go with me to the Serenity Seasons Resort tonight? Besta's singing in the lounge. You gotta see her, Irv."

"I gotta eat and then I gotta nap."

That evening Irv decided to go see Besta. What else did he have to do? He put on a nice plain blue sports shirt, expensive black dress slacks, and a pair of Bruno Magli loafers. This was as dressed up as Irv had been in months.

Slim put him to shame. He wore a white linen suit, a white silk shirt open at the neck, an eighteen-karat-gold Taurus bull icon around his neck, and red alligator shoes on his feet.

Irv laughed when he saw his friend. "You're back," he said.

"Damn right. And it feels good."

They got in the back of the Mercedes SUV. Up front were Rashan and another bodyguard who did the driving. The road wound along the mountainside. The sun was setting into the sea and the sky had turned golden. The newfound energy emanating from Slim was getting to Irv. He felt happy.

The Serenity Seasons Resort was the most exclusive on the island. It was decorated with thirties-style bamboo furniture. The lobby looked like a movie set where Humphrey Bogart was about to walk in at any moment. The clientele were rich white businessmen, some traveling alone, some with families. The lounge, just off the lobby, was a cozy posh room with floral wallpaper on three sides. The bandstand was set up on the fourth side, where open doors gave way to the beach. Blue lights radiating from the hotel roof illuminated the crashing waves. Beyond the singer onstage was a great expanse of sand, sea, and starlit sky.

"That's Besta," said Slim to Irv as they entered the lounge. "That's my girl."

The two men took seats at a table in the back. Their bodyguards seated themselves at a table just behind them. Besta was singing a song that Irv did not know. He didn't really relate to her style. He had made a fortune in the music business without knowing music. He had hired others to figure out who had talent. It wasn't that he didn't appreciate music; it just rarely moved him.

He did, however, appreciate Besta's body. She was short and stacked and obviously comfortable with her shape. The expression that came to Irv's mind was pleasantly plump. She was also sassy. She had a sexy attitude. She wore a black pageboy wig that neatly framed her face. Her eyes sparkled. She seemed to be saying, *I know what you want. Maybe I'll give it to you and maybe I won't. Stick around and see.*

Irv could see why Slim was smitten, but he wasn't. Her voice was strong, her tight orange-and-green dress showed off her considerable curves, she was professional enough in her presentation, yet all that wasn't enough to keep Irv's interest until . . .

"Now, friends," she said to the audience of perhaps twenty-five or thirty people, "I'm going to surprise you with a song that you didn't expect to hear in Jamaica. My mother taught it to me, and she heard it sung by Billie Holiday. It's a song about a mother, so I when sing it, I think of mine. She's been gone now for many years, but she lives in my heart, just as I believe all our mothers live in our hearts. It's called 'My Yiddishe Momme.'"

Irv's heart started hammering. Had he heard right? Was this woman talking about a song that he—Irv Wasserman—had heard as a young kid growing up in the Jewish ghetto of Chicago? This was a song that Irv's own mother loved and played over and again, by a singer named Sophie Tucker. Irv had memorized Tucker's version. The words were simple; they were a child's lament for a dead mother.

The child longs for the mother's love, longs to touch and hold and kiss the mother who provided him sweet solace.

Besta sang the song a cappella. Just as she began, trade winds began blowing in from the sea just beyond the open doors. The song floated on those winds. Irv closed his eyes and saw his own mother. "My Yiddishe momme," sang Besta, "I need her more than ever now." Her voice shattered the hard shell covering Irv's soul. Her voice took his breath away. He didn't know what to do. His first thought was that he would break into tears. He couldn't let that happen. He had never cried in public. He didn't know what that would look like. He couldn't imagine it. He was afraid that were he to start crying, he wouldn't be able to stop. He couldn't picture himself weeping like a child. He couldn't stand the humiliation. And yet as the song went on, the emotion built up inside him. The walls of his heart, like a dam overwhelmed by a storm, were about to break. He had to get up to leave.

He hurried to the bathroom, Rashan behind him, and barely made it inside a stall, where he shut the door, put his head in his hands, and sobbed like he hadn't sobbed since the death of his mother. He muffled the sound of his cries, but the weeping wouldn't stop. Standing outside the stall, Rashan asked Irv whether he was all right. When no answer came and Rashan heard nothing but sobs, he understood that Irv needed to be left alone. Five minutes later, when he finally emerged, Irv's eyes were red. He went to the sink to wash his face. By the time he returned to the table, Besta was sitting there next to Slim, who introduced her to Irv.

"Charles told me about you," she said. "He said you're his friend, and I sang the song for you. I was hoping you knew it."

"I know it," said Irv, still sniffling. "I know it good."

"And you liked it?"

"It was my . . ." Irv fought to keep his composure. "It was my mother's favorite."

"Beautiful," said Slim. "Ain't ever seen you so emotional, good brother. I told you Besta brings it. Girlfriend brings it with all she got."

"We all miss our moms, don't we?" asked Besta. "Tell me about yours, Irv. You don't mind if I call you Irv, do you?"

"No, sweetheart, you can call me Irv. But my mother, well, that's a long story. Tonight we're here to celebrate the future, not the past."

"Now you're talking," said Slim.

"Charles told me that you were once in the music business, Irv," said Besta.

Irv nodded.

"And he said you were quite an important force in the industry," Besta added.

"I wouldn't go that far."

"He's modest," said Slim.

"Most great men are," said Besta.

"I'm not great," Irv retorted. "And I'm not modest. But I do have to say that I'm moved, young lady. You have a tremendous talent and you know how to sell a song."

"I knew she'd sell your cold-blooded ass, Irv," said Slim. "I fuckin' knew it."

"I wasn't trying to sell anybody," said Besta. "I was just expressing something deep in my soul. It was a message, Irv, from my soul to yours."

"The message was delivered," Irv said. "And I'm feeling that the world needs more messages like that. The world needs to know about your talent."

"Does that mean you're going back into business?" asked Slim.

"It means *we're* going back into business," said Irv. "The Besta business."

Tokyo

Beauty didn't understand why this time she felt compelled to meet her biological father. Last time she was in Tokyo and Kato had located him, she was furious. She refused to see him. He was, after all, the man who had impregnated and then abandoned her mother, Isabel Long. He had disappeared off the map—never writing her once, never bothering to see after her welfare. He was a dog. To him, Isabel Long was nothing more than a mistress. And when Isabel suffered a cruel death from cancer when Beauty was eleven, he still remained silent. Not a word. Not even a sympathy card. Beauty's attitude toward her father had remained constant: *Fuck him!* So why, especially on this trip, was she about to meet him?

It had to do with what everyone was calling her nervous exhaustion. The episode in Paris that led to the cancellation of her wedding was still shrouded in mystery. When Kato decided not to reschedule the wedding Beauty was relieved, even if she didn't let him know. The staff that had come to facilitate the events, the hundreds of guests, and the many media reps had all left Paris in a state of confusion and frustration. During those days that Beauty was missing, no one was willing to wait around. No one could say where she was or what was happening. It was a messy business that made Kato look weak and inept.

He and Beauty flew from Paris to New York, where for two months they barely spoke. Kato was furious but couldn't express his anger. How can you get angry with a person who suffered a nervous breakdown? But *was* it a nervous breakdown or a manipulation? Was this sleepwalking business Beauty's way of getting out of a wedding that she really didn't want? After all, she had agreed to marry him only as a way to save Power. Kato had tried to erase that fact from his mind, to convince himself that Beauty did in fact have real love for him. He had wanted to believe that even if Power's life hadn't been on the line, she would have married him anyway. But that belief was shattered by what had happened in Paris.

It's one thing to see your fiancée disappear because of some unexplained psychological episode. But Beauty's blasé attitude *after* the episode—her lack of regret—only added to Kato's doubts about her sincerity. She apologized, she said the right words, but her heart wasn't in it. Kato felt that her heart had been lightened by the experience. She seemed at ease.

Beauty couldn't deny that was she relieved. In New York, she turned her attention to the Young Beauty line of clothing and in-store boutiques that she had developed for the chain. It was, in fact, one of the only profitable areas in an operation that was experiencing alarmingly lagging sales. Making matters worse, ever since the Paris fiasco Kato struggled even more with his role as chief operating officer of this enormous business.

Solomon Getz, the man Kato appointed vice president of merchandising, saw that struggle firsthand. He was the one who reported Kato's difficulties to Beauty. The conversation had taken place over a quiet lunch at Peacock Alley, the restaurant at the Waldorf-Astoria on Park Avenue, the day before Beauty and Kato were to leave for Tokyo.

"I don't want you to get any more upset," said Solomon. "You've been through a lot."

"I feel fine," said Beauty. "All that happened in Paris is behind me. But I know that Kato isn't feeling fine at all. That's why I convinced him to take this trip to Tokyo with me. His parents are there, and he finds his parents comforting."

"Didn't he have to take on his parents in order to do this Bloom/Fine deal?"

"He did," said Beauty, "but once it happened, they got behind him."

"I'm afraid they're about the only ones behind him. I'm telling you this, Beauty, because you're my friend and I want to prepare you."

"Prepare me for what?"

"I don't think he has the skills to pull this off. His entire upper-tier management is in revolt."

"Including you?"

"Because of you, I've stayed neutral. But I understand their panic."

"Panic over what?" she asked.

"His mismanagement is running the company into the ground. He's made one bad decision after another. He took over a failing Nordstrom location in Minneapolis and spent a fortune refurbishing it as an upscale Bloom's. The market is not there to support it. Sales have been miserable. He closed down the Boston store just when it looked like it was about to turn around, and here in New York the flagship store is being ignored. With Saks, Barneys, Bloomingdale's, and Bergdorf Goodman right around the corner, we're getting clobbered. You can't afford to lag behind in the middle of Manhattan. You've seen that yourself."

"I've mentioned that to him, Solomon, but he's been distant."

"And you haven't?" Solomon asked his friend.

"Well, I've been busy with my own line."

"It's the only line that this store is presenting in a fresh and attractive way. You need to get him to focus, Beauty, or else it'll be too late. The numbers are dismal. His backers can't be happy."

Beauty thought about those backers, the men who saved Power, and wondered whether Kato would see them in Japan.

"Have you reset a date for the wedding?" asked Solomon.

"Not yet."

"Is that because of you or him?"

"Both of us, I suppose."

"I don't understand."

"To tell you the truth, Solomon, I don't either. It's just a strange period for us. We're leaving each other alone. And I'm not sure that's bad."

"I'm not sure that's good, Beauty."

"Well, I'm certain things will get out sorted out in Tokyo. I have a feeling that Tokyo will help us both get a handle on what's happening."

But Tokyo only added to the emotional distance between them. They had a penthouse suite at the Rising Star, a fifty-story hotel that towered over a scramble crossing thought to be the busiest intersection in the world. Beauty loved the location, the hub of young fashion in Japan. Kato wanted something more secluded but was too distracted with other matters to argue with Beauty.

While Kato was depressed, Beauty was excited. More than any culture, the Japanese understood preteen and teen fashion. As bold innovators in that market, they inspired Beauty. She ran from one designer workshop to another; she ran from one store to another, whether a giant operation like Matsuzakaya or the smallest boutique down an alley in Roppongi. Beauty was convinced that no people on earth shopped with as much passionate energy as the Japanese. In Tokyo, she was happy to lose herself in the world of retail.

Meanwhile, it was that world that led Beauty back to her biological father. She was walking through Harajuku, a section of Tokyo famous for street fashion and outlandish style. In her mind, she was considering the strange contradiction of how, on one hand, the Japanese were conformists and cultural copycats, but at the same time, they created outrageous and edgy fashion like no one else.

That thought was going through her head when her eyes were drawn to a large store with the name, in huge orange letters, THE ATL. Though it was common for Japanese retailers to adopt Americanized names, she was surprised to see the abbreviation for Atlanta. She had seen a score of such stores, like Blue Genes, Hippity Hop, Rap It Up, and Beatz. For many years the Japanese had been infatuated with the hip-hop style of African Americans. This, though, was something else.

The store, filled with clothing designed for young teens, was fabulous. Jeans were deconstructed and reconstructed with patches of blue leather and red wool. Hoodies were created in a combination of fabrics—silk and satin, cotton and crinkly polyester—and crazy colors like Popsicle orange and neon green. Skirts were made from a combination of sackcloth and gabardine. Floppy hats with huge crowns and wide brims bore the bold abstract designs of painters like Jackson Pollock. Beauty loved what she saw. She took out her notepad and began jotting down ideas.

Then she looked up and saw a man who looked just like her.

Fortunately, he didn't see her. He was across the store speaking to one of the clerks. He had her cheekbones, her eyes, her hands, her gestures, her stature, her everything. Beauty knew she was looking at her father. She remembered that when Kato had located him he'd said his name was Akira Matsui and that he owned a clothing store for teens in Harajuku. This had to be him.

For a second, she considered introducing herself. Maybe the shock would give him a heart attack. Maybe the heart attack would kill him.

Maybe the whole episode would give her great satisfaction and pay him back for treating her mom like dirt. She took a step in his direction, but then changed her mind. She didn't want the confrontation. She didn't want to be in his presence. She turned around, and before he could get a look at her, she hurried out the door.

The thought, though, didn't leave her mind. She now knew the exact location of her father, and she couldn't stop considering the coincidence of how he and she were both in the same line of work. She also couldn't deny the fact that his taste was brilliant. She wanted to know the name of his designer. She couldn't imagine it was him. These clothes had a woman's sensibility. He must have hired a designer and yet—to his credit—he had the taste to recognize the designer's advanced aesthetic. Despite her certainty that he was a low-down dog, he had to be an interesting man to run a store this avant-garde.

When Kato arrived at their suite that night, he was exhausted. Usually he asked her about her day, but all he could do was fix himself a drink and collapse on the couch.

"What's wrong?" she asked.

"Finances," he said. "It's always finances."

"What about finances?"

"I don't want to worry you."

"Saying that," said Beauty, "only worries me more."

"I'm sorry. I just don't know what to say—or do."

Beauty hadn't seen Kato fall into this kind of despair before. She wanted to probe more, but she knew that the kindest thing was to leave him alone. She walked over to the window that looked down at the scramble crossing. The lights of the electric city were screaming. People were streaming in every direction. It was seven o'clock and she wanted to enter that stream. She didn't want to stay in the suite with a depressed Kato.

"Want to go out to eat?" she asked.

"I'll just order up food. Tell me what you want."

"I think I want to go out for a while."

"Fine," he said, not bothering to argue.

"I won't be long."

"Fine," he repeated, almost as though he didn't care.

She went to the bedroom and selected an especially edgy outfit, fuchsia toreador pants and a flowing black poncho-style top—both her own designs. She was just about to walk out when she looked in the closet and saw an Atlanta Braves baseball cap that she had taken to wear on the plane. She put it on her head and walked past Kato, who, still collapsed on the couch, didn't bother to look up or say good-bye.

The elevator music, accompanying her on the fifty-story ride down, was a Muzak version of Prince's "Little Red Corvette." When she exited the hotel and hit the street, she knew exactly where she was going even if she couldn't explain why.

Akira Matsui saw his daughter walk through the door of his store. He had not the least doubt that it was her. In fact, he had been waiting for this moment ever since Kato Yamamoto had called him last year. He knew that the young merchant prince was living with his daughter, and he had been hoping that she would seek him out.

He was thrilled to see her—thrilled to see that she was as beautiful as her mother, thrilled to see the exquisite marriage of Asian and African American features, thrilled that her attire was not only in synch with the clothes he sold but perhaps even more advanced. He walked over to her, extended his hand, and called her by her birth name. "Welcome, Tanya," he said in barely accented English.

Beauty did not take his hand. "No one calls me that," she said.

"I know that's the name your mother gave you. And I welcome you to this store. I welcome you to Japan."

"I don't need your welcome, and I didn't come here to see you. I came to see your clothes. I want to meet your designer."

"She is a woman your age, and I'm happy to introduce you. But first can we talk in my office for a short while?"

"What is there to talk about?"

"How lives, lost for twenty-two years, may now be found."

"The subject doesn't interest me."

"Let's sit and have a cup of tea. Then I'll take you to the designer."

Beauty's father's voice had a soothing and beguiling quality. He beckoned her with a gentleness she hadn't expected. She'd thought he'd speak crudely and be embarrassed by her presence. She had been waiting for the worst. She took up his offer and followed him to his office.

Akira Matsui worked in an office above the store. The walls were light blond wood, the floors covered in large square stones in contrasting browns, beiges, and light yellows. Four starkly elegant sculptures of black-and-silver metal, original works of the Japanese-American artist Isamu Noguchi, sat in the four corners. Matsui's desk was a large slab of gray marble held up by legs of distressed steel. Beauty had to admit that his taste was perfect—austere, simple, and artistic. She sat in an armless chair of off-white vintage leather. He sat across from her in an identical chair.

"I have been following your life closely," said Matsui.

"Not close enough. You've never called me in your entire life—not once."

"Out of consideration."

Beauty laughed. "You're confusing negligence with consideration."

"My calls would have only confused you."

"Well, there certainly isn't any confusion now. You slept with Isabel Long, you made promises, and when she became pregnant, you jumped on the first plane back to Tokyo. It's all clear."

"Not as clear as you might think. You see, Isabel always knew I had another family here in Tokyo. I was clear about that from the start of our relationship."

"That's a convenient position to take now," said Beauty. "But I don't believe you."

"I sent support."

"I don't believe you."

"I have records to prove it."

"Records can be faked."

"I have letters from your mother, thanking me for my help. There was no bitterness in her letters. You can read them if you like."

"Letters can be falsified. I'm not interested in reading any fake letters."

"You will recognize the sincerity of her tone," said Matsui.

"Look," said Beauty, "let's cut the crap. If you really cared, at the very least you would have come to her funeral."

"I didn't learn about her passing until two months after she was gone. By then, I was sure my appearance would do nothing but upset you. The Yamamotos had told me that you were being cared for by Charlotte Clay. I knew she was a good woman and that you would be in good hands. I also sent her money to help support you."

"What am I supposed to do? Thank you for all your wonderful support? You were glad to live your life without me. I've been glad to live my life without you. I've come here solely for business reasons. Your line of clothes interests me. I want to meet your designer."

"She'll want to meet you."

"Is she here?"

Matsui looked at his watch. "Eight thirty," he said. "She should be here. She likes to work late. Her workroom is right above us."

Beauty followed her father up to a higher floor. When he opened the door to the workroom, a woman got up from her drawing board and looked in their direction. It was clear that she had no sight in her vacant eyes. She recognized Matsui's footsteps but not the person who had entered with him.

"Who are you with?" she asked.

"Your sister," he answered.

Opening Day at Turner Field

Ted Turner himself had just left the private box overlooking the baseball field he had built. He had shaken hands with everyone there, including Ajay Lock and his wife, Louella. Despite the fact that it was a sporting event, Ajay was dressed in a banker's blue chalk-striped suit and his wife was in a tweed gray-and-black St. John ensemble. In the midst of his campaign, he wanted to look mayoral at all times. Louella, always elegantly groomed, played the part of the good wife. While Turner hadn't endorsed Ajay for mayor, he had taken the time to come by Southern Security's box at Turner Field to wish the candidate well.

Power observed all this from the corner of the box. Because of the many well-wishers and supporters passing through, he had not yet approached Lock. This was, in fact, the first time he had seen Ajay in person. He had looked at his pictures in the paper and watched him campaign on television, but those images didn't convey the man's distinguished bearing. His middle-of-the-road positions went over well with voters on the left and right. Few doubted that he would be the city's next chief executive.

Power patiently waited while Lock continued to glad-hand. Power was in no hurry. He loved baseball. He had been a Braves fan since birth. He had idolized David Justice and lived and died with the team's fortunes. What better way to pass the time than to relax in prime seats and watch his boys start a new season?

During a lull in the action on and off the field, Power walked over to the mayoral candidate and introduced himself. Louella was busy talking to a prominent preacher who had dropped by to say hello.

"Paul Clay," he said. "A pleasure to meet you."

"My pleasure, Mr. Clay," said Ajay.

"I'm a friend of Ed Kingston."

"Ed's a good man," said Lock.

"I've known Ed awhile. I met him through one of your customers, Charles Simmons."

Power saw that he had gotten Ajay's attention, even if Ajay tried to hide his disdain at hearing Slim's name.

"Of course, Charles. And what did you say your name was?"

"Paul Clay. They call me Power."

"Well, Mr. Clay. Thanks for stopping by to say hello."

"There's one quick matter I wanted to mention. Will only take a second. I was turned down for financing that would enable me to save Simmons's operations."

"I do remember Ed showing me that file, yes. Sorry about that. But business is business. Atlanta doesn't lack for resources, though. Others will surely help you."

"No one will touch this, Mr. Lock, and you know it. Simmons's reputation guarantees that."

Discomfort began to set in. Ajay stood up. "Well, again, nice to have met you. I'm afraid my wife and I have another obligation."

"Perhaps we can meet in your office later this week," said Power. The calm boldness in Power's voice surprised Lock.

"There's nothing to meet about, Mr. Clay. Your application has been denied. Such decisions are final."

"Maybe yes, maybe no. But, beyond that matter, there is the relationship between Professor Marcus Copeland and your daughter Skyla that requires your attention."

The last statement stopped Ajay. "What in hell are you talking about?" he asked in a lowered voice. "How do you know Copeland? And what does he have to do with Skyla?"

"We'll discuss all that when you find the time to meet with me."

"How do you know Skyla?" asked the banker.

"She works for me."

The very next day, at eleven A.M., Power was ushered into the magisterial office of Ajay Lock in the Southern Security Bank Building. Out of respect to his host's high position, Power was dressed in a blue blazer, blue tie, and pleated beige slacks. Lock wore a gray vested suit.

"Be brief, Mr. Clay, I don't have much time," said Ajay bluntly.

"Please, sir, call me Power."

"What is this business about my daughter?"

"She works for me."

"You don't know what you're talking about. She's a student at Georgia Tech. She's a top student."

"She's also one of my top earners. She's been a professional escort for the past five weeks. Your economic adviser, Professor Copeland, was one of her first clients. He became obsessed with her—and still is."

Lock's eyes went wide, and his breathing became heavy. "I don't believe any of this," he said. "This is a fabrication. You've been hired by my opponent. I'll have you arrested."

"For what?"

"Blackmail."

"I haven't asked you for a thing."

"You will, and you'll get nothing," said Ajay. "This is a ruse."

"I have detailed records," Power replied. "My records are meticulous. You can go over the documentation any time you like."

"My daughter would never engage in such work."

"You're wrong. She enjoys it. And part of that enjoyment comes from knowing how vulnerable it makes you."

"And as for Coleman, he's never met my daughter."

"He hadn't until he called the agency requesting an escort. Believe me when I tell you, Mr. Lock, that I didn't set him up with Skyla intentionally. It was pure coincidence. Now he won't leave her alone. He texts and calls night and day. Haven't you wondered why he's practically moved from Palo Alto to Atlanta?"

"To help me with my campaign."

"Did you ask him to move here?"

"That was his idea."

"That's my point."

Lock's intercom rang. The voice of his assistant said, "Professor Copeland on the line."

"Tell him I'll call him back," said Lock.

"He says it's extremely urgent," said the assistant.

"I'll call him back," Lock repeated, "and please don't disturb me again." He asked Power, "Does Copeland know that you know?"

"Copeland knows that she's your daughter," said Power.

"Did she tell him?"

"She didn't have to. He's been to your house. He saw her photo."

"Oh, shit . . . ," said Lock, seeing his political future evaporate in front of him.

"And Skyla, of course, discovered that he's one of your economic advisers," said Power. "She liked the irony of that but doesn't really like the professor. I've had to tell him to back off."

"And will he?" asked Ajay.

"He'll have to. He has a career that could go up in smoke. As do you."

"What would anyone gain by releasing this information?" asked Lock.

"Nothing," said Power. "Nothing at all."

"And you, I presume, are the only one capable of preventing that release."

"I am, sir."

"And the price of that containment?"

"No price. Just your approval of the financial package that will allow me to take over the Simmons enterprises spread across the city."

"You're talking about some twelve million dollars."

"As I told Ed Kingston when I first made the proposal, it has all the hallmarks of a profitable partnership for your bank."

Ajay Lock looked at Power and spoke with the decisiveness that characterizes all successful executives.

"I'll make certain the professor goes back to Stanford—and stays there," said the mayoral candidate. "As far as my daughter is concerned, I'll need your guarantee that this entire sordid matter will be kept in strictest confidence. Additionally, I'll need your guarantee that my daughter will discontinue her work for you and for anyone else in your field."

"What makes you think I can control her like that?"

"Knowing my daughter as I do, I presume she has fallen in love with you and will do anything you ask of her."

Ajay wasn't wrong—and Power knew it.

"As long as you control her," said the banker, "you'll get what you want from me."

Blue Harmony

The yacht floated along the coast of Key Largo. It was sunset, and the sky had turned a dreamy shade of pink that, to Slim's eyes, matched the pink eye shadow that highlighted Besta's glowing complexion. She was dressed to kill, but, then again, Besta was always dressed to kill. She was a woman who understood that, despite a culture that worshipped thin, many men still worshipped curves. Slim had become her worshipper because, even after two weeks of bedding her, he still hadn't suffered the premature ejaculation that had plagued him for so long. She had turned him into a new man, and there was nothing he wouldn't do for her.

Irv Wasserman was glad to be along for the ride. In fact, he was paying for the ride. He had hired a captain and crew and chartered a grand yacht, the *Blue Harmony,* for two weeks. He chose the enormous boat not because it held four bedrooms, four baths, and an ornate dining room with a floor of Italian travertine, but principally because of the state-of-the-art recording studio situated on the middle deck.

"I'm not a creative person," Irv told Besta and Slim when they had all been discussing the best time and place to record the singer. "I don't have anything to say about the music. The business part is different. I'll have a lot to say about that. But the music is your department. However, hearing Besta talk about how she wants to make music to make people forget their problems, I'm thinking she needs to make that music in a problem-less place. You mentioned Miami, Slim, but Miami is filled with problems. These days hoodlums are running Miami. New York is worse. Don't even mention L.A. And I sure as hell don't wanna go back to Chicago, just like you got no interest in going to Atlanta. So I say we record in the middle of the ocean. Some clever guy has probably built a studio on a yacht. Let's find that yacht and go sailing the seven seas while you make your record."

Besta ran over to kiss Irv.

"He don't need that much sugar," Slim said, a wave of jealousy passing over him.

"After how you keep dipping in my bowl," said Besta to Slim, "ain't much sugar left."

It didn't take Irv long to find the *Blue Harmony,* a studio yacht that had been used by everyone from Tina Turner to Trey Songz. Besta had been getting tracks from an R & B producer who called himself Up. With the assurance that Up was gay, Slim agreed that he and his engineer should spend two weeks on the yacht, recording Besta's vocals.

Up, a handsome medium-brown-skinned black man in his mid-twenties with long dreads and smiling eyes, didn't seem gay—but he also didn't seem interested in Besta as a sexual partner. He was all about the music. Up's engineer was Althea, a nerdy young black woman with thick glasses and a Boston accent. She was a whiz in the studio. When not working, she got busy perfecting her newest audio software innovation.

The weather was gentle, warm enough during the day, cool enough at night. The *Blue Harmony* sailed along in a smooth rhythm to the bedroom R & B being recorded in the studio. Besta said that her songs were inspired by Slim. She put words to Up's melodies. Her stories had a common theme: "You Last Longest," "Baby, Wait Till I Come," "Your Love Don't Fade," "The Man in My Dreams (Is the Man in My Bed)." Slim sat next to Althea as, on the other side of the glass, Besta sang her heart out. She seemed to be singing to Slim. Meanwhile, Irv stayed in his bedroom, watched baseball games on television, and enjoyed long naps. For the sake of everyone's security, Rashan was on board, always alert.

Up and Althea kept to themselves in the studio while Slim, Irv, and Besta were served lunch on the upper deck.

"I'm the luckiest girl in the world," said Besta, her breasts straining against her super-tight pink jersey halter. The outlines of her erect nipples could not have been clearer. Slim loved how they looked. Irv was indifferent. He recognized Slim's miraculous sexual rebirth and was happy for his friend. He derived satisfaction from the fact that he had brought Slim back from the brink of madness. He'd gotten him to the hospital in Miami, he'd taken him to Jamaica, he'd found him a good therapist in Dr. Mapploroot, and, through Irv's employee Rashan, Slim had found God and Besta. *Good for Slim,* Irv thought to himself. *Good for me. At least I've done something for my fellow man.*

Besta had also done something for Irv. She had brought back memories of his own mother and restored emotional and physical health to his friend Slim. How then could he—Irv—not return the favor by helping Besta?

Besta seemed to embody happiness itself. She exuded optimism. She was a talker but also a generous conversationalist. She sensed that Slim and Irv did not want to talk about their pasts, so instead she questioned them about their interests—what foods they liked, what baseball teams Irv followed, where Slim got his great taste in clothes. She was a flatterer, but her flattery felt sincere. She was also candid in revealing her own history. As they ate a succulent whitefish caught only hours before and baked by the ship's Bahamian cook, she told them how she had wound up in Jamaica.

She was born in Cleveland, where her father was a barber. Her mom, a Jamaican and devout Christian, worked in a bank. Her folks divorced when Besta was twelve. She and her mom moved to Kingston, where she did well in high school and attended a two-year college. At

the encouragement of her conservative mother, she studied hotel management. Her dream, though, was to sing. Her idol was Whitney Houston. She found a way to express her talent by singing in outdoor clubs
and, on occasion, in the resort where she worked as assistant manager.
Her mother knew of none of this, and when Besta finally confessed that
she had in fact been singing popular music in public and had found
producers willing to record her, the conversation was difficult.

"Are you going to bed with these producers?" her mother had asked.

"Not both, of course not," said Besta.

"Are you going to bed with one of them?"

Besta's lack of response was as good as saying yes.

"We'll send her flowers," said Slim. "Give me your mom's address
and I'll send her a hundred red roses, just to thank her for giving birth
to Besta."

Besta laughed. "I'm not sure she'd appreciate that."

"Why not?"

"Because she'd think you were trying to buy her too."

The word "too" shook Slim. "*Too?*" he asked. "You think I've
bought you?"

"If you have, you sure as hell didn't pay enough," said Besta, trying
to laugh it off.

"Everyone is for sale," said Irv. "Everyone is a seller, and everyone
is a buyer. We buy records, we buy producers, we buy singers, we buy
friendship. We're traders. That's what people do."

"You see," said Besta, "your friend Irv is a wise one."

"And, Besta," said Irv, "believe me, sweetheart, when I tell you
that we're going to buy you the stardom you deserve."

"You hear that, Slim? Irv is ready to go to work."

"I think that you and me," said Slim, "are ready for a little after-
lunch nap."

"A naughty nap?" asked Besta.

"Why the fuck not?" asked Slim.

Sisters

Ryoko Matsui looked nothing like her half sister, Beauty. She was somewhat homely, short in stature, and shy by nature. She had been blind since age six and overprotected by her mother. Unlike Beauty, whose mother was African American, Ryoko's mother was Akira's plain-faced Japanese wife of forty years, a woman to whom he had never been faithful.

Ryoko had been homeschooled by English and French tutors. She spoke three languages fluently. At an early age, she had displayed unusual artistic talent. For years, her parents were convinced that she was going to become a painter, but then in her early teens she began drawing dresses and skirts as though she could actually see them. She became obsessed with fabrics and spent many hours with her father as he inspected bolts of cotton, silk, and polyester as part of his work in the fashion industry.

Her parents had tried to arrange friendships between Ryoko and men but she never seemed interested. She showed no interest in romance, only design. She had no knowledge of her father's romantic life outside his marriage and it was only last year, when her mother died, that Akira had told her that he had fathered another daughter who lived in America. Ryoko was both shocked and curious. She wanted to know all about her half sibling. When Akira said that Tanya also worked in fashion, Ryoko insisted that they meet. Akira explained that, because he had abandoned Tanya in order to preserve his family in Tokyo, Tanya had no interest in meeting him. "That will change one day," said Ryoko, a soft-spoken woman. "Every girl wants to know her father."

The moment that Akira announced that Tanya was in the room, Ryoko jumped up and opened her arms.

"My sister!" she said. "Please come here so I can feel your face."

Still stunned by the revelation, Beauty walked over to Ryoko, who gently ran her fingers over her face.

"You are beautiful," she said. "That is why they don't call you Tanya. They call you Beauty, don't they?"

"You know that?"

"They read me the fashion magazines that come from America."

Beauty sat in a chair next to Ryoko's drawing board. While they spoke, Ryoko held her sister's hand.

"I am so lucky you came here," said Ryoko. "I have dreamed of meeting you."

"I didn't know you were here," said Beauty. "I didn't know that you existed."

"I realize that. Our father has divided his life into many compartments. He didn't tell me about you until my own mother died."

"And your own mother never knew?"

"Never," said Ryoko. "It might have made her die even earlier."

Akira began to break in. "I'm sorry—"

"Please, Father," Ryoko said in Japanese. "Leave me and my sister to ourselves so we may speak."

Happy the women were getting along so beautifully, Akira left the room.

"How old are you?" asked Beauty.

"Twenty-two. And you?"

"Twenty-two."

When they compared their birthdays, they learned they were born two weeks apart. Beauty was the oldest.

"My father had two daughters with two different women within days of each other," said Ryoko. "Isn't that amazing?"

"Incredible," said Beauty.

"Does that make you angry at him?"

"I'm too shocked to say. How about you?"

"I'm so happy at finding you it's hard to be angry. Should I call you Tanya or Beauty?"

"Most everyone calls me Beauty."

"And you design like I do?"

"Not as well you as do. Are all the clothes in this store your designs?"

"Yes. Do you like them?"

"I love them, Ryoko. I love them very much. I walked into the store because of your designs. They drew me in."

Ryoko squeezed her sister's hand. "Let me see what you're wearing," she said.

"You want me to describe my clothes?"

"It's easier for me to feel them. I need to touch the fabric."

As Ryoko's fingers explored Beauty's outfit, she nodded her head and smiled. "I see," she kept saying. "I see very clearly. We have similar visions. We like the wild side of fashion, don't we? It's amazing. I could have designed the very clothes you are wearing."

"It's scary," said Beauty. "I feel like I could have—or wish I could have—designed the clothes in this store."

"Of course you could have," said Ryoko. "You did! Through me! And I designed your clothes through you!"

The conversation went on for another thirty minutes, the sisters exchanging ideas about new dresses and skirts, overcoats and raincoats, hats and shoes. It was though they were of a single mind. They couldn't believe how incredibly close their fashion sensibilities were.

"You must talk to our father," said Ryoko. "You ask him to find a way for us to work together."

"We don't need his permission. You can work with me whenever you like. I have my own line. I have absolute creative freedom. We can start collaborating right now. In fact, I'd love for you to come back with me to New York."

"Oh, I could never leave Tokyo, Beauty. I could never leave Father."

"You've not been out of the country?"

"Once to China, but the trip did not go well. I became ill. I'm very used to living in the home where I was born. I've never lived anywhere else."

"And yet you design with a great international flair. Surely you've been exposed to the fashions of other cultures."

"Only in my imagination," said Ryoko.

"Well, I'm here often. And I can come here more often. And we can speak on the phone and use the computer. I see you have a computer."

"Yes, it talks to me."

"That's wonderful."

"I think you're wonderful, Beauty. I think you have made me very happy."

Beauty took her sister's hand and brought it to her lips.

A few minutes later she was in Akira's office.

"What did you think of Ryoko?" he asked.

"She's amazing," said Beauty.

"I think she's a genius. But then again, you are too. Both my daughters have extraordinary gifts."

"Do you think you could convince her to come back to New York with me?" asked Beauty.

"I don't think so. Because of her blindness, she has been very sheltered. She has a strong artistic soul, but physically she is not strong."

"I could hire someone to care for her full-time. That would be no problem."

"You have other problems, I'm afraid," said Akira.

Beauty didn't understand this last remark. After meeting Ryoko, her bitterness at her father had dissipated a bit. She was so grateful to have discovered her sister that her heart was light and forgiving. But what did he mean by "other problems"?

"I'm talking about Kato Yamamoto and his precarious position at Bloom/Fine."

"Why precarious?" asked Beauty. "And what do you know about that?"

"I know a great deal. You see, the people who financed his enterprise initially financed me as well. When I went into business for myself, I was told that they had an interest in investing in fashion. They lent me the money. They were extremely involved in my business until I was able to pay them back—with a healthy profit. Even then, though, they insisted on being my partner. That's why I know who they are and understand how they work. And from what I've been told, they are extremely unhappy with your fiancé. He has not only cost them millions by what they consider his mismanagement, he has disrespected them. Because his operation is situated in America, he feels that he can ignore their demands. He keeps them at a distance and acts as though he is above reproach. He is not. And I must warn you, my daughter, that their reproaches are severe."

"Kato can take care of himself," she said.

"Perhaps. But I wouldn't want you to get hurt. This organization is powerful beyond any other in Japan. Powerful and ruthless."

"I want to spend more time with my sister," said Beauty, ignoring Akira's last remark.

"And you will. You will see her whenever you wish. You may come to the house to visit."

"No, I'm more comfortable seeing her here."

"Is tomorrow too soon?"

"Tomorrow would be good. I'll be back in the afternoon. There's more I want to discuss with her."

"I know she'll be looking forward to it."

Beauty left the store and walked into the neon night. Tokyo, always abuzz, seemed filled with joy. Beauty was filled with joy. For most of her life she'd been unsuccessful in making friends with other women. They were jealous of her. Even at work, she found it easier to get along with men. At the same time, she had longed for a close relationship with a woman her age. And now, to find that person in the form of a sister who shared her passion and talent . . . well, it was almost too wonderful.

As she sat in the back of a cab and watched the crowds—walking along the grand boulevards, stopping by nightclubs and noodle houses, streaming into sushi bars and pachinko parlors—she briefly thought of her father's warning. How much trouble was Kato really in? Could it be as bad as Akira had said? For now, though, she simply didn't want to think about it. She wanted to enjoy the afterglow of having met her sister, Ryoko. As a result, her life was richer. Her life was better than ever.

When the cab was a few blocks away from the scramble crossing, the locale of the Rising Star Hotel, the driver had to stop. The police had blocked off traffic. Beauty thought there must have been an accident. She got out and walked the rest of the way. When she came to the hotel, she saw a half-dozen police cars. There was a great commotion. Even the entrance to the hotel was blocked off. Out front she saw the hotel concierge.

"What has happened?" she asked.

"A terrible thing," he said.

"What?"

"A man jumped to his death."

"From this hotel?"

"I'm afraid so."

Beauty felt panic in her throat. "Has he been identified?"

"Not yet."

"When will they let guests back into the hotel?"

"I'm not sure."

She stood outside for another hour until the police lines came down. She ran into the lobby and called for the elevator. When the doors opened, she stepped inside and saw a policeman standing there. She started to press the button for the penthouse.

"You stay in penthouse suite?" he asked in broken English.

"Yes," Beauty answered.

"Please, you come with me."

THE PAYOFF

The Power Building

On Marietta Street, not far from the CNN headquarters in down-town Atlanta, the sign outside the five-story structure was dis-played in a bold black script. Power had thought of using the name Paul Clay Enterprises instead but decided to go with Power. That was, after all, his brand. Besides, the name suited the situation. It was a power move that got him this handsome modern building and all the thriving businesses that it held.

A year had passed since his confrontation with Ajay Lock. Spring had come and gone, summer was brutal, fall mild, and win-ter harsh. Now April showers were coming down. Power got up from his desk and looked outside. He liked the sound of the rain. The drops hit the window of his office with a steadiness that reflected the steadiness of his life this past year. Everything had fallen into place.

Ajay had been elected mayor of Atlanta and Ed Kingston had taken over as head of Southern Security. Ed had made it clear that Power would have all the resources he needed.

"Don't know how you were able to impress that man," Ed said after getting word that the bank had agreed to go into business with

Power, "but he thinks you're God's gift to this city's business future. What the hell did you tell him?"

"He understands profitability, Ed. That's all there is to it."

Of course there was a lot more to it than that. The essential element was Skyla, the daughter Ajay could never control, the same daughter whose behavior could have ruined his image and career forever, to say nothing of his campaign for political office. Skyla—her job as an escort and her relationship to Ajay's economic adviser Professor Marcus Copeland—was the absolute bane of Ajay's life. If someone could control her, his life might be kept from unraveling. If not, his life was doomed.

Power turned out to be the man who could control Skyla. The fact that she had unexpectedly fallen madly in love with him changed her completely. For the first time in her life, she was willing to submit to a man. Power would have liked to return her love. He recognized it as unrelenting and sincere. He knew that falling for Skyla would help him forget Beauty, the only woman he had ever loved. He tried to love Skyla because he knew that it made good sense, professionally and personally. She was fine. She was smart. She had his interests at heart. She was an asset to his life in all ways. But deep down, he knew his heart wasn't free.

And so he went along with the program—not so much out of love but out of practicality. He saw that by making Skyla behave he'd have all the financial resources he required.

At first she thought she'd play a game of prostitute/pimp with Power. He could order her around and use her as a sex worker. In rebelling against her stifling upper-middle-class background, she found the role exciting. Power, on the other hand, didn't get off on it and, more important, understood that he needed to put a leash on her.

"I'll do whatever you want," she had told him.

"I want you out of this business."

"Why?" she asked. "I can make you money."

"You can make me more money by keeping a low profile—or even no profile."

"Because of my father?"

"What else? If you want to help me, you'll stop being a goddamn embarrassment to him."

"Does that mean I'll get to move in with you?"

"Whoa—not so fast, baby girl."

"You're moving pretty fast yourself. You want to get your hands on Daddy's money and you want nothing to get in your way. Well, the way to get me out of the way is to let me in."

"You're already in, Skyla."

"I mean all the way in. I want to live with you. I want to be with you every day. I can help you with these businesses you're trying to run. I'm the top finance student at Georgia Tech. I've inherited my father's gift for understanding profit. It's a win-win for you, Power. You win my love, you win my body, you win my brains, and you win my father's backing. How can you say no?"

Power thought about it for a few seconds. "I can't," he said. "I'm saying yes."

That night Skyla packed up her things, abandoned her apartment, and moved in with Power. She'd never been so happy. As a lover, he was the first man with whom she had earth-shattering orgasms. Other men had loved her longer and harder, but she was never able to surrender to them. She responded to Power's strength in an entirely different way. She took in his strength without resisting. Her only desire was to make him happy. When they loved, she went wild. When she came, she screamed out his name.

He couldn't tell her, though, that despite the physical ecstasy he gave her, he wasn't loving her. He was loving Beauty. Fortunately, she knew little about Power's history. She had no idea that Beauty even existed.

The first year they lived together had gone well. Skyla agreed to leave escorting. Power found a way to make sure Professor Copeland caused no problems. He found him another young coed who fit the professor's preferred profile. With that out of the way, and with Ajay's bank backing him, he set out to accomplish his goal: Take over where Slim left off.

There were restaurants, car washes, barbershops, beauty salons, wig stores, and a large funeral parlor. Power was able to get these businesses up and running again. He decided that the escort business was too notorious to maintain. He was afraid it might undermine Ajay and Ed's goodwill, and so he asked Holly if she wouldn't mind turning it over to another manager in Atlanta. As one of Power's biggest fans, Holly was happy to help. She had watched—and encouraged—Power's relationship with Skyla. She knew the best thing for Power was to build a wholly legitimate empire. He should have nothing to do with selling women, sex, or drugs. Slim's gambling parlors remained closed, along with his other illegal holdings.

Skyla's cohabitation with Power improved her relationship with her father. He realized Power's calming influence and was delighted to give his daughter tips on real estate opportunities in the city. As a banker and then as mayor, he knew what land was earmarked for development. He could point Skyla and her boyfriend to rich opportunities where apartment complexes, shopping strips, and major malls were in the planning stages. He also advised them that a successful fast food chain selling artisan pizzas was looking for a franchisee. Power bought four of these locations, and within two months, they were turning a healthy profit.

It didn't stop there. With the bank's backing, Power built the biggest and most luxurious workout center in the city. It featured an indoor track, pool, basketball court, and boxing ring. He also found the funding to renovate an old movie house in downtown Atlanta and turn it into a concert venue. That was Skyla's idea.

Skyla had many ideas. Her business sense was super-sharp. She wanted to make her man happy—and she knew that the best way to do that was to make him money. Deep in her soul she knew that he didn't love her as she loved him. She repeatedly asked him whether there was another love in his life. She sensed some loss, a need in him that she couldn't fulfill. But that realization only motivated Skyla more; she had to prove her absolute necessity. As long as she remained essential to Power's operation, her place next to him was secure.

Power slowly began to have second thoughts about Skyla's obsession with him. Ultimately, it could mean trouble. He tried to level with her; he told her that he liked her but carefully avoided the word "love." She used the word all the time. That made him uncomfortable, but the rapid flow of events had him capitulating. He let her move in. Seeing her brilliance, he let her into his plans. Suddenly she was up in his bed and up in his business. He had a new life that took off like a rocket. If it weren't for Skyla, it wouldn't have taken off at all.

For large chunks of time—sometimes a few hours, sometimes even an entire day—Power was free of thoughts of Beauty. It had been months since he had tried to reach out to her; he no longer looked for the latest news about where she was living and what she was doing. He left her alone. Life was fine, or at least tolerable, without her.

This morning, for example, he was reading a report indicating that the Power Theater, his renovated movie palace, would be ready to go by the Fourth of July. Skyla had found a booking agent to work up a schedule of performers, a mix between known and up-and-coming acts. He saw big names like Mary J. Blige and Chris Brown. He hadn't heard of any of the up-and-coming acts, but as he perused the list, he noticed someone called Besta was opening for John Legend. On Besta's contract the name IW Management Group was listed. He remembered that was one of the umbrellas under which Irv Wasserman had managed acts when he was still in the music business. But that firm had been dormant for years, even before Irv retired from all his operations and moved to Florida. Power thought there was no way in the world that Irv Wasserman would ever return to management, especially for a new R & B singer without a reputation or a label.

No, this IW Management couldn't be Wasserman. To build up a new act required the energy and tireless commitment of a young man. Wasserman was a tired old man. This was probably nothing more than a coincidence, but it was worth looking into. Power's curiosity was triggered.

Hong Kong

t's more exciting than New York," said Beauty.

"Tell me about it. Tell me everything you see," said Ryoko.

"Well, from where we are, I see the harbor. The light of the moon has turned the water white. I also see a jumble of skyscrapers that look like lollipops reaching up to the sky. You like lollipops, don't you?"

"Yes, yes," said Ryoko. "They are red and green and yellow and blue, aren't they? Are these buildings the color of lollipops?"

"Not during the day, but now at night they're lit with colored lights. There's every color of the rainbow. On some of the buildings huge advertisements are displayed. Some of them are forty stories tall."

"What are they for?"

"One is advertising a Cadillac Escalade. Another is for a camera company. Then there's one for Calvin Klein clothes. And there's one for our new Two Sisters store."

"With the logo we designed?" asked Ryoko.

"The logo is larger than life. Two sisters, arm in arm."

"I can't wait to go down to the store."

"We'll go right after lunch."

"Do you think it will be a success here in China?"

"I do."

"Do you think it's edgy enough for Hong Kong?"

"Don't you remember what Seiji said? 'You girls didn't just design edgy, you're off the edge entirely'?"

"Do you think Seiji understands fashion?"

"I think he understands business," said Beauty. "I think he's very smart."

"Is that why you married him?"

"I married him . . . well, I married him because he asked me," Beauty confessed.

"Hadn't Kato asked you as well? Weren't you supposed to marry him?"

"That's when I became sick."

"Because you didn't want to marry him?"

"It's amazing how well you know me," said Beauty.

"I know you like a sister knows a sister. I wasn't surprised when you agreed to marry Seiji."

"Why do you say that?"

"Because," said Ryoko, "you knew he would take care of us."

"But our father has always taken care of you."

"Not in this way. Not in a way that lets me show the entire world what I can do with clothes. You have that same dream, and you decided Seiji can make that dream come true."

The two women were seated in the dining room of the lavish Macau Suite atop the Mandarin Oriental Hotel. Beauty had convinced Ryoko to let Beauty accompany her to Hong Kong, a city Ryoko had visited as a little girl. During that trip, she had become ill and was reluctant to ever leave Tokyo again. In the company of her sister, though, she felt protected. There was also the added attraction of shopping at Hong Kong's avant-garde boutiques with Beauty and meeting the Chinese designers that Ryoko had been reading about.

Traveling on Seiji's private jet, a Gulfstream G550, meant the trip would be hassle-free.

Beauty had desperately wanted to bring Ryoko along. Her sister anchored her emotions in a way that no one since Anita Ward, her late mentor, had been able to. She wanted to be with her all the time, especially in the aftermath of her sudden marriage to Seiji Aoi.

It had been thirteen months since Beauty had returned to the Rising Star Hotel and learned that Kato had jumped to his death in the scramble crossing. The shock was tremendous. That evening she was taken to the police station, where she had to fill out paperwork. Reporters were everywhere, looking to speak with her. Kato's parents showed up, but they were too distraught to speak. The day after her son's suicide, Mrs. Yamamoto suffered a debilitating stroke. Mr. Yamamoto fell apart and was taken to the mental ward of a retirement home in Kyoto, never to be heard from again.

Beauty had no choice but to turn to Akira Matsui, her biological dad. Alone in Tokyo, she felt assaulted on all sides. The press was after her for a story; Bloom/Fine executives, scurrying to consolidate their position in what appeared a doomed empire, were calling her night and day. She needed the refuge that Akira provided. He moved her into his home in a bedroom next to her sister, Ryoko. That setting provided her the security she so urgently required.

Ryoko was wonderfully kind and understanding. She sat with her sister for hours on end. And while Ryoko could feel her sister's anxiety about the terrible end to Kato's life, she couldn't detect real grief. Even though Ryoko wouldn't say it to anyone—not even to Beauty— she felt her sister experiencing relief. That's when she realized that Beauty's marriage to Kato had been based on practicality, not love.

Their father, Akira, realized the same thing. He had known all along that his daughter had cut some kind of deal with Kato. In his conversations with both Kato and Beauty, Akira realized that the relationship, at least from Beauty's vantage point, had to do with business. That's why he had not tried to hide the truth from Beauty when she came to him two weeks after Kato's death and asked about the rumors that Kato had not jumped to his death but had been pushed.

"I do not know the truth," Akira told Beauty, "but I do not discount that theory."

Akira was sipping tea with his two daughters on a delicate table of bamboo in the beautifully manicured garden that Akira's late wife had cultivated in the backyard of their villa outside Tokyo. Cherry blossoms were in full bloom. Pink-and-white flowers were everywhere.

"Who would do that to him?" asked Beauty.

"That is a naïve question," said Akira. "I think you know the answer."

"Simply because he had not turned a profit?"

"Much more than that. He had costs them millions—and, even worse, he thought he could ignore them. Yakuza is an organization that cannot be ignored. I know that through personal experience."

"They own you like they owned Kato?" asked Beauty.

"I told you before how they helped when I went out on my own and continue to be my partners. Because my business is profitable, they leave me alone. I make them money, I show them respect, and I have no trouble with them."

"And you've known all about this, Ryoko?" Beauty asked.

"My father has confided in me over the years," said Ryoko, revealing a toughness Beauty had not initially seen. "I've come to understand the brutal ways of the business world. I've learned that we all need protection."

"Then you know what they did to Kato," said Beauty. "You know that they killed him."

"I only know that they are not interested in harming you," said Akira.

"How do you know that?"

"I have been told."

"By whom?"

"Seiji Aoi."

"Who is he?"

"Son of Rin Aoi."

"I don't know these people," said Beauty.

"Kato knew them well. They were the people who helped him buy Bloom/Fine. They were his backers."

"And his killers," said Beauty.

Ryoko noted the lack of emotion in her sister's voice. Akira noted it as well. He saw that she wanted to know about the Aoi family.

"They are the most powerful family in all Asia," said Akira. "Their worldwide reach is enormous."

"I know," she said. "They saved my brother's life."

"Your brother?"

"Power. I call him my brother even though he's not. He's the son of Charlotte Clay, the woman who adopted me when my mother died and you didn't bother to come to her funeral."

"I didn't know about that," said Ryoko.

"You know now," said Beauty.

"I regret that," said Akira, "as I regret so much in my life. But we are here today as a family, are we not? We are here today to help each other and make up for the past."

"How do you propose to do that?" asked Beauty.

"I want to introduce you to Seiji Aoi. He very much wants to meet you."

"I'm sure he's vulgar and ugly."

"Not at all," said Ryoko. "He's young and beautiful. At least that's what all the newspapers say. He is a movie star. He plays elegant gangsters who wear gorgeous clothes and get the sexiest women. He is a sensation because the public knows who his father is."

"How old is he?" asked Beauty.

"Thirty-eight, perhaps thirty-nine," said Akira. "His father is sick and dying. That's why Seiji has stopped acting. He has been designated to take over his father's business. He has been trained to do so ever since he was a young boy."

"Have you met him?" asked Beauty.

"Only once, and he was most charming."

"I've gone to see all his movies," said Ryoko. "I love his voice and imagine the handsome features of his face. Women swoon. Just hearing the love scenes, I have swooned. He's every woman's fantasy."

"I'm afraid he is not a fantasy of mine."

"Only because you didn't grow up in Japan, Beauty," said Ryoko. "Instead of Seiji, think of Johnny Depp. They say he is the Japanese Johnny Depp. But they say more handsome than Johnny Depp. More—how do you say? Sultry?"

"I think you want to meet him," Akira told Beauty.

"You can't think for me," she told her father. "You don't know me that well."

"But maybe *I* can think a little for you," said Ryoko in her gentle but firm way. "And I also think you want to meet him. Maybe you and I, we meet him together. Maybe that will make it easier."

"And what's the purpose of this meeting?" asked Beauty.

"We won't know until it happens," Ryoko answered. "Life is a mystery, is it not? Isn't it a mystery that you and I met when we did? Well, this might be another one of those mystery meetings. Maybe this is a man you are destined to meet."

"You sound like you really want to meet him yourself, Ryoko," said Beauty.

"I do. He's a movie star. Who doesn't want to meet a movie star?"

Before agreeing to meet Seiji, Beauty asked to see his movies. Ryoko had them all on DVD. The first, shot when Seiji was barely twenty, showed him as a street urchin who found his way into the center of a Japanese crime ring. If anything, Ryoko had understated the case for Seiji. He was more than good-looking; he was drop-dead handsome, with penetrating brown eyes, chiseled features, a powerful chin, a wide sensuous mouth, broad shoulders, thick black wavy hair, an impressive five-foot-ten-inch frame.

Beauty sat with her sister and watched on the wide-screen TV in the den. Because the film was in Japanese, Ryoko translated as it went along. She not only rendered Seiji's words in English, she described the scene. Although blind, she saw the film as vividly as Beauty. How was that possible?

"Others have described the movie to me," Ryoko told Beauty. "And I have listened to each film a dozen times."

Seiji transfixed Beauty. His eyes—liquid, faraway, dreamy—were extraordinary. It didn't matter what he was saying; it was enough to look into those eyes. He also moved beautifully. In the beginning of the story, he was an innocent. But when he moved into the world of crime, he became a killer. His first murder—shooting a rival mobster through the heart—was sudden and absolutely convincing. He didn't blink. His eyes went from hot to cold. He was merciless in this execution, and his indifference in murdering a man added to his mystery. It was, of course, the love scenes that had made Seiji a star. In those, where the audience was treated to a long look at his sinuous torso, his athleticism was on full display. Beauty could not help but be moved.

The other films documented Seiji moving through his twenties into his thirties. His looks became more striking. His face matured, his body hardened, his presence on the screen grew more dynamic. Producers put him in roles that dramatized his passionate need for sex and violence. The two were wed. But it was always men he killed, never women, and women he loved, never men. In one film, he was a corrupt banker who ran an international cartel of thieves; in another, he was a prisoner who time after time made impossible escapes so he might make love to the many women waiting for him; and in the most spectacular and self-reflective of all, he was an actor whose producer, an underground warlord, was exploiting his talents to make a fortune. In the climactic scene, Seiji murders his exploitative boss by ever so slowly cutting his throat with an ancient samurai sword.

"So do you want to meet him now?" said Ryoko after the final scene of the final movie.

"I'm curious, yes," admitted Beauty.

"Father will arrange it. And is it okay if I come along?"

"I wouldn't have it any other way," said Beauty. "You are my sister. You are the one leading me to him."

"Isn't that an expression you have in English?" asked Ryoko. "Don't you say, 'The blind leading the blind'?"

Beauty laughed, her thoughts already on the impending meeting.

The meeting took place in an exclusive sushi bar in the Ginza. Seiji sent a car for the sisters. When told that Ryoko would be coming along, he had no objections. He knew about Akira's talented Japanese daughter and how she had been reunited with her long-lost American sister. He understood that the two women couldn't spend enough time together. He looked forward to meeting them both.

Beauty's most fervent wish was that Seiji would make her forget Power. No man had been able to do that before, but Seiji could well be the first. He had the look, the charisma, the mystery, the body, the fame, the fortune, yes, and even the power. If he could replace Power in her romantic and erotic mind, he could well be the man she was looking for.

She considered the fact that he might also be the man who had eliminated Kato. On one hand, such an act had to be considered cruel and tragic. On the other hand, Kato's absence had not sent Beauty into a state of mourning. Kato had loved her, yes; he had sacrificed for her and helped set her up for success in the world of fashion. But at no time and in no way had she loved the man. She had barely even liked him. He was ambitious but dull. As a lover, he was lackluster. As a conversationalist, he put her to sleep. He was a businessman, and not a particularly imaginative one at that. She felt terrible that he had suffered such a horrible death, but when her sister had asked whether she really missed him, Beauty couldn't lie. She couldn't say that she did.

Seiji arrived at the sushi bar with an entourage. Four wide-bodied men in black suits and black ties surrounded him. They were broad enough to be sumo wrestlers. Seiji was much taller than them, so his head towered above his protectors. Everyone in the restaurant noted the entrance. The place was buzzing. He was, after all, among the most famous men in Japan. The first thing Beauty noticed was his flowing mane of shiny black hair. His hair was his best feature. His eyes searched the room until he spotted Beauty and her sister. He smiled and whispered something to his men. Two of them escorted Beauty and Ryoko to a private room in the back while the two others followed with Seiji in tow.

The walls of the room were covered with ancient Japanese fans hand-painted with scenes of snowfalls on temples and sunshine on gardens. They sat on cushions on the floor before a low table of antique marble—Seiji in the middle and Beauty and Ryoko on either side. The four big men guarded the door.

Thrilled to be meeting Seiji, Ryoko told him in Japanese, "It is our honor to be here, and if you like I will translate into English. I'm afraid my sister has not yet learned Japanese."

"My English, not great," said Seiji in English, taking the blind woman's hand, "but I try. Maybe I make myself understood."

"Your English is wonderful compared to my Japanese," said Beauty, noting how Seiji had endeared himself to her sister.

"Ryoko, I know your work," he told her. "Your father has showed me. You make all Japan proud. You design with your heart."

"My father is prejudiced."

"He may be, but I am not, dear Ryoko. You have gifts. Great gifts."

"Have you seen my sister's line?" she asked the movie star.

"Young Beauty. Yes," said Seiji. "I know Young Beauty. It is profit center in stores where there are no profits."

For several seconds, silence prevailed. No one quite knew what to say next. Beauty felt the man's strong charisma. He spoke with tremendous self-assurance. He knew who he was and what he wanted. She liked that attitude in a man. But she also wasn't sure of how to direct the conversation. After all, she was sitting next to the person who in all probability had been responsible for Kato's death.

Sensing all that, Seiji said, "I sorry for your loss, Miss Beauty. Very sad loss. I know Kato, not for very long, but I meet him last year. Nice man. Good man."

"Thank you," was all Beauty could think to say.

"I have shown Beauty all your movies," said Ryoko, moving to a happier topic.

"Oh, no," said Seiji.

"Why do you say that?" asked Beauty. "You don't like your movies?"

"My movies not me. I act. Maybe I act too good. People think . . . they say, you are that man in the movies. But that not me."

"Who are you then?" asked Beauty, deciding to push the envelope.

"I like this question," said Seiji. "This is a thinking question. We talk, but first we must eat. I order for everyone. That okay?"

Beauty had no objections, but she still wanted to hear his answer to her question.

After ordering a thousand dollars' worth of exotic raw fish and several bottles of the world's best sake, Seiji gave it a try. "I am man who looks for love."

"What kind of love?" asked Beauty.

"Love of woman."

"You must have had the love of thousands of women."

"No, that is desire. Yes, maybe the women, they do desire me. They see the movie and they want the man. But love is not desire."

"Then what is love?" asked Beauty.

"Love," said Seiji in his even-toned voice, "love, it is union."

"That's beautiful," said Ryoko. "That's true."

"In love you join," said Seiji. "Like you and your sister, Miss Beauty. You have love, and you have joined. There is bond. Close bond. Nothing can separate. Time, distance—they make no difference. No separation, no space between two things, one thing—that is love."

Beauty thought of Power—a thought she did not want to entertain, but it came to her anyway. Why was she thinking of Power at a moment when this Japanese move star was commanding the room? Ryoko, who wore rhinestone-encrusted white-framed dark glasses for the occasion, hung on his every word. Beauty was impressed by what he was saying, and yet her mind drifted.

The evening went on. Seiji offered up delightful conversation. He had much to say about American cinema. He discussed De Niro and DiCaprio and Pacino and Denzel Washington. He knew all the directors and told them about the times he'd been asked to come to Hollywood. He had refused, he said, because he knew he wouldn't go over well with American audiences. He realized his limitations and was convinced his appeal was restricted to Asians. Americans didn't get him. The Asian acting style was nuanced in a very different way. A raised eyebrow meant one thing in Tokyo and another in Texas.

"Have you been to Texas?" Seiji asked Beauty.

"To Dallas, yes," she said.

"And you know cowboys?"

"No."

"They say I should make the cowboy movie. I have learned the lasso, but the hat, it is not good on me."

Ryoko laughed and said, "I think you can make any movie you like."

"But now no more movies. No more fun. We work now."

"And exactly what kind of work do you do?" asked Beauty with a strong touch of sarcasm in her voice.

"Business," said Seiji. "I am business."

"And what kind of business?"

"We have banking. Many real estates. In Canada, in United States, in Australia. In many countries where English is spoken. That is why my English, it must be better."

"Your English is fine," Ryoko told Seiji.

"All this time, I never go with English woman. No English girl-friend. So I invite you, Miss Beauty, to where we have home, private island called Tojo, not too far."

"Actually, I'm not English, I'm American," said Beauty.

"Of course, I know that. Please accept invitation."

"Is this a family invitation? Does it include my father and sister?"

"Yes, yes, whole family invited. Soon you see a new world. My world."

A week later Beauty was in that world. She, Ryoko, and Akira were flown over in a private jet to a small island just off the coast of Japan. The terrain was rocky and the compound, designed in the style of a Japanese palace, commanded a view of the Pacific. In all her travels, Beauty had seen nothing like it. It was from another century. Seiji explained that most of the Meiji-era palaces, on which the Tojo compound was based, had been destroyed during World War II. His father, Rin Aoi, sought to restore an era when his nation's might was at its height. Thus he spent some $60 million in constructing an edifice that, along with its exquisite gardens, occupied forty acres. The palace, filled with crystal chandeliers and ballroom-size rooms covered with ancient tapestries and gilded mirrors, had twelve bedrooms and ten bathrooms. A staff of thirty was on call twenty-four hours a day. At the northern end of the island a runway had been built to accommodate Aoi's fleet of planes. There was also a barracks on the island that housed a private army of twenty-five highly trained soldiers.

As Beauty, Ryoko, and Akira were driven from the airstrip up the steep hillside to the palace above, Beauty described to her sister everything she saw. When they reached the house, Seiji greeted them at the main entrance and took them on an extended tour. It was then that Akira asked to pay his respects to Rin.

"Father is not well," said Seiji in Japanese.

"I understand," said Akira. "And I would not want to add to his discomfort. Please tell him that I offer him all my respect."

"He has, however, asked me to introduce him to Miss Beauty."

Beauty, who did not understand what was being said, saw a quizzical look on the faces of her father and sister.

"What is he saying?" she asked Ryoko.

Seiji answered her directly. "Please," he said, "you come and meet my father."

"Of course," said Beauty.

While an older woman dressed in a traditional robe of silver and gold escorted Ryoko and Akira to their bedrooms, Beauty followed Seiji down a long hallway. On the walls were images of Japanese warlords from past centuries. The hallway seemed to go on forever. At the very end they stood before a set of magnificent black wood double doors covered with carvings. The carved scenes were of great battles in which enemies of the warlord were mutilated in a variety of ways. Seiji knocked once and immediately the enormous doors opened.

The room, as long as a football field, was filled with people dressed in ancient Japanese costumes, both women and men. Music that sounded strange to Beauty's ears was being played on stringed instruments she had never before seen. Ocean winds blew through open windows. On long bamboo poles oversized silk flags with intricate Japanese lettering billowed in the breeze. In the midst of the colorful scene was a canopied bed whose frame was fashioned from a precious metal reflecting the light of the sun.

Seiji walked Beauty over to the side of the bed that held Rin Aoi, a small man whose eyes were closed and whose breathing was labored. Three elderly women attended him. Seiji leaned down and whispered into his ear. Slowly the old man opened his eyes and saw Beauty. Unexpectedly, his lips formed a beautiful smile. He held out his hand to her. She took it.

In a hushed tone, he said a few words to her in Japanese.

"Please tell me what he said," Beauty said to Seiji.

"'You are welcome, and I accept you to my family. I accept you as my daughter.'"

He held Beauty's hand tightly, and when he let go all life left him. He died at the moment, and for the next several days all focus was on his funeral.

The night after the final burial ceremony, Seiji came to Beauty's bedroom.

"My father accepted you," he told her. "I accept you. I ask you to marry me."

"Last time I was to marry," she said, "the affair was broadcast to the world. The marriage became a news story, and I did not react well. This time, if I do marry, it must be private. No preparations, no guests. My sister, my father, your family. No one else. That is my demand."

"And so it shall be," said Seiji.

When Beauty told Ryoko the news, her sister broke into tears.

"I knew it!" she said. "He loved you the first time he saw you! You have done for me, Beauty, what I could never have done for myself. You must tell me everything, even what it was like to be loved by him."

"That hasn't happened."

"I'm surprised. You marry a man without loving him first?"

"This is a different kind of marriage. This marriage is about money."

"But aren't you curious about how he loves?"

"Not entirely."

Beauty spoke the truth. At this point, sex was not a priority. She realized that she was marrying one of the richest men in Asia—and that was enough.

When she did invite him into her bed, he stood before her and said, "I want you to look at me first. And then, in this mirror, I want to look at you looking at me."

She had no problem with the ritual. He slowly undressed, thinking that the revelation of his body would thrill her. His body was superb—his long limbs, his tight muscles, his erect stature—but she did not finding it thrilling. He did. He couldn't stop staring in the mirror. He posed, as though he was being photographed. He was adamant that she keep her eyes on him. The sight of his own physique excited him enormously. When, after fifteen minutes of admiring himself, he finally climbed into bed and slipped Beauty's nightgown over her head, he kissed her passionately but kept sneaking glances at the mirror. His lovemaking was fine, neither too timid nor aggressive. He had been with dozens of women, perhaps hundreds, and understood the female physique. He gave her pleasure, but still, he did not thrill her.

Beauty's thrills came only in memories of being with Power.

The sexual union with Seiji had taken place eleven months ago. As a result of her marriage to him, everything in Beauty's life and the life of her father and sister had changed. Seiji had promised them, and for all indications was giving them, the world. He immediately agreed to Akira's plan to open four other stores in Tokyo and one in Hong Kong. Two Sisters had become a high-fashion chain in a matter of months. In terms of construction, redesign, and staffing, Seiji had worked miracles. Because of his influence with unions and government officials, everything seemed to happen overnight. His resources were limitless. All Beauty and Ryoko had to do was design the clothes.

If individually they worked with tremendous intensity, together they were five times as energized. As a perfectly harmonious team, they pushed each other's creativity to new heights. They laughed as they worked, they exchanged ideas, they extended their reach into the outer limits of fashion. Their blouses and dresses, their skirts and sweaters and scarves and pantsuits, looked like works of modern art. The styles were sleek, loose, flowing, often overstated, slyly funky, and always marked by a certain casual ease that characterized their relationship. Each piece had a personality—friendly and daring.

The grand opening of the Hong Kong store, on the street level of the tallest skyscraper in the most madcap shopping city of the world, was a much-heralded event. Seiji had pulled out all the stops. He had hired Frank Gehry, the celebrated American architect who had designed the Guggenheim Museum in Spain and the Disney Concert Hall in Los Angeles. Gehry rendered the exterior of the store in sheets of undulating metal, each sheet carrying the Two Sisters logo. The interior was super-sleek, with floors of shiny titanium and walls painted by Asia's most outrageous post-punk graffiti artists, whose scenes of urban life—street signs and street vendors, subways and motor scooters—added to the electric buzz. Dance music charged the exceedingly large space—twenty-three thousand square feet—and the salespeople were notable for their wild hairdos done up in yellow, green, and shocking pink.

The official opening was at eight P.M. on a Saturday. By seven, the sisters were dressed. Beauty wore a retro taffeta turquoise dress. Ryoko wore a jagged-hemmed skirt of distressed denim dotted with discarded pieces of costume jewelry, splashy fake emeralds and sapphires. Her blouse carried reproductions of menus from Hong Kong's favorite fast food restaurants. As a token of love, Beauty had designed a special pair of dark glasses for her sister—cat's-eye shades whose frames were fashioned from elephant tusks.

The mayors of Hong Kong, Beijing, Tokyo, and Shanghai were set to attend. Seiji had invited every major Asian film star. Brad Pitt and Angelina Jolie, who were filming in China, had promised to show up. An army of publicists had been hired to control—and heighten—the media frenzy. An army of security guards had been hired to maintain some semblance of order. Business had kept Seiji in Tokyo until the actual day of the opening—Beauty, Ryoko, and Akira had flown in earlier—but he was due to pick up the sisters and their dad in their suite at seven thirty and accompany them to the store.

At seven thirty-five a man came in with a message for Akira. Ryoko overheard the message. Beauty saw Ryoko's face turn a sickly color.

"What is it?" asked Beauty.

Still in shock, Ryoko answered "Seiji was taken to prison."

"You Last the Longest"

You last the longest, baby, I swear you do," said Besta.

"That's just a song."

"Not just any song, *your* song."

"Besta, you've changed my life. You've made me a new man."

"You've made me a new woman, honey. Loving like yours don't come 'round but once a lifetime. I wouldn't be where I am without it."

"Wait a minute, woman," he said. "You're saying it's only professional gratitude that got me into your bed?"

"No, sir. It's you being a man among boys. You taking charge—out there in the world and right here between the sheets."

"You know I've had my problems."

"So you say, darling. But I've had me quite a few men, and I'm good at figuring out who's had problems and who hasn't. And I'm here to tell you, sugar, that if you have had problems, you don't got none no more."

He laughed and snuggled next to her. Their naked bodies still tingled with sexual energy.

"You ready go to again?" she asked.

"Ready, willing, and able."

"Well, I now know where you got your name. You always up."

Up kissed her open mouth. Minutes later, he gave her what she was pleading for. Before daylight peeked through the curtains, they were at it again.

"How long has it been since you first met Besta?" Irv asked Slim.

The two men were smoking cigars on the patio of Irv's Boca Raton mansion, protected by high gates on all sides. Rashan, chief of security, had beefed up his staff to three other men the moment Irv decided to return to the music business. The Boca residence was Irv's most recent, acquired largely because its former owner, a notorious drug dealer, had equipped it with the highest-tech surveillance equipment on the market.

"Been over a year now," said Slim.

"And has she ever given you the slightest reason not to trust her?"

"No, can't say she has."

"And you're still fucking her regularly?"

"Well, not as much as when we first met, but yeah, man, I'm still boning her good."

"Then what the hell you worried about?" asked Irv.

"She didn't want me up in Nashville while she was recording."

"What were you doing while she was recording?"

"Nothing. Just looking at her sweet ass and big tits."

"Then she's right. Leave her alone and let her sing. Women get tired of men looking at their ass and tits."

"Not this one."

"Look, Slim, if you wanted to stay you should have stayed."

"But I didn't want to make the bitch unhappy. I know that when she's in the studio, she don't like no distractions."

"Then you did the right thing."

"I still don't like leaving her up there alone with the producer."

"You said he's queer."

"Ain't you ever heard of a half queer, a cat who likes pussy as much as dick?"

"Don't they call that a bisexual?"

"I ain't buying that he don't like no pussy. When they work together, they hardly need to talk. They just look at each and know what to do."

"That's just good chemistry between artistic types."

"But it leaves my ass out in the cold."

"You forgetting about our trip to Chicago and New York? You forgetting our meeting with those Internet music people? We've been setting her up real good. We're gearing up this label with her as the featured artist. How many more acts we got? Four? Five?"

"Five," said Slim. "Besta, a white rock group, that young boy, that young girl, and the Latin chick."

"And the A & R guy we stole from Sony, he knows what he's doing, don't he?"

"He don't appreciate Besta enough. He don't believe in her like I do."

"He doesn't have to," said Irv. "We got the money behind her."

"Think I should get on a plane and go back to Nashville tonight?" asked Slim.

"No, leave her alone, Slim. You gotta learn to trust."

"Coming from you that's saying something. You're the mother-fucker who always says don't trust no one."

"And you're the one who said you finally met a woman you *can* trust. And also she's the woman who solved your sex problems. If you can't trust her, who can you trust?"

"I trust you, Irv. I seen what you done for me. You made me your partner on this music thing and you been dealing with me straight. You straightened my bread to where I can move around again. It ain't where it was, but it's enough so I'm back on my feet. It's to the point where I'm ready to go back to Atlanta and fuck up that little bitch who took my shit."

"I thought we weren't gonna talk about Power."

"Have you heard me talking about him? Haven't I done what you said? Haven't I left it alone?"

"So there's no reason to start up now."

"Except," said Slim, exhaling a long stream of smoke from his Cuban cigar, "that motherfucker got all my businesses tied up like they're his."

"They *are* his. He got the bank to back him. You had to run, Slim. There was no way you could've stayed. You had to go away and get well. While you were gone, he moved in. You can't blame him for that."

"I could kill him for that."

"Not a good idea."

"I could at least fuck him up the way he fucked me up."

"You tried that once, and he found a way out. He's smart."

"If he's smart, it's because I taught him to be smart. It wasn't him, though. It was that Jap half sister of his. That's the bitch who saved his ass, her and the connection to the gooks."

"That's a connection to be taken seriously. I'm telling you, Slim, you did good to run."

"I didn't run 'cause I was scared."

"I didn't say you were scared. You were sick."

"You talk like I was a mental case," said Slim.

"What would you call it?"

"I'm better now. I'm a hundred percent, wouldn't you say?"

"I wouldn't take you on as my business partner if I thought you were still crazy."

"So it's not crazy for me not to catch a flight to Nashville tonight and check up on my bitch?"

"Your call, not mine."

The conversation happened after the men had enjoyed a large lunch of crab cakes and Cuban beer. As a result, Irv was ready to nap. He had trouble sleeping at night, but never during the day. He cherished his midday naps.

When he got to his bedroom and saw that the maid had prepared his bed just the way he liked—pillows fluffed, sheets turned back, easy-listening music on the radio—he was pleased. He wasn't pleased, though, when the phone rang. The ID said the call was from outside the country. He almost wasn't going to answer it when curiosity got the best of him.

"Dad, it's Judy."

Irv's heart sank. He hadn't spoken to his daughter in over a year. For the most part, he'd been able to forget about her. That was a relief. When he had tried to reach her, he never got through. Now that she was calling, he figured there was only one reason—she needed money.

"Where are you, Judy?"

"Bahrain."

"Still with the Arabs."

"The Arabs are beautiful people."

"I'm sure, when they're not looking to kill Jews."

"I didn't call to talk about politics, Daddy. I called to see how you are."

"I'm amazed you got this number."

"It wasn't easy. But how are you? How's your health?"

"I'm fine."

"You never let me explain what happened back in Chicago," said Judy, referring to the fact that, in Irv's view, she had conspired with his chief financial man to steal his money.

"Why explain?" he asked. "That's over with."

"But it's important that you see I was trying to help you."

"Fine, Judy. You were trying to help me."

"Do you believe me?"

"I believe I want to take a nap."

"I want to see you."

"I won't be coming to Bahrain any time soon."

"But I'll come to you."

Irv said nothing.

"I would have come earlier but I've had some money problems," said Judy.

Oy, thought Irv, *here it comes. Money problems.* "How could you have money problems when your Arab prince has more money than God?"

"All the protests over here against the government hurt his family. Somehow his family lost all their money."

"It happens."

"But it wasn't fair."

"Life's not fair, Judy. I don't have to tell you that."

"We need your help."

"*We?* I don't even know this Arab man."

"You'd like him. He's your kind of guy, Daddy."

"I'm sure," Irv said sarcastically.

"Right now, though, we're desperate. We're actually in hiding. His life might be at risk. We need to get out of here."

Irv remained silent.

"Can you send us money? The best thing would be to send a private plane with a pilot you could give the money to. That way he could fly us out of here. It's easier to leave on a private plane than a commercial one."

Still silence on Irv's part.

"Well?" asked Judy.

"Well what?"

"Can you do it?"

"I can. You know that or you wouldn't call. But will I? That's another question."

"My life is in danger."

"I thought his life was in danger."

"Being with him, I'm endangering my own life."

"Then get away from him. If you want, I'll prepay a ticket for you. You can fly out on a commercial airline."

"And leave Habib?"

"That's the idea."

"I can't," she said.

"Can't or won't?"

"Won't. I love him. Trust me, he's a good man."

"If he is, that makes him the first good man you've ever found."

"How about Power?"

"He wasn't your man. He worked for me. And, believe me, he's had trouble of his own."

"I need you to do this for me, Daddy. I need you to fly in a plane and get us out of here."

"You know what that would cost?"

"Are you saying that my life isn't worth that much?"

"I'm saying I don't hear from you for over a year. You run over to the land of our enemies. You get a rich boyfriend. I have no idea what you're doing with your life. And then when your life falls apart, after ignoring me—not knowing whether I'm alive or dead—you call up and say, 'Send me a jet plane so me and my Arab lover man can fly away'?"

"You have to say yes. I'm your daughter."

"Don't tell me what I have to say."

"If you don't say yes and you read about me with my throat slit, you'll feel guilty for the rest of your life."

"Maybe yes, maybe no. When you thought I had lost my senses and tried to rob me blind, did you feel guilty when you got caught?"

"No, because you never understood the circumstances."

"I understood everything. I'm going to hang up, Judy."

"Just like that? With my life on the line?"

"Your Arab boyfriend, he'll save you."

"You can't do this, Daddy."

Irv hung up and said out loud to the empty room, "I just did."

Irv's afternoon naps were usually deep and dreamless. This sleep, though, was disquieting. It felt like he had dreamed himself inside an action film. The action was nonstop. He was being chased by his first wife and Judy's mother, Ginny Calzolari, who wielded a knife in her hand. Irv managed to outrun her, but when he turned the corner he saw a bulldozer being driven at him. The driver was John Mackey, his late first lieutenant who had tried to swindle him. The bulldozer was coming right at him, and when Irv turned to run, there was Judy heading toward him with an army of Arabs wielding swords and screaming for his head. He woke up in a sweat.

"Goddamn you, Judy," he said. "Get out of my dream."

But when he closed his eyes and fell back into unconsciousness, she was there again. This time she was a roller derby star, racing around the track in skates, knocking other women to the ground. The other women included Dr. Trina Mapploroot and Besta, who couldn't get out of her way in time. They would get up, but only to be elbowed by Judy as she thundered her way around the ring again. Irv tried to warn them that his daughter was deadly and without pity, but his cries could not be heard over the heavy metal band that played in the stands. Again and again, Dr. Mapploroot and Besta were decked by Judy until their heads were bloodied and their bodies mutilated. When they were too weak to get up, Judy skated over them, the blades on her skates made from knives. Eventually she sliced their bodies with her skates and cut their heads from their torsos. Irv woke up in horror.

"You look like you saw a ghost," Slim told him when, after his disquieting nap, he went to the den, where the television was showing the aftermath of a horse race. "That tip you gave me paid off," said Slim. "That Arab horse, Desert Wind, you said would win just tore up the track. I'm giving you half of the hundred grand I just won."

"Forget about it," said Irv. "I didn't put up no money. It's your bet, your winnings."

"Never had no one treat me like you, Irv. Never really had a friend before."

Irv was about to say, "Me either," but didn't. He asked the cook to make a light salad for dinner. He wasn't feeling good.

"I'm not going to Nashville," Slim said. "I'm listening to you. I'm not going to be crazy."

"Good," said Irv. "It's good not to be crazy."

Later the men had dinner together on the patio. They watched the cloudless sky turn from light blue to dark blue to black.

"I'm going to bed early," Irv announced.

"Go ahead," said Slim. "You'll feel better in the morning."

Irv did. His dream had been free of Judy and her mother. His dream had been about Slim. He was in his father's country of Ukraine. Jews were being hunted and slaughtered. His parents had fled and hid him in the closet. Soldiers entered his house. Irv, a small boy, could hear them stomping through the house. They got closer and closer to the closet. When they opened the door little Irv looked out and saw their murderous eyes, their rifles pointed directly at him. As they were about to shoot, though, Slim busted down the front door and, with a machine gun, began mowing down the soldiers. He killed them all. Irv was now no longer a child. He was a grown man. He embraced Slim and thanked him for saving his life. Slim took one of his two matching diamond wristbands and gave it to Irv.

"This is for you," Slim said in the dream. "You are my brother."

At breakfast the next morning, Irv was still dazzled by his dream. Slim came to the table in his silk robe with "SS" stitched across the front lapel.

"Irv," he said. "Been thinking. If you won't take the fifty grand from me, you gotta take this."

Slim took off one of his two matching diamond wristbands and gave it to Slim.

"You're my brother," he said.

Amazed, Irv took the wristband and put it on. It fit. Later that day he called his high-priced well-connected lawyer, who had offices in New York, London, and Geneva.

"I want to change my will," he said. "I'm cutting out my daughter. Nothing for my daughter. I'm giving everything to Slim."

The Power Theater

The dressing room is beautiful, baby," Besta told Slim, who was on the phone in Miami. "I wish you were here to see it."

"I ain't going back to that fucked-up city ever," said Slim, "and I'm still pissed you didn't listen to me and scratch it off your tour."

"Look, Slim, you got an issue with Atlanta. I don't. My single wasn't doing anything in New York or Chicago, but bam—just like that—'You Last the Longest' blew up in Atlanta. Atlanta loves me. How could I have scratched Atlanta?"

"Easy. The more they don't see you, the more they want you."

"But I want them, baby. These are my first fans."

"Maybe, but there are better places to play than that fucked-up old movie theater."

"Are you kidding? It's fabulous. My dressing room is a suite, all blue velvet, a big sofa, a wet bar, and a mirror that wraps around the room. This Power Theater—"

Slim broke in, saying, "I don't want to hear the fuckin' name."

"I know you got issues with that boy, Slim, but he does seem to have taste, least judging by how he spruced up this place."

"I want you out on the first plane to Miami tomorrow morning."

"No problem, sugar. I'll be in your loving arms tomorrow night."

"Sooner you out of Atlanta, the better."

"I hear you, Slim."

"How's Up?"

"Good. Been a blessing to have him on keyboards onstage every night."

"He ain't coming to Miami with you, is he?"

"No, sir. He'll be going back to San Francisco."

"That where his boyfriend lives?"

"Suppose so, Slim. Haven't asked."

"Well, don't. No need to get into his personal stuff. You and him got a musical thing happening. Keep it there."

"Aye-aye, captain."

"You making fun of me, Besta?"

"Just being obedient—that's all. You take care and give Irv a big fat kiss for me. Love you, baby," said Besta.

"Back at ya," said Slim before hanging up.

"The way you talk to that man," said Up, stretched out in his underwear on the couch in Besta's dressing room, "I know you have a future in acting. You got me to believe you."

"Look here," said Besta, "ain't nothing wrong with making an old man feel good about himself. Now help me strap on my bra, will you, Up?"

"I like it off."

"I know you do."

"We have time?" he asked.

"Ninety minutes before we go on. Your love lasts longest, but it don't last no ninety minutes."

"Let's see," said Up as Besta slipped out of her panties and walked his way.

Seventy minutes later, when the Bentley pulled up to the front of the theater and Power and Skyla got out, all heads turned. People took their cell phones, lifted them high over the crowd, and started snapping pictures of the couple. As a result of hiring Atlanta's most effective public relations agency, Power's profile was high. The *Atlanta Journal-Constitution* ran a feature on his unprecedented success. *Atlanta Finance* magazine named him Young Businessman of the Year. He served on two of Mayor Ajay Lock's advisory boards dealing with underprivileged children and inner-city education.

The PR firm encouraged Power to go public with the fact that he was living—and in partnership—with the mayor's daughter, described by the press as fashionable, beautiful, and brilliant. She also continued her studies at Georgia Tech, where she maintained an A average. Together they represented the best of young Atlanta. The notion that Power had once been associated with the notorious Charles "Slim" Simmons was a forgotten fact. Slim was the past, Power the present and future of the city. He had taken failing businesses and, with the help of Skyla, brought them back to life. As a mover and shaker, he was light-years ahead of any of his colleagues.

Power hadn't told Skyla that he suspected Besta was connected to Irv Wasserman. There was no reason to. Like Power, Skyla had heard and liked the single they were playing on the radio. Like Power, Skyla was a music fan and enjoyed an evening out. Besides, it wasn't really Besta they had come to see; it was Bruno Mars.

The Power couple were dressed in black—Power in a slim-fitting double-breasted suit with a white silk collarless shirt open at the neck, Skyla in a tight black dress with a side vent high on her thigh and strapless top that brought attention to the two-carat pear-shaped white diamond that hung from her neck. They greeted a horde of well-wishers as they made their way to the front row, took their seats, and awaited the opening act.

Besta's backup band, the Up-Towners, was tight, the keyboardist and leader a handsome dude with long dreads. Besta came out in a blousy chartreuse jumpsuit and a retro Afro wig. She sang in the soar-

ing soul style of Aretha and Chaka Khan but, given the Up-Towners'
hip-hoppish beats, with a street attitude that felt current. She unasham-
edly moved her ample frame with bold sexuality. Her smile was electric
and her songs, all about the endless pleasure of good loving, captivated
the audience, who were up on their feet, Power and Skyla included.

"She's great," Skyla shouted to Power as Besta sang "You Last the
Longest."

"Badder than Jennifer Hudson?" Power asked his girlfriend.

"I think so," said Skyla. "I think she's the bomb."

"You want to meet her between sets?" asked Power.

"Sure."

After thirty-five minutes, Besta left the stage to a standing ova-
tion. On their way to her dressing room, Power and Skyla stopped in
to say hey to Bruno Mars, who was getting ready for his star turn.

In the hallway, Power spotted Up.

"Great show," he told the keyboardist. "I'm Power Clay and this is
my friend Skyla."

"Power as in the Power Theater?" asked Up.

"Yes, sir. How were the acoustics for you?"

"Outta sight," said Up. "Nice to meet y'all. Thanks for having us,
man. I'm sure Besta wants to say thanks too."

"Let me ask you something before we go in there," said Power.
"This IW Management. Who's behind that?"

"Old-school cat who was off the scene for a while. Used to be big
in Chicago. Irv Wasserman."

Power's heart started hammering against his chest. He hid his
emotions and said, "No kidding. How did that happen?"

"Down in Jamaica. Besta was gigging around the island when
Wasserman heard her . . . no, I take that back. Wasn't Wasserman who
heard her first, it was this other cat. Dude called Simmons. Slim Simmons. Besta got the man's nose wide open. He's her manager. Or I
guess you could say him and Wasserman are co-managing."

Skyla saw the shock in Power's eyes. She knew about Slim but not about Wasserman. Power hadn't shared that part of his story with her.

"Come on in," said Up, opening the door to Besta's dressing room. "Let me introduce you."

Besta had changed into a red robe. Her wig was off was and her hair was covered with a white silk turban.

"Who is this beautiful couple?" she asked, her face beaming with a warm smile.

"This here is our host," said Up. "This is Power, the man who owns the theater, and this is his fine lady."

"And what's your name, sugar?" asked Besta.

"Skyla."

"Well, Skyla and Power, y'all look like *Ebony*'s couple of the year. And I can't tell you how much I love your theater. It is really is magnificent."

"Don't want to take up much of your time, Besta . . . ," Power began to say.

"Hell no, y'all wanna go out and hear Bruno. Me too. I'll be watching the brother from the wings."

"We just wanted to say how much we loved you," said Power. "We love your songs and we love your singing."

"Well, isn't that a sweet thing to say, young brother, especially coming from someone like you."

"Before we go," said Power, "I'm just wondering if we might talk to you later this evening, after the show."

"Would love to, sugar. You have something specific in mind?"

"I'm starting a booking agency—in addition to a management firm and label. We're interested in new talent. I don't know if you have any contractual obligations."

"Nothing I can't get out of," she said matter-of-factly. "Would love to talk to y'all later."

Milan, Italy

Teatro Barbieri was considered one of the jewels of the Italian Renaissance. It was constructed nearly five hundred years ago and closed for a five-year restoration at a cost of seventy million euros. Its reopening was a grand occasion, and using that occasion to showcase Two Sisters' new fashion line was a phenomenal coup. The world press was waiting.

"The press will be disappointed," said Akira Matsui as he walked into his daughters' suite at the Hotel Principe di Savoia. "But the show has been canceled."

"What!" exclaimed Beauty. "You said everything was in place—that Seiji is out of prison."

"He is out," said Akira, "and it's been proven that one faction of the government, hostile to his family, did maliciously prosecute him. A more sympathetic government board has overturned those charges, but his adversaries have managed to tie up much of his money and he feels that it's a mistake to show a line that, even if well received, may not be deliverable."

"No!" Beauty shouted. "For a multibillion-dollar enterprise not to be able to support a relatively small retail line . . . why, that's absurd. He controls an entire chain of luxury stores."

"No longer," said Akira. "Those stores have been sold."

"Fine/Bloom?"

"The entire chain. Bought by Saks Fifth Avenue."

"You have to be kidding."

"Bought at a bargain price," said Akira. "Seiji's group suffered a tremendous loss. But the cash was necessary."

"For what?" asked Beauty.

"I'm not privy to the details of the Aoi operation. We are a minuscule part of their holdings."

"I'm his wife, goddamn it," said Beauty. "That's hardly minuscule."

"He thought it be best if you went to New York," said Akira. "I received a wire from him just now saying that you should go to New York and wait."

"Wait for what?"

"For him, I suppose."

"And where do I stay?"

"He owns a building on the Upper East Side. The top two floors are his."

"He owns a building and he's canceling our line?" asked Beauty, now fuming. "None of this makes sense."

"He will explain. Meanwhile, he has made your reservations to leave tomorrow."

"I'm not going without Ryoko," said Beauty.

Ryoko had been listening carefully. She was neither naïve nor overly moralistic. Through her father, she had come to understand the cold ways of the business world. She appreciated those ways because they enabled her to live a life as a pure designer. She had been able to experiment—and enjoy success—because of the people who funded her father. The fact that those people had run into problems did not surprise her. And the fact that Seiji had been singled out to take the heat for his family operation also came as no surprise.

Seiji had become Ryoko's brother-in-law—a notion that, despite his reputation and recent arrest, still thrilled her. The sudden arrival of her sister, Beauty, and all that went with her, continued to be a source of marvel. Ryoko had gone from working alone in a room to traveling the world with a glamorous woman married to a glamorous man. She was living a fairy tale. It might not be her fairy tale, but she was delighted to live it all the same.

"This will all work out," she told Beauty. "I trust that Seiji will see his way clear to giving us what we want. I'm sure of it."

"And you're willing to go to New York with me?"

"I've been to Hong Kong and it was wonderful. All this week I've loved Milan, and I see no reason why I won't adore New York."

"You will, I promise," said Beauty.

"Then it's settled," said Ryoko.

"And you're not crushed that we won't be showing our line—all those dresses that were sewn, the models we hired, the beautiful set that was designed?"

"I'm disappointed, Beauty, but no, not crushed. There is always next season and the season after. That's why fashion is so great. The seasons never stop. We just need to be a little more patient."

Beauty considered her sister's statement. Patience. Of course you can never have too much. But hadn't Beauty been patient enough? She had been patient with Anita Ward in New York; with Soo Kim in Los Angeles and Soo's Italian husband, Primo Dalla Torre; with Kato Yamamoto—she had paid her dues. In marrying a man touted as the most powerful in Japan, she figured that her patience had finally paid off. She and her sister would be bankrolled for the rest of their creative lives. She'd been certain that within a few months she'd be elevated to CEO of Fine/Bloom. From there, given Seiji's endless money, she'd move up to even more ambitious ventures.

Now all that had suddenly changed, just as it had suddenly changed with Anita, Soo, Primo, and Kato. Time after time, was it Beauty's fate to reach the top, only to slide back down to the bottom?

But this could hardly be called the bottom. Seiji owned his own building in the most expensive section of Manhattan. Her place was at the top of the building, not the bottom. Far worse things had happened to her. And yet, given her past, she couldn't help but fantasize about a future in which, shortly after she arrived in New York, someone would arrive with an eviction notice. When she read the news on her computer, would she see that Seiji was convicted on some other charge and would be spending the rest of his life in prison?

Beauty's heart was heavy. She would do what she had to do. She always did. At the same time, she always thought of Power. But he was lost in his world, just as she was lost in hers. To extricate herself from her current situation was impossible.

Her mind went back to New York, when Power had begged her to come to Atlanta. She said no. She chose Kato. And when Kato was gone, she chose Seiji. Both choices had tremendous consequences. They took her farther away from Power. She had hoped they would take her where she wanted to be. But now, in this storm of mental confusion, she no longer knew where she wanted to be.

Beauty did know, though, that she needed to reconnect with her friend Solomon Getz. As soon as she and Ryoko arrived in New York, she called her friend and asked him, "You still have a job?"

"Do you?" Solomon asked back.

"I don't know."

"I don't either."

"So we're in the same place," said Beauty.

"No. You're in Milan showing your new line and I'm in New York waiting to get axed."

"No, I'm back. My line was canceled. The show is off."

"So we *are* in the same place."

"I'm at Seiji's place."

"He has a town house here?"

"A building. I want you to come over. I want you to meet my sister."

"You brought her?"

"She's part of my life now. You'll love her."

"Tell me what he looks like," Ryoko asked Beauty before Solomon arrived.

"He's handsome. Curly hair, brown eyes, strong build. Former Israeli soldier. First person I met in New York when I arrived as a sixteen-year-old. That was only seven years ago. Feels like seven hundred."

"A former lover?"

"Oh, no," said Beauty. "He's gay. His boyfriend is Amir, from Jordan. He's wonderful. They're both wonderful."

"How did you meet them?" asked Ryoko.

Beauty told the story—of how Solomon had been Anita Ward's driver; how he worked his way up the ladder at Bloom's, only to be fired; how he and Amir moved to Chicago to start over again; how, after the death of Primo Dalla Torre and Anita Ward, she had gone to Chicago to be with Solomon and Amir; how, nurtured by a loving cohort of gay men, she had been able to regroup in Chicago; how her job at Claire's had brought her back to Atlanta and her affair with Kato had brought her back to New York, where, in the aftermath of the Yamamoto purchase of Bloom's, Solomon was given a key executive position.

"So you have helped each other," said Ryoko.

"Always," Beauty said. "He's my brother."

"Then he's mine as well."

At that moment, Beauty thought of Power. For all that had transpired, there was still no man with whom she was closer, at least in her secret heart. And yet that secret was something she still hadn't shared with Ryoko. She wondered why. Was it shame that kept her love for

Power hidden from her sister? Or was she afraid that once Ryoko heard the truth, she would encourage Beauty to run to him? Even worse, would Ryoko, who adored Seiji, find fault with Beauty for being obsessed with another man?

When the door opened and Solomon and Amir appeared, they embraced Beauty.

"You must be jet-lagged, sweetheart," said Amir, a demure gentleman with a thin frame and graceful gait. "You've been through so much."

"Come meet Ryoko."

Ryoko was seated at the enormous dining room table, where she was drinking a cup of green tea. She rose as the company approached her. She extended her hand, and they each took it warmly. Amir kissed her on one cheek, Solomon the other.

"Beauty has told me about you both," she said. "Your friendship has meant so much to my sister."

"Not as much as it has meant to us," said Solomon. "We adore her."

"And I adore Japan," said Amir, who began telling Ryoko about the year he spent studying music in Tokyo. His Japanese wasn't perfect, but it was good enough to tell the story to Ryoko in her native language. Meanwhile, Solomon and Beauty wandered into the living room and sat close to each other on the couch.

"How big is this place?" Solomon asked.

"Two stories. So far I've counted five bedrooms."

"This is Seiji's taste?" He looked around at the furnishings—heavy drapes, huge antique Japanese vases, woodblock prints, scrolls, and fans encased in fanciful frames.

"I'm sure it's his decorator, not him."

"What's he like, this husband of yours?"

"He's a star."

"A diva?"

"Yes. He likes attention. Apparently his father did not. His father was low-key, and from what Ryoko tells me, Seiji's recent imprisonment had to do with his refusal to stay out of the limelight."

"And now his little empire is falling apart."

"It's hardly little, Solomon. I think his resources are vast."

"Not vast enough to hold on to Fine/Bloom."

"That's only one of his family's many investments. But you still haven't told me, what have the new owners told you?"

"Just heard today. Clean sweep of top management."

Beauty took Solomon's hand and said, "I'm so sorry."

"When it comes to the retail business, at this point we're all war veterans. I'll survive. But it's not me I'm worried about, Beauty, it's you. You got yourself in another situation."

Beauty sighed. Several seconds passed before she finally said, "We're old pros by now."

"We are, but I still have to ask you—what do you think you're doing?"

"Surviving, Solomon. That's what we're all trying to do."

"No one believes in you more than me. I saw your talent from the start. I saw this brilliant teenage girl with energy and drive and knew that nothing and no one would get in her way. You *are* a survivor, baby, and you've survived some rough blows. But the blows have gotten rougher and more dangerous and now I'm really worried."

"I'm fine."

"You say that, but one husband is dead—"

"I never married Kato."

"Sorry, one *boyfriend* is dead and now your new husband, whom you barely know—"

"I know that the man is completely devoted to me."

"Marrying the professional to the personal can be lethal."

"You and I have done it for years, Solomon. We're friends, yet we help each other in business however we can."

"We're not sleeping together."

"What difference does sex make?"

"All the difference in the world. It changes the chemistry. It makes a relationship combustible, explosive. The thing can blow up at any minute."

"What *thing* are you talking about?"

"Your life, Beauty."

"My life is what it is."

"It needs to change. You need to stop running."

"Running from what?"

"Love."

"Oh, please, Solomon. You don't know me as well as you think you do."

"I know you pretty goddamn well. I know that after you saved him, you ran from him. And I know you're still running. I think you need to stop. You need to change course."

"I can't change who I am."

"You can if you want to."

"And why should I want to?"

"Because you're heading in a dark direction."

"Finding out that I have an amazing sister in Tokyo with an amazing heart and talent—was that a dark direction?"

"That was beautiful, but where are you going now?"

"I'm going to show you some of the samples of our line."

"I've seen many of them—they're great, I agree. I love Two Sisters. I applaud what you're doing with Ryoko. But I'm not talking about Ryoko. I'm talking about Seiji Aoi and the world he represents. I'm urging you to get out of that world before it's too late."

"Just like that?" asked Beauty.

"Just like that," Solomon repeated.

Beauty didn't reply. She looked in the direction of the dining room, where Ryoko and Amir were deep in discussion. She thought about where she had been and where she was—back in New York, back in another precarious situation, back to a future with no certainty.

"I'm sorry I cost you your job, Solomon."

"You got me my job, Beauty. I don't care about losing it. I care about losing you."

"That's not going to happen. I have a family now—a father, a sister."

"And a husband?"

"Yes, a husband."

"Whose work and whereabouts are unclear."

"My work is clear and so are my whereabouts. I'm back in New York, where my sister and I are going to design clothes like this industry has never seen before. My goal is to make Two Sisters successful—and I'll do whatever it takes to achieve that goal."

Cali

It had been years since Slim had been to San Francisco. The last time he'd gone was with his late lieutenant Andre Gee. That was the trip when he'd been looking to forge a deal with a major West Coast drug supplier. The negotiations had broken down and, in frustration, Slim had blamed it all on Andre's severe stutter.

"I told you not to open your fuckin' mouth," Slim had said after the meeting had ended.

"They a-a-a-a-a-a-asked me a q-q-q-q-q-q-uestion," Dre had said.

"Yeah, but when you couldn't get the answer out, they thought you were a retard. They didn't wanna do business with me if I worked with a fuckin' retard."

When Slim thought back to that episode he hardly recognized himself. He had been a cruel man. He had been a murderous man. He had lost sight of reality. He had seen the entire world coming at him. He had fought and slaughtered anyone who was part of that world. He was sorry. In the church of Father Noel Peters he had repented and received salvation. God had rewarded him with Besta. She had given him not only purpose but strength in bed. She had even written a song about his lasting power, the song had become a hit, and he had flown from Miami to San Francisco to see her sing that song at an outdoor festival where Ne-Yo was headlining.

Slim didn't give two shits about fuckin' Ne-Yo. He didn't care about Bruno Mars or Trey Songz or any of these boys young enough to be his grandkids. His kind of soul music was Smokey Robinson and Marvin Gaye. But Slim realized that these young boys were making money, and to have Besta open their shows was the right move. She was being exposed to a young audience who had started buying her songs on iTunes in such quantities that Slim and Irv decided it was time to shoot a video. Picturesque San Francisco was the perfect spot.

Slim had to admit that Up was the right producer and musical director for Besta. He had that hip-hop swag. He wore oversized Akoo hoodies in apple red and metallic blue. His baggy jeans hung down low and his flipped-to-the-side baseball cap read HUSTLIN' IZ MY LIFE. He had a look that Slim wanted to believe appealed to sissies. Besta said that Up was gay, but Slim hadn't seen him with any boyfriend.

"That's cause he don't mess with sex when he's working," Besta told him. "He disciplines his Up-Towners like they in the army. That's why the band has such a good snap. The boy's all business."

There was no doubt that the Besta/Up music business had been good. And when Slim was around, Up was respectful. He called him "boss." He heeded Slim's suggestions, even when he thought they were dumb. Up knew who he was working for.

Slim had no complaints. He and Irv were spending a huge amount of money on building up Besta, but that felt good. Life had purpose again. Irv had reached out to old contacts in the music business who were happy to do him a solid. Those contacts had come through. Besta wasn't yet a star, but she was on her way.

Slim's plane landed in time for him to get to the afternoon sound check. That night's concert was being held on a giant stage at Golden Gate Park. When he arrived, he saw that Besta was going over her material with Up. They stood close together—as would be expected—

but when they caught sight of Slim, they suddenly moved away from each other. Why?

"Hey, baby," Besta yelled from the stage. "Great to see you."

"Great to be seen," said Slim, whose healthy mental condition over the past months had resulted in a weight gain. To hide his stomach, he wore a loose-fitting double-breasted green suit of light wool. A gaudy gold chain hung over his black Versace T-shirt. His Ferragamo alligators cost $1,500, and the diamonds in his ears were each a half carat.

He walked up to the stage, where Besta gave him a big hug.

"Hey, Mr. Slim," said Up. "What's goin' on?"

"All good," said Slim, a stern look on his face.

"Something's bad," Slim told Irv. He was calling his partner in Miami from the suite he was sharing with Besta at the Fairmont hotel, high atop Nob Hill. "When I turn my back, I feel like the whole band is laughing at me. All those Up-Towners, those kids, like they know something I don't."

"You're imagining stuff again, Slim. This isn't good. You have a good situation with this lady. Leave it like that."

"And this Up. I don't like him. Something's not right with him."

"He's a queer," said Irv. "Queers have problems."

"He don't act like no queer."

"What do queers act like?"

"They act like bitches."

"Not all of them. Some of them act normal. I had a bookkeeper, Melvin Steinberg. As a young man, he played baseball in the minor leagues. Almost made the White Sox. Had season tickets to the White Sox. Good-looking guy. Dressed regular. Talked regular. No sissy stuff. Not a hint. And then one day I learn him and Sol Livinsky, my dentist, are living together and sleeping in the same bed. Could have knocked me over with a feather. You understand what I'm saying, Slim?"

"I'm going to fire him."

"Fire Up?"

"I'm doing it today."

"And what about the concert? Who's gonna play for her?"

"I'll find another piano player."

"Who knows her arrangements? Slim, it's his band. You're about to ruin everything."

"I'll wait till after the concert—then I'll fire his ass."

"You're not thinking straight. This is the man who produced her. He wrote songs with her. One of those songs is on the charts. He's a key to her success."

"He wants to fuck her. Or maybe he already has."

"I don't like this talk, Slim, I really don't. I'm afraid you're getting sick again. That's not good, especially after all we've been through. You don't want to slip back. You don't want to get sick."

"Something's happening here, Irv. I can feel it in my gut. If you were here, you'd feel it too."

"All right, here's what we'll do. Where's the next gig?"

"L.A."

"Fine. I'll meet you, Besta, and Up in L.A. I'll fly out and see if I see what you see."

"You'd do that for me, Irv?"

"I want to put your mind at ease, Slim. I don't want you getting sick again. Let me assess the situation. If it's rotten, we'll do what we have to do. And if it's not, we can move ahead."

"That would mean a lot to me, Irv."

"Just promise you'll forget about this business until I get to California."

"I promise."

Slim broke his promise. Watching Besta shoot the video in San Francisco, he couldn't lose the thought that something was wrong.

The video itself was straight-ahead: a series of shots of Besta riding a cable car lip-synching her song followed by a series of shots of Besta in a soundstage bedroom. In the cable-car shots, she'd be wearing a skintight black pantsuit; in the interior ones, she'd be wearing a revealing black negligee.

Just before the day of filming, the director looked over the story-board and said, "Something's missing. I think we need to put a love interest in these shots."

"Why?" asked Slim, who was in on all the meetings. "She's making love to the camera. She's making love to all the men watching the fuckin' video. That's better than making love to one man."

"I'm not sure," said the director. "Women watching these videos like to see a handsome man. He has to be really fine."

Besta didn't comment. She could see Slim, who was paying for the shoot, was getting a little crazy.

"Besides," said Slim, "it's too late. You should have thought of this before. You got no actors, you got no models."

"There's that guy in Besta's band," said the director. "Isn't he the bandleader?"

"Up?" asked Slim.

"Up, that's his name. He's a terrific-looking guy. He looks like a model. We'll just get him."

Slim exploded. "Fuck no!"

"Did I say something wrong?" asked the director.

"You sure as shit did. That kid ain't no actor."

"We don't need an actor, Mr. Simmons. We just need an attractive male."

"That motherfucker is ugly as sin," said Slim. "He's got a face like a dog."

Besta knew better than to intervene. She kept quiet.

The director sighed. "Look, Mr. Simmons, you're paying me good money to give you a video that sells the song. I can do it without a male interest, and that would be fine. But we're going to have more impact if I do it with a guy in some of the shots."

"What do you think, Besta?" asked Slim.

"I know you know best, Daddy. You call the shots any way you wanna. I'm cool either way."

Slim stopped to think—he thought about what Irv had told him;

he was comforted by the fact that Irv was coming out tomorrow to meet them in L.A. He calmed himself down and told the director, "Okay, if you think it'll help."

By the end of the day of shooting, Slim felt like he was losing it. He knew in his gut that he hadn't been imagining anything, that the sexual vibe between Besta and Up was real.

During the shoot on the cable car, they looked at each other like they wanted to fuck. It wasn't just acting. And even though they never touched, their eyes said it all. The scenes in the bedroom were even worse. They not only touched, they kissed. She was in this thin negligee with her tits showing; he was on her bed wearing nothing but running shorts.

"Keep your fuckin' mouths closed when you kiss!" Slim yelled from behind the camera. "You don't need to open your mouths."

"I didn't like any of that," Slim told Besta when the day was over and they were back in their suite.

"Up was thinking about kissing a boy, not me," she said.

"It didn't look that way to me."

"Well, you don't gotta look at it no more. It's all in the can. And we alone. Been waiting for this moment all day, sugar."

"So he just warmed you up for me?" asked Slim.

"He's cold as ice. I don't need no warming up when I'm in a room all alone with you."

She kissed Slim hard, pressing herself against him. He got hard and she led him to the bed. She undressed him, he undressed her, and they went at it. A second after he slipped it in, though, he came.

"Goddamn it to hell!" Slim screamed. "It's happening again."

"No problem, baby," said Besta, trying to comfort him. "It ain't no thing."

"Hasn't happened since I met you. Why the fuck is it happening now?"

"Don't let it throw you, daddy. Come on, let's just cuddle up in here."

"Don't wanna cuddle. Wanna fuck."

"We'll fuck again. We got all night."

But when an hour later, after some champagne and good weed, they tried again, he came again—seconds after he entered her.

She tried to reassure him, but he was inconsolable. He didn't know what to do.

The L.A. gig was a big deal. Besta was opening for Chris Brown at the Hollywood Bowl. This was the final leg of the campaign, devised by the booking agent hired by Irv and Slim, to introduce Besta to live audiences. So far it was working. "You Last the Longest" had gone top twenty R & B. With the soon-to-be-released video, it was likely to go top ten. Besta was blowing up.

Irv was flying in. Slim was so eager to see him that he went with the driver to the airport. First thing, he told Irv about the video and the sexual heat between Besta and Up.

"Why in hell did you go to the shoot?" asked Irv as the car sat in traffic on the 405. "Of course that would drive you crazy. You shouldn't have gone."

"Well, I went," said Slim, "and I'm glad I did. I saw that my thinking hasn't been wrong."

"Well, stop thinking, Slim, and just relax. I'm here. I'll look things over. You trust me, don't you?"

"With my life, Irv. You saved my fuckin' life."

Irv went to his suite at the Montage hotel in Beverly Hills to nap. Slim and Besta were on the same floor. The show wasn't until the next day, and that night Irv proposed that the three of them—himself, Slim, and Besta—have dinner. Slim agreed. They went to Crustacean, a celebrity-friendly upscale seafood restaurant.

After wine, salads, lobster, and dessert, Besta excused herself to go to the ladies' room.

"What do you think?" asked Slim.

"I think she's crazy about you," said Irv. "She looks at you like you're Jesus. She treats you like a king."

"She's putting on an act for you."

"It's a pretty good act," said Irv.

"That's what I'm scared of."

"You don't need to be scared of nothing," said Irv. "I'm looking into this further. I'm meeting Up for breakfast—just me and him alone. Then I'm going to their rehearsal to see how Up and Besta are together."

"If they know you're there, they'll act like nothing's happening."

"They won't know I'm there. I set up the rehearsal at a studio where they got a one-way mirror. I'll be watching and they won't know it."

"Good," said Slim. "You'll see."

Next day, after his breakfast meeting with Up and his clandestine presence at the rehearsal, Irv went back to the hotel for his afternoon nap. He saw six different messages from Slim, asking Irv to call him.

"Will you please calm the fuck down?" said Irv when he reached Slim. "You been calling every five minutes."

"I gotta know. What'd you see?"

"At breakfast I saw a dedicated musician who didn't do anything but talk about music and how he's writing new songs for Besta."

"I told you—he's into her."

"As an artist, yes. As a woman, he couldn't care less. The kid wants to make money. He wants hits."

"How about the rehearsal?"

"Completely professional."

"Are you sure they didn't know you were there?" asked Slim.

"Positive. I watched them for over an hour. He never so much as touched her. She's a product to him, not a piece of ass. I guarantee you, Slim. You got nothing to worry about. There's nothing there."

"I'm not sure you're the right guy to judge this kind of shit," said Slim. "You aren't the romantic type. You said so yourself. You haven't been good at romance."

"Then why did you want me to come out here and look over the situation?"

"Because I was sure you'd see the truth."

"The truth is that nothing's happening," said Irv.

"I don't believe that."

"You don't believe me? You think I have some hidden agenda?"

"I don't know what to believe."

"Slim, listen to me. This thing is getting you sick. Just put it out of your mind. This woman loves you. This woman can sing. This woman is doing nothing wrong."

"If loving you is wrong," Besta told Up, "then I don't want to do right."

He laughed and said, "Ain't those lyrics to an old song?"

"It's a song I'm singing to you, darling. You rockin' my boat and rockin' it hard."

They were in Up's room at the Farmer's Daughter Hotel on Fairfax Avenue, some four miles away from the Montage hotel. After rehearsal, they had waited for the band to leave before driving over for an afternoon delight.

"We should have waited till Slim leaves town," said Up.

"He's busy with Irv."

"I like Irv. He's OG. Them old-school gangsters are cool."

"Long as they get what they want."

"I hate that you gotta keep giving it to Slim," said Up.

"It ain't about nothing," said Besta. "Second he smells pussy, he busts his nut."

Up broke out laughing. "Well, whatever might be off about these old men, they got us this far."

"And I'm thinking that this young boy," said Besta, "this Power over in Atlanta, he gonna take us the rest of the way."

Bone's

As she rode with Power to the Buckhead restaurant where they were meeting her parents, Skyla was silent. She was thinking about the nature of love.

Love had surprised her. It wasn't part of her expectations or plans. And yet here she was, deeply in love with a man she wanted to believe was slowly beginning to love her. There was, of course, the possibility that she was fooling herself. Skyla was smart; she understood self-delusion. But she was also a woman who had been swept up by an obsession with the man who sat next to her in the backseat of the blue-and-silver Maybach 62, the sleek German sedan driven by Jordan Gee, younger brother of Andre Gee, Slim's murdered lieutenant and loyal friend to Power.

She loved how Power had slipped into his role as a business titan; she loved how he had leaned on her advice; she loved how comfortably he assumed his new role as man of the hour. She loved everything about him. She had worked night and day to give him everything he wanted. She knew that Power, a good and decent man, was appreciative, and that his appreciation was turning into love.

Gazing out the window, Power wasn't thinking of Skyla; he was thinking of the ironic fact that Bone's, their destination, was the restaurant where Power had seen Andre Gee for the last time. That's where Andre had taken him to dinner just before Power's departure for New York, where Slim had first set up his job with Holly Windsor. That was the night Dre warned him not to return to Atlanta. Dre never said why, but Power felt how deeply Dre cared about him. Dre was a fiercely loyal man, and his loyalty to Slim resulted in his death.

Like his brother Andre, Jordan had played football for the Falcons, where he'd been a starting tackle for five years. After retirement, he worked at a Mercedes dealership. That's where Power ran into him. He told Power he was better at driving cars than selling them, which was when Power immediately gave him the job. Jordan knew all about his late brother's devotion to Power and was excited at the prospect of working for a man Dre had loved. From the start, the Jordan–Power bond was unbreakable.

When Dre had taken Power to Bone's, they had eaten in a private room. This time, though, Power's dinner was anything *but* private. The mayor commanded a center table where everyone could see him. After all, it wasn't every evening that the mayor came to dine. And Ajay Lock was a man who liked to seen.

The Locks were already at the table when Power and Skyla arrived. Ajay gave Power a firm handshake while his daughter kissed her mom on the cheek. She did not kiss her father. Since Skyla had hooked up with Power, she and her father had forged an uneasy peace. For her part, Louella was grateful that the image of her happy family had been miraculously maintained.

The men were dressed in suits—the mayor with a tie, Power with an open collar. The women were attired in sophisticated cocktail dresses—Louella's was black, Skyla's was dark brown. Louella wore a double strand of cultured pearls. Skyla wore an arty necklace fashioned from old typewriter keys. Ajay ordered vintage French wine. He and Power began discussing the prospect of expanding the

Hartsfield-Jackson Atlanta International Airport and the business opportunities that would create in the adjacent area. Louella and Skyla talked about Nicki Minaj's recent appearance on *The Wendy Williams Show*. Skyla liked her; Louella didn't. The wine arrived, then the salads, the soup, the steaks, the sides. The small talk continued, and it wasn't until dessert that the real reason for the dinner became apparent.

The mayor was in the middle of discussing his rise in the popularity polls when his daughter abruptly stopped him.

"That's great," she said with some sarcasm, "but we didn't really invite you here to discuss politics."

That silenced her father.

"Whatever the reason," said Louella, "we're delighted to be with you and Power."

"Well, the reason will make you even more delighted," said Skyla.

"What is it, dear?" asked Louella.

"We're having a baby."

A week ago, when he learned the news, Power had reconciled himself to the situation. Skyla would never consider an abortion and, as far as he was concerned, it was her choice. In his soul, he had always dreamed of having a child with Beauty—but that wasn't happening. Skyla was happening, and he had no choice but to go along with the program.

"That's wonderful, dear," said Louella. "Simply wonderful."

Ajay smiled before saying, "There's nothing I'd like more than to be a grandfather. And nothing I'd rather do than to throw you the most sensational engagement party this city has ever seen."

"No one's said anything about getting married," said Skyla.

Louella looked down at her chocolate cake. Power ate a bite of lemon sorbet.

"What do you have against marriage, Power?" asked Ajay.

"Nothing, sir," he said.

"Daddy," Skyla said, breaking in, "don't pressure Power like that."

"No pressure," said Power.

"You aren't against marriage?" Skyla asked Power.

"I have no real attitude about it," he said.

"You don't?" asked Skyla, who up until this point had been reluctant to mention marriage to Power. Their relationship was going great, and she didn't want to rock the boat. But suddenly, in this improbable setting, the topic was on the table and Power, to Skyla's surprise, was not adamantly opposed. She was about to say something when she realized that, in a strange way, her parents were doing the work for her.

"Well," said the mayor, "if you have no objections—and you seem to have none, Power—then I don't see any reason why we can't start planning this engagement party. I can have my staff put it together in a week's time. I wouldn't be surprised if the governor himself attended."

"That's a marvelous idea, Ajay," said Louella. "What do you think, Power?"

Several seconds of silence.

"Well . . . ," he said, "I'm not opposed."

"Great," said the mayor. "It's a done deal."

Skyla looked for a smile on Power's face. She looked for a sign of happiness in his eyes. But there were no indications that Power was remotely happy. He displayed only indifference.

Is this how he proposes? Skyla asked herself. *By going along with my father's plan for a party?* She began to say something but thought better of it. Why stir up trouble, especially with her folks at the table?

After the dinner was over, after a date for the engagement party was set, the couples went their separate ways. In the backseat of the Maybach, with Jordan behind the wheel, Skyla and Power sat in silence until she finally said, "You don't have to do it, you know."

"I know."

"Only if you want to."

"I told your dad I would."

"But that's still not saying you want to."

"It's fine, Skyla, it really is."

"It's a big deal."

"I realize that."

"But it feels like you're doing it just for convenience."

"I'm doing it because it'll make everyone happy."

"Including you?"

"It won't make me unhappy."

"Damn it, Power!" Skyla said, exploding. "You don't get married in order to not be unhappy. You get married because you're in love."

"If you'd rather not get married . . ."

"You know I want to get married. You know how much I love you. You know this is my dream come true."

"Then that's great," said Power. "It's great I'm making you happy. That makes me happy."

"And what about the love part?"

"I love making you happy."

"That's not the same as saying you love me, Power."

"If it makes you happy, I'll say that I love you."

Skyla sighed, realizing that was about as good as it was going to get.

That night they made love—or rather, Skyla made love to Power. Their sexual relationship had settled on her as the aggressor. This was something new for Power, but he didn't mind. He saw that she liked it, and as she took charge, as she took him in her mouth for extraordinarily long periods of time, it allowed his mind to dwell elsewhere.

She fell asleep before him. His mind was active with thoughts of that evening. Was he being too passive? Was he foolish to marry a woman he knew he didn't love? Or would it in fact be foolish *not* to marry her? She was the perfect partner with the perfectly connected parents. Since she had joined him in a domestic union, her wildness had dissipated. Her energy had all been channeled into advancing his agenda. Why not marry her? Why not seal the deal, since this was the best deal he had ever gotten so far in a life marked by a slew of lousy deals? Things were moving ahead; business was booming; his world was calm. Why not solidify his situation with a formal engagement and proper marriage?

From the other room, he thought he heard the sound of his cell phone. He looked at the clock by his nightstand. Midnight. He wondered who would be calling at midnight. He got out of bed and found his phone attached to the charger on the kitchen counter. The ID read PRIVATE. Out of curiosity, he picked it up.

"Power?" said the voice on the other end.

"Yes."

"It's Irv Wasserman."

"Irv . . . I'm surprised. You okay?"

"I'm fine. I want to come see you."

"Well, my life has changed a lot. I'm not sure—"

"I know what's happening in your life and I'm glad. What I have to say won't change any of it. It'll just make it better. I'm coming to Atlanta tomorrow for a few hours. I'll be at the Renaissance Concourse hotel by the airport. We'll have a late lunch in my room. Come by at two."

Irv spoke with the authority of a boss. Power recognized that as the same authority that had given him many orders in the past—orders he had always obeyed. He and Irv had never suffered a falling-out. At the same time, Irv's sudden call messed up Power's mind. He had just been thinking of how smoothly things were going. He had just adjusted to the fact of his engagement. Now this. The better part of wisdom told him to tell Irv no.

But curiosity overwhelmed caution and Power said, "I'll be there."

"Japanese Finance Minister Murdered"

The sudden sale of Seiji's building on the Upper East Side upset Beauty far more than Ryoko. Beauty sensed a growing danger in the abrupt changes in Seiji's life, while Ryoko felt she was in the middle of one of Seiji's movies. After being protected by her dad for so long, Ryoko loved this new life. The more adventurous, the better.

One day Ryoko and Beauty were situated on the top two floors of an elegant high-rise apartment building and the next they were transferred to a large three-story house on a tree-lined street in the Park Slope section of Brooklyn. Tastefully furnished, the domicile nonetheless had a fortress-like feeling. Seiji had arranged for a construction firm to build a concrete wall in front and a high gate in back. Exterior surveillance cameras were installed and bars were put on all the first-floor windows. A military-standard alarm system could be activated from every room, even the bathrooms, and six highly trained, fully armed Japanese security men worked long shifts to secure the dwelling 24/7.

All these arrangements were made while Seiji was still in Tokyo. He called Beauty every day to discuss these plans, and his tone was always calm and matter-of-fact.

"No danger," he said. "Moves matter of precaution. You be more comfortable in these new quarters."

"Can you explain why the move is necessary?" she asked her husband, who increasingly felt more like a stranger to her.

"I arrive and then explain."

"When will that be?"

"Shortly."

"Shortly" turned from one week to two, and two to three. In the meantime, though, Seiji made good on his promise and spared no expense in turning the entire third floor of the Park Slope house into a design studio for Beauty and Ryoko. Mannequins were brought in along with drawing boards made of teakwood, sophisticated computers equipped with up-to-date software, and a battery of voice-recognition devices designed specifically for the blind.

In addition to the security force, Seiji had arranged for a staff of four workers to be at the sisters' beck and call. If Beauty or Ryoko wanted a particular bolt of fabric from the Garment District in Manhattan, they had only to ask. A full-time cook commanded the kitchen. On Seiji's orders, the basement had been turned into a plush in-home theater with an enormous screen and access to any movie that the women wanted to watch. Naturally the complete collection of Seiji's films was there on Blu-ray.

The sisters had everything they could want—except for one thing. They were not allowed to leave.

"This temporary situation," explained Seiji, who had not seen Beauty for over a month. "I promise."

"But if there's no danger," she asked, "why such drastic restrictions?"

"My concern is you, your sister. You be safe. I arrive shortly and—"

"You used that word before, Seiji."

"And I use again, but I speak truth. I be there shortly and we go out. We free."

Beauty sought clarity by calling her father, Akira, who was back in Tokyo. But Akira spoke only in generalities.

"There is great confusion in our government," he explained. "Great changes are happening and I'm just hoping that it all goes well for Seiji."

"You sound like you have doubts," said Beauty.

"I have confidence in Seiji. He's a smart man, and I'm counting on him to resolve the situation. But the difficulty is that Rin Aoi was the most brilliant man this country has ever known, and now that he is gone, his enemies sense a weakness in his organization. Seiji is trying to prove that such a weakness does not exist."

"How does he prove that?"

"I can't tell you specifically, Beauty, but he has his ways. He will get through this. I have confidence. I also have confidence that you are caring for your sister."

"It's really the other way around. She's caring for me."

"She adores you. Is she doing all right in New York?"

"She's thriving. Her ideas for the new season are incredible. Far better than the line we were forced to cancel in Milan."

"So you see, it's all working out."

"I want to believe that."

"There's no reason not to."

During conversations like this, Beauty felt—at least for a few seconds—that she had a real father. She could release long-held resentments and begin to appreciate having a caring parent. Those feelings, though, were not permanent. Deep down, she couldn't entirely forget or forgive him for what he had done to her mother. Yes, he had shown up at the right time in her life; yes, through him she had discovered a sister whom she loved; and yes, he had connected her to the all-powerful man she had married. But she couldn't help wondering whether Akira Matsui had done all this more for himself than for her.

By arranging her meeting with Seiji, he had ingratiated himself with the Aoi family. And when his daughter married Seiji, Akira had actually entered the family, thus raising his status and bringing him close to the center of authority.

Compared to Seiji Aoi, Kato Yamamoto was a relatively easy man to understand. He was the son of wealthy merchants whose ambition to expand his parents' holdings exceeded his ability. He stumbled into a world where he was naïve and in over his head. His incompetence cost him his life.

Seiji was a different animal entirely. He was a star. As a dashing and ruthless antihero in big-screen dramas, he had won over the hearts of the Japanese people. Until his arrest, he had appeared invincible. And although he was probably the purest narcissist Beauty had ever encountered, his narcissism was easy to tolerate. Its obviousness made it manageable. As both man and lover, he needed to be admired. He needed to be seen. The mirror was his best friend. He admired himself in the mirror of Beauty's eyes, and though he was undoubtedly taken by her own physical charms, she had to do little to make him happy. It was enough to look at him.

On this Monday morning, though, five weeks into her strangely secluded life in Brooklyn, two startling developments took place, one after another. The first was the page-one headline she read in the online edition of the *New York Times*: JAPANESE FINANCE MINISTER MURDERED. The article said the assassination was carried out by a car bomb. The minister, his aide, and his driver were blown to bits. It went on to say that this particular official had been adamant in undermining the finances of a crime syndicate headed by the Aoi family. The minister's investigation had led to the recent imprisonment of Seiji Aoi, currently free on bond and awaiting trial. A link between the bombing and Aoi, though, could not be established.

A half hour after Beauty finished the article, the phone rang.

"I arrive," said Seiji.

"You *will* arrive or you *have* arrived?" asked Beauty.

"I call from my car. We there soon."

Forty minutes later, the door to the third-floor studio opened and Seiji, dressed in a long black coat and green felt fedora, entered as an actor enters the stage. He face was flush with confidence. He walked over to Beauty and stood directly in front of her, as though he was posing. Finally he embraced her. Ryoko, who had been working at her drawing board, made her way over so that she, too, might embrace him. He opened his arms and accepted her warmly.

"Two sisters," he said. "Beautiful."

"You are beautiful," said Ryoko to Seiji.

Beauty said nothing.

That evening, when he made love to her in the master bedroom suite, she still said nothing.

In the morning, he said that all was well. They would all be going into Manhattan for dinner and a show.

"You know this *Jersey Boys*?" asked Seiji.

"The Broadway musical?"

"They say it very good."

"You want to see *Jersey Boys*?" asked Beauty.

"Yes. It is about America. I need to learn America. From now on, I stay in America."

The Potter's House

Slim had never been much of a churchgoer, but since the encounter with Father Noel Peters he would occasionally get up early on a Sunday morning and make his way to a house of God. He liked megachurches because the seats were comfortable, the choirs were good, and the preachers were spirited. He knew Bishop T. D. Jakes from television and was eager to hear him in person.

The Saturday-night gig in Dallas had gone well. Besta was one of two opening acts for Kelly Rowland, and the crowd, people in their twenties and thirties, cheered at the sound of the signature guitar riff opening "You Last the Longest." The song had gone top five R & B. The Texas date represented the last stop on the tour in which Besta was an auxiliary attraction for major stars. Slim's hope was that the next tour might find Besta headlining.

Irv had helped him. Slim knew Irv to be highly skeptical of others, so his reassurance that all was well with Besta meant a lot. Slim was also happy that immediately after the Dallas gig Up flew off to Memphis, leaving him alone with Besta. When Slim suggested that they go to the late service at the Potter's House and postpone their return trip to Florida until Monday morning, Besta was quick to agree.

"If we right with God," she said, "what can go wrong?"

Slim was certain that Bishop T. D. Jakes was right with God. He commanded the stage of the Potter's House, where seventy-five hundred worshippers followed his every word. A large man with a booming voice, he preached in the old-school style, where storytelling was an emotional experience. He had his parishioners waving and standing and shouting. He spoke of David, the king who started out as a shepherd shoveling sheep dung; David, who had the guts to face Goliath; David, who, in spite of Saul's jealousy, revered his leader; David, who was both poet and warrior; David the adulterer; David the champion of the oppressed; David, a man of contradictions and conflicts; and finally David, a man with a heart for God.

"Are you David?" asked Bishop Jakes. "Can you embrace his vision? Can you feel his passion for the Lord? Can you identify with his dilemmas?"

Slim rose out of his seat and cried, "Yes, I can! You go on and preach, Bishop!"

As the preacher grew more intense, so was Slim's reaction. Like David, he had been born an underdog. Like David, he had risen above his station. Slim once had commanded men. Slim once had an army at his beck and call. Slim was no stranger to power. Slim was no stranger to God. God was his constant companion. God had brought him to Irv, who had helped restore his right mind. Besta had done the same. She had helped restore his manhood, and even though his sex problem had recurred, he had conquered the problem once and would conquer it again. God was good. This woman sitting by his side was good. She was grateful for all Slim had done for her. She would never abandon him and, according to Irv, she wasn't two-timing him.

"Put your faith in God," said the bishop, "and God will see you through."

Slim put his faith in God.

A few hours after the service, back at the W Hotel, he put his manhood in Besta and was able to love her for at least a few minutes.

"You last the longest," she began singing in his ear, even as she thought of Up.

Slim slept on the flight from Dallas to Miami. When he opened his eyes before landing, he saw that Besta was not seated beside him. He looked around and saw that she had gone to the coach section, where she was chatting amicably with Rashan and the other body-guard who'd been traveling with Slim. He trusted Rashan, but the other guy was new. He was a hunky Latino, a former cop who walked with a strong swagger and seemed awfully goddamn pleased about his good looks. When Slim went to coach to fetch Besta, he heard the new guy say that he was being featured in a Hunk-of-the-Month catalog as Mr. June.

"You pose shirtless?" asked Besta, who had her back to Slim as he walked up the aisle.

"Why the fuck should you care?" asked Slim, surprising Besta with his sudden appearance.

"Oh, I really don't," said Besta.

"You act like you do."

Besta played off Slim's jealousy and headed back to first class. Before Slim left Rashan and his new man, he whispered in Rashan's ear, "I don't like this asshole. Fire him soon as we get home."

When they got home, Slim was surprised that Irv wasn't there.

"Where'd he go?" he asked.

"Not sure," said Rashan.

"Who's traveling with him?"

"He brought a couple of the guys."

"Funny he wouldn't say anything to me about not being here," Slim mused.

"Well, it ain't like you're married to the man," said Besta.

"He usually lets me know where he is."

"I wouldn't worry about it, baby," she said.

"I won't."

He did. Later that day he wandered into Irv's bedroom and looked through the pieces of paper on his nightstand. He saw a bunch of notes with several phone numbers. They all had one thing in common—404, the Atlanta area code.

Now why the fuck would Irv be making all these calls to Atlanta?

The knock at the door came precisely at two P.M.

"You look terrific, kid," Irv told Power.

"You look well yourself," Power said, reciprocating.

"You look like a regular executive. The suit and everything. At least they don't make you wear a tie."

"That won't be happening any time soon."

"Sit down," said Irv. "Make yourself comfortable. I'm just about to order up lunch."

Irv had booked the presidential suite of the Renaissance Concourse hotel adjacent to the Atlanta airport. Seeing Power was the only purpose of this trip—and he wanted to get in and out quickly. Two men from Rashan's staff, traveling with Irv, were quartered in an adjoining room.

"I'm having salmon and a salad. How about you, Power?"

"Sounds good."

"Want a beer?"

"Just a Diet Coke."

"Diet Coke is no good for you," said Irv.

"Make it iced tea."

Irv ordered the food and settled in an easy chair across the couch from Power.

"I'm glad you came. I really am."

"What are you doing in Atlanta, Irv?"

"I came to see you."

"I'm flattered."

"You should be. I can't remember the last trip I made just to say hello to another person."

"I'm guessing," said Power, "that you came to say more than hello."

"I came to say something wonderful has happened."

"I know you're back in the music business."

"That's not the wonderful part. The wonderful part is that your uncle is well."

"Who's my uncle?"

"Slim."

"He's not my uncle, Irv. He's my mother's murderer—"

"Now, now, let's not go down that path. He acted like your uncle. He loved you like an uncle. And he still does."

"Is that why you went into business with him, because of his love for me?" Power asked sarcastically.

"I didn't go into business with him—not at first. He showed up in Miami as a crazy man. I put him away in an institution. I had him locked up. And when the doctors examined him, they told me that I was right. The man is crazy. He's out of his fuckin' mind. He's a certified paranoiac lunatic. That's what the doctors said, Power. They said the only way he'll survive is if he takes these medicines and gets someone to care for him night and day. So you know what? I volunteered."

"Why in hell would you do that, Irv?"

"Why? Why is a good question. I'm not sure. Maybe because when I needed help Slim helped me. That's one reason. Another is that I saw myself in him. I got crazy myself. I got paranoid."

"It wasn't paranoia. It was real, what had happened to you. Your guy and your daughter tried to steal."

"But my mind didn't stop there, Power. My mind saw the whole world trying to steal from me. My mind was sick. Slim's mind was sick."

"That motherfucker was born sick. He's a sick piece of shit."

"He's no longer sick."

"Who cares?"

"He's changed. I'm telling you. And this is coming from a man, an old Jew, who never believes anyone can change. But I've watched him, Power, I've been there to see the changes. Do you want to hear about them?"

"No."

"I can understand that. Anyone can understand that. The food's arriving. Let's eat and talk about something else."

The men walked to the dining room, where a waiter served their salmon and salad.

"How's Judy?" asked Power.

"This is what you want to talk about?" asked Irv.

"Just trying to be polite."

"Judy is fucking some Arab—that's how Judy is. She hasn't changed. She's seen more dicks than my urologist. And she's still trying to get my money. Can you believe it?"

"I was hoping she'd changed."

"Like I said, Power, no one changes. We're born one way, and that's how we stay."

"I think I'm changing."

"How?"

"I'm getting married."

"Mazel tov. To the mayor's daughter?"

"So you know about that?"

"It's in the Atlanta papers. I read the papers. I keep up."

"Business is good," said Power.

"The businesses you took from Slim."

"The businesses Slim left when he ran out of town."

Irv took a bite of salmon, chewed carefully, and said, "That's why I'm here. I think it's time you and Slim went back into business."

"That will never happen."

"You say that now, but your heart can change."

"You just said no one changes."

"You and Slim, Power. You two are the exceptions. You're like father and son, and it pains me to see this misunderstanding go on."

"Murder is no misunderstanding. Slim is a cold-blooded murderer. Ain't more to it than that."

"There's much more. I say that because I know you both. I've seen you both in action. You need each other."

"I need Slim like I need cancer."

"Sometimes we don't understand our own needs."

"I don't understand you, Irv, I really don't. The last time I saw you, you talked about being alone in the world. Remember that painting you gave me of that guy on the little boat in the middle of the ocean with no one around him?"

"You still have it?"

"Yes. But that's not the point. The point is that you had retired from the world. Now here you come, flying into town, telling me how Slim is reformed, a changed man who wants to work with me."

"I didn't say that," said Irv. "He doesn't know I'm here. I just came to check the temperature."

"Cold as ice," said Power. "If I see him, I'll fuckin' kill him."

"Not the most welcoming attitude."

"What other attitude should I have?"

"Can I tell you a story, Power?"

"When have I ever stopped you from telling your stories, Irv?"

"Did I ever tell you about my brother, Louis Samuel Wasserman?"

"Yes," said Power. "The one who went to Yale and wound up in jail."

"A financial genius on Wall Street who gets his throat cut in federal prison by some two-bit junkie convict. He bled to death right there in the prison yard."

"It's a sad story."

"But it doesn't have to be your story, Power."

"It's not. I'm not going to prison."

"But you're involved with the kind of fancy wheeler-dealer money men who will bring you down."

"The mayor? The president of Atlanta's biggest bank?"

"He'll be the first to go. Mark my words."

"I don't see it."

"Most of us don't see the help we need. Slim didn't see the help he needed, but I gave him that help. I helped change his life for the good. Now I want to do that with you. I want us all working together. I feel like we're family."

"I have respect for you, Irv, and I don't want to sound mean. But I have to say that you're deluding yourself. Slim's an evil low-down worthless douchebag piece of shit, and the more I can do to hurt him, the happier I'll be."

Irv pushed aside his salmon, took a sip of iced tea, and looked Power in his eyes. The old man saw it was hopeless and decided to say nothing else. The meeting was over.

Slim had Rashan call all the numbers he had seen on the slip of paper in Irv's bedroom. Each one was a former business associate of Slim's in Atlanta. That was puzzling. The last number, though, was more than puzzling; it was startling. It set off all the alarms in Slim's brain. It was the number to Power's office in Atlanta.

Slim went to find Rashan, who was in the kitchen making coffee.

"Give me the cell number for one of your guys who's with Irv."

Rashan gave him the number for Leo Koles.

Slim dialed it.

"Leo?" he asked.

"Yes."

"How's the weather in Atlanta?'

"Pretty nice."

Slim hung up.

Irv was in Atlanta. Irv was meeting with Power behind Slim's back. Something was happening. Something was very wrong. Forces were conspiring against him. His best friend was turning against him.

New Woman

Arm in arm, Beauty and Ryoko entered the office building of the hottest fashion magazine in America. Its editor, Lena Pearl, a former designer, had briefly mentored Beauty at the behest of Anita Ward. That was when Lena was riding high with a successful line of her own. That line, though, fell as quickly as it rose, and Lena went bankrupt. A resourceful and highly educated woman, she reinvented herself as a journalist and found backers for a slick publication that quickly found a readership and advertisers.

Beauty was delighted to catch up with Lena. After all, Lena had not only encouraged Beauty's creativity, she had urged her to broaden her outlook by taking a number of college courses. Beauty liked her enormously.

When the receptionist told the sisters that Lena was ready to see them, Beauty led Ryoko down the hallway to a corner office filled with paper, clothes, drawing boards, and computers.

Lena rose immediately and came from behind her desk to give Beauty a hug.

"Meet my sister," said Beauty. "This is Ryoko."

Lena hugged Ryoko as well. The sisters sat on an overstuffed canvas-covered couch while Lena leaned against her desk. She was a short woman, perhaps twenty pounds overweight. Her entire wardrobe consisted of loose-fitting outfits, all in black. Even though she was in her forties, her hair was white. She favored lots of makeup—bright red lipstick and heavy eye shadow. Her large oval-shaped black eyeglass frames contrasted nicely with her white hair.

"It's fabulous to see you both," she said. "I can't tell you how happy I am that you came in."

"No happier than I am," said Beauty.

Beauty meant those words. The weeks preceding this meeting had been rough. Seiji had been preoccupied with establishing his American presence. He had left Tokyo with his fortune, which had nearly been frozen by his political enemies in Japan. He did what he had to do to get hold of those funds but no longer trusted a government that nearly did him in. He decided to invest deeply in financial institutions in the United States, where banks, big-time Realtors, and even politicians were far friendlier. As a result, though, he had no interest in retail or fashion. That was an area that Kato Yamamoto had screwed up royally. Seiji concluded enough was enough.

"But where does that leave me and Ryoko?" Beauty had asked him when, a few days after arriving in Brooklyn, he announced his decision to avoid the world of clothes.

"It's fine that you do it," he said. "Ryoko, she is a good drawer. You too. Clothes are very nice. I like them. You make whatever you like. I get people to help you sew."

"But we want to put out the collection we were about to show in Milan," said Beauty. "We were ready to launch Two Sisters."

"Launch is when a rocket goes into space. Is that right ?" asked Seiji.

"Yes."

"To build rocket costs fortune. And then it crashes."

"Our line wouldn't crash," Beauty said insistently. "It will sell."

"That is not my business. My business is making money with other money. You find other money for your Two Sisters, then all is fine."

"The whole point—" Beauty began to say, but stopped herself before she expressed the full thought: *The whole point of marrying you was to use your money.*

Seiji's English wasn't good enough to complete her sentence for her. He saw she was frustrated but reasoned that she was resourceful. She also had much to look forward to. Seiji was in the process of buying a large estate in Greenwich, Connecticut—a sprawling eight-bedroom ranch home on ten acres complete with indoor pool, tennis court, and private pond—that would surely satisfy her restlessness. He went to the computer and proudly showed Beauty photos of the place, where, within a few weeks, construction of the security walls and fences would be complete. She acted excited but couldn't have cared less. She had seen enough opulence to last the rest of her life. Beyond the annoying recurring dreams concerning Power, her single passion involved fashion. With her talented sibling, she was certain that she could achieve the international success that had long been her goal.

Attaining that goal, though, suddenly became complicated. The one resource of which she'd been certain was gone. How do you get the world to notice a collection without publicly showing it?

"In Japan," Ryoko told Beauty, "sometimes the magazines show fantasy collections. I remember my mother describing those to me when I was a little girl. In my mind, I would imagine what the clothes looked like. That's when I fell in love with fashion."

"Fantasy collection." The term fascinated Beauty. Of course she had the clothes that she and Ryoko had designed for the Milan show, but they could go beyond that. Utilizing advanced software programs, they could design a fantasy collection. Once those designs were finished, Beauty would have a product she could present to a magazine. And when she read in the *New York Times* that Lena Pearl had started *New Woman,* her plan fell into place. Lena was one of the most open-minded people she had ever met, a woman with a creative heart. Years back, Lena was the one who had told Beauty, "The imaginary world feeds the real world. Were it not for poetry and music, literature and art, the real world would be drab and gray. The best fashion designers must understand poetry as much as business."

When Beauty first saw Ryoko's designs in their father's store in Tokyo, Lena's words had come to mind.

"When it comes to designing clothes," she told Lena as their meeting began, "my sister is a poet. Can I tell you the story of how we met?"

"Of course. I'm excited to hear it. When I downloaded those sketches you sent, I was floored. Your imagination is really running wild."

"*Our* imagination," Beauty said, correcting her. "Without Ryoko, I could never have found this kind of freedom."

"I have to admit that I'm envious," said Lena. "When I lost my line, I spent some time looking for a creative partner who might help spark new ideas. When I couldn't find anyone, I had to pack it in. So now I'm living vicariously through other designers. It's not a bad job, though."

"It's a great job, Lena, and I'm sure I have just the story for you."

"Please tell it."

Beauty told it, but not in its full form. Her version was highly edited. She told Lena that she and Ryoko had the same dad without mentioning the fact that he had deserted her mother, Isabel. She glossed over the episode of her life concerning Kato Yamamoto as well as the debacle in Milan. Her story was all about finding and joining up with her long-lost sister.

"And it's my sister," said Beauty, "who first mentioned the idea of a fantasy collection. I think it'd be better, Lena, if Ryoko told you about her childhood experience with those collections in Japanese magazines."

Ryoko spoke of those collections with tremendous conviction.

She described them in precise and colorful details. Her sincerity shined through.

"That's beautiful," said Lena. "Are you proposing a fantasy collection for *New Woman*?"

"Yes," said Beauty.

"You want to use the magazine to find financing to make the fantasy come true?" asked Lena.

"Am I that transparent?" asked Beauty.

"Well, there's nothing wrong with that. It serves my purpose as well. I need fresh ideas, and you and Ryoko have a truly wonderful human-interest story to accompany the collection. I'd like to do a major spread. I think it'll be sensational, Beauty."

It was.

When the eight-page spread was published eight weeks later, it became the talk of the industry. The word was out. By virtue of their sketches and several actual garments photographed on real-life models, Two Sisters was thought to be the most avant-garde collection of the decade. Beauty and Ryoko had expanded beyond designs for teens to women as well.

The intense phase of their work had begun as soon as they left Lena Pearl's office. That very weekend the estate in Greenwich was ready and the move gave the sisters added inspiration. The woodsy acreage was dense and the foliage beautiful. Between long sessions that yielded one new idea after another, they took leisurely walks around the grounds and sat on a wrought iron bench that faced a pond. Seiji had bought dozens of black ducks and white swans that splashed and swam as the women fell into a deep discussion.

"Are you angry at Seiji?" asked Ryoko.

"Angry for what?"

"Angry for not giving you the money he promised."

"I don't have time for anger," said Beauty. "Anger just gets in the way."

Ryoko took her sister's hand and said, "That's why I love you so much. You have a big heart."

"It's not my heart, Ryoko. It's my head. My head tells me that if we want to achieve what we need to achieve, we have to focus. Anger wouldn't let me focus."

"Then you forgive him for everything he's done?" asked Ryoko.

Beauty paused before answering.

"What do you mean by that?" she asked Ryoko.

"All I mean is that he's a man who gets confused, I believe, by the parts he's played in the movies and the part he now has to play in real life. Because I've seen all his movies many times, I know how deeply he played those roles. He became those characters. When his father died, he could no longer pretend. He had to be real in the real world. And I think that's been hard for him. Underneath it all, though, I don't think he's a bad man."

"I understand that you love him, Ryoko. And that's perfectly fine. I know you love him more than I do."

"I love him in ways that you can't, Beauty, but believe me, I'm not jealous of you. I'm glad for you. You've made this dream of mine come true."

"I wish I could give him to you."

"He doesn't see me," said Ryoko, "any more than I see him."

"He doesn't see me either," said Beauty. "To be honest, he really only sees himself."

"What do you mean by that?"

"Can I tell you something I've never told you before?"

"Of course. You can tell me anything."

"When we make love, he has to have a large mirror by the side of his bed so he can watch himself."

Ryoko moved her head from side to side as she absorbed the idea.

"Maybe he wants to see how beautiful you are," she said.

"No, Ryoko, I've watched him. He's watching himself. He needs to see his own beauty."

"That is so strange. Now there's something I must tell you. It's about the time I had a boyfriend when I was nineteen. He was my first. I can't say he was attractive but I imagined him to be Seiji Aoi. He had a voice like Seiji's, so it was easy to pretend. I know his body was not Seiji's—he was chubby with small hands and many chins—but that didn't stop me from imagining. I imagined so hard that all my fear of having sex disappeared and I accepted him."

"Did you enjoy it?"

"Oh, yes. So much so that I may have scared him."

Beauty laughed.

"It think it was also the first time for him. But he learned quickly. We both did."

"And were there others?"

"For a while, yes. He told some of his friends, and soon I had many suitors."

"And did you accept them all?"

"Many of them, yes."

"And did you enjoy them as well?"

"I did as long as I could pretend they were Seiji. But soon the pretending didn't work and the enjoyment stopped."

"Did our father know about all this?"

"He was always at the store. He and mother were always trying to arrange meetings between me and respectable boys, but those boys didn't interest me. I liked the bad boys who wanted sex and sex alone."

"And your mother didn't know?"

"My mother thought I was this shy little blind girl interested in nothing but sketching dresses."

"And how about now? Now are you interested in being with men? Are you interested in meeting new men? I could arrange that. If that would make you happy, I'd love to arrange that."

"You are sweet, Beauty. But like you, I want to focus now and think about other things later."

Beauty was pleased. She was glad that her sister spoke to her so openly, and also surprised that her life was wilder than she had imagined. It was good to know that her sister, despite being sheltered, had found the courage to explore sensual pleasure. There was more to Ryoko than met the eye.

Ryoko's inner eye, her sense of the visual, astounded Beauty. Maybe it was because her blindness freed her from the reality of mundane sight. Or maybe it was simply a gift that few are given. But even those times when Beauty initiated a design—say, a poncho-style winter shawl—Ryoko took it to another place, giving it dramatically ragged edges or configuring it with a crazy Scottish plaid of red, green, and yellow. Ryoko's fabulous hat stylings were inspired by Southern black church ladies whom she had never seen but heard described. She could take a retro disco skirt and turn it into a template for an evening gown; conversely, she could take a formal evening gown and cut it down into something daring for the dance floor. When the concepts went over the top, Beauty was there to tame them. Ryoko didn't mind. She knew that her sister's grasp of the American market, the audience they had to capture before any other, was profound. Besides, Beauty was coming up with boldly original ideas of her own—asymmetrical blouses, inside-out topcoats with viscose linings fashioned in multicolored floral patterns, scarves stitched together from a half-dozen different fabrics.

Content that the sisters had found something to occupy their time, Seiji was convinced his new American life was on an even keel. When the spread on Beauty and Ryoko appeared in *New Woman,* he looked it over quickly and smiled.

"Very good" was all he said,

The sisters were waiting for bigger praise, but if Seiji wasn't into it, others were. Solomon Getz was convinced that the notoriety would bring Beauty the backers she needed and began looking for interested parties with big bucks. He wanted nothing more than to work for Two Sisters, and if finding them financing would help make that happen, he was their man.

At the same time, Seiji was connecting with important moneyed people in every major American market. A team of shrewd lawyers, who had enjoyed a relationship with syndicates in New York, decided that branching out to a syndicate recently relocated from Tokyo might prove profitable. They made introductions for Seiji to meet a number of key players.

"Is this man a banker?" Seiji asked Herman Kiner, his Wall Street lawyer, who had set up a dinner with a gentleman who would be in New York for a few days.

"He was a banker," the lawyer explained. "Now he's mayor of Atlanta."

New Birth

Slim knew that Rashan liked him. He was the man, after all, who suggested that Slim see Dr. Mapperoot; he was also the one who introduced Slim to Father Noel Peters. Rashan was there when Slim met Besta. And Irv had never objected when Rashan switched priorities and began traveling with Slim rather than staying with Irv. But all this wasn't enough for Slim. He had to be sure. He had to buy Rashan's absolute loyalty.

"I'm going to make you a wealthy man," Slim told Rashan before Irv returned from Atlanta.

"You don't have to do that," said Rashan. "Mr. Wasserman has made my life very comfortable."

"Fuck comfort," said Slim. "You're gonna be rich. I'm gonna deposit a hundred thousand dollars in your bank account by the end of this month. And that's only the start."

"I don't understand why—"

"I need you to see that right now you're the most important motherfucker I know. You're the only one who can tell me—who can show me—what's going on. I need you to do things for me that I can't ask no one else. If you do them right, and I know fuckin' well you will, you'll earn everything I'm giving you."

"What do you need, Mr. Simmons?"

"I need the truth, son. I need you to get me the truth."

Irv Wasserman thought he would nap on the flight from Atlanta to Miami. As the plane flew through a bank of dark clouds, he closed his eyes. He sought sleep but sleep wouldn't come. His mind was on Power.

Given Irv's history with the young man, he had been certain his mission would prove successful. He trusted that Power liked and respected him. Years back, when Power had saved his life, Irv had expressed gratitude by mentoring him like a son. Power had been the first to acknowledge that Irv had taught him a great deal. Because the two men were bonded, Irv had been convinced that Power would heed his advice.

Irv could not have been more mistaken. His attempt to bridge the gap between Power and Slim had failed miserably. *Strange,* thought Irv, *how much this meant to me.* In his old age, in light of his own fractured family, Irv longed to be an instrument of reconciliation. He was emotionally invested in Slim's rehabilitation. The wound between Slim and Slim's surrogate son was painful, and Irv badly wanted it healed. So when he realized that Power's fury was too great to bury, he found himself heartbroken.

The flight attendant came by with a cart of drinks. Irv asked for tea with two sugars and low-fat milk. He took a few sips and sighed at the thought of the sad fiasco. But at least Slim had found a good woman—that was a positive. And at least the two of them—Slim and Irv—had reinvigorated their lives by going into music together. Another positive. Before Slim came along, Irv had been drowning in a sea of boredom. At least now he was afloat. If he couldn't bring Slim and Power back together, at least he had brought Slim back to sanity. There's only so much one man can do.

"I think this Power cat is on the move," said Up, who had called Besta in Miami from his mama's house in Memphis.

"That's my gut feeling too," said Besta. "He's young and sharp."

"And he's got Atlanta dialed up. He owns the city."

"Or his father-in-law does."

"You see who he's already signed to his label?"

"I know. Platinum acts."

"Besides," said Up, "as a music town, Atlanta kicks Miami's ass."

"You preaching to the choir, boy," said Besta. "It's just a matter of how I get outta here."

"Business is business. You tell Slim you got a better contract."

"Slim don't play that shit. He old-school. He'll hurt you before he'll let you go. Besides, him and Irv already got me locked into a contract."

"Fuck them old geezers. Let 'em sue. Power, he got lawyers that'll scare the shit out of 'em."

"Irv and Slim don't scare easy."

"Don't matter none. Happens all the time in the music game. Better offer come round, you grab it. That's how it works."

"I know you right, Up, but I still gotta be careful."

"Ain't a matter of being careful, baby. It's more a matter of getting outta there—and in a hurry."

"What'd you learn?" Slim asked Rashan.

"The man Mr. Wasserman went to see is called Paul Clay."

"Power," Slim said under his breath. "Fuckin' Power. Where'd they meet?"

"In Mr. Wasserman's hotel room."

"For how long?" Slim asked.

"A little more than two hours."

"When does Irv's plane land?"

"Not till eleven P.M."

"What time is it now?"

"A little after nine."

"Where's Besta?"

"Here I am, sugar," she said as she walked in the living room.

"Why you all dressed up?" asked Slim.

"New Birth is having that ten P.M. service you wanted to go to?"

"New Birth?"

"That megachurch you like where they got the instant replays on the giant screens when the people get baptized. You know, the one where the preacher sings like Teddy Pendergrass? The one you liked."

"Oh yeah, I forgot we were going. I'm not in the mood."

"God will put you in the mood. He'll change your mood."

"Not tonight he won't," said Slim.

"I feel like some praise and worship."

"Go on, then," said Slim. "Rashan will have one of the boys drive you. Better that I talk to Irv when no one's here."

"No problem, baby. By the time I get back, I'll be all prayed up and ready to rock."

Besta left and Slim got to thinking. His mind got to working overtime. He imagined the plots that Irv and Power were hatching. He imagined their conspiracies. As the thoughts assaulted him, he began to sweat. His breathing shortened and at times he felt dizzy. He closed his eyes and thought he heard his blood start to boil.

"Check the airport," he told Rashan. "See if the plane landed."

A few minutes later, Rashan reported that the plane was delayed. Thunderstorms diverted the flight. It might not get in for another couple of hours. Slim was bone tired. His mind was exhausted from going over the devilish scenarios that Irv and Power were devising. From the couch, he picked up the remote control and flipped through the sports channels. Nothing held his interest. He asked Rashan if there was an update on Irv's flight. The delay was going to be even longer. Slim was determined to stay up. He'd confront Irv as soon as he walked through the door. He had to. He couldn't wait till the morning. He had to know what lie Irv would tell, what lame excuse, what bullshit he'd offer to hide the truth. Irv was the one who always said that you can't trust anyone—not even your best friend. And Irv, Slim's best friend, was right. Slim couldn't trust him, shouldn't have trusted him, would never trust the motherfucker again.

In spite of all efforts to stay awake, by two A.M. Slim nodded out. When he woke up and saw daylight streaming through the windows, he didn't know where he was or what had happened. Where was Irv? Where was Besta?

When he heard noises from the kitchen, he rubbed the sleep from his eyes and went there to see who it was. Irv was sitting at the counter with a cup of coffee set before him.

"You must have been dead tired last night," said Irv. "I've never known you to fall asleep on the couch."

"What time is it?"

"Ten A.M."

"I slept that long?" asked Slim.

"You probably needed it. Where's Besta?"

"Probably in bed."

"Have some coffee," said Irv.

"I don't want no coffee."

"All right, then don't have no coffee."

"How was Atlanta?"

"Not good," said Irv.

"You surprised I know that you went there?"

"Why should I be surprised? I didn't try to hide it."

"How about your meeting with Power?"

"Did he call you?" asked Irv with a glimmer of hope in his tired eyes.

"Why the fuck should he call me?"

"Because I asked him to."

"Why the fuck would you ask him to?"

"Because you guys need each other. You love each other."

The statement surprised Slim. He knew Irv would be concocting some cover-up excuse, but this was one he hadn't expected.

"*You're* the one who wants to go into business with Power," said Slim. "*You're* the one who's looking to fuck me over. He's using you to pay me back and fuck me over. And you're using him."

Irv didn't bat an eye. His only response was to laugh. "That don't even make no goddamn sense," he said. "Why should I be interested in going into business with Power? What does that kid got that I need?"

"Money."

"I got money."

"Yeah, but maybe now he's got more."

"A lot of people have more than me, but I ain't looking to go into business with them. I'm looking for peace of mind. And I'm looking for you, my friend, to have your peace of mind. That won't happen until you and Power forgive each other and make nice."

"You're talkin' bullshit."

"I'm talking sense, solid common sense," said Irv, "and you god-damn well know it. Don't go off on one of your sick mind trips. Don't get crazy and start seeing plots when there ain't none. You've come too far, Slim, to go back to the nuthouse. You got a real friend in me. You got a good woman in Besta. And even though Power ain't ready to talk now, I think he will be soon. If I have anything to do with it, you'll get your son back."

Irv's words did little to temper Slim's emotions. Inside, Slim was thinking overtime, double time, triple time. Inside, Slim was feeling frantic and confused. He called for Rashan.

"Get Besta in here," Slim ordered.

"She's not here," said Rashan.

"What do you mean, *she's not here*? When did she get back from church?"

"She never did."

"What are you talking about?"

"After the services, the driver was waiting for her outside and she never showed."

"Where is she?" asked Slim, his heart thumping against his chest. "Where did the bitch go?"

"I don't know," said Rashan.

"Where did you send her?" Slim asked Irv.

"I got nowhere to send her," said Irv. "I got nothing to do with her."

"The hell you don't!" Slim finally let loose and screamed. "It's Power! She probably went to Power. You set it up, you motherfucker! You set up this whole motherfuckin' thing!"

Cascade Heights

I f you want to cancel the engagement party," said Skyla, "you can."

"Why would I do that?" asked Power.

"There's no reason for us to get married."

They were leaving the doctor's office, where Skyla had just been told that, in her first trimester, she had miscarried. Her sadness was profound.

"The baby wasn't the only reason we were getting married," said Power.

"I think it was. You don't have to pretend it wasn't."

"The engagement party will make you feel better."

"That's not a good enough reason," said Skyla.

"It'll make a lot of people happy."

"Including you?" she asked.

Power hesitated before answering. He thought of the grief she experienced in losing the baby and said, "Yes, including me."

"Are you insisting, Power?"

"Yes, I'm insisting. The party's still on. Matter of fact, I already have an idea for the wedding."

A week later Jordan Gee drove the couple to Cascade Heights.

The notion of taking over Slim's ultramodern house, now into foreclosure, had crossed Power's mind several times. He liked the concept of actually owning the property where he had come under Slim's tutelage. The move would dot the "i" on "irony" and complete the circle. These had been Power's training grounds, the setting of his birth as a protégé and his near death as an enemy.

"What do you think?" he asked Skyla as they began walking around the property.

"The statues and interior design are atrocious," she said, "but the architecture itself is clean. It's very streamlined. Everything inside, though, would have to go. The insides require a major do-over."

"Are you willing?" asked Power.

"Why are you asking me?"

"I guess I see it as a great project. You have great taste, and I'd like to have the place redone in a classier style. Besides, it'll cheer you up."

"You think so?"

"I know so," said Power.

"Well, it's nice of you to care."

"How long do you think it would take?"

"I'd have to ask the contractor," said Skyla.

"There aren't any walls to knock down."

"Exactly. I think it could be done in a couple of months."

"In time for our wedding?" asked Power.

"Here?"

"Why not? Here's as good as anywhere."

"Dad says he wanted the grand ballroom of the Ritz-Carlton."

"It's our wedding, not his."

"But he's paying for it."

"I can pay for my own wedding. I want it here."

"Why is that so important to you?"

"You know why."

"Not long ago you were saying that the Slim thing is behind you. Then all of a sudden this Besta woman comes along and all can you talk about is Slim. You're preoccupied with a man who everyone knows was a lowlife."

"I once lived in this house on someone else's terms," he said. "Now I want to live here on my terms."

"And that means getting married on this very spot?"

"Yes, this very spot."

This was the spot where Power and Beauty had last lived together. And although she hadn't stayed long before running off to New York, the house held some powerful memories of her presence. In Power's mind, marrying another woman in this very location would help him erase those memories. He wanted to shut down that part of him that continued to hold hope for him and Beauty. Marrying Skyla would help erase that hope. He also knew that, given the press coverage the wedding was guaranteed, Slim would see the images of his old home in the hands of the protégé whom he tried to kill.

Slim would also soon learn that another protégé, Besta, was also no longer his. The takeover of Slim's home, businesses, and lady was better revenge that outright murder. These were moves guaranteed to torture the man who considered himself a chess master. How many times had Slim told Power that no one could outthink or outmaneuver him? *Well, think again, Mr. Simmons,* thought Power. *Your shit is over. Your day has come and gone. You gonna be worse than dead. You gonna be alive to watch your own destruction. You gonna have to live with a humiliation that's gonna make you wanna die.*

Ajay Lock liked being mayor. He was a born leader. Certainly he was a born businessman, and leading a bank hadn't been enough to satisfy his insatiable ego. Mayor was more like it, but perhaps even that wasn't enough. Governor sounded better. Before that, though, there was a city to run and a term or two during which he would prove his executive genius.

Ajay understood that while Atlanta was the cultural and economic center of the South, money always meant more than art. And when it came to money, Lock had genius. He understood the greatest American art form of all—using money to make more money. As head of a bank, he had great freedom in working his magic. As mayor, that freedom was practically limitless, especially if the mayor wasn't intimidated by the needlessly strict rules of financial engagement. Ajay Lock was not a stickler for rules. And while it was true that he had run for mayor to feed his ego, an even bigger reason had do with the mean green. As bank president, he earned handsomely. But as mayor, he could make a fortune.

As he sat in his office on a Monday morning and looked at the week ahead, he saw a calendar filled with meetings—zoning committees, conferences with the police and fire chiefs, panels with the utility board and the director of cultural affairs. Before he got started with these pressing matters, though, he had scheduled an appointment with a man who had come highly recommended by Herman Kiner, prominent Wall Street attorney.

"Seiji Aoi," said the lawyer, "was perhaps the biggest movie star in Asia before retiring from films on the death of his father. Now he runs his dad's businesses, which, by the way, have a global reach and a billion-dollar-plus net worth. Most of that money was invested in Japanese enterprises, but after some problems with the government, he's moved his money and is currently looking to park it in the right place. He's especially interested in American cities like Houston, Dallas, and Atlanta. That's why you came to mind, Ajay. He wants to continue his game plan, the one that until recently worked so well for him in Japan, where he partners up with politicians uniquely positioned to identify and guarantee growth opportunities."

The mayor was glad to meet the gentleman. Through discreet

inquiries he had learned that the Aoi family money was tied to questionable activities, but those dealings had been restricted to Asia. In America, Seiji was clean. Ajay saw no reason not to hear what the man had to say.

Kiner, a portly man with a wide face and pale blue eyes covered by rimless glasses, accompanied Seiji to the meeting. They greeted Lock cordially and accepted his invitation to join him in the private conference room adjoining his office. Coffee was served.

"If you prefer tea," Ajay told Seiji, "we have a wide selection."

"Thank you, but I already have the American habit of coffee. Strong coffee very good."

The pleasantries over, the men got down to business.

"I understand you're looking to invest in Atlanta's future," said the mayor, "and we're looking for future-thinking investors. That's why I've been thinking about a project on the west side of our city in a neighborhood that has long suffered from neglect. Some years back when a popular nightclub called Charlie's Disco burned down, the neighborhood went down with it. Not only was the nightclub never rebuilt, the surrounding blocks fell into disrepair and the buildings were abandoned. My plan is simple—to build a multistory urban mall on that land. I have no doubt that major retailers will come to the table. There are large parcels of land in the vicinity that can be purchased for a song."

"A song?" asked Seiji.

"By 'a song,'" said Herman Kiner, "the mayor means quite inexpensively."

"Yes," said Ajay, "and the potential for gentrification in the area surrounding the mall would be tremendous. High-end apartment complexes, town homes, all sorts of innovative urban dwellings could be constructed that would attract an up-and-coming demographic. Those are people with the money to rent and buy in a newly revised neighborhood with easy access to what will be a showcase urban mall."

"I have architect, very good friend, Japanese man," said Seiji. "He win awards. His mall won prize in Amsterdam. Very modern."

"I'd welcome his design. As a member of the urban redevelopment board, I'm always on the outlook for innovative design."

"I like," said Seiji. "I speak more with Mr. Kiner and we do business. Yes, yes, I like."

"Well, that's just great. We're looking forward to seeing more of you, Mr. Aoi—"

"Seiji, please. You call me Seiji."

"Like I said, we're very hospitable here in Atlanta. Matter of fact I'd love to invite you to the wedding of my daughter next month."

"Very nice," said Seiji.

"Are you married, Seiji?" asked Ajay.

"Yes, wife very beautiful."

"Well, then, I hope to see her at the wedding as well. You'll receive a formal invitation in the mail. It'll be a wonderful occasion and a chance for you to meet not only my daughter and son-in-law but our city's most prominent leaders."

The Late Show

Irv Wasserman liked Letterman more than Leno. Leno could be funny, but he played the part of the nice guy. Irv preferred Letterman's off-the-wall brand of humor. Besides, tonight Jerry Seinfeld was Letterman's guest. When it came to being off-the-wall, no one was better than Seinfeld.

Irv's routine was pretty much the same. Dinner at eight followed by a cigar on the patio. Usually Slim joined him both for the food and the smoke, but ever since Besta had left, Slim had been sulking. Irv understood and to a large degree was baffled. Given how much they had done for her, why would she up and leave like that? It made no sense. Neither did Slim's accusation that she had gone over to Power's side. It was just Slim's paranoia.

Letterman's monologue wasn't particularly good, and had Seinfeld not been scheduled to appear later on the show, Irv probably would have turned off the TV and gone to sleep. Even the prospect of seeing the comic, though, wasn't enough to keep his eyes open. When he first nodded off, he caught himself and sat back up in bed. The second time it happened, he simply drifted off into deep slumber.

"You filthy little motherfucker."

Irv opened his eyes and saw Slim standing over him, his single diamond wristband sparkling in the light of the lamp on his bed stand.

"What are you mouthing off about?" asked Irv, slowly coming out of his sleep. The TV was still on. Craig Ferguson's *Late Late Show* was about to go off the air. Irv was annoyed he had missed Jerry Seinfeld.

"She's in Atlanta," said Slim.

"Who's in Atlanta?"

"The bitch."

"What bitch?"

"Besta. Besta went to Atlanta. Yesterday she went to Power's office. He's got a music company and she's gonna sing for him. You set this up."

"Where you getting your information from?"

"Rashan. He hired people. They located her. They followed her. I even got pictures."

"That stupid bitch," said Irv, shaking his head.

"Very fuckin' stupid for you to trust her. Did you really think I was too stupid to figure this out?"

"Figure what out?"

"The three of you—the bitch, Power, and you. I blame them, and I'll fuck up both of them, but I blame you the most. You're the brains behind it."

"Calm the fuck down, Slim. You're getting all crazy in the head again."

"Am I? You wanna see the fuckin' pictures of her coming out of Power's office?"

"No. But I had nothing to do with that."

"Then what were you doing talking to Power just a week before all this shit came down?"

"I told you, Slim. I wanted you guys to get back together. I still do."

"That's a lie."

"Why the fuck should I lie to you?" asked Irv. "What's in it for me? You think I want Power to steal Besta from you? What would that give me?"

"A bigger share of the money when she hits it big."

"Look, you dumb bastard, why in hell do I give two shits about that kind of money? When I die you get all my money."

"How dumb do you think I am?" asked Slim.

"Pretty fuckin' dumb if you think I'm screwing you. You wanna see my goddamn will?"

"Something you wrote up to fool me even more? No, I ain't looking at no fake will."

"Think about it, Slim. You know me. You know that I ain't leaving my money to my crazy daughter who tried to screw me. I ain't leaving it to my ex-wife who I hate with a passion. I got no one else. I'm leaving it to you. I'm telling you the fuckin' truth."

"Well," said Slim, "there's only way to find out."

Irv saw what was happening, tried to resist, but Slim was too quick. He took a pillow and, with murderous force, pressed it against Irv's face. Weak in body, Irv had no chance against a man nearly a hundred pounds heavier than him.

A minute passed, then two, then three, while Irv emitted a series of moans, muffled groans, and anguished cries. His legs twitched, his arms flailed, and finally, after five full minutes, he surrendered.

"Fuckin' asshole," said Slim as he saw that all life had drained from his former friend. "Rot in hell."

Craig Ferguson was saying good night.

Slim looked down at Irv. He was glad the motherfucker was dead. One less enemy. But there were others, and they would all be coming for him. They would be coming at him from all sides. But he'd be ready. He'd mount his defenses. He'd go on offense. He'd build up an arsenal. He'd hire soldiers. He'd build an army. And once the battle plan was in place, he'd move his troops. He'd take down every last scumbag who even thought of going against him. He'd wipe out the rest of those fools who thought they had him where they wanted him.

No fucking around.

No mercy.

The chess master was in control.

The chess master couldn't be beat.

The chess master had a war plan, neat and simple:

Scorch the fuckin' earth.

The Power Plant

D o you like the song?" asked Besta as she sat in the control room of the brand-new studio Power had just built. She, Power, and Up had just heard a playback of Besta's latest vocals.

"I think it's hot," said Power. "Where'd you get the track?"

"Up," said Besta, pointing to her keyboardist lover. "Up got him the fattest tracks."

"I also gotta say, man," Up said, "that this here Power Plant is the most amazing studio I've ever seen."

"Thanks," said Power before asking Besta, "You calling it 'I Put a Move on You'?"

"That's the hook, honey," she said. "That's the title."

"I guess that's the story of you and Slim," said Power with undisguised satisfaction.

"I wasn't thinking that. But if the shoe fits . . ."

"He's not gonna be happy when he hears it," said Power.

"He couldn't have been happy when I didn't bother coming home. But that's the way love goes. Here today, gone tomorrow. You feel me?"

"You worried about what he might do?" asked Power, looking for insight into Besta's understanding of Slim.

"Maybe he'll cry a river," she said, "and maybe he'll find another bitch. I don't really care. Him and Irv, they're two old men with nothing to do and nowhere to go."

"He'll know where to go now," said Power. "He'll come looking for you."

"Do I look worried?" she asked.

"No, but I think you'd be wise to look for protection."

"I got protection," said Besta. "I got you. Can I be honest with you, Power?"

"Sure."

"I know about what went down between you and Slim. I know you were once his boy. And I know he can't like how you came out of the thing a lot bigger than he is. That's one of the reasons I'm here. I like big. I want big. And in addition to how you gonna promote me—and I do believe that you will promote the shit outta me, even if it's only to show up Slim—I also gotta believe you gonna protect me."

"Twenty-four/seven," Power told her.

"That's what I'm talkin' 'bout!" Besta exclaimed before turning to Up and saying, "Didn't I tell you that Power's our man?"

"Word," said Up.

"What about the legalities?" asked Besta.

"I've never known Slim to worry about legalities," said Power. "All the time I worked for him all I heard him say was that contracts weren't worth the paper they were written on. Contracts are meant to be broken. And the contract that I read between you and him is not especially binding. I wouldn't worry about it."

"I ain't worried about nothing," said Besta, "except making hits."

"From what I hear, you've already cut one since you been here in Atlanta. Do a few more and we'll be ready to drop the record. Radio's already been primed."

"My time is prime time," said Besta. "I'm ready right now."

That night Power brought home an early version of "I Put a Move on You." Skyla loved it.

"You look happy," she told her fiancé.

"I like this singer," he said. "She's got spunk. I think she's about to break out."

"You want her to sing at our wedding?"

"That's an interesting idea, Skyla. Hadn't thought of it. Yes, I do. You pick the song."

"No, you pick it. You're the music man."

"I'll think of something. Did your parents ever give you the guest list?"

"It's on your desk in the den."

"How many?"

"Over three hundred."

"Holy shit."

"Holy matrimony," Skyla said, correcting him.

"Ajay okay with having it up at Slim's old house?"

"You mean our new house."

"Whatever."

"Daddy and Mommy went up to take a look at it. They were impressed. They want to build a huge tent in the backyard in case it rains."

"Cool."

"The governor's coming."

"Cool."

"Maybe the president."

"I doubt that."

"You know the mayor. He's connected."

"Not that connected," said Power.

"You'd be surprised. All sorts of foreign dignitaries are coming. Captains of industry from Russia, Saudi Arabia, Greece, Japan."

"Who's coming from Japan?" asked Power.

"I told you. The list is on your desk."

Power felt a twinge when he heard the word "Japan." He went to the den and picked up the list. His eyes went down the names until he saw Mr. and Mrs. Seiji Aoi. He went to his computer and began searching.

He knew that after the death of Kato Yamamoto, Beauty had married again. He had tried to stop himself from wondering why she had so quickly taken another husband. He knew it'd be easy to let the thought preoccupy him, and so he fought against it. Then, by chance, he had caught an Internet item mentioning that the former Tanya Long—Beauty's real name—was marrying a Japanese movie star turned businessman. He thought the name was something like "Seiji" but couldn't be sure. Immediately he Googled Seiji Aoi and, sure enough, there were images, not only of his handsome face as he appeared in various films, but shots of him with Beauty by his side.

Beauty! Coming to his wedding! That was crazy! That was wrong! Why in hell would her husband's name be on his in-laws' guest list? What could possibly be his connection to the Locks? None of it made sense. He picked up the phone and called the mayor.

"How's my favorite son-in-law?" asked Ajay.

"A little puzzled," said Power. "Looking over your guest list and wondering why you want to invite Seiji Aoi."

"New friend of mine. Business associate. Wonderful guy. You'll meet him. You'll love him."

"Did you meet his wife?"

"No. Why?"

"Just wondering."

"You have any objections?"

"It's just that you hardly know the guy."

"I hardly know a third of the people on that list, Power. That's not the point."

"What is the point?"

"You get to have the wedding in your new house and we get to invite whoever we want."

Power had no comeback. Why argue? It was probably a waste of time, because when Beauty learned about the invitation she'd turn it down. He couldn't see Beauty coming to his wedding—especially when she saw that the address was the very house she had fled.

As he said good-bye to Lock, Power saw another call was coming through. The ID said "Private." Usually he didn't pick up on unlisted numbers.

"Power?"

"Yo."

"This is Judy Wasserman."

"Judy. Wow. It's been a while."

"Have you heard about my dad?"

"No. Why? Is anything wrong? I recently saw him."

"Where?"

"He came to Atlanta."

"How did he look?"

"Fine."

"Well, he's not fine. He's dead."

"Dead? I can't believe it."

"They found me in Dubai."

"You're calling from Dubai?"

"I'm flying to Chicago tonight. The body is being shipped from Miami. Did you know he was living in Miami?"

"Didn't you?"

"Every time I tried to locate him, he was living somewhere else. I tried to get back in his life. I loved him. He was my father. If you only knew the real story, Power."

I know the real goddamn story, Power said to himself. *I watched it firsthand. All you cared about was his money. You never stopped trying to steal.*

At the same time, the woman's father had just died and there was no need to be cruel.

"I'm sorry, Judy," he said. "I really am. I liked Irv."

"He adored you. You were his son."

"He was good to me."

"I'm sure he left you something. There's a lawyer in Chicago who has his will. He's going to read it after the burial. You gotta come. You gotta meet me there."

"I don't think so."

"Why? You just said that you loved him. I need you there, Power. There's no one else. He had no one. No friends."

"He had one friend."

"Who?"

"A guy named Charles Simmons."

"Who's that?" asked Judy.

"He's the guy who set me up with Irv. They call him Slim."

"A brother?"

"An older brother."

"OG?"

"You could say that."

"What was he doing with Irv?"

"He had mental problems and Irv brought him back. At least that's what Irv said. Personally, I hate the motherfucker. I don't know what Irv saw in him. Except maybe Irv was lonely and needed a friend."

"Doesn't sound like my father."

"Men change in old age."

"I still need you to come to Chicago."

"I'm about to get married, Judy."

"It ain't about that, Power. I'm about to get married myself. I got a new boyfriend. The old one was trash, but this new one is gold. He's building the tallest skyscraper in the world right in the middle of Dubai. He's got his own plane. We'll stop by and pick you up. You gotta be with me when we bury Dad. I gotta have someone there I trust."

"If Slim's there—"

"Fuck Slim," said Judy. "If you're worried about protection, Masud has a veritable army. You've never seen protection like this before. Will you come? Will you do it out of respect to a man who respected you?"

"I need to think about it," said Power.

"The more you think, you more you'll realize you need to be there."

"Mr. and Mrs. Seiji Aoi Are Cordially Invited . . ."

Beauty read the invitation for the fourth time. She ran her fingers over the raised letters. She tried to deny the impact that this piece of paper was having, but she couldn't. She had been standing but had to sit down. Alone in the living room of the estate in Greenwich, Connecticut, that she shared with her husband, Ryoko, and a staff of servants and security men, Beauty plopped down on the couch. She found these facts difficult to process—first, that Power was marrying; second, that the marriage was to take place at Slim's former address; and third, that she and her husband had been invited.

Had Power somehow reconciled with Slim? That couldn't be. Their murderous relationship could never be repaired. Had Power bought Slim's house to spite him? Possibly. But why marry there? And beyond being the daughter of the mayor of Atlanta, who was this Skyla? Had Power married her for some political advantage? Surely it couldn't have been love. But why not? Wasn't Power capable of loving someone other than Beauty? Beauty assumed he wasn't. But why? Was that because she was incapable of loving anyone but Power? Was she prepared to admit that most disturbing truth?

"Ah," said Seiji, who came into the living room holding a mug of hot tea. "Here you are. Good morning."

"Good morning."

"You see invitation. Good. We go."

"I can't."

"You must."

"Sorry, Seiji, Ryoko and I have a meeting that weekend in Dallas with the investment group behind Two Sisters."

"That's good," said Seiji, "but you postpone meeting."

"Not a good idea."

"Bad idea to miss the wedding. This man, the mayor, very important to me."

"Why?"

"Important man, Beauty, important business all over Atlanta. He wants a partner. I am glad to shake his hand and work with him."

"Have you met his daughter?"

"No."

"Or her fiancé?"

"Don't know anyone in Atlanta except the mayor. I like him. Strong, smart. You will like him."

"I'll meet him another time."

"This time is best time. Arrangements already made. No discussion. Just enjoyment at wedding."

Satisfied that his position was clear, Seiji left the room before Beauty could protest any further.

She could of course simply refuse. But hadn't she done just that? And hadn't he ignored her refusal? She had never defied her husband before. She had no reason to. He had been content to see her and Ryoko go off and find funding for their enterprise without him. He was proud of the two sisters; he admired their independence of spirit. The publicity garnered by his wife's fashion enterprise added to his own prestige. He had married wisely. He enjoyed the media attention.

The articles on Beauty never failed to mention that she was married to a famous Japanese movie star.

Beauty appreciated that her marriage was working well. Seiji left them alone. He had his business; she had hers. He was polite in all his dealings with her. In the bedroom, as long as she was willing to watch him watch himself in the various mirrors he had strategically set up, there were no conflicts. Sex was not exciting, but neither was it painful. It was all about Seiji getting off on Seiji. Beauty's only orgasms came with thoughts of Power. Otherwise she faked it. Seiji never knew the difference. When, on occasion, he asked her to watch him masturbate, she agreed. The ritual seemed childish to her, but what the hell. At least he had no interest in violence or pain.

The demand that she attend this wedding in Atlanta was unusual for him. Beauty didn't quite know how to respond. She wasn't about to attend Power's wedding—that much was certain—but she needed to think about the best way to reapproach Seiji with her refusal.

"Seiji just told me about your upcoming trip to Atlanta," Ryoko said a few hours later as Beauty helped her to the kitchen table that faced the garden and woods beyond.

"I'm not sure about that . . ."

"Atlanta holds many bad memories for you," said Ryoko. "This I know. But a wedding, that's a celebration."

"This just isn't any wedding."

"I know, it's the mayor's daughter. Do you know her?"

"I don't."

"How about the man she's marrying?" asked Ryoko. "Do you know him?"

The question—so direct and simple—required a simple and direct answer.

"Yes."

"Oh," said Ryoko. "Do you know him well?"

Another simple question, another simple answer.

"Yes."

"Is he nice?"

Not such a simple question.

"Well . . . yes."

"How do you know him?"

"He's Power. My brother. Remember I told you about my brother?"

"Yes!"

Beauty had mentioned that her brother had been saved by the Yakuza but never told her sister the full story. In fact, she'd never told anyone the full story. But then again, she had never known a sibling—unless Power could be considered a sibling.

As Beauty began telling the tale, though, she began editing out key details—but then stopped. Why edit when she was speaking to the one woman in the world who never judged her? She needed to say what she had never said.

"I slept with my brother. I did it because I wanted to. I'd always wanted to. And after doing it, it's been hard for me to think of anything else."

"But he's not your brother. He had a different father and mother. Am I right?" asked Ryoko.

"Technically, yes, but he was raised as my brother."

"Just for five years. I understand, Beauty, but it's not technical at all. It's physical. You do not have common blood."

"We had a common mother."

"Your adopted mother. Not your real mother."

"She became my real mother. Power became my real brother."

"And so did the love you felt for him—the love he felt for you—that was real as well."

"I've been ashamed ever since it happened that first time—but not ashamed enough to keep it from happening again."

"When did it happen again?" Ryoko asked.

"When Kato got in touch with Seiji's family. When Slim was looking to murder Power. After all that, he came to New York. It happened in New York behind Kato's back."

"Did Kato ever know?"

"He probably suspected, but I don't think he knew."

"Was it as powerful the second time as the first?"

"More powerful," Beauty admitted.

"Did you think about leaving Kato?"

"Power wanted me to, but I couldn't. I knew it was wrong."

"You keep saying that, Beauty, but I don't see the wrong."

"I don't see it," Beauty said. "I *feel* it."

Ryoko said nothing.

"So you see why I can't go to the wedding," Beauty added.

"Before we discuss that, let me ask you another question. Does Seiji know that it was his people who saved Power—and that Power is the same man who is being married in Atlanta?"

"I don't know, Ryoko. What do you think?"

"I'm not sure. His father's organization is large. When Kato made the request, Seiji was still acting in films. It may not have been that large an operation to merit his attention."

"But his father, Rin Aoi, must have known."

"Probably, but his father is dead. I doubt if he made his son aware of his every single action. There must have been actions like that all over the world."

"You're right," said Beauty. "If Seiji had made the connection between Kato, me, and Power, we would have heard about it by now."

"Given all that, I think it'd be good for you to go to the wedding."

"Why do you say that, Ryoko?"

"One reason is to keep things going smoothly. And there's another reason. I can't remember the word, Beauty, but there's an expression in English that means you've come to the end of something that has been long and complicated and needs to be over."

"Closure?"

"Yes, closure. That's what you need. He is getting married. You are already married. You will meet his wife. He will meet your husband. You will both see that you have good lives, good mates. You will wish him well, and he will wish you well. And after all that, maybe you will have peace of mind."

Beauty thought about what Ryoko had just said. *Closure*. That sounded great. That even sounded possible. But was it? Would seeing Power happily married end her endless thoughts about him? Would knowing that he was committing to a woman finally free her of the obsession with a man who both was and was not her brother?

But how could she return to Slim's house? That would be too much.

"Maybe that's part of the closure," said Ryoko after Beauty had explained to her why the locale of the wedding only added to her reluctance to attend. "Maybe, in beginning his new life, he needs to have the wedding there to put the past behind him."

Beauty thought for a few seconds. She looked at her sister before taking her hand. "Thank you," she said. "I never thought about that before."

"You never had a sister before."

Beauty leaned over and kissed Ryoko on the cheek.

Later that day she began to think about what she would wear to the wedding.

Two questions haunted Power: whether Beauty would attend his wedding and whether he should attend Irv's funeral.

He had no control over the first question. But seeing Seiji Aoi's name on the guest list did prompt him to research the man on the Internet. There were dozens of entries and articles on him in English and hundreds of thousands in Japanese. A translation app allowed him to read the Japanese.

The conclusion was clear—he was a film star whose father had controlled a large faction of the Yakuza crime syndicate. When his father had died, Seiji stopped making movies and took over the family business. Key political figures had tried to bring down that business. He had been jailed for tax evasion but not held for long. After his release, the minister of finance, the man behind his accusation, was assassinated. A signal had been sent. Then, though, rather than stick around Tokyo, Seiji moved his operation to New York. Now he was doing business with Power's future father-in-law.

And where did Beauty fit in all this? Seiji had married her shortly after his father's demise and the strange suicide of Kato Yamamoto. Power had met Kato in New York. He hardly seemed like the kind of guy who would leap to his death from the penthouse of a fancy Tokyo hotel. He seemed like a straight-up business guy. But if some of those articles Power read were right, and if Kato had found financing for the buyout of Bloom's from organized crime in Japan, Kato surely had a relationship with Seiji. Maybe it was Seiji's muscle that had saved Power. Maybe it was Beauty who had forced Kato to force Seiji to rescue Power that day in the very house where Power and Skyla would soon be married.

Pieces of the puzzle, though, were still missing. If Kato's death resulted from murder and not suicide, was Seiji involved? Did he have Kato killed so he could get to Beauty? Was he obsessed with Beauty the way Kato had been—and the way Power still was? Was it all about Beauty? Wasn't it *always* about Beauty?

Power wondered whether their lives, no matter how far apart they lived or how different the paths they chose, would forever be linked.

In any event, it was Beauty's choice—not his. She would accompany her husband to the wedding or she wouldn't. Power desperately wanted her to attend—and desperately wanted her not to.

The second question—whether to attend Wasserman's funeral—was personal as well as professional. On the personal side, for whatever had been wrong with Irv, Power liked the man. On the professional side, because Irv had always liked Power, there was every reason to believe that there might be a considerable inheritance to claim. Knowing Irv's antipathy for his daughter, Power doubted whether he would have left her much. There were no other family members and no friends except for Slim, and Power couldn't see Irv giving Slim even a small part of his fortune. God only knew the extent of that fortune. Power was curious to know the total worth. He didn't need the money—his own situation in Atlanta was exceedingly prosperous—but all the same, if many more millions were coming his way, why not learn about it firsthand?

He would do it quickly. He would urge Judy to arrange a meeting with the lawyer the day after the funeral. He would have to spend only one night in Chicago. He would bring ample protection on the chance that Slim might show. And if Slim did show, so much the better.

Power was no longer scared of the man who had both mentored and attempted to murder him. He had, after all, taken over Slim's world; he had expanded that world; he was hooked up to Atlanta's power elite in a way that Slim never was; he was slicker than Slim; he was smarter. Power had gone beyond anything Slim could ever imagine.

Why not look him in the eye and tell him just that?

Why not glean the satisfaction of letting this evil motherfucker know that he had outdone him in every possible way?

In the Matter of the Estate of Irving Jacob Wasserman

Power thought he was dreaming. He felt a naked body, a woman's body, beside him in bed. It wasn't Skyla, because the woman's breasts were far bigger. Her breasts were enormous. This woman was shorter and wore a different perfume and came at him with her mouth with different energy. This woman was Judy! Fuckin' Judy! Judy was on top of him and he was inside her and only hours ago they had been at her old man's funeral with her boyfriend Masud.

"What the hell are you doing?" he asked.

"I'm fucking you, that's what I'm doing! Keep it up! Keep it in!"

Still not quite sure if this was real life or a dream, Power kept it up and kept it in until Judy rode him all the way to her climax. She screamed when she came and asked for more. More excited than he was confused, he gave her what she wanted, again and again.

"Oh God," she said when it was over, "did I need that."

"How'd you get in here?"

"When I said I was your wife, they gave me a key."

"What about your boyfriend?"

"He's gay."

"Then why the fuck are you marrying him?" asked Power.

"Ever heard of a beard? I'm his beard."

"Can an Arab man marry a Jew?"

"He's a rebel. He doesn't like his family. When he came of age and got his money, he told them to get screwed. He was going his own way."

"Then why can't he tell them he's gay?"

"Being with a Jewish broad is one thing. But admitting that you're queer is another. In his world, he has to keep up appearances."

"And he doesn't mind you fucking around?"

"He likes it. He'd like to watch us do it, though he'd be checking out you, not me. I could arrange that."

"Don't even think about it," Power said adamantly.

Judy laughed. "Well, on one condition. We fuck again before we see the lawyer."

"Judy . . ." Power began to complain.

"Quit beefing. You know you love it."

You had to be blind not to see that Masud was gay. He was far more feminine than Judy, a quiet man of thin build, soft hands, dark eyes, and a hesitant smile. He dressed in Western garb, a bluish-gray Armani suit, an open-neck tab-collar white silk shirt, and black Gucci loafers. He carried a Louis Vuitton leather bag that looked more like a purse than a business case.

The three of them—Masud, Judy, and Power—sat in the backseat of the Rolls-Royce touring car that drove from Chicago's Peninsula hotel to the office of attorney Ian Shipman in suburban Evanston, Illinois. Two separate vans of security men—one in front, one behind—safeguarded the passengers. Judy was seated between the two men. Masud was busy speaking to one of his boyfriends on his $6,000 Vertu Constellation mobile phone. As he chattered in Arabic, he looked out the window, absorbed by the conversation. Judy took the opportunity to slip her hand into Power's trousers. She gave him a squeeze. Power pushed her hand away. This bitch was crazy.

Power thought back to last night's lovemaking marathon and the funeral that had preceded it. The service was held in the small chapel of a Jewish synagogue. No one had been in attendance except Judy, Power, and a rabbi. Power was shocked. The rabbi hadn't even known Irv.

"He's a rent-a-rabbi," said Judy. "Paid by the hour."

Power's mind flooded with memories. He thought back to the first time he'd met Irv. That was the evening Irving Jacob Wasserman was being honored in the grand ballroom of the Hilton Hotel. The mayor himself had been there. Of course that was the same evening Power had saved Irv from the gunfire of a disgruntled woman, Evelyn Meadows, who claimed that Wasserman had cheated her dead husband, soul singer Johnnie Meadows. There was no doubt that Irv had a checkered past, but the presence of so many dignitaries had impressed Power deeply. Did not one of them think well enough of Irv to show up at his funeral? Apparently not. There was no music, no flowers, no eulogies. The rabbi read a few prayers in Hebrew. From there, accompanied by the two security vans, they drove to a cemetery outside the city and laid the old man to rest.

That was yesterday. Today, on this way to Irv's lawyer, Power was still reliving his Chicago memories—the loft Irv got him when he first arrived, the way Judy had fucked him in that loft just as she had fucked him in his room last night; Judy's salon, Hair Is Where It's At; Judy's beefy boyfriend Dwayne "Ace" Foster and his Mad Muscles gym; how Foster was murdered; how Judy had wanted to take over Le Beef, the restaurant once owned by her mother; how Irv had Power working in his office, side by side with John Mackey, the trusted consigliere who, along with Judy, had unsuccessfully schemed to screw Wasserman out of a fortune—the very fortune whose fate would soon be revealed.

The caravan arrived at the lawyer's two-story brick building at two P.M., right on time. The bodyguards got out to secure the surrounding area. After a few minutes, they gave Masud, Judy, and Power the all-clear.

The attorney's office had an English atmosphere, dark wood, leather furniture, heavy drapes. Shipman had been raised in London and educated at Princeton. He was in his seventies, a formal man in a three-piece suit and black polka-dotted bow tie. He was slightly stooped, with tired watery blue eyes and an indifferent manner of speech.

He was surprised to see that Power and Masud had accompanied Judy.

"This one is like his son," Judy told Shipman, pointing to Power. "And this one's my boyfriend. We came in all the way from Dubai."

"Well, shall we get started?" asked the lawyer.

"Shoot," said Judy.

They sat at a carved antique conference table situated in the corner of the L-shaped office. The lawyer opened a folder.

"It's very precise," Shipman said, addressing Judy. "Your father was extremely clear in the matter of his last will and testament. To support his statements, he not only had these papers notarized and witnessed by three attorneys in Miami, he also enclosed a certificate from a Dr. Trina Mapploroot, stating that he was in perfect mental health at the time he formulated the will."

"Good," said Judy. "So how much?"

"The worth of his estate?" asked the attorney.

"The bottom line," said Judy. "Give us the bottom line."

"Give or take," said Shipman, "some thirty million dollars."

"Wow," said Judy, all smiles. Masud was smiling as well. "I told you," Judy said to Masud. "I told you that the old man didn't fuck around. Did he leave any to Power here?" asked Judy.

"I'm afraid not," answered Shipman.

"Don't worry, baby," said Judy, "we'll give you a good taste—just for being here, just for showing all that respect and love. So when do all these funds get transferred?"

"The process has already begun."

"I already set up a new bank account here in Chicago," said Judy. "Is that where the money will be going?"

"I'm afraid not."

"Why not?"

"Because it's all going to a Mr. Charles Simmons."

"No fuckin' way!" Judy screamed. "That can't be right!"

"Right or wrong isn't the issue," said Ian Shipman. "The issue is a legal one, and from a legal point of view, his will is ironclad. It cannot and will not be altered in any way."

Tuscaloosa

Maybe it was because his mother's family had been raised in rural Alabama, but Slim had always followed the Crimson Tide. He loved the University of Alabama's famous football team. For years he had taken the trip from Atlanta to the school's campus in Tuscaloosa for the big games. After the death of Charlotte Clay, he had taken Power along on several trips where they cheered from seats on the fifty-yard line.

Slim was comfortable in Tuscaloosa. It was close to Atlanta without being too close. It was the perfect place to set up an operation—a counterattack—without drawing anyone's attention. Tuscaloosa was a low-key college town, quaint and quiet, filled with historical buildings and tree-lined streets, the last spot where the law would look for a mastermind to engineer a plan to retake what was rightly his.

The plan was simple: Buy a large house on the same respectable street where the university deans and professors lived. Open several retail operations—a frozen-yogurt store near campus, an upscale barbecue restaurant in a middle-class black neighborhood, a sandwich shop near the downtown courthouse, a beer-and-burger emporium in the airport. Whether they proved profitable or not, these legitimate businesses would explain his presence in the city. They would also explain his need to buy an inexpensive industrial-style warehouse on the edge of town as a place to headquarter his operations.

His chief adviser was Clarence Avery, an attorney who had a history with Slim. At Harvard, Avery had edited the *Law Review*. After graduating, he moved back to Atlanta, where he was considered a brilliant brother with a fabulous future. After a decade of working for the city's most prestigious law firm, though, Clarence grew restless. Advising some of the city's wealthiest citizens, Avery dreamed of great wealth for himself. Greed trumped caution and he soon began plotting several extralegal schemes. One, involving insurance claims, garnered him a few million. He was riding high until a crafty associate district attorney caught on. It looked like Clarence was through. A long jail sentence seemed inevitable. His only hope was Slim Simmons, who had the district attorney, the associate's boss, in his back pocket.

Those were the days when Slim's political pull was at its strongest. He made the charges against Avery go away, but only on the condition—this was the DA's demand—that Clarence no longer practice in Georgia. Tuscaloosa appealed to Avery for the same reasons it appealed to Slim. The attorney needed an off-the-radar spot to reestablish himself. It took a decade, but by the time Slim arrived in the sleepy college town Clarence had a thriving practice in personal-injury work. He hadn't achieved his long-term goal of wealth, but, thanks to Slim, he had avoided losing his freedom and license.

The two men were excited to renew their relationship. Avery saw Slim as a powerhouse, a man who defied all the rules and yet, time and again, managed to avoid even the smallest penalties. If anyone could outsmart the law, it was Charles "Slim" Simmons.

Clarence's presence in Tuscaloosa was a key motivation for Slim to move there. Although he had a healthy respect for his own smarts, Slim knew that his plan to rebuild his empire required an astute legal mind. Besides, Avery owed Slim his very life. He'd do anything for Slim. And the fact that Clarence had a corrupt nature made Slim like him even more.

Their first meeting was at Clarence's house on Honeysuckle Lane. It was large—a two-story home with white columns and an expansive front lawn—without being pretentious. Avery was only too happy to invite Slim to dinner.

Clarence, who had just turned forty, had put on considerable weight since Slim had seen him last. He was dark-skinned man with a wide nose, a small mouth, and a thick neck. No one would call him handsome. His eyes were his best feature—chestnut brown, alert, and focused. He spoke with a thick Georgia accent and greeted Slim warmly.

"Brother Charles," he said. "Welcome. Come meet the wife and kids."

Slim was surprised to see that the wife was white. He hadn't remembered that Clarence favored vanilla. The kids were young—the girl nine, the little boy seven—and Clara, their mother, was nearly as heavy as her husband. The food was bland, the children noisy, and after dessert Slim was only too glad to retire to Avery's den, where the two men could speak in private.

"Sorry the food was lacking," said Clarence, "but that's what you get for marrying a white woman. Inferior cooking."

Slim laughed and said, "Looks like you're doing all right."

"Doing fine, Charles," said Clarence as he settled back in a La-Z-Boy recliner and offered Slim a cigar and cognac. The men lit up and started to sip.

"Surprised to see me in Alabama?" asked Slim.

"Surprised and delighted."

"You gonna ask me what I'm doing here?"

"I don't have to, sir. You're gonna tell me."

"I came to get ready."

"Preparation is always advisable. But might I ask, ready for what?"

"Atlanta. I'm going back. I'm taking back what is rightfully mine."

"I know you departed in great haste."

"I got away with my fuckin' life—that's all that matters. They didn't get me. And they ain't gonna."

"Your attitude is commendable, Charles. Your spirit is intact."

"You need to hear my plans, Clarence, and tell me if I'm crazy."

"You're the least crazy man I know," said Avery. "I'm just curious about the state of your resources."

"My resources? You won't believe my fuckin' resources."

"Am I to presume that means they are considerable?"

Slim took a toke from his cigar and a deep swallow of cognac before busting out in loud laughter.

"We're obviously talking millions," said the lawyer.

Slim's laugh got even louder.

"Tens of millions?" asked Clarence.

Slim didn't even bother answering. He just finished off his cognac and said, "Give me another shot."

He drained the second drink in nothing flat.

"Well, sir," said Avery, "I'm glad you've done so well for yourself, Charles."

"You have no idea. No fuckin' idea."

"Last time I talked with Ed Kingston at Southern Security, he said that your solvency was in question."

"Fuck Ed Kingston. If I wanted to, I could buy the bank and throw the motherfucker off the goddamn roof."

"I wouldn't do that if I were you, Charles. Ed's a friend of mine. A dear friend. He's also a man who could help you in your plans."

"When the shit started hitting the fan in Atlanta, Kingston ran from me. I hate the bastard."

"I understand. He was answering to Lock, a man he despises. Lock got everything Ed wanted—the presidency of the bank and the mayoralty. Lock is the man who built up your boy Power. His daughter is the young woman Power's marrying. But you know all that, right?"

"No, but I know it now. Tell me more."

"Not much to tell, Charles. Lock found a way to assign your assets to Power. He's made Power a multimillionaire. Take down Lock and you take down Power."

"And Ed Kingston can do that?"

"I believe he can help. Psychologically, he's motivated. Politically, he's angling to take on Lock in the next mayoral election. All he lacks are the financial resources. Recently he's reached out to me to see if I can find him a money man."

"Tell him you've got your man. Tell Ed Kingston to get his ass down to Tuscaloosa so I can tell him in person."

Slim didn't remember dreaming until he moved to Tuscaloosa.

When it came to sleep, his history was checkered. During his last days in Atlanta, when he was compelled to purge his enemies, he suffered through many restless nights, but after his recovery in Miami and Jamaica, sleep came easily. Making love with Besta had helped considerably. His reward was a sound night's sleep. But when Irv and Besta betrayed him and conspired with Power, his sleep troubles began again. So restless were his nights that he needed strong sleep medicine—a twenty-milligram dose of Ambien—to knock him out. Without the pills, he couldn't stop thinking of how he had been done in.

The incredible news about Irv's fortune now left Slim in a state of exhilarated confusion. At first he thought the call from Ian Shipman in Chicago was a prank. But when the funds were actually transferred, when the money started rolling in—the stocks, bonds, treasury notes, certificates of deposit, cash, deeds of ownership to property ranging from office buildings in Denver, Colorado, to apartment complexes in Dublin, Ireland—Slim realized Irv had told him the truth. He had left him everything.

But why? Why would a man who had betrayed him turn around and award him with his inheritance? It made no sense until Slim saw the angle. Eventually Slim always saw the angles.

Irv had written this will so that when Slim challenged him—as, in fact, Slim had done—Irv could point to the will and prove his devotion to Slim. Irv figured that Slim would take him up on the challenge. If Slim had seen the will he'd no longer have doubted or harmed Irv. Once Irv proved his loyalty, he'd immediately call the lawyer and change the will to disinherit Slim.

Slim was pleased that he hadn't challenged Irv. He was pleased that he hadn't asked to see a will that was there only to fool him. He was especially pleased to have done the one thing that Irv hadn't counted on—kill the bastard. In murdering that conniving motherfucker, he not only paid him back for his underhanded dealing with Power, he got to him before he could change his will. A double fuckin' victory!

Everything had changed for the better. Everything was great. The thought of controlling $30 million did wonders for a man's peace of mind. Now sleep came easily to Slim—deep sleep where, upon awakening, he could remember every last detail of last night's dream:

He lived in a penthouse atop the tallest tower in Atlanta. The tower was painted red. His penthouse was a combination apartment and disco. It was his old Charlie's Disco. Everyone was there. All his former friends. Power was an infant. His mother, Charlotte Clay, fed him at her breast. Beauty was a topless waitress. Irv was the cashier behind the bar, counting the money. Wanda Washington was the cigarette girl. Besta was a stripper on the pole. The customers were Jamaicans dressed in beach garb. Dr. Trina Mappleroot arrived with a class of students. They sat in a corner of the apartment and she read them books.

At one point Power morphed from being an infant to a grown

man. He ran up to Slim and told him that the place was on fire. Slim didn't believe him.

"Don't you smell the smoke?" asked Power.

"I don't smell shit," said Slim.

"You *are* shit!" Power screamed.

Power attacked him. Slim took out his razor blade and went for Power's throat, but just before he could cut him, the place filled with smoke. Children were yelling. Dr. Mappleroot opened a window so the children could escape. Besta spread wings and flew out the window as a giant bird. Beauty fell on the floor and was trampled by the customers—there were thousands of customers—trying to escape the building. In the chaos, Slim searched for Power. Where the fuck was he? Slim slashed every man he saw. He killed every man except for the one who had morphed back into an infant suckling at his mother's breast. That mother was Charlotte Clay and her infant was Power.

When Slim awoke, his mind was drained. He felt frustration. But it was just a dream, and dreams don't mean shit.

The Ensemble of Ensembles

Once it was decided that Beauty was going to attend Power's wedding in Atlanta, the two sisters went to work immediately. At first, Beauty thought her outfit should be low-key. Ryoko disagreed. She argued that they should take advantage of the high-profile nature of the event. The press would be there, and they would gravitate toward the most extravagantly stylish. The publicity would benefit Two Sisters. Beauty knew that Ryoko was right.

They began working with red—a long red satin overcoat, with a pointy high collar and narrow lapels, which fell to the top of the ankles. Under the coat was a sheer red blouse through which Beauty's breasts, firm enough to need no bra, were tantalizingly visible. The red satin skirt stopped just above her knees to highlight red mesh hose fashioned in a pattern of swirling circles. Red leather lace-up high-heel ankle boots completed the ensemble.

"Is it too wild?" asked Beauty when she tried it on the first time.

Running her hands over the coat, Ryoko replied, "Maybe not wild enough."

Beauty laughed. "It couldn't be any wilder. What do you think Seiji will say?"

"He'll like it. He'll say you look like one of his costars in a movie."
That's just what Seiji said.

"You are advertisement for Two Sisters!" he exclaimed with a
broad smile. "Everyone notices you. They notice you, not bride. But
wedding, it is two months away. Why hurry?"

"We wanted to make sure you liked it," Ryoko told her brother-
in-law in Japanese, "before we produced the final product. If you like
it, we want to design a tuxedo for you."

"You wouldn't make me wear red, would you?"

"We wouldn't make you wear anything you didn't like. But a red
tuxedo might be interesting. Would red be too much for you?"

"You would have to show me the design. A red tuxedo, a black tie,
and a black cummerbund. Maybe I would look so good photographers
would take pictures of me and not my wife."

"Not a chance," said Ryoko. "You'd be a matching set. You're a
couple. You belong together."

When Seiji kissed his sister-in-law on both cheeks, she smiled
radiantly.

"Thank you," Ryoko told Seiji. "Thank you for caring for my
sister."

At six foot eight, Ed Kingston had to shop at the Big and Tall men's
shop. Fortunately, the store carried Hugo Boss, Ed's favorite designer.
After his drive back from Tuscaloosa, he barely had time to stop in
the shop and pick up the double-breasted blue blazer that he had
special-ordered to wear to tonight's engagement party for Power and
Skyla. He realized that the affair, hosted by the mayor at the Inter-
Continental hotel in Buckhead, was to compensate people like Ed
who hadn't made the wedding guest list. That was fine. Ajay could
snub him all he liked. Ed was finally in a position to get what he
wanted.

As he drove home, he called his girlfriend Kim to say he'd be by to get her in two hours. His next call was to Clarence Avery.

"How was the trip back?" asked Clarence.

"Quick," said Ed. "Just getting ready for the big party tonight."

"Wish I could be there."

"No you don't, Clarence."

"Well, at least I could get a look at Skyla Lock. I hear she's something."

"What did Slim say about our meeting?"

"Not much. But that's good. If Simmons has something bad to say, you hear about it right away. If he has something good to say, he keeps quiet."

"I still get the feeling he hates my guts."

"He hates everyone's guts. You don't think he loves me, do you? But he's at the point where he needs at least a couple of people to work with."

"But is his money real? Have you had time to check it out? How do we know he's not full of shit?"

"Turns out I have a Chicago connection who put me in touch with Ian Shipman, the estate lawyer for Irving Wasserman. He confirmed everything Slim said."

"What's the estate's actual worth?"

"Thirty million."

"You're kidding."

"And Slim is sole heir."

"And the money's clean?"

"Clean as a whistle. And it's all Slim's. This Wasserman had a bulletproof will that anticipated every possible challenge."

"Wow."

"That's what I said."

"So he really does have the means to do what he was talking about yesterday."

"It'll work. I think his plan to start up a number of shadow companies will put him in the position he wants. He'll buy back his properties from Power."

"You really think Power will sell?"

"Why not? You'll bring the deals to him. You'll show him how he'll make a reasonable profit on every transaction—and you'll also demonstrate how the value on each of these properties is about to plunge. He'll be grateful for the inside information."

"And he won't see Slim's sleight of hand behind this?" asked Ed.

"Not coming from you," said Clarence. "Far as he's concerned, you and Slim are on the outs. Besides, he sees you as Ajay's man at the bank. You've never told Power your real feelings about Lock, have you?"

"Why would I?" asked Ed.

"That's just my point. He'll have no idea that you're manipulating the paperwork to show that this inside info is coming from the mayor."

"The mayor will never survive the scandal, Clarence. It's almost too easy."

"The best plans are always easy," said Avery. "They're the ones that work."

"You sound awfully confident, counselor."

"You've got the details of every dirty deal Lock has ever made. I've got Slim ready to spend millions to bring down Power. What else do we need?"

"Good timing."

"The timing couldn't be better," the lawyer explained with extreme confidence. "When egotists like Lock and Power are riding high, they're at their most vulnerable. They're convinced that their own shit doesn't stink. That's when they're cruising for a bruising. And believe me, Ed, our good friend Slim is fixing to bruise those guys like they've never been bruised before."

Avery's words left Ed with mixed feelings.

Even though Slim had once helped him, Ed never liked the man. He needed him, he used him, but he didn't trust him. Ed had seen Slim go off for the slightest reason. He had watched him flip from charming to violent because someone had used a word he didn't like. Yesterday in Tuscaloosa Slim seemed crazier than ever to Ed; he was more volatile, closer to the brink of violence. Driving back to Atlanta, Ed had felt Slim had little tolerance for him, not to mention fondness. He had never once looked Ed in the eye. He had not said a gracious word. All this had convinced Ed that avoiding Slim was the wisest course. Yet, during this call with Avery a few seconds ago, the words "thirty million dollars" had Ed reconsidering.

Clarence might be right. With that kind of money at his disposal, Slim shouldn't be avoided. He shouldn't be taken lightly. He should be listened to, catered to, and cultivated.

By the time Ed and Kim arrived at the InterContinental, the party was at a fever pitch. A smooth jazz band was playing instrumental versions of Lionel Richie hits. Uniformed waiters and waitresses carried around trays of shrimp, beef, and lobster. Champagne poured freely. Cameras were flashing. Everyone who was anyone was there. The buzz was intense. As a high-ranking executive of a major bank and former city councilman, Ed demanded some attention of his own. So did his date, Kim, who had reigned as Miss Atlanta two years earlier. But it wasn't until Ed approached Power to offer his congratulations that the cameras really started to click.

"Can I get a picture of you two gentlemen together?" asked the society photographer for the *Atlanta Journal-Constitution*.

"Sure," said Power, "Ed's an old friend. Even if he did think I was a lousy loan risk."

"Can I quote you?" asked the reporter.

"No," said Power. "That was a joke. Ed's my homey."

With arms around one another like old friends, Power and Ed stood together for several shots.

When the Atlanta newspaper arrived in Tuscaloosa, Slim quickly turned through the pages until he saw the article on Power's engagement party. There were many photos, but the one that caught Slim's attention was the shot of Power and Ed. As he studied the picture carefully, rage built up inside him until he picked up the phone and called Clarence Avery.

"Ed's gone over to Power's side," Slim told the lawyer.

"What are you talking about, Charles?"

"You see the *Journal-Constitution,* the article on Power's engagement party?"

"I'm looking at it right now."

"See Ed and Power?"

"Yes."

"Power's bought him. I can see it in Ed's eyes. Power fuckin' owns him."

"No, Charles," said Clarence. "Ed is merely—"

"Don't bullshit me, man. I know what I see. And I see it in Ed's fuckin' eyes. He's looking at me and he's laughing at me. He's telling Power what we're up to. He's working behind our backs."

"That's not logical."

"You telling me I'm making up this shit?"

Avery hesitated before answering. Slim was hot and Clarence certainly didn't want to raise his temperature. He needed to reply cautiously. His words had to be measured.

"I've known Ed a very long time," Clarence said in an exceedingly calm voice. "And I can vouch for him."

"That don't mean shit to me."

"He had to attend the party, Charles. He had no choice. To snub Ajay or Power would have gained us nothing."

"Yeah, but Power saw him coming. He knew that Ed had just been here with you and me."

"How would he know that?"

"He ain't stupid. Whatever he learned he learned from me. And that's something I would have figured out. When he saw Ed was our man, he took him off to the side and bought him—that's what he did—he bought the motherfucker and told him not to say nothing to us. Act like it's all good with us, but meanwhile the asshole is working as Power's man. Can't you see that?"

"Not really, Charles."

"If you can't see that, maybe you're in on it with them."

"What would be the purpose of that?"

"To fuck me out of my money. No one else knows how much there is. You're the only one."

Clarence Avery understood enough of human nature to know there was no arguing with Slim—at least not now.

"I realize that a man in your position can't be too careful—and I respect that. If you like, I can suggest ways to check up on Ed's loyalty."

"Fuck Ed. Ed's dead meat."

The Guyots

Rashan Guyot, the man in charge of Slim's ever-expanding security force, had been brought up in the abject poverty of Trench Town, the Jamaican neighborhood where Father Noel Peters preached. Rashan knew several local musicians who had gone on to fame and wealth, though he had never imagined that he himself would ever be wealthy.

As a boy, Rashan displayed no obvious talents. He was not musical and showed no intellectual gifts at school. The youngest of three brothers, he was, in the words of a cruel friend of his father's, "the runt of the litter." His brothers, like his father, were big and strong, while he was small and wiry. He didn't seem to belong to the Guyot family.

Brother Paul, closest to Rashan in age, was nine years his senior. Brother Deon was eleven years older, brother Jude thirteen years older. They and their dad, Lucas, were a tight team from which Rashan felt excluded. While he was a kid, his brothers worked with their father. He stayed home with his mother, Melea, the only family member who gave him any attention. His dad and siblings, caught up in their work, barely acknowledged his existence.

Rashan never stopped wondering about the nature of their job.

When he asked, he was told only, "It's man's work." Sometimes his mom would say, "It's work I pray you'll never have to do."

"I want to do it," said Rashan. "I want to do what my brothers are doing."

Melea took her baby in her arms and pressed him to her breast. "You are our special child," she said, "born at a special time. You don't need to do what your father or brothers are doing. God is protecting you from all that."

It didn't take long to understand that his brothers and father ran drugs. Rashan saw their guns and bags stuffed with marijuana. One of his schoolmates, an especially precocious boy, told him that they worked for Tayon Baylor, a notorious crime boss. When Rashan asked his mother whether that was true, she said he was too young to ask such questions.

On the evening of his eleventh birthday, Melea had cooked dinner and baked a cake. The two of them waited for the rest of the family to arrive, but at ten P.M. no one had returned.

"They are busy tonight," said Rashan's mother. "We will celebrate tomorrow."

Rashan began to cry. Melea's reassurance that his father and brothers loved him dearly fell on deaf ears. He knew they didn't care.

When he awoke the next morning, the men were still not there. Melea grew alarmed. She ran to the neighbors to see if anyone knew of their whereabouts. She ordered Rashan to stay home from school. He had never seen her in such a panic. It wasn't until early the next evening that a man came to speak with her. Rashan tried to eavesdrop but couldn't make out the words. After the man left, Melea walked over to Rashan with her arms extended. She cried for him to embrace her. Her eyes looked different. Her eyes looked like all life had been drained from them. Before she reached Rashan, her arms still extended, she suddenly collapsed. From that moment on, the eleven-year-old boy was never the same.

As a thirty-five-year-old living in the same house as Slim Simmons in Tuscaloosa, Alabama, Rashan Guyot looked back at his life with wonder. He wondered if his father and brothers had been killed in retaliation for a drug deal gone bad or whether it was a preemptive move on the part of a murderous rival. He wondered why, despite his father's work, the family never had money and why he had made his sons work with him. He wondered why the grisly details of their murder were so eagerly reported to him by his schoolmates—that their throats had been slashed and their bodies left to rot in a back alley.

He wondered why, after all they'd been through, after he and his mother had moved to Miami and found work, she suddenly fell ill. She required an expensive operation to remove a cancer in her throat. Raising money for her treatment had seemed impossible.

Then, according to Rashan's beliefs, God intervened.

After learning of the prohibitive cost of the operation, mother and son returned to the cheap motel where they had been staying. The news had devastated her. "All I want to do is sleep," she said. Rashan was certain that her crippling depression had returned. He put her to bed, wiped tears from her eyes, and went for a walk. He had to clear his head.

It was a sweltering summer afternoon in Miami. The sun was oppressive. Rashan felt a terrible fear. There was no way he could save his mother. He had been helpless to save his father and brothers, but when he grew up and gained confidence, he swore to protect his mother from all harm, just as she had protected him. Now that confidence was gone. It was just the two of them alone in a world where money meant the difference between life and death.

He walked aimlessly. He wandered into a park, his apprehension deepening. He couldn't imagine life without his mother. Dark thoughts were assaulting him, one after another, when he noticed an old man peacefully reading a newspaper as he sat on a bench. Out of nowhere, two thugs, who hadn't seen Rashan, menacingly approached the elderly gentlemen. One grabbed him by the collar of his shirt. The other stuck a gun in his stomach. For reasons he couldn't explain, Rashan snapped. He flew into action. He attacked from behind, catching the thugs by surprise. His first move was to knock the gun to the ground before pulverizing the first assailant with a vicious punch that crushed his Adam's apple; then he delivered a lethal upper-cut, catching the second thug's chin and practically decapitating him. Both muggers were down for the count. The old man was stunned.

"You are obviously well trained," said Irv Wasserman.

"Yes," said Rashan. "I was in the Jamaican army."

"I own a house in Jamaica. I love it there."

"It's my home and the home of my mother."

"Do you need work?"

"Yes. But I need money for my mother. I need money very badly."

"That is not a problem. I have all you need."

Irv had seen Rashan as a sign. He had been lonely in Florida and look-ing for a change. Like Power, Rashan had saved his life. Irv had no choice but to embrace the moment as a minor miracle. While mov-ing mother and son into his large luxurious high-rise apartment, he made arrangements for Melea's operation. At the same time, Irv fired his current security chief, who was not particularly sharp, and hired Rashan to replace him. Melea's operation was successful. And it was during Melea's extended post-op recovery that Slim arrived in Miami.

The minute Melea and Rashan met Simmons they were struck by his likeness to Lucas Guyot. They also sympathized with his mental condition. His sickness was not unlike the kind Melea had endured. They became emotionally invested in his recovery. And because that recovery had been due in large part to people who had personally helped Melea—Dr. Trina Mapplroot and Father Noel Peters—she and Rashan celebrated Slim's improvement with enormous gratitude. That gratitude deepened when Slim trusted Rashan as his confidante and made good on his promise to give him a hundred thousand dollars.

Rashan had not been in the room when Slim had suffocated Irv. He accepted the explanation that the old man died of a heart attack. He also accepted Slim's notion that Irv had betrayed him. It was Rashan, after all, who discovered that Irv had met with Power and that shortly after that, Besta had gone to Power's camp in Atlanta.

Because Rashan was convinced that his father and brother had been murdered due to their lowly status—they were mere workers in a large criminal system—he felt protected by Slim. He liked being next to the big boss.

It came as no surprise, then, that when Slim moved to Tuscaloosa he brought along the two people he trusted most—Melea, to run his household, and Rashan, to form his army.

The idea of amassing a small private army to secure Slim's operations and deal with his enemies, wherever they might be, was the most exciting assignment of Rashan's life. For all practical purposes, Slim had become a powerful and wealthy version of his father. Rashan would fight to keep him alive at any cost. There was nothing he would not do for the man.

With limitless funds at his command, Rashan could hire and arm whomever he wanted. He could train them, promote them, or dismiss them according to his assessment of their worth. He had in essence become a general, a powerful man himself. He took his role seriously, and every assignment, no matter how bloody, would be carried out with deadly devotion.

"It's going to be rough for a while," said Slim after he got off the phone with Clarence Avery and continued to stare at the photo of Ed Kingston and Power in the *Atlanta Journal-Constitution*. "Very fuckin' rough."

"Give me the word," said Rashan, "and we'll do whatever needs to be done."

The Connecticut Prime Cut Club

Because Seiji Aoi looked down to see that his wife was calling him on his cell phone, the bullet missed him by a fraction of an inch, entering the ear and ripping through the brain matter of Matsaharu Aoi, Seiji's first cousin, who had arrived in America that very morning. Along with the other gentlemen who had been seated at a long table in a private dining room of the most exclusive eatery in Greenwich, Connecticut, Seiji hit the floor. The room was sprayed with gunfire coming through two different windows. When Seiji's two security men came running into the room, they were shot to death. Seiji had not thought to secure the outside perimeter of the restaurant. He hadn't given the least thought to being attacked. Since coming to the United States, there had been no incidents whatsoever. Seiji was convinced that his problems in Tokyo had not followed him to the eastern coast of the United States. He had lowered his guard.

Were it not for the fact that a police squad car happened to be patrolling the street where the Connecticut Prime Cut Club was situated, the gunmen would have met their goal of murdering everyone at the table, Seiji included. Sirens stopped the killers in their tracks. As it was, five of Seiji's guests, including his cousin, died—three in the restaurant and two later that same night in the hospital. The assailants fled into the night, leaving virtually no evidence behind. Seiji walked away without a scratch.

He thought immediately of Beauty. He remembered that she and Ryoko were in Manhattan, having dinner with Solomon Getz. He called her cell and she answered on the first ring.

"Let me speak, must speak with Ryoko," he said, realizing he was too discombobulated to express himself in English. He needed the ease of speaking his native tongue.

"Are you two all right?" he asked his sister-in-law in Japanese.

"We are at a restaurant. We are fine."

"You must leave immediately."

"Why?"

"Don't ask. Just get up and leave. Do you have a driver?"

"No. We came in a cab with Solomon Getz."

"You must get away from him immediately."

"He's Beauty's best friend."

"No one is a friend, Ryoko. Our enemies have arrived on these shores. They can be anywhere. They are everywhere."

"Why are you talking like this?"

"My cousin Matsaharu is dead. Others as well. They came to get me. My wife saved my life."

"I don't understand."

"I put my head down to look at the phone when she called me. That's why the bullet flew past me. Do you know why she called?"

"I'll ask her."

"Don't. Not now. Doesn't matter. Just leave there. Leave this Getz man. Take a cab. Don't come back to Connecticut. Connecticut is dangerous. They are here. They are all around. Go to a hotel. Don't tell me which one. Not on the phone. Check in and stay there. I'll be in touch."

Ryoko felt fear mixed with excitement. She felt as though she was living in one of the Seiji Aoi films that she loved so well. She was in a movie with her favorite movie star.

The next day, watching the morning news on TV from his home in Tuscaloosa, Slim was startled to see Beauty's face on the screen. She was standing next to a Japanese man referred to as her husband. His name was Seiji Aoi. The reporter detailed an attack on him at a restaurant in Greenwich, Connecticut, that left five people dead. He was described as a Japanese film star whose family reportedly had ties to organized crime.

Slim's mind started to churn. He didn't take the facts at face value. He looked for the subtext, and the subtext was obvious. Because of Beauty's involvement, Power had to be involved as well. That motherfucker was still hooked up with the fuckin' Japanese Mafia, the same Mafia that had saved his ass when Slim had him cornered. Or maybe it was a different Mafia. Maybe different factions of the Mafia were fighting each other. It didn't matter. All that counted was that this bastard, through his bastard sister, was still playing war games. But that was a good thing. Because if he was in the middle of one war, he had to be preoccupied. The chess master sensed that Power's position was weak. It was time to finally eliminate a player that should have been eliminated long ago. It was time to strike.

Mayor Ajay Lock watched the same broadcast and immediately picked up the phone to call Herman Kiner.

"What the hell . . . ," said Ajay.

"All is well. My client was unharmed."

"But the scandal—"

"What scandal? He was merely in the wrong place at the wrong time."

"It's being reported as a gangland attack."

"It's being misreported. I can assure you, it's nothing of the kind."

"You told me he was clean, Herman."

"Clean as a whistle."

"I want out of the deal."

"It's a little late for that, Mr. Mayor. The deal is done. But you have nothing to worry about. There are three layers between you and Seiji."

"Good. Let's keep it that way. I don't want to see him. I don't want him at my daughter's wedding."

"It's a little late for that as well. He told me how pleased he was to be invited. He and his wife are coming."

"Uninvite him."

"That's not exactly within my jurisdiction, Mr. Mayor."

"Then I'll do it."

"I wouldn't advise that."

"Why not?"

"The reasons are obvious. This is not a man you want to antagonize."

"I don't want him there, Herman."

"He's a movie star and his wife's a high-fashion powerhouse."

"Somehow I'm going to get word to him that he can't attend."

"All that will do is draw more attention to your relationship with him. He doesn't like humiliation, and you won't like being on his bad side. You do not want to know about this guy's bad side."

When Power saw the news report, his first thought was of Beauty. He had to reach her. It wasn't easy, but he finally remembered Solomon Getz. Getz, terribly concerned for Beauty's welfare himself, felt Power's genuine apprehension and gave him her cell.

The minute Beauty heard Power's voice, she went to another emotional place. She was already shaken by Seiji's near assassination. But this call sparked something even stronger.

"Are you all right?" Power asked.

"I'm . . . I'm fine. What about you?"

He felt tenderness in her voice, concern, even love. "I'm okay, but how about you? Where are you? I'm worried sick."

"Don't worry. I'm in New York."

"Do you need to get out? Do you need help, Beauty?"

"Really, there's nothing to worry about. No one has ever been more protected."

"That's what you thought with your last husband."

"Kato and I never married."

"They got to him, though, didn't they?" asked Power.

"I'm not certain."

"I can send for you."

"No need to. I'm coming there. We're coming to your wedding."

Power wanted to say, *It should be our wedding,* but the words stayed locked in his mind. He hoped Beauty shared that same silent thought.

"Tell me about your bride," said Beauty, trying to change the subject, but Power's mind couldn't be changed.

"You need to get out of that situation," he said.

"And move into what situation?" she asked.

"Just get out—now—it's no good, Beauty, it's not safe."

"I've never been safer."

"I don't believe that," said Power.

Beauty wasn't about to admit that she didn't believe it either.

"I'm happy for you, Power," was all she said. "Happy you found someone to love."

Power wanted to say that he hadn't found love at all. He wanted to say that he still thought of Beauty night and day.

"Are you in love with your husband?" he asked.

Beauty wanted to say that she hadn't found love either. She wanted to admit that her fantasies were all focused on Power.

"I'm not good at defining love," she said.

"So the answer is no."

"And what's your answer?" she asked. "If you're not marrying for love, why are you marrying?"

"Who said I wasn't marrying for love?"

"I assumed that . . ." Beauty didn't know how to complete her thought.

Even on the phone, even during this disconcerting conversation of half questions and half answers, both Power and Beauty were turned on. But beyond the physical signs of the overpowering heat that their dialogue generated, both their hearts felt on fire.

"I want to see you," Power said.

"Well," said Beauty, "I . . . I want to see you too."

"Don't Stop Till You Get Enough"

Ed Kingston grew up on Michael Jackson, and because VH1 was having a Michael Jackson video marathon, he had his television set on that station. Ed loved all the MJ jams—from "ABC" and "The Love You Save" to *Off the Wall*, *Thriller*, and *Bad*. It was a good way to relax on a Saturday morning. Kim had just gone back to her place after spending the night. The bump and grind had been great and Ed was feeling good. After watching Michael's video for "You Are Not Alone," his plan was to go to the private gym in the high-rise where he lived.

When the phone rang, he saw Clarence Avery's name on the ID but decided not to answer. He had his MJ groove on and didn't want to be disturbed.

"Hope you're there, Ed," said Clarence through the answering machine, "because I had a disturbing call with Slim. He thinks he's onto you. He may even think he's onto me. We may have to consider a preemptive strike. I have contacts in Asia who could be helpful."

Ed turned off the television and picked up the phone.

"What are you talking about?" he asked Avery.

"Glad you're there. Slim's convinced you've betrayed him—he's sure you're in cahoots with Power."

"What the hell makes him think that?"

"The picture in the paper of the two of you."

"That didn't mean shit."

"Tell it to Slim."

"I thought the whole point of going to the party was to keep Power and Ajay off guard."

"That was my explanation, but he didn't buy it."

"Well then, fuck him. If he gets crazy, there's nothing we can do about it."

"There might be something we *have* to do about it," said Clarence.

"Like what?" asked Ed.

"I used the word 'preemptive.'"

"I'm not exactly in that line of business."

"Not until now. This is a question of survival, Ed. I have contacts. In fact, a group from Japan is over here right now on another matter."

"I'm not getting involved," said Ed.

"You already are," Clarence told him.

Ed put down the phone. It wasn't anything he was going to worry about now. Not today. Today was Saturday and he was going to work out. The workout Kim gave him last night reminded him he needed to stay in shape.

He changed into his gym gear and told himself to forget about Slim. Except he couldn't. Slim was a psycho. Ed had watched him operate for many years and knew he was no one to mess with. When Ed had refused to deal with Slim and passed his account over to Ajay, he had felt Slim's rage. Slim was not a man who forgave and forgot. On the other hand, for all his dirty money—and God knew there was a ton of it—Slim had no political base and little financial sophistication. He needed brainy guys like Clarence Avery and Ed Kingston. His return to Atlanta depended on making smart alliances. Slim needed Ed more than Ed needed Slim.

Right now, though, Ed needed an intense workout. The combination of loving on Kim and stressing over Slim required a good half hour on the treadmill and forty minutes with the weights. The building's private gym was often empty and today was no exception. He put in ear buds and dialed up his iPod to old-school rap—Public Enemy, 2 Live Crew, Master P. He cranked up the volume and started running. His goal was to run four miles in thirty minutes. With the treadmill humming and Chuck D spitting, Ed focused on the feat in front of him: He got deep into the groove of the run until the rest of the world was gone. He blocked out everything but moving his feet in a steady rhythm. The rap helped. The rap pushed him on. The rap was so loud that he didn't hear the man walk into the gym, didn't see him pick up a seventy-pound dumbbell and walk right behind him, didn't know what had hit him when the weight came down directly on his head and crushed his skull—not once or twice but six separate times.

By the time Rashan Guyot walked out the door, Ed had stopped breathing.

Hearing about his friend's murder the next day, Clarence Avery fell into a state of shock. He kept hearing Slim's words when they had spoken last.

"Fuck Ed," Slim had told the lawyer. "Ed's dead meat."

Slim's Revenge

The mayor was panicked. He was also deeply confused. He didn't believe the reports that the brutal murder of Ed Kingston was the random act of a deranged man. Ajay was convinced it had something to do with Seiji Aoi. In his feverish mind, Lock knew that he could look at it one of two ways:

The men who tried to assassinate Seiji had also killed Ed. They were sending the mayor a message—*You mess with Seiji, we mess with you. Just as we knocked off men close to him, we knocked off a guy close to you.*

The other explanation was that Seiji's men murdered Ed. Maybe Seiji's lawyer Herman Kiner had told his client that Lock was reluctant to continue to do business with him; maybe Kiner had told Seiji that Lock didn't even want him at Skyla's wedding; and maybe Ed's murder was Seiji's furious reaction, his way of saying to the mayor, *Don't take me lightly.*

Either explanation gave Lock cold chills.

He immediately called Kiner.

"Have you heard?" he asked the lawyer.

"I saw something about a murder in Atlanta. An officer at your bank."

"The man who worked directly under me."

"I'm sorry to hear that," said Kiner.

"That's all you have to say?"

"What else can I say?"

"You can explain Seiji's role in all this."

"I can assure you, he has no role."

"And it's purely coincidental that days after someone tries to kill him, my man is killed."

"Purely, yes."

"I don't believe it."

"I can't control your beliefs. But I do know the facts."

"And what are the fuckin' facts, Herman?"

"The two unfortunate events are not related."

"And you expect me to believe that?"

"Believe what you like, Mr. Mayor. If you'll excuse me, I have another call."

Lock's next call was to Power.

"I need to see you," he told his future son-in-law.

"I'm actually just outside on my way up to see *you*," said Power.

Five minutes later the men were holed up in the mayor's private office.

"Do you know who did it?" asked Lock.

"Slim Simmons."

"I don't think so," said Ajay. "I think it's coming from this character Seiji Aoi. It's him or his people."

"Slim had supported Ed for political office. He gave him money. But when Slim needed the bank's support, Ed wasn't there for him."

"But I was," said Lock. "I took care of that sleazy bastard."

"Which is why you're safe."

"I sure as hell don't feel safe. We need to do something—something quick."

"Like what?"

"Cancel your wedding."

"What will that achieve?"

"It will keep Seiji out of Atlanta."

It will also keep me from seeing Beauty, thought Power.

"You'll be breaking your daughter's heart," said Power.

"She'll get over it."

"And what reason do we give?"

"You'll think of something, Power."

"I can think of nothing—except that you're scared shitless."

"If you had any sense, you'd be scared too."

"Scared of what?" asked Power.

"The Yakuza, Slim's old mob—you tell me. All I know is that it makes no sense to have this wedding up at Slim's old house."

"It's my house now."

"And it's your goddamn ego that's driving you."

"The wedding's a week away, Ajay. You really expect me to ditch it?"

"I do."

"Well, don't hold your breath."

"You gotta do something to keep Seiji and his people out of Atlanta."

"*I* have to do something? I'm not the guy who got involved with the motherfucker to begin with."

"I'll talk to Skyla."

"You have every right to. You're her dad. But good luck on getting her to cancel our wedding."

"Something has to be done."

"You're right," said Power. "You have to calm your ass down. You don't want to get a heart attack and miss your daughter's wedding."

Power left the mayor's office feeling strangely cocky. It wasn't that Ed's murder did not affect him. But it wasn't fear that he felt; it was almost relief. If Slim was about to make a move, Power would be ready. If Slim thought he could take back Atlanta, the man was delusional. Power was more in control than ever. He had Slim's city, he had Slim's woman, and he even had Slim's house. That house, symbol of all that was once Slim's, was the proper setting for crowning Power prince of Atlanta. The house was an armed fortress. Jordan Gee, Power's head of security, had a big enough militia to protect the president of the United States, never mind the mayor. The governor, due to attend, would have his own security.

Jordan, who had been waiting for Power outside the mayor's office, accompanied him to the car and sat next to him in the backseat as Ted Blake, a former marine and Jordan's number-two man, drove to their next appointment. Still lost in thought about next week's wedding, Power felt his phone vibrate. The ID read "Caller Unknown." Power had a feeling, and so he hit "accept."

His feeling was right.

"Are you all right?" asked Beauty.

"Why wouldn't I be?"

"I read about the murder of that man who works at your father-in-law's bank."

"He's not my father-in-law yet."

"That's just a technicality," said Beauty.

"No," said Power. "That's a sure-enough fact."

"Are you considering walking out on the wedding?"

"Are you asking me to?"

"Power, I'm just calling to make sure you're all right."

There was more concern and intimacy in Beauty's voice than Power had heard since they had made love in New York.

"I'm fine," he said.

"Didn't Ed Kingston have something to do with Slim? Wasn't he Slim's man on the city council?"

"At one time or another, every politician in Atlanta had something to do with Slim."

"So Slim's back in Atlanta."

"I don't know where Slim is," said Power

"And you're still not worried?" asked Beauty.

"I'm just eager for you to get here. I'm eager to see you."

I can't wait to see you, Beauty was on the verge of saying, but instead stayed silent.

"I need to go," she finally said.

"I need to say that I'm glad you called. I want you to call more. I want to call you more."

"You won't need to," said Beauty. "We'll be together soon."

He loved the sound of those words; he relished the breathiness of her voice against his ear. He was aroused in every way possible—and he sensed that Beauty was aroused as well.

"We'll be together soon," she said again.

"Damn right," he replied.

Rashan and his crew returned to Tuscaloosa in good shape. Their mission was accomplished. Item one had been Ed Kingston. Item two had been Kingston's answering machine. Item three had been obtaining a copy of the wedding guest list by slipping a thousand dollars to one of the mayor's secretaries.

In the seclusion of his warehouse office, with Clarence Avery sitting across his desk, Slim switched on Ed's answering machine. He had heard this message before but wanted to hear it again—this time with Clarence in the room. That's why he'd had one of his men forcibly bring Avery to the warehouse.

The voice on the message machine was Clarence's. The voice could not be clearer.

The voice said, "Hope you're there, Ed, because I had a disturbing call with Slim. He thinks he's onto you. He may even think he's onto me. We may have to consider a preemptive strike. I have contacts in Asia who could be helpful."

After the message played, Slim lit up a cigar, leaned back in his chair, stared at the ceiling, and said nothing. He was eager to hear Avery's bullshit explanation. This was going to be good.

298 / Tip "T.I." Harris with David Ritz

His heart beating wildly, his forehead wet with sweat, Clarence was quick to respond. "The operative word, Charles," he said, "is "'thinks.' You'll note that I said you *think* you're onto Ed. You may even *think* you're onto me. On your part, those thoughts would be erroneous. I was merely concerned about your thought process. For you to be *truly* onto us would let you see that we all have common goals. We are all on the same side. Any thoughts contrary to that— thoughts that may lead you to believe we have anything but your best interests in mind—would be misinterpretations."

Slim laughed. The laugh gave Clarence shivers.

"Are you following me, Charles?" asked the lawyer. "Are you seeing my point?"

Slim blew a perfect circle of smoke that floated up to the ceiling. He still had nothing to say.

"By 'preemptive strike,'" Avery went on to say, "I merely meant that we need to address you directly—as I am doing now—so that you do not come to any wrong conclusions. By 'preemptive strike' I was referring to a meeting such as this when, in the name of candor and goodwill, we clarify our absolute support for you. The Asians I refer to are a group of financiers from Seoul, Korea, who have contacted me about business opportunities in Atlanta. Once I explain to you— and I'm prepared to do so right now—the extent of their resources and willingness to partner up with us, you'll understand with even greater clarity that we're all on the same team."

Slim took another puff of his cigar. This time the smoke circle broke up quickly. He still didn't say a word.

"Any questions you'd like to ask me, Charles? I'd be delighted to discuss any aspect of our dealings."

More silence.

Twenty seconds later, Slim picked up a piece of paper and handed it to Clarence.

"What's this?" asked Avery.

Slim finally spoke. "The guest list for Power's wedding."

"Oh," was all Clarence managed to say.

"See the names Mr. and Mrs. Seiji Aoi?"

"I do," said Avery.

"Those wouldn't be the goddamn fuckin' Asians that you, Ed, and Power had in mind, would they?"

"I can assure you, Charles, that I've had no contact with Power— none whatsoever. And no, Mr. Aoi is Japanese, not Korean."

"So you know him."

"I do not. I've never met the gentleman."

Slim laughed again.

"You're a funny motherfucker," he told Avery. "You really are. You got bullshit on top of bullshit. But right now I don't got no time for no more bullshit. Right now blowing a hole in your head ain't gonna do me no good. Tuscaloosa is a little place and blowing a hole in your head is gonna make a big noise. I don't need no big noise. I just need for you to get on a plane and go to that bitch that you've been fucking in Memphis."

"What bitch?" asked Clarence.

"The one that's waiting for you in Memphis. People understand a man running after pussy. Pussy can be so good to make a man leave his wife and kids. That's what you doing. You running off to Memphis to catch up with this bitch. She's waiting for you. I just hope nothing happens to you while you're there. Memphis is a dangerous town."

"Charles, this is insane, this is—"

"Plane's waiting for you. Private jet. You flown on a private jet before? It's cool 'cause you don't gotta go through no security at the airport. Have fun, Clarence. Your bitch is waiting."

Before Avery could object any further, two of Rashan's men came to drive him to the private airport just out of town. Before they boarded the plane, though, the attorney shit his pants.

. . . .

"Ryoko needs to go with us," Beauty told Seiji three days before the wedding.

"But your sister . . . not invited," he said.

"I can get her invited."

"How you do that?"

"I just can."

"Not so easy."

"Easy for me. I know the bridegroom."

"This Paul Clay? How you know him?"

"I just do. From when I was a kid in Atlanta. I know him. He'll be happy to add Ryoko to the guest list."

"Why it so important Ryoko come?"

"I don't want to leave her alone here. I want her with me. With us," said Beauty.

"I not understand."

"You don't have to understand. I'll take care of this."

"Who is Paul Clay?"

"A man—that's all. The man who's getting married."

"You like him?"

"Well, yes . . . no . . . I mean, he's getting married and it'll be a beautiful wedding and I don't want Ryoko to miss it."

Seiji looked puzzled and a little concerned. "Have Ryoko come here. She explain to me in Japanese."

Beauty helped Ryoko into the room. She answered her brother-in-law's questions with reassuring confidence. No, Beauty had no real interest in Paul Clay; yes, Beauty did want her to come along for sisterly companionship; and yes, after what had happened at the Connecticut Prime Cut Club, Beauty had been on edge—they all had—and it would be nice if they all could go to Atlanta together.

Ryoko's explanation satisfied Seiji. He said, however, it was better that he call the mayor himself to put Ryoko on the guest list. There was no reason for Beauty to bother the bridegroom. Seiji was certain that the mayor would accommodate him.

After her talk with Seiji, Ryoko felt her way to the kitchen, where Beauty was sitting alone.

"What did Seiji ask you?" asked Beauty.

"He asked about Power."

"And what did you say?"

"Nothing of what I knew. I said Paul Clay means nothing to you."

"And he believed you? He still doesn't know how Power was saved by his father's organization?"

"He doesn't seem to."

"Sit next to me," said Beauty. "Let me make you some tea."

"I'd like that."

Beauty helped Ryoko to the table before going to the stove to boil the water. A few minutes later she came back with a cup of hot green tea that she placed before her sister.

"We talked till four A.M. last night," said Beauty. "You must be tired."

"I'm fine," said Ryoko. "I don't need much sleep. Are you feeling the same way today that you felt last night?"

"That it's dangerous for me to see Power?"

"Yes."

"I am feeling that way, but . . ."

Ryoko finished the sentence for her sister. "But the danger is exciting."

"I wouldn't use that word," said Beauty.

"Maybe the word is 'stimulating.' Is that the right word?"

Beauty broke into a small smile. "You know me," she told her sister. "You know me well."

"Anyone who has heard you speak from your heart would tell you what I'm telling you now—you love the man you call Power."

"And that still bothers you?" asked Beauty.

"It still worries me. I don't expect you to feel about Seiji the way I do. He is a hero in my culture, not yours. And I know that you are not happy that he has not supported Two Sisters with his money the way you had expected. You are with him for practical reasons—reasons that no longer appear very practical. And because I understand all this, I worry. I worry about what you will do in Atlanta. Now I start wondering whether it's really a good idea to go. I thought it would be closure. But now it seems like it's a reopening. Why are you going, Beauty?"

"I'm going because Seiji and I were invited."

"You could have easily declined. And I also wonder why you are taking me. I wonder if you're taking me so I'll be there to urge you not to do anything dangerous."

"Is that what you would urge, Ryoko?"

"I don't know."

"And you see leaving Seiji as dangerous?"

"It's one thing to leave him for a man you truly love. But it's another to leave him *at the wedding* of the man you truly love."

Beauty took Ryoko's hand and said, "I can't remember when I haven't lived with danger. And I also can't remember when I have lived with love."

"Yet you've done well living without love."

"Have I?"

"Only you can answer that."

"I don't know. I really don't."

"But yet you still want to go to Atlanta."

"I have to."

"Why is this Seiji Aoi calling and insisting that his sister-in-law come to the wedding?" Ajay asked Power over the phone.

Power was immediately drawn to the question. He had closely followed the articles about Two Sisters and knew that Ryoko was approximately Beauty's age. He also knew that she was the blind daughter of Beauty's biological father in Japan. He further knew that the sisters, having discovered each other, had grown close enough to forge a creative and business bond. Knowing all this, though, he still didn't understand why Seiji was insisting that Ryoko come to Atlanta.

"Do you think she's dangerous?" asked Ajay.

"In what way?"

"I don't know. I don't know anything about these people. She might be a killer."

"She's blind."

"The blind can kill. Maybe her blindness is a ruse. Maybe she's going to lead the attack."

"You're paranoid as a motherfucker," said Power.

"Paranoid? After what happened in Connecticut? After what happened to Ed? I hardly think so."

"So you didn't add her to the guest list."

"Of course I did. I had to. Do you think I want to incense Seiji? If it wouldn't infuriate my daughter and make the two of you look like fools, I'd cancel this goddamn wedding—no matter what the world might think. I have a dark feeling about it."

"Feelings change."

"Mine are only getting darker."

"Lighten up. It's all good," said Power, who felt great about Ryoko's arrival. He wanted to meet her and find out why it was so important to Seiji—or Beauty—that she come along.

The day before the wedding Power went up to Cascade Heights to check out final preparations for the ceremony in his new home. The plan was to move in after he and Skyla honeymooned in Bermuda.

The transformation was great. The gaudy gates had been replaced with elegant ones in burnished wood. The interior design of the house itself, once glitzy, was toned down and tasteful. That was all Skyla's doing. She had changed the white walls to beige, removed the golden mirrors and the sculpture of a life-size mermaid swimming over a waterfall. The wild animals that Slim had kept caged in the yard were long gone. Shiny hardwood floors were now covered with soft chestnut-brown carpet. The feeling was warm and inviting.

Out back an enormous tent had been constructed and three hundred plus folding chairs were already in place. A bandstand had been built and a rehearsal was under way. Besta, Up, and the Up-Towners were playing Luther Vandross's "Here and Now," the well-worn wedding song. When they saw Power, they stopped to greet him.

"How we sound, baby?" Besta asked Power.

"Beautiful."

"Party's gonna be off the hook," said Up. "Thanks for asking us to play."

"Wouldn't have it any other way," said Power.

"We'll have 'em crying," Besta promised, "and then we'll have 'em dancing."

"I know you will," Power said in agreement as he left the tent and walked the grounds, which were already being swept, inch by inch, by dozens of security technicians. He wandered over to the area where Slim's four-car garage had stood. Above the garage had been the apartment where Power had lived—and faced death. In redoing the estate, Power insisted that the structure be demolished and replaced by a garden.

Walking through the garden, fragrant with rows of red roses, he thought of the days behind him and the days ahead. He thought of tomorrow, and of Beauty.

. . . .

Across town, in her suite at Atlanta's Four Seasons Hotel, Beauty dreamt of being with Power, in a cave facing the ocean. Outside a torrential rain soaked the beach. She and Power stayed in the cave as they watched angry waves crash against the shore. The scene was thrilling, the lovemaking endless.

She awoke before Seiji and went to the sitting room. Ryoko was already there, still in her robe.

"You're up early," said Beauty.

"You too. You've been dreaming."

"How can you tell?"

"I can feel it. I can read in your spirit that you've been dreaming of him."

Beauty said nothing.

"Have you called him yet?" Ryoko asked.

"No."

"Will you?"

"I don't know."

"The wedding is at four," said Ryoko.

"It's not even seven A.M. We have lots of time. We have a few hours before we need to worry about getting dressed."

It wasn't yet seven A.M. when Power left his bedroom and went to the kitchen to call Beauty. He was almost through dialing when Skyla walked in.

"Who you calling?" she asked, all smiles.

"The security people."

"We're going to have more soldiers and cops than guests," said Skyla. "It's crazy."

"It *is* kind of crazy," he said in agreement as he put down his phone.

"What happened to your call, Power?"

"I'll do it later."

Skyla spent the morning in hair and makeup. A crew of stylists had left the set of a Halle Berry movie to fly in for the job.

Skyla had never been happier. She had never imagined—especially during those wild years of acting out—that she'd want a royal princess wedding. And yet that's exactly what she was getting. As the stylists worked on her face and hair, her $75,000 custom-designed Vera Wang wedding dress was being steamed. On TV the weatherman said the day would be 75 and sunny. This was her day, her wedding, her man. This was perfection.

In Tuscaloosa, Slim took his mind off the wedding by going to his bedroom, where a woman awaited him. Experience had taught him to make love in the morning. That's when the chances of coming too soon decreased. Because he knew he'd be in a celebratory mood, he had arranged for this particular lady, a prostitute from Birmingham, to arrive at nine A.M., when he'd be fresh and ready to go.

He selected her from a gallery of photographs sent over the Internet. She caught his eye because she looked like Besta—short and stacked. He wanted to take no chances and arranged to talk with her on the phone before agreeing to her $2,000 price. Her speaking voice was sweet, and after a short discussion, he was satisfied that he could satisfy her.

When he opened the door to his bedroom, he saw her slouched against his dresser. Her pose was provocative. Her outfit consisted of a bra and thong, both sheer black. The bra was too small for her exceptionally voluminous breasts and the thong barely covered her clean-shaven pussy.

Slim got hard and she went to her knees, thinking he wanted to be serviced. He didn't. He undressed himself and waved her over to the bed. She got on her back and spread her arms and legs open.

"Bra off or on?" she asked.

"Off," he answered.

"Thong on or off?"

"Off."

He approached her naked body confidently. He fingered her with something less than tenderness. She was wet.

"Good," he said. "Gonna bone you, bitch, like you never been boned before."

"Do it, daddy. Fuck me good."

The minute he went in, though, he went off.

Infuriated, he viciously slapped her face. "You filthy cunt!" he screamed. "I thought you knew how to fuck a man."

"Sorry, daddy, I—!"

"Shut the fuck up," he spat before hitting her again, this time with his closed fist. He broke her jaw. Slim didn't give a shit. He looked at his watch and saw that the wedding was still a few hours away. Maybe there was a ball game on TV that would kill the time. When the lady began crying that she needed a doctor, Slim ignored her, walking out and slamming the door behind him.

The cars began arriving at the Cascade Heights estate of Paul Clay and his future wife as early as three fifteen P.M. By then everything was well in order. Before entering the grounds, each vehicle was subject to a thorough inspection while the passengers got out and walked through a sophisticated scanning device. The security men apologized effusively for the inconvenience, but the mayor would have it no other way. Furthermore, he had arranged with the governor to have military helicopters patrolling the airspace above Cascade Heights, ensuring that there would be no mischief from on high.

Leonard Sudavico had recently endured two profound hardships. First, his company, which developed software for the insurance industry, had declared bankruptcy, and then his wife had taken their infant son and nine-year-old twin daughters and left for good. He was alone in a big fancy house that he could not afford.

So three weeks ago when he was offered $2 million for the home, a fair price, he quickly accepted. The buyer was unidentified, but that hardly mattered; the terms were cash and possession within a week. He didn't understand the buyer's eagerness. The house needed work. There were other, far more attractive homes for sale in Cascade Heights. But no matter; Sudavico was glad to be gone before the wedding of the mayor's daughter caused traffic headaches for the local residents.

By three forty-five P.M. nearly all of the three-hundred-plus guests had arrived and were enjoying sparkling water and juice on the great lawn in front of the freshly repainted house. It was a splendid turnout—the men in tuxedos, the women in fabulous gowns. The city's most prominent citizens were there to celebrate. The weather was ideal, the sunshine abundant. Upstairs in the master bedroom, Skyla was in the final stages of getting dressed. She looked exquisite.

"Is Power here?" her mom asked.

"I don't know," said Skyla. "We came separately, and I left before him."

In the pool house, where Power was to dress, his entourage was concerned. He hadn't arrived. The cell phone belonging to Jordan Gee, who was driving Power, was not responding.

Three fifty P.M. The wedding would have to start a little late. No big deal.

Seiji Aoi could be spotted on the great lawn. Wearing this red tuxedo, he felt foolish not being with his wife. His outfit was designed to go with hers. Without her, he had the sensation of being a target. Surrounded by four of his own security men, he was speaking on his cell phone to his security guard back at the hotel.

"It's ridiculous that they couldn't be ready in time," said Seiji. "It's ridiculous to be standing here without my wife."

"She and Ryoko left some time ago," said the security man. "They should be arriving any second."

"I called her but there's no answer."

"I assure you, sir, nothing is wrong. They're on their way."

Four P.M. came and went.

Five after four. No Power, no Beauty.

Four ten. Power and Beauty still missing.

Skyla was told that Power wasn't there. She felt sick in her stomach.

Seiji was furious. Where in hell was his wife? Where was his sister-in-law? What was happening?

Four twenty P.M. A flurry of calls to Power, a flurry of calls to Beauty. No response. The guests began to mill about nervously. There was an ominous feeling in the air. They walked into the tent and took their seats.

Four thirty P.M. No announcement was made. The guests faced the flower-laden altar. Besta sang a hymn while Up accompanied her on a grand piano.

Four forty P.M. Besta sang another hymn. Everyone knew something was wrong. How long did they wait? The mayor was going crazy inside, as was the mayor's wife, as was their daughter. Seiji could barely contain his rage. He was turning as red as his red tuxedo.

Four fifty P.M. Jordan Gee drove past the gates of Slim's old estate, but Power was not in the backseat.

Four fifty-five P.M. Ryoko, seated alone in the back of a Rolls sedan, was driven through those same gates.

One minute after five. The seated guests were told that the ceremony would begin shortly. A little more patience was required.

Five after five. Besta sang the fourth hymn of the afternoon.

Five ten P.M. A ground-to-ground cruise missile, launched from a tractor installed in the backyard of Leonard Sudavico's former home by Rashan and a crew of technicians from Afghanistan, exploded onto the Paul Clay estate in the exact spot where the life-size mermaid had once swum in the waterfall. The horrific explosion could be heard fifty miles away.

Eight P.M. A special edition of the *Atlanta Journal-Constitution,* published hours later, called it the worst catastrophe in the city's modern history.

Nine P.M. Rashan arrived in Tuscaloosa and handed the special edition of the paper to Slim.

Given what had transpired that morning with the whore from Birmingham, Slim was in a lousy mood. But the headline changed all that. As he scanned it, he broke out into a broad smile: MISSILE MASSACRE IN CASCADE HEIGHTS! HUNDREDS DEAD!

That smile, though, vanished when he read the second paragraph. "Several of the survivors reported that the groom had not yet arrived. There is no word of his whereabouts."

Slim grabbed a pistol and blasted his hundred-inch flat-screen Sony to smithereens.

Power and Beauty had driven out of Atlanta with the radio off. No music, no news, no knowledge of the mayhem they had missed. Nothing but the pleasingly persistent roar of Power's Porsche hugging the highway. They weren't sure where they were going. They didn't care. Being together was enough.

The sun had set, turning the sky orange, then pink, then purple, then faint gray before fading to black. The top was down, the stars brilliant, the road ahead open and wide.

Power and Beauty, hand in hand, heading out to forever.

Acknowledgments

David Ritz would like to thank Tip, Esi Sogah, Lynn Grady, Jason Geters, David Vigliano, my loving family—Roberta, Alison, Jessica, Charlotte, Nins, James, Isaac, Jim, Henry, Pops, Elizabeth, and Esther—and loving friends, Harry Weinger, Herb Powell, and Alan Eisenstock. Thank you, Jesus.

Keep reading to
see where the saga began
in
Power & Beauty.
Available now.

The Nightmare, the Dream

It was a Saturday in June, nine o'clock in the morning, when the explosion hit. It rocked our little apartment in Conway Court; rocked our whole neighborhood; rocked my world and flipped the script on our lives.

After that morning, just two months before my sister and I turned sixteen, nothing was ever the same.

At first I thought it was a terrorist attack. But why the hell would terrorists be launching attacks on niggas on the west side of the ATL?

"It's Charlie's Disco!" my sister started screaming. "I can see it from here!"

Charlie's Disco sat right across the street from where we stayed. Charlie's Disco was run by Moms's friend, Charles "Slim" Simmons. Moms helped Slim with his bookkeeping. Sometimes when she was working in his office above the club she'd let me sit downstairs at the bar and drink lemonade. I liked that. I liked being inside the smoky club with the black leather booths and plush ruby-red carpet. I studied the disco ball that hung over the dance floor and imagined what it was like when the place was packed with the flashy pimps, hustlers, and hos—Slim's best customers.

But Moms would never allow me in there when the place was packed. Moms knew better. After all, she started out as a waitress at Slim's. She said Slim was always good to her, but Moms wanted to do better. Moms went to night school to learn bookkeeping so she could buy me and my sister, Beauty, nicer clothes. Moms put money away in our college fund. Moms always said she was raising me to be a polite Southern gentleman. People said Moms was the only woman Slim respected. Everyone respected Moms.

"Where's Mom?" I yelled, jumping out of bed when the explosion hit.

"I don't know, Power," Beauty said, her voice shaking. "She mentioned something about going over to see Slim."

My heart started racing. My brain started panicking.

Moms couldn't be at Slim's.

Moms had to be okay.

Just last night Moms had made us dinner. Just last night Moms had helped us with our math homework and read out loud from the Bible.

Moms was a young woman, healthy and strong. Moms hadn't gone over to Charlie's this morning. She probably just went shopping. Moms was fine.

I threw on some sweats and, together with Beauty, ran across the street.

Holy shit!

Charlie's was ablaze. Biggest fire I'd ever seen up close. The heat was incredible. Fire trucks, firemen, cops, folks milling around, everyone trying to figure out what the fuck had happened.

"Anyone inside?" someone asked.

"They pulled out one body. The woman was dead."

The woman was dead.

Beauty and I heard the words at the same time.

"Can't be Moms," I said to my sister. "Moms went shopping."

Beauty didn't speak, but I knew what she was thinking.

"Moms is probably already home by now," I said.

Beauty ran over to the firemen and started asking questions. The fireman directed her to a cop. The cop said something that made Beauty's eyes go wide. She put her hand over her mouth. She started screaming. I ran over there.

"What'd he say?" I asked.

"He's gonna take us to the hospital. We gotta get to the hospital."

After that, my brain went blurry. Riding in the cop car. Sirens screaming. Arriving at the ER. Running through the hospital. Looking for doctors. Talking to nurses. Going up and down hallways until we finally found the one doctor who asked the question that I didn't wanna hear.

"Are you related to Charlotte Clay?"

"She's our mother," said Beauty.

"I'm afraid she's gone."

"Gone where?" I asked. "Gone to Macon? Gone back to where she was born in Alabama? Gone *where*, motherfucker?" I was losing it.

"She's dead," the doctor said.

"Can't be dead!" I started hollering. *"Must be another woman. My mother went shopping. She didn't go to no Slim's. Not that time of morning. She'd have nothing to do with Slim that time of morning. It's all a big mistake!"*

The doctor put his arm around me. I pushed him away and screamed even louder. *"Fuckin' hospitals get shit mixed up all the time! Fuckin' hospitals can't keep nothing straight! That woman who died ain't my mother!"*

"Would you like to identify her?" the doctor asked.

I couldn't.

Beauty could.

Beauty went into the room.

I stayed behind.

Beauty came out, shaking and weeping, running to me, falling in my arms.

"She's gone." Beauty was crying.

My heart was hammering so hard it felt like it was coming out my chest.

"She's gone," Beauty said again. She looked up at me and asked, "How we gonna live without her? How are we going to make it, Power?"

Relatives and friends called. Relatives and friends came by. The crib was packed when we got back home. But we made it clear that we really couldn't be with anyone. Seeing other folks weeping and sobbing was too much. We told them that we appreciated their concern, but we needed to be alone.

No mother. Just sister and brother.

That night, the first night without Moms, Beauty slipped into my bed. She was crying so hard her body was shaking. Her shaking didn't stop until I held her.

She wasn't my blood. Beauty had African-American/Asian blood. She had Asian eyes, Asian skin. Mom had adopted her five years ago when we were both eleven. But she was still my sister. Didn't matter that she was beautiful; didn't matter that she had a killer body that every boy in school was looking to tap. I knew that I couldn't see her that way. Moms always said, "You gotta watch her back, boy, not her backside. She's family. And never forget it." But at times I did forget it. I took me more than a few peeks in the keyhole when she undressed at night. And I caught her taking more than a few peeks at me coming out of the shower.

Sometimes—well, more than sometimes—*most* times when I jerked off, I saw Beauty in my mind. In my mind, I did everything to Beauty to make her scream out my name. But that was fantasy. When it came to reality, I did what Moms told me to do.

But tonight Moms's body was at the funeral home, and Beauty's body was next to mine. She had come to my bed. She needed to be held. I needed to be held. We needed to do something to make this new and horrible fear go away. The fear was all over us.

The midnight hour came down on us.

We were alone in the crib without our mother.

We were alone in bed.

Beauty brought her mouth to my mouth.

I had never tasted her mouth before. It was soft, sweet. I pressed my lips against hers. I felt her tongue touching mine. I felt her opening her heart, her mind, her soul.

I knew it was wrong.

She knew it was wrong.

We were crying out to each other.

Moms was gone, Moms was dead, we were alive, we were holding each other, feeling each other in a way we'd always wanted to but never had.

We couldn't.

We shouldn't.

But the horror and the confusion of losing the most important person in our universe had turned our universe upside down. The person who made sense of the world, the person who kept us safe, the person who gave us the rules was no longer there. The rules were no longer there.

We could do what we wanted.

In our confusion, our pain, our fucked-up fear, we faced each other that night in bed. We did what we had longed to do.

It was not the first time for Beauty, and it was not the first time for me. But it might as well have been.

Once we started, we couldn't stop. It was crazy. My mind couldn't stop saying *crazy crazy crazy crazy* but my body wasn't listening, my body didn't care, my body fought off my mind.

For five years we had fought for Moms's attention. We had teased and taunted each other to the point of tears. For five years we were rivals.

Now we were lovers, loving so deep and with such crazy don't-stop don't-ever-stop passion that I wasn't even sure it was really happening.

I had fallen into a dream. I was loving Beauty in a dream. In a dream, we were doing everything we had long dreamed of.

But when I woke up, the dream was there next to me.

I was naked.

She was naked.

The dream was not a dream.

The dream was real. The nightmare of Moms's death was real. Our reaction to her death now seemed like a nightmare.

"Power," Beauty said to me, "we can never tell anyone. We can never do this again."

"I'll never say a word."

"Never," she said. *"Never ever!"*

Slim

I'll take care of everything."

Those were the first words of the first person who showed up at our doorstep the day after the night everything changed.

"Don't you worry," said Charles "Slim" Simmons. "I'll take care of everything. Your mama was my best friend. I treasured her like a precious jewel. She was my heart and her kids ain't gonna want for nothing—not now, not ever."

We were in the front room of our small apartment. Beauty was sitting in front of the television, staring at a blank screen. She wasn't even looking at Slim. It was a hot day, and she was dressed in cutoff jeans and a T-shirt. She wasn't even looking at me.

I was looking at Slim.

He was about my height—this year I'd shot up to five eleven—and where I was thin and wiry, he was big-boned and thirty pounds too heavy. He had a belly on him. I guess he'd been slim when he was young. At forty-five, he looked his age. He had good hair that he styled in silky waves. I got kinky hair that I cut short to my scalp. His skin was light tan; mine is dark like Moms's. His eyes were green; mine are brown. He wore an open-collar blue silk shirt, black alligator low-top boots, a fancy Monte Carlo Panama fedora, and a sleek slice of dazzling ice on each wrist. Matching diamond wristbands were his trademarks.

Slim wasn't a smiling man. He had a serious vibe, a take-care-of-business vibe, and before this day, he had never given me a second's worth of attention.

"Just got back from Cutler Jefferson's funeral home," he said. "Cutler's my friend from grade school. I said, 'Cutler, give this great lady the send-off she deserves. Lay her out in satin and ermine. Make her even more beautiful in glory than she was in life. Set out your best coffin, the one made in hand-polished mahogany where the hardware is fourteen-karat gold. You dealing with a queen, Cutler. You dealing with royalty. Spare no expense.' This here tragedy happened in my place. This here accident, where the gas heater blew up and caused this terrible explosion, this thing was something so unbelievable that only God knows why. She didn't deserve this. You kids know that. You know it better than anyone. Your mama was a sure-enough angel of the Lord. She's gone, but I'm here, and I'm here to set things right for y'all."

I didn't know what to say or do.

Beauty kept looking down. She never did face Slim.

Slim saw Beauty. All men saw Beauty. She was just an inch or two shorter than me, and her long black lustrous hair fell halfway to her waist. Her almond-shaped eyes gave you a dreamy feeling; when she did look at you, it felt like she was writing a poem about you. She was small-waisted and slender like a model. Lots of models have small breasts, though. Beauty's breasts weren't small. They were perfectly proportioned to her body. They jutted out. They stayed up and out. She never wore a bra because she didn't need a bra. She had amazing breasts. Her lips were thin and her mouth wide. Her cheekbones turned up to the sky.

Her mama, Isabel Long, had worked alongside my mother in the bookkeeping department at Fine's Department Store for years. They lived in an apartment right next to ours. Beauty's daddy was some Japanese dude who knocked up Isabel and wanted nothing more to do with the whole affair. When Isabel died, my mother felt like she had no choice but to adopt the girl, whose name was Tanya. Even as a baby, Tanya was so gorgeous everyone called her Beauty. She and I grew up together. She was just like a sister.

At about the same time eleven-year-old Tanya came to live with us, my daddy, Paul, fell down at his job at the plant. He was just a young man, but a stroke did him in. He was in the hospital for only a week before he died. He was the one who called me Power. I'm Paul Jr., but when I fell in love with the Power Rangers at age three, Daddy renamed me after my favorite toys.

"Power," said Slim, "I'm taking you and your sister outta here. I'm taking you to my crib. You gonna live with me."

For the first time, Beauty looked up. She stared straight at Slim. Her eyes looked at him like he was some kind of devil. She didn't say anything. She didn't have to.

"I got six bedrooms and I only use one," Slim said. "You'll have your own bedroom and your own bathroom. One of the bedrooms has a canopy bed and a little room right next to it with a vanity table, the kind where women put on their makeup and do all that womanly shit. That'll be your room, Beauty. You gonna love it. Power, I'm putting you in the room above the garage. It's like a private apartment, with its own entrance and everything. You'll come and go as you please. If you wanna bring your bitches up in there, I got no problem. Youngbloods gonna do what they gonna do."

I didn't know what to say, so I didn't say anything.

"I gotta slide outta here," said Slim. "I'll be back later with all the details on the funeral. The funeral will be something no one will ever forget. My man Cutler is going to turn this funeral *out*. So start packing up your things. I'll have one of my boys come by with a pickup and take your suitcases over to my place whenever you're ready. God bless you both. God bless your beautiful mother. I loved that lady, and nothing in this world can stop me from making sure that her kids get every last goddamn thing they need."

Wanda Washington

After Slim left, time hung heavy on our heads.

What could we say?

The shock of Moms's death had caught us up in a terrible grief. The grief was choking us. The fact that we had slept together fucked with our minds. The guilt was choking us. Grief and guilt were all over us; we couldn't even look at each other.

I was sitting on the couch. Beauty was sitting on a kitchen chair, her back to me. The morning was hot. The TV was off. The windows were open. A neighbor across the way was screaming at his wife so loud we could hear every last word.

"Bitch!" he yelled. "Why do you care if I get home at four A.M.? You ain't giving up no good pussy anyway!"

"That's 'cause that sad old dick of yours can't stay up long enough to please no normal woman. You out there foolin' with them freaks."

I got up and closed the windows, muffling the fight.

Finally Beauty spoke, although she still wouldn't look at me. "I'm not going to live with him."

"Why not?"

"He's a grease ball."

"Moms liked him."

"Moms liked everyone. She had a generous heart. But she saw through him. That's why she never married him."

"He's a powerful dude," I said. "He owns half the barbershops in the city. Plus all those car washes and hot-wing joints."

"He's a gangsta."

"Moms was looking to help him. Now he's looking to help us. That's all there is to it. What else we gonna do?"

"Stay here."

"Just the two of us? And live like a couple?"

"Don't put it like that, Power. Don't ever say that. That's never going to happen again. *Ever.*"

"I understand, but I'm saying it's going to look funny."

"I couldn't care less how it looks. I know what I want to do and where I want to live—and it's not with Slim Simmons. I'm not going anywhere near that man."

Beauty got up, went to her bedroom, and closed the door behind her.

A half hour later, the doorbell rang.

I looked out the window and saw Wanda Washington standing there carrying great platters of food. I opened the door.

"Hey, Power," she said, "I brought y'all some eats. Should last you a few days. Got all sorts of treats here."

Wanda walked in the house like she owned it. She went right to the kitchen, opened the refrigerator, and started putting the food away.

"Where's Beauty, baby?" she asked.

"In her bedroom."

She sat down on the couch and motioned for me to sit down next to her. Miss Washington was a heavyset woman. Her cheeks were chubby and her friendly eyes sparkled. Her mouth was fixed into a permanent smile. She was incapable of *not* smiling. She wore a heavy perfume and a fancy wig that flipped up on the side. She owned

Wanda's Wigs, and she always claimed that she was her own best advertisement. She wore a different wig every day.

"Get Beauty in here," she said. "I want her sitting with us."

"Beauty!" I cried. "Miss Washington is here."

When Beauty walked in, Wanda got up and hugged her.

"Now you sit down here next to me, baby. We gonna pray. We gonna say, Father God, we here to praise you, we here to give you the glory, we here to thank you for this new day that you made, we here to say that we love you with all our hearts, even though our hearts are broken and souls messed up. These children don't got no mama, Lord, and they hurting. Oh, they hurting real bad. Their hearts are crying, Father God, their hearts are crying worse than they ever cried before. We live in this mean ol' world, Father, and things happen that we don't understand. We don't understand why this wonderful woman, their mama and my friend, Charlotte Clay, gotta be gone so soon. We don't know why you took her, Lord, and we don't know why you left her children to fend for themselves. But we trust you, Father God, yes we do. We know you got our backs. We know you got the master plan. We know that everything happens for a reason, even if we can't understand that reason. And we don't understand. We're filled with hurt. Oh, the hurt goes deep. The hurt is all over us. We crying real tears, Father—"

At this point we were all crying. Beauty and I broke down. Wanda spoke through sobs.

"We crying and we trying, Lord. We trying to pick ourselves up and look life right in the eye. Life without these children's mama. Life without my friend Charlotte. We doing our best, Lord. We know we can't lose our minds. We can't hide from life. Life goes on, yes it do. We got things to do, Father God. This boy Power, Lord, he's a brilliant student. He plays basketball on the school team and he's a star. Keep him strong. Keep him righteous. And sister Beauty, she's a special child, a special young woman. She can sew, Lord. She can sew like a woman who's been sewing her whole life. She makes her own designs and she sews them herself. You gave her talent, Father, so let that talent blossom. Let these children prosper. Let them find the strength to go on. They got to go on. Got to keep bringing it. Your will is for us to spread your love. To love each other like you love us. Psalms says, 'Weeping may endure for the night, but joy will come in the morning.' Bring us that joy. Even in the midst of pain, let us feel your joy. You are our joy, our bright morning star, our shining prince of peace, our all in all. Bring us peace, Father God. In the name of your precious son, Jesus, bring us what we need to run this race. Amen."

"Amen," I echoed.

"Amen," Beauty whispered.

"Now let's eat," said Wanda, getting up from the couch and heading for the kitchen. "I'm heating up a lasagna that's gonna hurt your mouth. You ain't never tasted nothing like it."

Moms loved Wanda, and of course, we couldn't help but love her too. Moms was a humble woman of few words. She dressed tastefully. Wanda's taste was different. She wore too-tight pantsuits, like the green-and-purple getup she wore today that didn't hide any of her fat. She didn't care. Moms loved that Wanda didn't care. She liked women like Wanda who, unlike herself, weren't at all conservative and quiet. She got a kick out of Wanda. Moms always said that Wanda, like Beauty's blood mother, Isabel, was a friend she could count on.

"Count on me to get y'all through this," said Wanda while serving us big portions of her meaty lasagna. "And count on Slim."

"He was here this morning," I said.

"I know he was. He told me that he was coming. I told him it was too soon, but you can't tell Slim nothing."

"He wants us to move into his house," I said.

"Well, I think that's mighty generous of him. That's like when he bought me my wig store."

"I didn't know that it was Slim who bought it," said Beauty.

"He owns it. I work for him. But I make him a pretty penny, so he leaves me alone to run it as I please. He's a rough man, Slim is, but he's not a bad man. He's got good in him, and I know damn well he wants to take good care of y'all."

"I'm not going," Beauty flatly declared.

"I can sure enough understand how you feel, sweetheart. Leaving this place is not going to be easy."

"It's not going to happen," Beauty reiterated.

"Charlotte always said, 'That Beauty's got a mind of her own. That child has her own ideas about things.' She respected that about you, Beauty. You a strong young woman. You got that streak of fire running through you. I got that same streak of fire running through me. And I tell you, girl, that ain't no bad thing. We need that streak of fire."

Beauty didn't respond.

"But in this day and age, we also need help. You gonna need a lot of help. Now Slim, he got him this house up in Cascade Heights. It's a big beautiful house, yes it is. With lots of room and lots of privacy. He can go about doing his business, and y'all can go about doing yours."

"I don't trust him," said Beauty.

"You don't got to, baby. I got my eye on that man at all times. I know him well. Hell, I talk to him practically every day. I see how he do. I know he's an operator. He can operate for good, and he can operate for bad. Right now, when it comes to y'all, he's operating for good. Besides, Beauty, I ain't letting you out of my sight. I want you with me at Wanda's Wigs. Summer's just begun and I'm gonna have you working down there every day. I wanna teach you the wig business, baby. You're a natural."

With that, Wanda went over and gave Beauty a great big hug. Beauty tried to fight back a smile, but she couldn't. No one could resist Wanda.

BOOKS BY TIP "T.I." HARRIS

TROUBLE & TRIUMPH
A Novel of Power & Beauty
with David Ritz

Available in Paperback and eBook

In this powerful follow-up to *Power & Beauty*, Power and his closest friend Beauty have fallen under the spell of Slim Simmons, a savvy Atlanta businessman. But Beauty recognizes the violence beneath Slim's charm. She escapes to the Big Apple to pursue fashion, though it comes at a steep price: turning her back on the boy she's come to love. To Power, Slim's world holds everything he thought he wanted: money, women, action. He discovers too late that Slim is a killer who will turn on anyone in his way. Unable to forget Power, Beauty is determined to risk everything for the only man she's ever loved. But is saving Power worth sacrificing herself—body and soul?

POWER & BEAUTY
A Love Story of Life on the Streets
with David Ritz

Available in Paperback and eBook

Tip Harris, better known as Grammy Award-winning, multi-platinum selling hip-hop artist and actor T.I., displays yet another side of his remarkable talents with *Power & Beauty*, a love story of life on the streets. Set in the dangerous shadows of Atlanta, Georgia, *Power & Beauty* is a dark, gritty story of sex, violence, hustling, and redemption centered around Paul "Power" Clay and Tanya "Beauty" Long—two kids facing long odds and lethal temptations, yet whose miraculous, unbreakable bond ultimately becomes their salvation. A love story, a crime story, a survival story, *Power & Beauty* bristles with an electrifying authenticity born of Tip "T.I." Harris's hard life on the streets. This is exhilarating, brutally honest, page-turning urban African-American fiction at its very best.